MEMOIRS OF A DEAD MAN

Hjalmar Bergman

HJALMAR BERGMAN (1883-1931) is one of the foremost Swedish authors and playwrights of the first decades of the twentieth century. His writing is rich in dreamlike symbolism, yet simultaneously strongly realistic – many of his books are firmly anchored in the Bergslagen district of central Sweden in which he grew up. Over the course of his career he built up a gallery of families and characters to whom he would return again and again, like Balzac, to compile a portrait of human society as he saw it. Bergman has been accused of a profound pessimism, yet his writing is suffused with a rich sense of life's ironies, and novels such as *Markurells i Wadköping* (1919, The Markurells of Wadköping), *Herr von Hancken* (1920) and *Farmor och Vår Herre* (1921, Grandmother and Our Lord) are today regarded as (tragi-)comic classics of Swedish literature. His concerns were existential, and his narratives multifaceted and psychologically acute – at times reminiscent of Dostoyevsky. Bergman travelled widely in Europe, and spent four unhappy months in Hollywood as a screenwriter in the 1920s. He suffered from chronic emotional insecurity, exacerbated by his ambiguous sexuality, and came to rely increasingly on alcohol and drugs. Exhausted by the effort of writing his final novel, *Clownen Jac* (Jac the Clown), about an artist whose creativity is dependent on fear, he died alone in Berlin on New Year's Day, 1931.

NEIL SMITH is a translator and editor living in Norfolk. He studied Scandinavian Studies at University College London, and lived in Stockholm for several years. He is currently deputy editor of *Swedish Book Review*.

KARIN PETHERICK taught Swedish literature at University College London for many years. Her doctoral thesis dealt with aspects of style in Hjalmar Bergman's novels, and she is currently working on a new edition of August Strindberg's *Ockulta dagboken* (Occult Diaries).

Some other books from Norvik Press

Victoria Benedictsson: *Money* (translated by Sarah Death)
Jens Bjørneboe: *Moment of Freedom* (translated by Esther Greenleaf Mürer)
Jens Bjørneboe: *Powderhouse* (translated by Esther Greenleaf Mürer)
Jens Bjørneboe: *The Silence* (translated by Esther Greenleaf Mürer)
Johan Borgen: *The Scapegoat* (translated by Elizabeth Rokkan)
Fredrika Bremer: *The Colonel's Family* (translated by Sarah Death)
Suzanne Brøgger: *A Fighting Pig's Too Tough to Eat* (translated by Marina Allemano)
Camilla Collett: *The District Governor's Daughters* (translated by Kirsten Seaver)
Kerstin Ekman: *Witches' Rings* (translated by Linda Schenck)
Kerstin Ekman: *The Spring* (translated by Linda Schenck)
Kerstin Ekman: *The Angel House* (translated by Sarah Death)
Kerstin Ekman: *City of Light* (translated by Linda Schenck)
Knut Hamsun: *Selected Letters* (2 vols.) (edited and translated by James McFarlane and Harald Næss)
P. C. Jersild: *A Living Soul* (translated by Rika Lesser)
Viivi Luik: *The Beauty of History* (translated by Hildi Hawkins) (2007)
Runar Schildt: *The Meat-Grinder and Other Stories* (translated by Anna-Liisa and Martin Murrell)
Amalie Skram: *Lucie* (translated by Katherine Hanson and Judith Messick)
Amalie and Erik Skram: *Caught in the Enchanter's Net: Selected Letters* (edited and translated by Janet Garton)
August Strindberg: *Tschandala* (translated by Peter Graves) (2007)
Hanne Marie Svendsen: *Under the Sun* (translated by Marina Allemano)
Hjalmar Söderberg: *Martin Birck's Youth* (translated by Tom Ellett)
Hjalmar Söderberg: *Selected Stories* (translated by Carl Lofmark)
Edith Södergran: *The Poet Who Created Herself: Selected Letters* (edited and translated by Silvester Mazzarella)
Helene Uri: *Honey Tongues* (translated by Kari Dickson) (2007)
Elin Wägner: *Penwoman* (translated by Sarah Death) (2007)

MEMOIRS OF A DEAD MAN

A Novel

by

Hjalmar Bergman

Translated from the Swedish by

Neil Smith

and with an afterword by

Karin Petherick

Norvik Press
2007

Originally published in Swedish by Bonniers Förlag under the title *En döds memoarer* (1918). This translation follows the text of the 1995 edition of the novel edited by Kerstin Dahlbäck and published by the Swedish Academy as part of its Swedish Classics series.

Translation © Neil Smith 2007.

The translator has asserted his moral right to be identified as the translator of the work.

Afterword © Karin Petherick 2007.

A catalogue record for this book is available from the British Library.
ISBN 10: 1-870041-65-8
ISBN 13: 978-1-870041-65-2
First published in 2007 by Norvik Press, University of East Anglia, Norwich NR4 7TJ.

Norvik Press gratefully acknowledges the financial assistance given by the Swedish Institute, the Anglo-Swedish Literary Foundation and the Arts Council (England) towards publication of this book.

Website: www.norvikpress.com
E-mail address: norvik.press@uea.ac.uk

Managing editors: Janet Garton, Michael Robinson, C. Claire Thomson.

Cover illustration: *Visit hos excentrisk dam* (Visit to the Home of an Eccentric Lady, 1921) by Nils von Dardel. The painting is reproduced and overprinted by kind permission © Nils von Dardel/BUS 2007. Reproduction © Moderna Museet

Cover design: Richard Johnson

Printed in the UK by Page Bros. (Norwich) Ltd, Norwich, UK

Contents

I
THE INHERITANCE AND THE LAW

1. Fält-Fältman-Arnberg and his Descendants 11
2. Arnberg's Tuberculin 36
3. The Bishop's Palace 77
4. Arnberg's Explosives 92
5. The Mirror 109
6. Hitrotorp 139

II
LÉONIE. AN INTERMEZZO   191

THE INHERITANCE AND THE PROMISE

1. Arnberg's Transatlantic 243
2. The Hôtel de Montsousonge 265
3. Mr Hansen Explains and Reconnects 291
4. The Four-Fold Reduction 306
5. Le Maschere da Capo 325

Afterword   344

Notes   351

This translation is respectfully dedicated to Messrs John Grainger and John Harrison, the teachers who first opened my eyes to the treasures of literature written in languages other than English.

NS

MEMOIRS OF A DEAD MAN
I

THE INHERITANCE AND THE LAW

'... So also that the vain ruminations of lost souls and the grave fears of sceptics praise Him and the plaints of the lost glorify Him ...'

David Rygelius the Elder: *Imitation and Observance of the Word*

Chapter 1

Fält-Fältman-Arnberg and his Descendants

> *I the Lord thy God am a jealous God –*
> Evidently.
> *Visiting the iniquity of the fathers upon the children unto the third and fourth generation –*
> Yes.
> *Of them that hate me.*

Them that hate me.

My father was an atheist. This caused a certain amount of offence in its day when as a young student in Upsala he challenged his uncle and future father-in-law, Julius Arnberg (at that time an associate professor but later Bishop of W.) to a public debate about the second and third clauses of our declaration of faith. My uncle and benefactor Dean David Rygelius the Younger has told me that it was this debate that was the true cause of my father's downfall. I take the liberty, however, of doubting this.

From what I now know, or believe myself to know, I must look for the cause further back in time.

My paternal great-great-grandfather, who called himself Fält, then Fältman, and finally Arnberg, was the son (albeit never acknowledged) of Count Arnfelt, the general who was involved in the conspiracy against King Gustav III. After the masked ball at the Opera the general withdrew forthwith to his estate, Frönsan, where Fält was some sort of bailiff or steward. He divided all his money and valuables into two parts and entrusted the larger of these to his steward for the benefit of the young count. With the remainder in his trunk he attempted to flee the country, but was murdered on a farm near the Norwegian border by his valet, one Battiste Léon. This is what my father has told me regarding the murder:

'The Count, exhausted after two long days' travel, stopped at about six o'clock at a farm some ten miles from the border. The Count went to bed at once. Later that evening an unidentified individual arrived and asked to speak to the valet. They had a long conversation, after which the unidentified man (Fält?) rode away again. At about two o'clock that night, when the farmspeople were sound asleep, the valet woke his master. He said that he had received news that the Count was being pursued: the greatest possible haste was of the essence. The Count got up at once and ordered him to prepare everything for his morning ablutions. Battiste advised him not to undertake anything that might delay them or wake the farmspeople; his toilette could surely be deferred. But the Count stroked the bristles on his chin and replied: "I do not wish to travel another day in this appalling condition." When he sat down in front of his mirror, a valuable piece made of hexagonal Venetian glass, upon whose silver frame the seven cardinal virtues were represented, he fell asleep and slept for the duration of the shave. Just as the valet was wiping the blade and putting it aside, the Count awoke with a start, and his dazed eyes met the valet's in the mirror. The Count exclaimed: "Battiste! What are you thinking? What are you up to?" The question came so unexpectedly that the valet fell to his knees and, in tears, confessed that a certain person (Fält?) had sought to persuade him to let the Count's trunk fall unnoticed onto the road during their journey that night. The Count became extremely agitated. "What treachery!" he cried. "What a despicable Judas!" He tried to stand up, but the powdering-gown, which also enclosed the back of the chair, hindered him. "What's this?" he cried. "Have you already bound me, you assassin!" Battiste stumbled to his feet and, with trembling fingers, began to loosen the knots. The Count watched him intently in the mirror. And once again their eyes met for a silent moment. Instead of loosening the knots, the valet put both hands on the strap and tightened it still further around the Count's throat. He completed the task with the razor-blade.

Memoirs of a Dead Man

'However,' my father went on, 'the story is not only uncorroborated, but also improbable. Since the valet never fell into the hands of the law, and consequently never registered a confession, and since the Count was found dead by the farmspeople, no-one, of course, has been able to stand witness. The one thing which makes it at all credible is the Count's emphatic cry: "What a traitor! What a despicable Judas!" He himself had of course come directly from an act of high treason. And from internal evidence such as this, my boy, we may discern the truth.'

So I do not know with any certainty the extent to which Fält was a Judas. But it is more than likely that he took possession of the funds entrusted to him by the Count. In 1793 a man by the name of Fältman established himself in Gothenburg as a shipping-agent and broker. His working capital seems to have been quite considerable. In spite of this, he felt obliged to seek a new place of refuge and a fresh name some five years later. In 1800 he is to be found in Ystad, already married to one of the daughters of the town's merchant class, and a partner in his father-in-law's business. In Ystad he adopted the name Arnberg. His wealth and reputation grew without interruption. In 1804 he became English vice-consul. He died in 1813, Knight Commander of the Vasa Order and Knight of the Order of the Pole Star.

There is, however, also a story from Ystad: in the year 1812 a British man o'war put into Ystad harbour, having been pursued by one or more French ships. The captain, Sir Mogens Feurfield, had on board a large sum of money, government funds, and, in order to secure the safety of this beyond all doubt, he had himself taken ashore where he sought out the English consul, with whom he deposited the money against an appropriate receipt. He stayed ashore one more day as a guest of the consul. Late in the evening of the second day the consul and one of his men accompanied Sir Mogens down to the harbour. The servant was to row him to his ship. It was a dark and windy February night. The consul lit the way down to the boat, took his leave and returned home. Some friends who had helped him entertain the foreign guest were still seated at the card-table. He sat down and, as he was shuffling the pack, told them why the captain had visited him, adding that he had eventually persuaded the captain to refrain from carrying out his intention. 'That was a shame,' one of the friends interjected, 'you might have got to keep the money for years and get some profit from it.' Arnberg smiled and replied: 'I have no use for other men's money, only my own.' After a hour playing cards the friends left and the consul went to bed. But the servant did not return that night. He was found the next day by the harbour, half-naked and half-dead. The boat had capsized, the servant had used the last of his strength to make it to shore, and Sir Mogens had gone to the bottom. And with him, according to testimony of the consul and his friends, went the war-chest. The case was closed, but that was not, however, the end of the matter. Some months later the aforementioned servant departed this life by his own hand. He was found in bed with his throat cut and, in his hand, a razor-blade which was apparently not his own, yet nor was it anyone else's. One curious fact that the unfortunate man's friends noticed in silence was that he was holding the blade in his left hand. Yet as far as they were aware he had not been left-handed. Indeed, they found this fact so peculiar that one night they dug up the coffin from its unconsecrated earth and placed it, with its lid removed, on a sort of *lit-de-parade* made of empty boxes beneath the consul's bedroom window. Then, hidden behind the boxes, they waited for dawn. As expected, they saw the consul, still in his night-gown, a night-cap on his head, pull up the blind. He pressed his forehead to the window-pane, peering up at the sky, checking the wind and weather. Then he lowered his gaze. He stood still for a few moments. Then the men saw him fumble for something with his hands, and assumed that he was looking for his spectacles. But suddenly he raised his hands and clutched at the air above his head, possibly to pull the blind down again. However, he fell backwards and was later found dead. According to his doctor he had suffered from a serious weakness of the heart for many years. The men's coarse and fateful prank demanded and received appropriate punishment.

That is practically all I know about my ancestor, Fält-Fältman-Arnberg. Nothing particularly honourable. He did, however, leave a considerable fortune to his son and – as far as I am aware – only child. Johan Ludvig was a credit to the family. In his younger years he was a scientist, chemist, physicist and metallurgist. He graduated from Lund and even became a senior lecturer in something, I am not sure what. But he soon left the university. He was unhappy in Skåne. He moved to Värmland and bought the ironworks at –dal, a property some ten miles from Frönsan, the Arnfelts' estate. (As a result of which our family once again came into contact with the Arnfelts.) 'In the doctor's day' –dal's works became one of the finest in Bergslagen. Only a few years ago I heard an old labourer speak admiringly of 'Arnberg's oven' – an object of whose merits I am admittedly unaware, nor do I even know what it was used for. Johan Ludvig was also a good and helpful man. He used to say: 'to help one's neighbour is to help oneself.' And he acted accordingly. It was thanks to him alone that the Arnfelts managed to hold on to Frönsan. He was also very affectionate towards his children. The only person who seems to have had any reason to speak ill of him was his wife, the poetically inclined daughter of a schoolmaster from Skara. (She had French or Walloon blood in her veins, and her maiden name was Claire Aurore Clémence Lebossu!) Towards her Johan Ludvig harboured serious misgivings, which, in his old age, hardened into the firm conviction that she wanted to poison him. Whence this suspicion towards the tender-hearted, romantic Claire Aurore Clémence? No-one could say, least of all Johan Ludvig. He gave no reason, he did not even seem angry or upset at his wife's alleged criminal intent. He regarded it as an inescapable fact. However he survived his spouse, and the fact that he really did die of poisoning some months later – as a result of a fatal confusion of medicine bottles – cannot, at any rate, be blamed on her.

On one daguerreotype, probably taken to mark their silver wedding, they sit hand in hand, innocently and affectionately looking into one another's eyes. And I imagine that what they saw in each other's eyes was something quite different to what General Arnfelt saw in those of his valet. Their children are grouped around them. Foremost stands their eldest son, my paternal grandfather, short and fat, with no neck, and a bushy black beard around his full, negroid lips. He stands there confidently, his legs rather far apart, with his right hand on his mother's shoulder. Between father and mother, his left hand on his mother's shoulder, his right on his father's, stands my great-uncle Julius (my great-uncle and maternal grandfather: which is to say, my father married his cousin). In the course of time he became a bishop, but here he is only a pious student with woolly hair and somewhat staring eyes. To the right of Johan Ludvig stands the third son, Leonard. In the portrait he seems to be a boy of twelve or thirteen. His trousers are clearly too tight, and he gives the impression that he is about to fall flat on his face. But he has hold of his father's arm with both hands. On stools in front of their parents sit Klara and Léonie. Léonie, the youngest, an absolute beauty. Died unmarried, where and when unknown. Klara, the ugliest of the children, married a Rygelius and went on to become the mother of my benefactor, Dean David Rygelius the Younger. She is holding her little sister by the hand and looking affectionately into her eyes, just like their father and mother.

On the whole, it is striking that they are all stretching out their arms to one another. The photographer must have been a rather sentimental and inept fellow. Or else the depth of family feeling was overwhelming. Or else there was some other reason.

The last time these children were gathered together was at my paternal grandfather's wedding. He was marrying Anna Maria Riis af Boskull, a tall, blond, handsome girl who had come to –dal in the capacity of Léonie's governess. Her father was a military accountant who belonged to an old family of public servants of lesser nobility who, despite centuries of toil in the service of the crown, had not succeeded in climbing many rungs of the social ladder. On the third day of the wedding, once most of the guests had left and only the five children, an old steward or book-keeper by the name of Grundberg, and perhaps one or two more intimate friends were seated around the table, my paternal grandfather stood up and proposed a toast to the dear departed, meaning his parents. The silver goblets were set out and the toast was drunk in silence and with feeling.

Memoirs of a Dead Man

Upon which Julius said:

'Well, my dear Ludvig, I've been waiting a long time for that toast!'

Now, my grandfather had a hot temper and, besides that, a poor head for drink. He exclaimed:

'Perhaps you would have preferred me to have proposed it yesterday, in front of indifferent strangers? That's rather tactless of you, my dear Julius. Priest you may be, but you still lack piety.'

My grandmother, the young bride, sought to calm the storm. She asked all manner of questions about her parents-in-law, and asked among other things what her mother-in-law's maiden name had been. When told, the thoughtless creature burst out laughing.

'Lebossu! That's just too silly! *Bossu* means hunchback, doesn't it!'

'Very tactful,' Julius muttered, 'very pious.'

And he said, reproachfully:

'Our mother's father was, thank the Lord, a respectable man. He was a schoolmaster in Skara.'

'That's a lie!' my grandfather shouted, banging his goblet on the table. 'You're lying, my dear Julius, you're lying!'

This outburst startled my grandmother to the extent that she exclaimed:

'Good Lord in heaven!'

At that Julius stood up, buttoned his cassock, and said:

'I have no desire to remain in a place where our dear mother's name is ridiculed and the Lord's name taken in vain.'

'Well, go then,' Grandfather cried.

But Klara and Léonie held their brother back and pulled him down onto his chair.

Grandfather said:

'I maintain that our mother's father was never a schoolmaster in Skara.'

They argued over this for a while, until old Grundberg interrupted:

'You're probably right, sir. The late mistress's father was French or Belgian. He came here to help the Doctor with his experiments, and he lived in the wing for a couple of years. I saw

17

him on many occasions, although he spent most of his time in the laboratory. It was as though he were anti-social. In the end the Doctor seemed to think he had become a nuisance, so he wrote to the family in France. And then the daughter came to collect him. But there wasn't much collecting done, but rather the reverse.'

'That's as may be,' Julius conceded. 'But afterwards he became a schoolmaster in Skara.'

'That's a lie!' Grandfather repeated. And Grundberg said:

'I have heard that he gave private lessons in Skara. And it is quite possible that he had some temporary post at the school. But I don't think he ever became a schoolmaster.'

'He's buried in Skara, that's all he ever had to do with Skara,' concluded Grandfather.

And the happy bride, my poor grandmother, could not resist scoffing:

'Poor Julius! That was rather a lesson, wasn't it?'

At which Julius stood up, left the room, ordered his horse and carriage to be fetched, and drove away without so much as taking leave of his brother and sister-in-law. To his sisters, who once again tried to make peace, he merely said:

'I cannot stay where my departed loved ones are insulted. I am sorry for Ludvig, but I cannot help him.'

This ridiculous quarrel about the King of Spain's beard proved to be decisive in my grandfather's fate. Until then he had managed the works at –dal for his father's estate, but in his anger at the disrupted wedding celebrations he now decided to buy out not only Julius but the others as well. This resulted in large mortgages and a chronic lack of capital. And, besides that, he was left to rely too much on his own advice.

My grandfather was incurably generous. Admittedly, he had changed his father's motto, 'to help one's neighbour is to help oneself', to the more passive: 'to harm one's neighbour is to harm oneself'. But this was merely a strategy deployed constantly and repeatedly against old Grundberg's grumbling. When at the end of the 1850s the two Count Arnfelts had their heads in the noose, Grundberg, still a tough old fellow in spite of his eighty-six or seven years, advised my grandfather to pull the rope quickly and take control of Frönsan himself. Among other things, this would have given the works at –dal the opportunity to regulate and better exploit its water supply. But no. To harm one's neighbour...

'Besides,' my grandfather said, smacking his swollen lips contentedly, 'besides, I have the honour of being distantly related to the Counts.'

And so he drove to Frönsan, and with still strong arms helped lift the two Counts, assisting the eldest to regain the status of his forefathers, and finding a position for the younger one, Adolf Otto, in a commercial firm associated with the works at –dal. And that was not all! When A. O. Arnfelt founded the Independent Bank of W. – one of the first in the country, and now one of the largest – Ironmaster Ludvig Arnberg headed the list of founder members. And there can be no doubt that it was not least his name that attracted creditors to the enterprise.

If I am not mistaken, this shows that the currently illustrious Arnfelt dynasty has the now assassinated Arnberg family to thank for its position. Any expression of gratitude was long in coming: but come it did.

Ludvig Arnberg was not a scientifically trained metallurgist like his father, still less was he a financier, and even less was he a pioneer of any sort. He was an industrious and conscientious foundry proprietor who thought his father's achievements the image of perfection, and sought to maintain them to the best of his abilities. But that which had been perfect 'in the doctor's day' became, however, less perfect with time, until finally it was really quite imperfect. He understood this and sought solace and refuge in his weakness. What could he do without capital? If only his siblings had left their shares of the inheritance in the business, if only that wretched Julius had been less short-tempered – if only! If that were the case, maybe he too could have performed miracles and perfected his late father's achievements.

He did not let this worry him, however. Debit and credit balanced one another tolerably enough, and this was sufficient for an old man like him. Especially for a man who could say: 'to harm one's neighbour is to harm oneself – and I've never done that.' He lived a happy and contented life on this earth for many years –

often somewhat intoxicated (because these were the days when people drank a lot), but even in the impetuosity of drink he retained his good, old-fashioned common-sense, instructing his sons, Johan and Otto, and giving them many maxims and rules of conduct, and always complimenting his wife on her beautiful hands – long, slender, white hands which were held to be a sign of noble birth.

But when he was approaching the age of sixty he received a visit from A. O. Arnfelt, who had dispensed with the title of Count and simply called himself Bank Director. It was a summer's day. A. O. was on his way to Frönsan, but as the road from the station happened to pass the works at –dal, and as he was tired after his journey, he decided to spend the night there. My grandfather, who suffered from hay-fever, was lying in his room with the windows and doors well sealed. My grandmother received him with open arms, overjoyed at having some occupation for her talkative tongue. Arnfelt directed the torrent of words. People have expressed surprise at the number of things he found time for. The explanation was probably that he understood how to make use of everything. He could with reason have had the English phrase 'Nothing too small' as the motto on his coat of arms. By the time dinner was over he probably knew more about the Arnbergs than the Arnbergs themselves knew. He asked to be shown around the works. My uncle and my father, then a newly-fledged student, were his guides. During the tour Arnfelt did not utter a word, apart from a few rather abrupt questions. The boys were in a cold sweat. Used to their father's good-natured garrulousness, they felt threatened by the visitor's taciturnity.

The demonstration over, Arnfelt took himself off to his host's room; the boys, who were dejectedly plodding after him, were stopped at the door with a single gesture. And the door was shut. Not to be opened again until about two o'clock that night, when Arnfelt went to his room. Early the next morning he continued his journey to Frönsan.

At about nine o'clock Grandfather came down to the dining room, sat down at once at the breakfast table and ate with a hearty appetite. He was pale through lack of sleep, but he was smiling.

Memoirs of a Dead Man

His family breathed out; they had been expecting something terrible, without really knowing why. When Grandfather had emptied his coffee-cup and wiped his negroid lips and his woolly, greying beard, he said:

'Do you know what? I dreamed about my dear father last night. Now what could that mean?'

Grandmother knew the answer to that: to dream of the dead meant hard times ahead.

'Well, my dear,' Grandfather said with a frown, 'surely that's a rather superficial way of looking at it.'

And with a energetic gesture, with truly military bearing, he pointed to the window with his napkin and added:

'No, it seems to me to imply that great changes are in the offing for –dal's works. And that my beloved father's accomplishments will live on for several generations yet.'

He revealed some of the many decisions that A. O.'s visit and their nocturnal conversation had brought about.

'But you haven't got any capital,' Grandmother said, picking up on an old theme. Grandfather pursed his lips, allowing himself the beginnings of a smile, and said with hard-won modesty:

'I don't think Ludvig Arnberg will be refused credit. That was Arnfelt's opinion, at least.'

And this turned out to be the case: Ludvig Arnberg was not refused credit. Whether this was because the local banks really did respect the name, or because they were following the directives of the Arnfelt bank, sufficient means were at any rate granted for the whole of –dal's works to be transformed. Grandfather's friends advised a slower tempo, but he was an old man, he was in a hurry. For three years he lived in a state of almost sinful happiness. In actual fact he was not labouring for the sake of future generations, but those of the past. He daily refrain was unchanging: 'If only Father could have seen this!' He excavated, he blasted, he built, he expanded, he perfected – all to delight the eyes of the dead. 'If only Father could have seen this!' He forgot about his sons, or at any rate my father, who spent those years in Upsala. He persuaded my uncle, a lieutenant, to obtain a discharge. He had need of his youthful energies – feeble though they were.

Thus the race to fulfil the imagined wishes of a dead man continued, until one day the time was deemed ripe and those concerned gave a sudden and sharp tug on the reins. My poor grandfather fell as good as instantly. He lay there floundering the way fallen horses are wont to. At Christmas my father returned home from Upsala. It was the very year when he caused a degree of scandal by challenging Uncle Julius, the professor, to a public debate about the declaration of faith. My father, who knew that Grandfather nurtured a small grudge against his brother, was pleased to be able to brag a little. But Grandfather listened with dismay. 'What sort of nonsense is this? Should a young pup like you blaspheme against the Word of God?' He went on:

'And so you've broken with Uncle Julius. Just when I needed his help.'

My father replied that the break was not, in all likelihood, terribly serious, particularly as he, my father, intended to announce his engagement to his cousin, the professor's eldest daughter, at Easter.

'Never,' my father said as he recounted all of this, 'never have I been so dumbfounded as I was then. And never have I so clearly seen how quickly and thoroughly a person, even an old person, can change. My father, my good-natured father, who usually approached every family occurrence with sentimental or mischievous amusement, wasted neither laughter nor tears on my news. For a while he stared blankly ahead, then suddenly grabbed my shoulder and said:

'"Then you're the one who shall get the money!"'

Yes, Ludvig Arnberg actually sent his son on an extraordinary mission to his brother Julius, newly-appointed bishop and his son's prospective father-in-law. It was a matter of saving –dal's works for the Arnberg family. The answer was no, a double no; one no to the suitor, another to the beggar. This was probably the first bitter chalice of humiliation my father had to swallow.

When Father returned to –dal, his mission unaccomplished, the place was deserted. Not a soul was to be seen. But in the small parlour he found his father, mother, brother and sister. They were sitting in complete silence, immobile, holding one another's hands. Just like in the picture. During the days that my father had been away the fatal blow had been dealt. Grandfather had written to A. O. Arnfelt asking for help, and humbly reminding him of the services he and his father had rendered the Arnfelts. It is probable that A. O. had merely been waiting for this letter. Some days later the Independent Bank, whose own claim was relatively insignificant, filed a petition of bankruptcy on Ludvig Arnberg. The bankruptcy aroused little surprise. In part because it was known that Grandfather's position was insecure, and partly because the methods of the Independent Bank were common knowledge. (These would, admittedly, seem childishly simple today – but we were all children once!)

My father quickly and concisely conveyed Uncle Julius's reply. Then even he settled down in the small parlour, stretching out his hands to his father, mother, brother and sister, becoming part of this second tragi-comic family group.

The group was soon split up. Grandfather, gouty and in an early second infancy, was cared for by his sister, Klara Rygelius, the Dean's wife, in Lillhammar. Grandmother, too, stayed at the parsonage for a while, but she soon fell out with her sister-in-law and went to stay with her eldest son, the former lieutenant, for whom Uncle Julius had procured a position within the poor relief in W. However, her son's lowly position and meagre income were poorly suited to my dear grandmother, and, when the Bishop's wife passed away at a convenient moment, she assumed the position of housekeeper in her brother-in-law's home. The Bishop, who had always loathed his sister-in-law, hereby gave proof of true Christian forbearance. She was, however, a fine and pleasant old lady, and the Bishop treated her with great respect. But Grandfather never saw his beloved Anne-Marie again – I know not why – and had to content himself with complimenting the beautiful hands that had enchanted his adult life in long, elegant letters.

My aunt, Aurora, was raised in the Bishop's home, became a teacher, and died young of tuberculosis.

–dal's works passed, after an interregnum of a year or two, into the hands of A. O. Arnfelt.

Johan Arnberg, my father, determined to regain the family home. During the spring before the catastrophe he had taken his bachelor's degree, with physics and chemistry as his main subjects. Instead of continuing his studies, he was now forced to make them bear fruit as soon as possible. He took a position as a teacher at an agricultural college, and two years later became the principal of a folk high school. He wrote essays in the academic press, articles for the daily newspapers, he translated, he made fair copies, he checked accounts. And he starved. All to collect a little capital. With this capital in his pocket he would leave for America. The King's Highway of nineteenth-century Sweden – to adoptive soil.

He had a woman who kept house for him. In the fullness of time she became my stepmother. Her name was Hedda: I have never heard what her surname was. That my father actually succeeded in scraping together between seven and eight thousand kronor through eight years' diligence and privation was doubtless thanks to her. She was without compare. She had a capacity to work as she slept, or sleep as she worked: bed was somewhere she lay on Sundays, and eating was something she did on feast-days. The rest was work. Yet she stole from my father incessantly. She took all that he succeeded in bringing home, either openly or behind his back, used it to pay off half of the most essential expenses, and hid the remainder. And whenever my father expressed some modest desire on his own, or, more often, on her account, she would reply:

'Oh no, Arnberg, we'll make reductions there!'

Where had she got that phrase from? Even later on, in my day, it was in daily use.

She and Father had a child, a daughter, my dear sister Anna. I know for a fact that my stepmother was fond of her. But if my father's success had been in question – she obstinately associated this with saving money – then she would have sacrificed the child. In fact she actually did as much. When my father wanted to marry her after Anna was born, she refused. 'We'll make reductions there, Arnberg.' And when my father showed himself to be as obstinate as her, she simply ran away with the child, kept herself hidden, and only surfaced again after my mother's death. That was what Hedda was like, and still is to this day, because she is still living up there in her ramshackle hovel.

Left all alone, my father decided to realise his American plan at once. He resigned his position and asked for leave of absence; he wrote a long farewell letter to his father, a shorter one to his mother, and went off to town with the two letters. In the letter to his father he had enclosed a small sum of money, and wished to register its postage. Just as he had picked up the receipt, an elderly gentleman approached the counter and asked if there were any letters for him.

'And your name, sir?' the clerk asked.

And the elderly man replied, rather severely:

'Please take note. Leonard Arnberg.'

My father stood motionless, his wallet in his hand. Leonard Arnberg! His uncle, the Doctor's youngest son, had borne that name. He had gone abroad shortly after completing his studies, had sent a few messages home, but finally had fallen completely silent. But on the other hand neither the name Arnberg nor Leonard was so unusual that a more plausible explanation could not be found.

But when the clerk replied that there were no letters for Leonard Arnberg, the old gentleman calmly hooked his arm under my father's and said:

'Put your wallet away, Johan, and keep me company for a while. I saw you come into the post office and followed you. I was not actually expecting any post.'

'Uncle Leonard!' my father exclaimed, thoroughly shocked. 'It really is Uncle Leonard!'

'Well, why should it not be me?' the old gentleman grumbled. 'So, Johan, you are thinking of going to America?'

'Have you just returned from there, perhaps?' my father asked.

'Give it a try, boy! Just give it a try!' the old man smiled grimly. Father glanced at his clothes and noted with a certain degree of relief that although they were, admittedly, old-fashioned and a little ridiculous, they were completely without fault. I ought to add that the only luxury that my father permitted himself throughout his life was a rather well-stocked and always impeccable wardrobe.

'And where are you thinking of going next, Uncle?' my father asked.

The old man stopped, rubbed my father's sleeve a few times, and said:

'Well. You see. I was planning to go to Lillhammar, to see your father. I want to see him again before he dies. There's something I should like to ask him about.'

Slowly wandering down the street, he went on:

'It concerns our father, Doctor Arnberg. He was, as you know, a wise, enterprising and gifted man. But in his old age he was afflicted with the *idée fixe* that his dear wife either wished to or was going to poison him. Take note – I say either wished to *or* was going to, in other words that she would somehow end up poisoning him. Well, there's nothing unusual in an old man becoming obsessed by an *idée fixe* in later years. But the strange thing is that our father really did die of poisoning. This is how it happened: for years he suffered from a complaint of the kidneys, and used to take Contrexéville for it. The bottle, which had a distinctive shape and naturally a label, was usually kept in the alcove in the stove in the bedroom. Well, one night, about four months after my mother's death, he felt the beginnings of colicky pains. He got up, took the bottle from the alcove, poured himself a glassful, and drank it. But the colic only got worse, and after two days of agony he passed away. All the symptoms pointed to arsenic poisoning, and an examination ascertained that the bottle contained an arsenic solution instead of Contrexéville. And that was that. But I should like to know who was responsible for keeping arsenic instead of Contrexéville in the bottle.'

'Was there no investigation?' my father asked.

'Yes and no,' Uncle Leonard replied. 'Ludvig conducted an examination, but I don't know what results he arrived at. Julius, on the other hand, did not want any trouble. And the old doctor at the foundry was, of course, an accommodating man. So that was that. But I want to ask Ludvig before he dies. And may the Lord be with us, my dear Johan.'

With that, the old gentleman let go of Father's arm and, without saying another word, stepped into the lobby of the City Hotel, where the doorman greeted him with an old-fashioned, ten-kronor bow.

'Well, he must have scraped a bit of money together over there,' thought Father, whose mind was full of images of the enchanted, golden land. And, thoroughly satisfied with this good omen, he set off home. The following evening he received a telegram from Lillhammar. After a severe attack of gout, Ludvig Arnberg had contracted pneumonia and was on his death-bed. My father set off as soon as he could. But arrived too late.

In Lillhammar parsonage were gathered, besides my father and the hosts, my grandmother and her eldest son Otto, the former lieutenant, Klara Rygelius's four children (including my benefactor, the current Dean of Lillhammar), as well as Bishop Arnberg with his two sons and daughter, Sabina, my father's former betrothed. A complete family gathering. They were all deeply moved, not least the Bishop. He embraced my father and humbly asked that all disagreements might be forgotten. Yes, family feeling flared up so strongly that it was hard for the gathering to break up. The Bishop's sons may have broken camp on the day of the funeral, but the others stayed in the parsonage for almost two weeks.

My father was so absorbed, partly in his grief, partly in his coming journey to America, and partly in the feelings aroused by seeing Sabina again that he had completely forgotten his strange meeting with Uncle Leonard. But one day it suddenly came back to him.

'Heavens!' he said. 'Uncle Leonard should have been at the funeral.'

'Uncle Leonard?' the Bishop repeated. 'No, brother Leonard has a valid reason for absence. He died more than twenty years ago.'

'But that can't be true,' Father objected, and told him about the meeting.

The Bishop said:

'You must have been dreaming, my boy. I know Leonard is

dead.'

'How do you know?'

The Bishop reflected for a moment, then said:

'Let us just say that I know.'

Father shrugged his shoulders.

'In that case it must have been his ghost that held my arm. He told me a strange story about Grandfather...'

But the Bishop threw up his hands. His face flared red beneath his woolly white hair.

'Enough of this nonsense! It's always the same! People who are too wise and too enlightened to believe in God believe in ghosts instead. It's the same old story.'

And he went out into the garden. Father wanted to go after him, but Grandmother held him back. She said:

'Now don't go upsetting Uncle Julius. You're spoiling everything!'

She told him how she had spent years slowly and carefully trying to induce His Lordship to look favourably upon Johan and Sabina. Recently she had finally succeeded in making him better disposed toward Johan, and after the affectionate atmosphere of the current gathering, she was in no doubt that events would take a turn for the better.

Scarcely had my father grasped this than he rushed out into the garden, took hold of the Bishop by the shoulder and said:

'My mother tells me that Your Lordship is starting to come to your senses!'

And he repeated his proposal of eight years' standing. The fine old gentleman, who could at times smile like a seraph or a cupid, smiled a smile that was somewhere between the two. And replied:

'Ah yes, of course! Sabina, Sabina! That might be one way to convert a superstitious heathen.'

He peered at him, and suddenly wrapped his arms around his neck and burst into tears, his eyes pressed hard against Father's shoulder. Father was both astounded and alarmed, because the Bishop, whilst extremely devout, was in no way prone to crying.

'It's nothing. Just a few tears I had in reserve for brother Ludvig. They should have come out at the funeral, but we priests at gravesides are like doctors at death-beds – it isn't the done thing for us to cry.'

He looked at my father again and said seriously, but without his usual bishop's tone – no, more like a normal, sinful person, someone who has been tested and not passed the test.

'Remember this, Johan! If there is anything pure in the Arnberg family, then keep it pure.'

My roguish father had difficulty suppressing a smile. Perhaps the Bishop noticed this. His tone became sullen and abrupt as usual.

'Well, I've had my eye on you. You're industrious and thrifty. That's always something. If it is the Lord's will, perhaps you'll end up a half-decent man.'

And, turning his back to him, he added, even more sullenly:

'Well, I've nothing against you talking to Sabina.'

From then on, family feeling surged still higher in the parsonage. The engagement may not have been announced, but they all knew about it, and were all happy. It was the case with members of the Arnberg family, just as with members of many other families, that they could be quite indifferent to one another, and they could despise one another. But let go of each other? – no. And the more that separated them, the more secure it felt when the bond was strengthened in some way or other.

The day before Father was due to leave he had another conversation with the Bishop. They agreed that Father should try his luck in America, that the Bishop should keep an eye on the family home and, if a favourable opportunity arose, buy it, either for himself or for Father, and, finally, that the engagement, or at least the wedding, should be postponed until Father had attained a relatively secure position either here or on the other side of the ocean.

All was well and good.

That evening they gathered for the last time around the stone table in the garden. The Bishop was reading. Grandmother was playing patience, Mrs Rygelius, the Dean's wife, was crocheting, the old Dean was sleeping the sleep of the righteous with his head on his wife's shoulder, covering her crocheting with his long white beard. His son, the priest (my benefactor), was playing dominoes with my uncle Otto. And my father and mother were sitting, naturally enough, hand in hand, gazing into each other's eyes.

Suddenly Uncle Otto turned to Father and said in a whisper, with a furtive glance at the Bishop:

'What was that story you were telling? That you'd met Uncle Leonard?'

Reluctantly, and rather absent-mindedly, Father repeated how he had met Leonard, and what he had said. Otto shook his head.

'It's very peculiar, certainly,' he muttered. 'But I could have told him a few things about Grandfather's death. Father told me the whole story. And it really is true that it was Grandmother who poisoned Grandfather...'

All of this was spoken in whispers: the Bishop noticed nothing, but old Rygelius woke up, because, as is well known, a whisper wakes people more surely than speech. The old man let out a deep sigh, stared about him, and, when he saw the gathering, his thoughts were perhaps guided back to the funeral. Because he sat up and said in a loud and urgent voice:

'Let us pray!'

The Bishop looked up and, while he sent a stern warning glance around the group, put his book down, took off his skullcap, and put his hands together. Old Rygelius recited the Lord's Prayer very slowly and a little hesitantly, as if he himself had begun to find his idea odd. His wife put aside her crocheting, Grandmother lay down her cards, Uncle Otto closed his eyes respectfully, but my poor father, over-eager as usual, grabbed his arm and said:

'Otto! What do you mean? What do you mean?'

The Dean fell silent at once, confused. The Bishop closed his eyes and continued the prayer in a loud voice until its end. Then he turned to my father.

'Johan – is it deliberate that you show a lack of respect by interrupting our prayer?'

But my father, who could think of nothing but what he had just been told, burst out:

'Uncle Julius! Do you know what Otto says? He says that it really was Grandmother who poisoned Grandfather.'

Otto shrank like a hare behind a rock. And Grandmother let out a deep-drawn sigh.

'Good Lord! Are we back to that again?'

My father went on:

'But how is this possible? Whatever do you mean, Otto!'

'I don't know anything,' Otto muttered. 'I just know that Father once said...'

'What are they talking about?' the Dean shouted in his wife's ear. Because, although Aunt Klara had grown stone-deaf in old age, he always sought explanations from her. She smiled.

'Well I don't know. But it must be something interesting.'

'It is indeed interesting,' agreed the Bishop. 'Materialists and atheists who believe in ghosts, and loving children who insult the memory of their parents.'

'I haven't insulted my parents!' Father interrupted.

The Bishop inclined his head politely.

'That's true. This is about your grandparents. And one cannot expect that respect should extend all the way to the second generation. However, the accused's son shall now ask leave to explain the matter. Unfortunately I cannot help the fact that the explanation is far too simple for modern tastes. Your grandmother kept a hen-house, as most housewives in the country probably do. Over time, the hen-house became infested with vermin, another fairly common occurrence. In order to remedy the problem she had the hen-house's walls, perches, and so on washed with an arsenic solution. And since there was not in those days such an excess of empty bottles as there was later in your dear father's time, she kept the arsenic in an empty Contrexéville bottle. I am prepared to vouch for the fact that with her exceptional sense of order she would have had a secure hiding place for the bottle. But she died. Your grandfather, weighed down with sorrow and age, no longer kept the servants on such short reins. A degree of disintegration could be discerned even then. Well, a servant – or why not your own father? – happens to find the bottle among your grandmother's things. And without examining the contents he puts the bottle in the place where Contrexéville water was usually kept. We know what fatal consequences this had. It is as simple as that.'

'It may well be,' Father admitted. 'But how do you explain Grandfather's decided conviction, his *idée fixe*, that he would be poisoned by his wife?'

'A strange coincidence,' Otto muttered.

But the Bishop said:

'I have never denied that some people have certain premonitions or forebodings of what may come to pass. But I reject the notion that we can draw from this any conclusion other than that God is omnipotent and that He is scarcely concerned with the laws that materialists lay down for His behaviour and actions...'

'Oh, Good Lord!' whimpered Grandmother, clasping her hands together. 'First the parents, then religion. The first is like a shower of rain, the second like a hail-storm. Julius, I beg you...'

'Of course,' the Bishop interrupted, 'let us leave this foolish religion, which had as its founder a mere carpenter's son, and let us concern ourselves with higher matters, as established by Ludvig Arnberg the foundry master. Yes, I know the family religion of the Arnbergs, I know about brother Ludvig's supposedly secret investigations. I know that we live only to redeem a crime. I know that that nice schoolmaster in Skara, Klemens Leo Lebossu, never was schoolmaster in Skara, nor did he belong to the Walloon family of Lebossu which arrived in Sweden during the seventeenth century. No, he was a mysterious Frenchman who tried to poison my father, and who finally charged his daughter, my mother, with carrying out the delicate task. And I know that the sacramental crime which, so to speak, constitutes our *raison d'être*, was that my grandfather enticed a certain Battiste Léon to murder their mutual master, General Arnfelt. And I also know – and this is the cardinal point of the new creed, a marvel of profundity! – that the aforementioned Battiste Léon was – a hunchback! *Il était bossu*! Lebossu! Do we need further evidence? The valet's name was Léon; our poor sister's name was Léonie. Our brother, who, naturally, is haunting us since – well, since he died – was called Leonard. Splendid! Why I am called Julius I do not yet know. But since my dear departed maternal grandfather was called Klemens Leo – note, Leo, Léon! – I can only assume that we poor Arnbergs are not satisfied with this valet's crime, but also have to bear the sins of at least three popes on our shoulders.

'Silence!' he suddenly commanded, although no-one had shown any sign of wishing to interrupt. 'This sickens me. It sickens me as a man, as a son, and as a man of God. I should like to vomit it up and be rid of it! Faith in Christ's divine lineage is dismissed with a simple reference to "empiricism" and "laws of nature", but people are willing to believe in table-turning and omens. The resurrection of the dead and a life after this are denied, but ghosts and lemures and vampires are permitted to exist! People don't believe in angels, but they believe in devils! Devil-worshippers! For centuries people fought the Kingdom of God with rationalism and materialism, but now those weapons are dulled. And so they grasp for spiritualism, mysticism. No, let's not mince our words – satanism! The Antichrist is showing his face. The time is ripe. My God, my God, I thank Thee for letting this breed of whores and sodomites perish in fire and blood! This breed of deceivers and self-deceivers! This breed of tricksters and fools! This breed of dangerous rogues and pathetic cattle!'

This vehement priestly declaration was received with unshaken tranquility of spirit by those present. The Dean combed his long beard, his son the priest continued his game of dominoes with Lieutenant Otto, Grandmother began to lay a new game of patience. And Father had been whispering sweet nothings in the ear of his beloved for a while already. But when the Bishop fell silent he realised that something ought to be said. And he said:

'You're so right, Uncle, so right. But nevertheless – how would you explain...'

'The peculiar Arnberg mysticism?' the Bishop interrupted. And went on in strident tones: 'That stems from your father. That was what made him a milksop all his life. That was what made him treat the Counts Arnfelt as though we were in their debt. And yet the reverse was the case, because our father had already proffered the master of Frönsan services which would have eradicated every possible debt. But Ludvig was a fool, and he got his reward. And if you want to know where he got his foolishness from, I can tell you that as well. He found it at the bottom of all of those bottles of rum and cognac. This mysticism is as simple as that when seen through the spectacles of a poor, superstitious priest.'

My father stood up and said:

'You are lacking in respect for the dead, Uncle Julius. Moreover, you lack respect for the man whose death you yourself caused, Uncle.'

'What?' exclaimed the Bishop. 'Now he's gone mad as well!'

'No,' said my father. 'I'm not mad. I reckon my father's death from the moment he was forced to leave the family home. After that he was one of the living dead, or a dead living man, whichever you prefer. You knew that even then, Uncle. Because when I had the honour of asking you for help on Father's behalf, I explained what the consequences of a refusal would be for Father personally. You can't refute that, if you care to cast your mind back. Uncle, you knew that Father would be broken spiritually – and physically too, for that matter – and the mysticism which you so sharply criticise was, of course, only a symptom of the beginnings of spiritual disintegration. You, who deny any responsibility for the murder of General Arnfelt, have thus committed a murder yourself, albeit in somewhat qualified form. That your conscience still showed signs of life at that point is proven by one event. When Mother moved from Otto's to the Bishop's Palace, she requested that Otto be allowed to have his father live with him. You refused to grant this. You didn't want to see the corpse, Uncle, until you were in a position to bury it, and use the reserve of tears that you spoke of earlier. But since then, your conscience has passed away, as is proven by the little speech you just made in honour of the murder victim. But a man whose conscience has died – is he really alive? No, my dear Uncle, in spite of all your priestly common sense, you would seem to be a dead man, a ghost. Indeed, more of a ghost than poor Leonard. At least he had one trait of the living – a desire to know the truth. It is as simple as that, seen through the spectacles of a poor atheist.'

While my father was speaking, the Bishop had been staring intently at his daughter. And what tormented him was certainly not so much Father's words as the fact that Sabina was holding my father's hand the whole while.

The Bishop stood up and said:

'Sabina – come along.'

My mother shook her head.

The Bishop stood for a moment, gazing into his daughter's eyes. He took a deep breath.

'I see,' he said, took his book, and left.

Grandmother continued to lay her patience, the priest and Otto played dominoes, the Dean combed his beard. But Aunt Klara, who had been crocheting, now and then casting a glance at the protagonists with an absent-minded smile, shook the threads from her hands and turned to her husband.

'David – what was the matter with Julius?'

'He – got – angry!' the Dean shouted.

'About what?' Aunt Klara asked.

The Dean twisted his silver beard, confused at having to explain something so complex to deaf ears.

'I – don't – know!' he shouted.

'Oh,' the deaf woman smiled, 'that's usually the way. Perhaps he didn't know either.'

'But you watch yourself, Johan!' she added, shaking her crochet-hook.

Chapter 2

Arnberg's Tuberculin

In 1890 an arcanum with the name 'Doctor Johan Arnberg's Tuberculin' was sent out from J. W. Grundberg's Medicinal and Chemical Laboratory in St. Paul, Minn., U.S.A. On the label was a picture of a terribly emaciated girl, kneeling in despair in front of a desk. Behind the desk sat a middle-aged man, holding a stethoscope in one hand, and resting his head, heavy with worry, upon the other. On this head rested a hand, and this hand belonged to an old man, a patriarch, whose halo and long, loose costume indicated that he numbered among the blessed. With his free hand he held out a sheet of paper to the worried man, paper on which the word *Tuberculin* was written. The worried man was identified as Dr J. Arnberg, and the patriarch as 'His grandfather, the Most Rev. J. L. Arnberg!'

The origins of the remarkable tuberculin were described in a brochure as follows: The renowned German professor Robert Koch had, whilst studying at Upsala University (!) as a young man, met the almost one hundred-year-old Archbishop Arnberg. Koch witnessed the venerable old man curing tuberculosis in the penultimate and even the final stage of the disease with a simple and safe medicine. Koch sought to become privy to the old man's secret, and was told that he, in whose parish (!) at least every other person suffered from this terrible disease, had devoted his whole life to investigating the true nature of tuberculosis. Eventually, as a result of his piety and his knowledge of the Talmud and other ancient Hebrew texts, he had uncovered a secret which could restore millions of suffering people to health and happiness. Arnberg offered to tell Koch of his discovery free of charge, but Koch, a proud man by nature (!), did not want to share the glory and the profits (!) with the Most Rev. Arnberg, and decided to make his own way. After a lifetime of hopeless toil, which had brought him to the edge of insanity (!), Koch had now released his tuberculin, so fêted in certain less scrupulous organs of the press, onto the market.

In the meantime, the venerable Arnberg had passed away, leaving a grandson, the renowned Dr Johan Arnberg, medicinal director of the world-famous J. W. Grundberg Laboratory, St. Paul, Minn., U.S.A. J. Arnberg had not only inherited great knowledge from his grandfather, but also an unimpeachable piety and inexhaustible love of his fellow man. It could almost be said that *the grandfather had been resurrected in the grandson*. He had also greeted the discovery of *tuberculinum Kochii* with selfless jubilation. But imagine his sorrow when he tested the medication in his practice for several months and found it did more harm than good. How he now regretted that he had not forced the obstinate (!!) old man to give up his secret on his death-bed! But his regret turned to terror when he one day discovered the first traces of the murderous disease in his only child, his beloved Anna. The world grew dark before his eyes. Following his forefathers' traditions, he sought refuge in the family Bible which he had inherited from his grandfather.

That he found among its pages a 'yellowed and almost disintegrated' recipe for 'the Archbishop's tuberculin' need not be recounted. I shall omit the instructions for use, as well as the long list of certifications, but must, however, cite the following:

–dal's foundry, Wermland, Sweden, 15th June 1890

J. Arnberg Esq.
St. Paul, Minn. U.S.A.

Please send ten cases of your tuberculin at once. I and the rest of my family regard you as our benefactor. *Your venerable grandfather* has saved us from ruin. Payment follows by return.
                        Count A. O. Arnfelt.
                        Banker.

(All the certifications are dated one year before the 'discovery' of the tuberculin. The brochure ends with the following leading question:

A complete course of Johan Arnberg's Tuberculin costs 25d. – a complete coffin costs 50d. – which do you choose?)

So much for the brochure: its fantastic story is, in actual fact, scarcely more fantastic than the true story of the origins of Arnberg's Tuberculin.

In 1885, two years after he had emigrated, Father went into partnership with J. W. Grundberg, a nephew of the faithful old retainer at –dal's works. Father became technical director of J. W. Grundberg's Laboratory, a chemical and engineering factory which mainly produced cosmetic treatments. The company, in which my father invested not only his meagre savings but also my mother's dowry, was going reasonably well, but not remarkably so.

Dr Arnberg's 'Amygdaline Paste' and 'Face Balm' recorded notable sales thanks to Grundberg's clever advertisements, but the profits were not great since production costs were high. As this was the time when the American market in arcane remedies was beginning to blossom and earn their creators fantastic sums, Grundberg proposed that the business be re-organised and that my father's already reasonably well-known name should front one or more humbug medicines. My father, however, refused in such strong terms that the suggestion was dropped.

In the spring of 1890 my parents travelled to Sweden at the behest of my grandfather. The Bishop, who had presumably become more accommodating over the years, wished to see his daughter again. Father, for his part, wished to see his mother again. My parents were both well received in the Bishop's Palace, where they remained the whole summer. No disputes arose between father-in-law and son-in-law, and, if any clouds threatened to sail onto the horizon, Grandmother sallied forth like a whirlwind and dispersed them with her chattering tongue. But one day, towards the start of autumn, the conversation turned to –dal. And the Bishop said:

'Well, Johan, by now you must have decided against trying to buy back –dal?'

My father smiled, and Mother replied:

'Decided against it? He lives for nothing else!'

'No,' Father confirmed, 'I really don't live for anything else. The fact that my father was forced to leave –dal as a bankrupt, that's the thorn in my flesh. Ideally I should like to strangle the men who did that, but as a civilised human being, and son-in-law of a bishop, I shall content myself with taking the spoils from A. O. Arnfelt's hands.'

The Bishop shook his head.

'That's false piety, that is,' he said. 'But since you persist in your madness, I should tell you that –dal's works is currently up for sale. I have an option on it.'

Father was beside himself with joy. Boyish as he still was, he embraced the old man and waltzed around with him. Grandmother, never late to join in with anything cheerful, exclaimed:

'So, my poor Ludvig is redressed at last! If he can see us now he must be smiling, the dear soul.'

But the Bishop dampened their spirits by telling them that the asking-price was almost seven hundred thousand kronor, more than three times the price Arnfelt had once paid.

And he added:

'Do you think you could manage that, my dear Johan?'

Father thought for a few moments, then replied:

'Yes, if you help me.'

The Bishop buttoned his coat.

'No, thank you,' he said. 'I'm too old for that sort of adventure. And besides, I think it wrong to encourage an *idée fixe* which will probably be your downfall in the end.'

'But it would be a way for you to atone for...,' began my father, until he was stopped by a terrible grimace from Grandmother. He went on:

'Well, perhaps I can get help from someone else. I shall write to my partner this very day. After all, his family comes from –dal, so he should still have an interest in the old place.'

Father wrote, and soon received a reply. J. W. Grundberg

informed him that in order to do his partner a favour, he would instruct the firm's homme d'affaires in Stockholm to purchase –dal, but that in return he demanded the right to manufacture and market a medicinal preparation of Arnberg's composition and bearing his name. If Father agreed to these terms, he was to telegraph the name of the preparation so that advertising could commence at once.

Father would surely have thought twice about this had the Bishop not informed him at the same time that A. O. Arnfelt had offered –dal to other buyers. In his haste, Father cabled the following reply to Grundberg:

Advertise Arnberg's Food. Children. Convalescents. Recipe, letter.

Arnberg.

With the notice of delivery in his hand, Father went into the Bishop's room, where His Grace was sitting surrounded by his womenfolk (my grandmother, my mother, my two unmarried aunts, and one maid). Father held out the sheet of paper to Mother and asked:

'Do you know what this is?'

'A notice of delivery.'

'Yes,' said Father, 'it's notice that the Arnberg family has recovered –dal.'

Great commotion! Mother embraced him, proud and happy. Grandmother burst into tears. The Bishop himself became a little affected and wished my father luck. But once he had had the story of the telegram explained to him, he said:

'It strikes me as being rather American. Just as long as you don't regret it.'

Father grew angry.

'I can assure you,' he said, 'that I intend to acquire –dal in an entirely honourable way. A nutritional preparation is no humbug.'

'I wasn't thinking of your preparation,' Grandfather objected. 'I was thinking of –dal. I don't believe that we Arnbergs are meant to own land.'

Memoirs of a Dead Man

'Just listen to that!' said Father triumphantly. 'The Bishop's become superstitious!'

The Bishop replied:

'Experience is not superstition. I saw my father invest immense sums of money in –dal without getting any corresponding gain from it. And I watched your father ruin himself.'

Father cut him off:

'All the more reason for me not to give up. It's my duty, and that's that.'

In spite of Grandfather's bad mood, the whole Arnberg family was in a state of fevered excitement. Even Uncle Otto, usually the Bishop's most humble servant, dared to praise my father openly, calling him a splendid fellow, and the worthy grandson of Johan Ludvig Arnberg. In her pride and joy in her son, Grandmother even became impertinent. She asked her brother-in-law if he were not tired of his crozier and crook, and wondered if she might offer him refuge in the family home. In any event, she herself intended to move there. She had been forcibly separated from her beloved Ludvig; this was practically a reunion. She was also the one who hit upon the glorious idea that a ceremonial procession should enter –dal as soon as Grundberg's homme d'affaires had signed the contract. Admittedly, the property would not be transferred until 14 March (and it was now the middle of August), but the main house was unoccupied and there was nothing to stop the new owners from entering the splendours of old just as the glory of autumn was showing them at their best. Father, Mother, Grandmother, Uncle Otto, and every Arnberg who felt for the honour of his forebears should take part in the procession. Yes, even Grandfather himself would be there, albeit in effigy. His portrait, painted during the last year at –dal (by the portrait painter Axel Borg, who otherwise specialised in paintings of elk), would have a place of honour in the family carriage, garlanded with oak-leaves representing the value of work. The elderly child went on fantasising in this vein, and Father, who was and would remain a child, found this all quite splendid.

'Idolatry,' muttered the Bishop. 'Ancestral worship. Idolatry!'

And that evening, when the happy clan sat conferring around

the table, deciding all the details of the programme of festivities, he said:

'Johan, being such a good son, you should also be a good father.'

Now, it was the case that my parents felt themselves to have reasons for hope that very summer, although admittedly these were as yet uncomfirmed. (This was in fact me, announcing my impending arrival to the world.) The Bishop's words made them awkward. Mother blushed, and exchanged a hasty, mischievous glance with Father. Father remained serious, and asked:

'How's that? What do you mean?'

The Bishop pulled out his wallet and extracted from it a photograph, which he passed to Father. It was of my half-sister Anna. A girl of seven or eight, thin, pale, suffering, with the broad nose, thick lips and slack features of a scrofulous child.

Father held it in front of him. Then he stood up, saying:

'You're right. I'm a fool.'

He went into his room. Mother wanted to follow him, but Grandfather held her back. He related the whole story, which my mother had not heard before. Father had never spoken about his child. Completely absorbed in his work, his ambition, his *idée fixe*, he had forgotten her.

Early that spring, shortly before my parents returned to Sweden, the Bishop had received a letter from my father's former housekeeper. The worthy Hedda wrote that she had managed to support herself and her child thus far. However, she had now been compelled to take employment as a cleaner on board a ship, and, as a consequence, had had to leave the child, and, as the child was in great need of care, she ventured to ask whether His Grace might give her some help out of pure compassion. Grandfather's reply had taken the form of a sum of money. Moreover, as soon as he was able he travelled to Gothenburg, where mother and daughter were then living, took the child to a doctor, and received confirmation that her condition was indeed troubling. With the doctor's help, he found her a place in a sanatorium for children on the west coast.

'And this,' concluded the Bishop, 'was in no way an attempt to

Memoirs of a Dead Man

alleviate the burden of responsibility on my son-in-law's shoulders. For I believe that we must all take responsibility for our deeds. No, I did it because, as the woman so wisely reminded me, there is such a thing as "pure compassion". Without reference to blood ties or any such nonsense.'

Mother said nothing. She went in to Father. He was lying on the bed, eyes closed, so still that he might have been asleep. My mother was quite calm and did not reproach him. But she demanded that he contact Hedda at once, and, if Hedda agreed, that they should take the child as their own. Father kissed her hands, and they said no more on the subject.

But once even this embarrassing matter seemed to have been settled in the best possible way, Father, incorrigible as ever, became happy as a sandboy once more. He wrote a dozen letters to Hedda, addressing them to different ports. He travelled to the sanatorium, and later told Mother that the girl was actually in radiant health, and that she merely needed a few helpings of Arnberg's Food to put some flesh on her bones.

'If I weren't such a hardened old atheist,' he laughed, 'then I'd be inclined to talk of a blessing from heaven. No sooner have I decided to create a nutritional preparation for children and convalescents, than I have a child who is a convalescent.'

And he worked tirelessly on his 'creation', postponing the ceremonial procession into –dal until a more suitable time. As soon as the recipe was ready, he sent it to Grundberg, along with a letter in which he described recent events. He described how the Bishop had discovered and saved his daughter, and how he himself was now happy that his preparation could help speed up the child's recovery. (He did actually believe in his own preparation.)

From this simple tale, Grundberg concocted his magnificent American advertisement.

Father also wrote that he did not intend to return to America until the following spring, and then only to wind up his affairs.

Late in November he received a reply from his partner. Grundberg wrote that production of Father's preparation had already commenced on a grand scale, but that the cost had proved so high that that a slight change in its composition had been necessary. He went on to say that since Father believed his preparation to be beneficial to convalescents, then surely it must also be excellent for the sick. He concluded by writing that he had taken the liberty of changing the name from 'Arnberg's Food' to 'Arnberg's Tuberculin'. Thanks to Professor Koch's widely reported discovery, 'Tuberculin' was a more powerful word than 'Food', and that psychological influences should not be ignored, etc., etc.

Perplexed and angry, Father picked up the brochure. He read it with growing astonishment: in the end, he was roaring with laughter. With the brochure in his hand, he rushed into the Bishop's room:

'There you are, Father-in-law!' he cried. 'See how how easy it is to become an archbishop in America!'

His Grace took the brochure, adjusted his spectacles with a smile, and read it. He was still smiling when he slowly put it down. But Father was beginning to feel uneasy.

He said:

'A bright lad, that Grundberg. Don't you think?'

'And you?' the Bishop suggested.

Father was offended.

'You surely don't imagine that I intend to allow...'

The Bishop laid his hand on the brochure.

'This is more or less what I've been expecting. I knew it would come, one way or the other. I have a little experience as far as America is concerned – and of what happens to Arnbergs in America. How many of these brochures do you suppose have been printed and distributed? How many portraits of "Arnberg and His Grandfather" do you imagine are on display in the American press? How many brochures in Swedish, Norwegian and Danish are going to flood into Scandinavia?'

'Naturally, I shall put a stop...'

But the Bishop interrupted him:

'I am not asking what you intend to do: I am asking what is going to happen. And what has already happened. Your father made mistakes; that was regrettable, but not, however, dishonourable. You have desired to rehabilitate your father's name – or whatever the phrase is – and you have committed a base act, a mean trick, a crime. Involuntarily, granted – but that does not diminish your responsibility. For pride and conceit may well weigh as heavily as ill intent. You wished to carry the fate of the Arnberg family on your shoulders, yet you could not even carry your own. Honourably, that is. You are a wretched fellow. Your father was an honourable wretch, you are dishonourable. That is the difference. Now go away, I don't wish to see you. You have made me a figure of ridicule, or something still worse. That I shall endure. But I do not wish to see you.'

That same evening my father travelled to Stockholm to see Grundberg's agent. It was true. He had received orders to prepare advertisements for Scandinavia. In the Swedish brochure, however, the Archbishop had been replaced by 'Dr J. L. Arnberg of –dal, the renowned scientist and healer'. Father forbade the agent to take any action at all until he had received further orders. Then he sent the following telegram:

Forbid advertisement, sales. Resign from company.

Arnberg.

The reply read:

Accept resignation from company.

Grundberg.

'What a relief!' Father thought. 'He's come to his senses. I daresay I shall lose –dal this time, but it can – and shall – be won some other way.'

He stayed in Stockholm for a week, planning his return to America, which he no longer wanted to put off. Deep down he was probably hoping that his partner would still help him with –dal, in spite of their differences. His hopes were reinforced when he heard from the agent that the purchase had been finalised in the name of his employer.

'What a relief!' Father thought once more, rubbing his hands.

The following morning the fatal advertisement was in all the newspapers.

Arnberg's Tuberculin.

And the whole wretched story.

Father took his leave of my mother and left her (and me, whose impending arrival was now known for a fact) at the Bishop's Palace. Mother gave him a letter; it was from Hedda, stamped in London, but with such an illegible sender's address that Father could not decipher it.

Hedda wrote that because Arnberg seemed to have come into such excellent fortune, and because Mrs Arnberg seemed to be such a kind-hearted person, it would be a source of eternal joy if they were to take care of Anna. 'Especially as I am in hospital and shall probably not get out alive. If you happen to pass through London on the return journey, Arnberg, it would be a pleasure to see you again, if I might dare to ask without offending your wife.'

Father, however, could not visit her in London. (The address was, as already mentioned, practically illegible.)

On Christmas Day he arrived in St. Paul, and went to find Grundberg. Not at home. For three weeks he wandered around the town. He came across the brochure wherever he went. And advertisements. And posters. And men carrying sandwich-boards. And camels with the terrible jar, larger than life, between their humps. And electric signs. And a procession of poor, pale, suffering children, each of them carrying in its hands a jar of Arnberg's Tuberculin, and led by a venerable old man, marching through the streets.

Eventually he did meet J. W. Grundberg.

'So, here you are,' his partner said, shaking his hand. And added:

'The settlement between us is ready to sign. You can come up to the office whenever you like.'

Father made his way to the factory: the director received him in his private office. Grundberg laid the papers out.

'By the way,' he said, 'your resignation came at just the right time. I'm thinking of selling up. Well, in a year or so. When sales of the Tuberculin start to dry up. It's going wonderfully at the moment.'

'So?' said Father.

'Well,' his partner continued, 'you were actually the one who gave me the idea. To return to the old country. I have, as you know, bought –dal. A lovely old estate, so to speak.'

'How dare you use my name and my preparation without my consent?' Father asked.

'It isn't your preparation,' Grundberg interrupted. 'As I wrote, I had to make substantial changes to the composition, which was ludicrously expensive. So the preparation is nothing to do with you.'

'What about the name, then?' my father shouted, no longer able to control himself. 'The name, you cheat! My honourable name!'

'Well I'm sure I don't know if I gave the Tuberculin an honourable name,' Grundberg replied. 'But in any case, it isn't yours.'

He rang the bell, and said to the office boy:

'Ask Mr Arnberg to come in.'

Father stared at him.

After a while slow, shuffling footsteps could be heard in the corridor that led to Father's old laboratory. The door opened. An old man, a very old man – no, the wreckage of a man – walked in. And bowed.

Grundberg smiled, and said:

'I'll leave you gentlemen alone.'

He went out. They were alone. Father did not move. The old man slowly stepped forward on unsteady legs. He wiped his face with a large red handkerchief, put on his pince-nez, and stared at Father.

'Oh, it's you, Johan,' he said.

The wreck was Uncle Leonard.

'How did you end up here, Uncle?' Father asked.

The old man replied:

'That's quite simple, my dear Johan. Mr Grundberg needed an Arnberg, he advertised for an Arnberg, and he got an Arnberg. He pays me a hundred dollars a month so that he can produce and sell my invention, Tuberculin.'

'But it's my invention!' Father shouted. 'It's my "Food" that that devil has renamed.'

'Yes,' the old man sighed, his hands and head starting to tremble. 'I know so little about all that. Of course I'm not an inventor. I just happened to read the advertisement. That Mr Grundberg needed an Arnberg. I'm sorry if I've upset you, Johan. But it's so rare for anyone to need an Arnberg.'

Father could not find the energy to curse the old man. He left him and ran around the factory, looking for Grundberg. And the more he ran and the more he had to search, the more furious he became. His eyes became bloodshot, his hair was standing on end, his fists clenched. He looked both dangerous and ridiculous at the same time (or so he thought later). In the end he began to shout, scream, roar:

'Grundberg, you cheat! Where are you? Where are you hiding? Rascal! Swindler!'

And he cried:

'My honourable name! My honourable name!'

The workers stared at him, shaking their heads, whispering and laughing behind his back.

But Father went on like a blind man, until he suddenly felt himself being held back by a powerful hand. He stopped at once and turned round. In front of him stood one of the workers, a Swedish-American, a calm, steady, solid lad who looked Father right in the eyes. And he said:

'Try to calm down, Mr Arnberg. You won't gain anything by getting excited.'

Father took a deep breath. He stayed where he was until the worker let go of his arm. Then he put his hand on his shoulder and said:

'You're a splendid chap. You know how to drive out evil spirits. What's your name?'

The man replied: 'Fält.'

Father said:

'I shall remember you. You've done me a favour.'

And he thought: 'Just keep calm, Johan Arnberg, and behave

Memoirs of a Dead Man

like a man, not some silly fool. What do you have to do? Be cold-blooded, and make a quick and wise decision. Well, that's not much to ask of a full-grown man. So just calm down.'

He walked thoughtfully through the rooms, across the yard, and into the office. Behind his desk sat J. W. Grundberg. When Father walked in he pulled out a small, blue-black object, and put it ostentatiously in front of him on the desk. Father pointed at the revolver and smiled. Grundberg blushed. (That fat, coarse, pale blue face could certainly blush – I've seen that for myself.)

Father sat down opposite him; after a while he said:

'Mr Grundberg, I've changed my mind. I will not resign from the company.'

'Is that so?' said Grundberg.

They sat in silence for a while, until Mr Grundberg resumed:

'I imagine, Mr Arnberg, that we would have trouble working together in the future.'

'Maybe,' Father admitted.

'Under the circumstances,' Grundberg went on, 'I should like to suggest that you buy me out of the business.'

Father was struck dumb. And in that moment of enlightenment he saw his whole future, saw himself as sole proprietor of Grundberg's Laboratory, as sole supplier of Arnberg's Paste, Arnberg's Face Balm, Arnberg's Food; he saw himself stepping ashore in Gothenburg a multi-millionaire, greeted by his mother and the Bishop, and he saw himself as the master of –dal.

But he said:

'You would probably be too expensive for me.'

Grundberg replied:

'We shall see. I shall let you know my price in a week.'

Every day that week Father made countless attempts to write to His Grace. On the seventh day he made his way to the office once more. Grundberg named his price: thirty-five thousand dollars.

The sum was greater than Father had hoped, but smaller than he had feared. He knew he could get hold of fifteen thousand there and then without any great difficulty, which left twenty. He wrote to the Bishop, explaining the situation in minute detail. He wrote that the purchase was the only way to prevent the disgraceful abuse of the Arnberg name. But when he came to describe Uncle Leonard's part in the shameful business, he felt oddly diffident and merely wrote that someone called Arnberg had allowed Grundberg the use of his name.

The Bishop replied:

'You are asking me for a loan of approximately seventy-five thousand kronor, which, more or less, is the amount which at best would fall to Sabina on my death. It is as difficult as it is objectionable to me to fulfil your wish. But since it seems to be the only way to repair the damage your stupidity has already caused, and the injury that our name has had to endure as a result, I shall do as you request. However, I wish to make it clear that my opinion of your abilities and wisdom has in no way changed for the better. And I make this express condition: that you find an effective way of preventing Grundberg from further abusing our good name.'

This was why, when the agreement between Father and his partner was being drawn up, Father said:

'I must ask that you make one commitment, Mr Grundberg. That you will not, under any circumstances, make use of my name, or Uncle Leonard's, or that of any other Arnberg, in the course of your future activities.'

Grundberg stood up and started to walk around the room; eventually he stopped in front of Father and laughed in his face.

'What on earth are you laughing at?' Father asked.

But Grundberg merely took out one of his thick, black cigars, bit the end off, lit it, and blew smoke in all directions. Only when Father's impatience had reached the desired level did he say:

'Well, you must forgive my laughter, Mr Arnberg, but I was actually rather surprised. I was certainly expecting you to make at least one condition. And, just between the two of us, I did pitch my price a little high. But I was expecting something else.'

'What? – What?' cried Father, bursting with impatience. 'Tell me!'

'Right. Well, for instance,' Grundberg went on, blowing out smoke, 'for instance, the right for you to purchase, at any time within a period of five, or, let's say, ten years, a certain ironworks in Värmland.'

Once again, Father was struck dumb. Tears came to his eyes. He leaped up and embraced his former partner. Even Grundberg appeared moved, and planted a kiss on Father's cheek. The lawyer and assembled witnesses stared at them, grinning, surprised at the tender scene. The Lord only knew, they had no idea who Father was, nor who Grundberg was, nor even what an ironworks in Värmland was.

Eventually Father said:

'We have never been friends, Grundberg. But we are now. Now I truly feel that we're friends.'

And when Grundberg tried to formulate the clause, he threw up his hands and cried:

'No, no! Nothing on paper between us. I trust your noble nature.'

But Grundberg held fast to his noble decision and guaranteed Father the right to buy –dal at a price of seven hundred thousand kronor at any time within the next ten years.

Father embraced him once more.

Because that was what my poor father was like.

A year passed.

Father was quite overwhelmed with work. He wrote to Mother every week and reported his progress. Arnberg's Paste and Balm were selling worse than before, but he was about to launch his strongest product, Arnberg's Food. As soon as this new product had got going, he would come and collect Mother and me.

Or that was the plan.

One day that factory worker, Fält, now a supervisor, came in to see Father in his office, and said:

'Mr Arnberg, do you remember that I once told you to keep your head?'

'Of course,' Father replied with a frown, because he was not fond of uninvited familiarity. But then he recalled the whole tragicomic scene and burst out laughing, saying:

'That was excellent advice, my dear Fält, and I took it to heart.'

'That's just what you didn't do,' said Fält. He took out a newspaper, opened it, and laid it out in front of Father, saying:

'If you'd kept a cool head that time and thought things through, then we might have avoided this sort of thing.'

Father looked.

It was the dreaded advertisement. Arnberg's Tuberculin! It was all there: Professor Koch, Dr Arnberg *and his grandfather, the Most Reverend* – The only difference was that the remarkable preparation was said to emanate from Dr L. Arnberg's Medicinal Laboratory.

In other words – while Father had been sweating to bring success and a good reputation to J. W. Grundberg's Chemical Laboratory, the eponymous Grundberg had set up a thoroughly bogus factory under the name 'Dr L. Arnberg's Medicinal Laboratory'.

Father felt the blood rush to his head, until he could no longer make out the print. But he said:

'We've done what we could. And been tricked. Fine, we won't worry about that. We've other things to think about. Now go, my dear Fält, and don't let me hear another word about this.'

And Father, summoning all his will-power, determined not to worry about it. He closed his eyes and ears, and all his senses, to Grundberg and Leonard Arnberg's dirty trick. He did not want his work disturbed. He thought: 'I won't let it bother me. I want to get rich, and I want to be master of –dal. I can do that because of the deal I struck with Grundberg. Nothing else matters.'

He carried on working.

One day he received a thick package from Sweden, bearing the Bishop's handwriting. Inside there was not a single written word, merely cuttings from newspapers, advertisements, articles about humbug medicines, among them one from a medical journal in which sorrow and surprise were expressed that a member of a well-known and respected Swedish family should be involved in such a disreputable enterprise.

Father threw the whole lot on to the fire.

'That doesn't bother me,' he thought. 'So long as I can live at –dal one day, then the rest of the world can wallow in the mire all it likes. Arnbergs and non-Arnbergs alike! I won't let it bother me.'

Then Mother wrote. She begged Father, for God's sake, to do all he could to placate the Bishop. Mother's position was already dreadful, and was threatening to become insufferable. She could no longer bear her father's mortification and disgust at his son-in-law.

But Father did not let even this bother him. He replied:

'Dear Sabina,

If a man is to reach his goal, he must make himself deaf, even dead, to everything else. I am nine tenths dead, and the one thing I still have power enough to do is, slowly but surely, to approach my goal.'

He still had confidence in his 'Food'. He would hear nothing of Grundberg, Uncle Leonard and their methods. This was, perhaps, less than wise. Because Grundberg had now gone so far as to appropriate Father's tried and tested products, Amygdaline Paste and Face Balm, claiming in advertisements that these products were only genuine if they came from the inventor's (Dr Arnberg's) own factory. With this he dealt his old company, J. W. Grundberg, a severe blow, one from which Father might have been able to recover with the help of the law. But he turned a deaf ear, and would hear nothing of his uncle and former partner.

Then one day he met Uncle Leonard, quite by chance, on a street in a poor part of town, where a group of children had gathered. The state of Uncle Leonard! Wretched beyond description. Thin as a scarecrow, limp as a rag, dirty as a negro, and hanging half-conscious on the arm of a police constable, who was steadily pulling him through the shrieking, laughing children. Father stopped in his tracks, and, blushing from top to toe, turned away and walked into a side-street. There he calmed down a little, and said to himself:

'What's this, Johan Arnberg? Are you ashamed of your uncle? You might as well be ashamed of yourself before you let yourself be ashamed by anyone else. The old man needs you.'

So he turned back and went up the constable.

'What's the old boy done?' he asked.

The constable, seeing that Father was neatly, even elegantly, dressed, replied:

'He was caught stealing.'

'From whom?' asked Father.

And the constable replied:

'From the prostitute he was visiting.'

The children shrieked and cheered and cried 'Urgh! Urgh!' And, in spite of the wretchedness of the situation, Father could not help but smile.

'Now listen here, my good man,' he said to the constable. 'Does this man look as if he visits women?'

He took the constable and his appendage with him into a bar. After a drink and five minutes' conversation, the constable went away several dollars richer. Father poured something strong inside Uncle Leonard. He came round, sneezed, blew his nose, and said quite coolly:

'Ah, it's you, dear John.'

'Yes, it is,' Father said, 'and you're coming home with me.'

Oh, that he had not done that!

When they got home, Father had him lie down on the sofa. And he asked:

'So what's all this nonsense then?'

The old man pulled a cushion under his head, made himself comfortable, and folded his hands on his stomach.

'Well, I wish I knew, dear John. I don't understand a thing. I was just sitting quietly with my lady friend – '

'Who was this lady friend?' Father asked.

The old man raised his head, stroking his beard thoughtfully, cupped his hand in front of his mouth and whispered:

'Her name is Mrs Feurfield.'

And he blinked, ground his teeth and made all manner of strange expressions.

'I see,' said Father. 'Well, it makes no difference to me what your friends are called. What happened next?'

'Well,' the old man went on, lying back down, 'the next thing that happened was that she suddenly jumped up and started shouting that I had robbed her. And a man came and threw me out, and another man came and took me away, and then you came, dear John, and poured whisky into me – and it wasn't good whisky, dear John.'

'Hmm,' Father said, 'what a shame. So how have you ended up like this? Has your partner gone and left you in the lurch?'

'Not at all,' Uncle Leonard assured him. 'Oh no, he gives me two hundred a month, regular as clockwork. But what good is that? Mrs Feurfield takes half, and the others take the rest, and the remainder goes on whisky. I won't deny that I like my whisky, dear John, but it has to be *good* whisky.'

'So what are we going to do with you now?' Father wondered. 'Shall I take you home, or are you going to stay here for the time being?'

The old man pondered this, then said:

'I think I'll stay with you, John. Because at home there's always someone who wants money from me. Now this one, now that one. One says his name is this, the next that his name is something else. But I'm always the one who has to pay. I really don't know what I've done to end up as the Arnberg family's treasurer in my old age. But there's no point worrying about that. I'll stay with you, dear John, until I've got my strength back.'

And stay he did. For weeks he lay on the sofa, dozing and drinking. He drank prodigious quantities, and Father did not try to stop him. It was pointless to try to reform the old wreck. Sometimes, when Father got back exhausted from the factory, he would take a glass to keep him company. And after a while he too began to acquire a taste for whisky. They would keep each other company, through whole nights, silent, thinking or dozing, each nursing his glass.

After a month or so had passed in this way, Uncle Leonard suddenly broke camp, washed, cleaned himself up, shaved, and sat down to rub the stains from his shabby suit. Father helped him: he dressed him from top to toe, and transformed him into a rather fine old gentleman. Black-clad, silver-haired, with ruddy cheeks and a pious smile on his lips, he looked just like an old priest. He admired his reflection in the mirror and said:

'Well, if Julius could see me now! Tell me, dear John, does the

Bishop ever speak of me?'

'He thinks that you're dead,' Father replied. 'I don't know why.'

Uncle Leonard laughed and said:

'No, dear John, he doesn't think I'm dead. He knows I'm dead. And he's right. I've been dead for almost thirty years.'

'For a dead man,' Father interrupted, laughing, 'I must say that you drink an awful lot of whisky!'

'Maybe,' the old man conceded. 'But there are many types of death. Dozens of them. There's physical death and spiritual, temporary and eternal. There's even civil death. And that's the case with me, dear John. I am dead in the civil sense. Leonard Arnberg died twenty-nine years ago. It was suicide. The Swedish vice-consul, Mr Feurfield, informed the family back in the old country. I myself informed the press, and received twelve fifty for my pains. Since then, it's not Leonard Arnberg but Leonard Fält who's been drinking the whisky.'

'Fält!' Father exclaimed. 'You're called Fält now, Uncle?'

The old man replied:

'It was my grandfather's name, *ante diem criminalis*. I assumed it *post diem expiationis*.'

Father was struck dumb; he started pacing about the room, beating his chest with his fist.

'I've got him now,' he cried, 'I've really got him now!'

The news that Uncle Leonard had officially 'passed away' thirty years ago and had not carried the name of Arnberg since then had given him an idea. He saw another chance to stop Grundberg's dishonourable use of the name. Another chance to appease the Bishop, to return with honour to Mother, to Grandmother, to everything from which he had been cut off. And he ran about the room, beating his chest. But Uncle Leonard said:

'Try to calm down, dear John. You won't gain anything by getting excited. I know perfectly well what you're thinking. You're going to set yourself against Grundberg. Do as you think best, dear John. But I warn you, Grundberg holds all the trump cards.'

Father went to a lawyer, explained the situation, received

encouragement.

The lawsuit between the proprietor of J. W. Grundberg's Chemical Laboratory, Dr Arnberg, and the proprietor of Arnberg's Medicinal Laboratory, J. W. Grundberg, lasted for three years, and swallowed my father's income and my parents' savings, every last penny. It is, however, probable that Father would have won in the end, because Uncle Leonard's testimony was decisive.

Leonard Fält, alias Arnberg, testified that he, at Grundberg's insistence, had assumed the name Arnberg, and that he under this name had signed a contract by which he gave up the right to manufacture certain chemical, cosmetic and medicinal preparations which were claimed – falsely – to be of Fält's, alias Arnberg's, invention. Grundberg's unreservedly expressed intention had been to gain control by these means of a name that was already tried and tested commercially with regard to the above-mentioned products. To the defence lawyer's question as to whether Fält was related to the Swedish Arnberg family, he conceded that this was indeed the case, but that he had no right whatsoever, nor, come to that, any responsibility, to bear the name for that reason. The Leonard Arnberg whose name he had assumed had taken his own life by drowning in 1863. This fact was supported by official documentation.

Other witnesses who confirmed Uncle Leonard's identity were his housekeeper or landlady of many years, Mrs Hansen; his intimate lady friend of thirty years, Mrs Feurfield, widow of the Swedish-Norwegian vice-consul, M. Feurfield; his intimate lady friend of twenty years, Miss Claire Aurore Clémence Léon; and finally his own son, Fält the supervisor.

After Uncle Leonard had testified, he returned to the sofa and the glass: he degenerated more and more, became slovenly and difficult. He was also in very low spirits. He said to Father:

'I've made a great sacrifice. Grundberg isn't paying me any more. If you can't give me two hundred a month, things will turn out badly for both of us – '

Father promised him two hundred dollars, and more besides. He thought he was saved. The case was dragging on, but once it was won, it would, in the first instance, put a stop to the wretched

Tuberculin scandal; secondly, it would give him a considerable sum in compensation; and, thirdly, it would relieve him of an untrustworthy competitor who was threatening to ruin him completely. With this in mind, Father felt justified in feeling optimistic. And when he was not always able to do so, he would join Uncle in a glass or two.

The old man lay on his sofa, hands folded on his beard or around the glass. He was scarcely ever properly awake, nor ever completely asleep. Sometimes he would mutter long strings of words, impossible to understand, without meaning, without context, noun after noun. But he always ended with an 'ah well, thank heavens', or 'well, thank goodness', or something like that. Sometimes he would raise his head a little, peer at Father, blink and grimace.

'Ah yes, John,' he would say. 'Ah yes.'

And Father would smile and nod. That was their conversation.

Over-exertion and the long, painful wait for a ruling in the case had meant that Father took a peculiar pleasure in the old man's listlessness and almost idiotic lethargy. The gloomy room in the evenings, the reclining figure, like the sculpture on an old tomb, the monotonous ramblings, the whisky – relaxation.

Once Father asked:

'What do you do with your money?'

And he might well ask, because Father supplied him with everything, and since the old man hardly ever moved, it was well-nigh impossible to understand how quickly the coins left his shabby leather purse.

Uncle Leonard replied:

'Well, you see, I have creditors.'

'Nonsense!' Father said. 'You must have been caught by tricksters, Uncle. Those creditors must be imposters.'

'What difference does it make,' the old man muttered, 'when I know I'm in debt?'

Father laughed. Yes, every now and then, as he sat there in the twilight watching the perpetually dozing old man, he would burst out laughing. 'What a life!' he would think. Sometimes he would have to get up and go over to the sofa, to let his finger-tips

Memoirs of a Dead Man

reassure him that a weak, uneven, slightly erratic flow of blood was still coursing through those hard, knotted veins.

And Father would think:

'How long are we actually alive? The boundary of death – where exactly does it run? Is it really just that feeble little trickle of blood that marks the difference between life and death?'

Yet another year passed. Father carried on working as before, but without pleasure, sluggishly, as though wading through pitch. He also wrote less often to Mother, and Mother answered his letters less often. She wrote so curtly and with so few words.

Then one day Grandfather, the Bishop, wrote. Father read the letter through once, twice, three times. Then he showed it to Uncle Leonard.

The Bishop wrote simply that if his son-in-law did not wish to be the cause of a complete break with his family, he should abandon the lawsuit immediately and seek a settlement with his former partner, J. W. Grundberg. That was all. No explanations.

Father asked:

'Can you understand what he means?'

It was late one evening: Uncle had drunk a considerable amount. This notwithstanding, he sat himself up, pushed back his hair, ran his fingers through his beard, blew his nose, wiped the sleep from his eyes, and said:

'Well, my dear John – the Bishop's abandoning you. That makes all the difference. What he means? He means that you should obey him. At once.'

'That's ridiculous!' Father cried, and starting to thump his chest (as he always did when he was upset). 'He must be mad. Am I to abandon a case I embarked upon largely for his sake? It's out of the question!'

He went into his bedroom, slamming the door behind him, undressed, went to bed, and fell asleep.

At about two o'clock that night he was woken by Uncle Leonard. The old man dressed in his best clothes: overcoat, top hat, cane and gloves.

'John,' he said, ' I wanted to ask you something. Can you get me a thousand dollars tomorrow or the day after?'

'What's that?' Father muttered, rubbing his eyes. 'What's all this? A thousand dollars! Like hell I can!'

'Are you quite sure?' asked Uncle Leonard.

'I'm quite sure I can't,' Father replied. 'And I'm even more sure that I don't want to.'

'I'll be off, then,' Uncle said.

'Where to?' Father asked.

'I'm going to see Grundberg,' Uncle replied, nodded, patted Father gently on the shoulder, and left. Father heard him open the front door, and then the soft whirring of the lift.

'Well, I'll be damned!' he muttered, then lay down and fell asleep again.

The following morning there was a terrible storm, snow and bitter cold. Father felt out of sorts and decided not to go to the factory. He paced about the room, and, once he had thoroughly aired the place after Uncle Leonard, he felt a bit lighter at heart.

He sat down at the desk and started a letter to Mother. He was in good humour and wanted to write something optimistic. 'Sabina could do with a few encouraging words,' he thought. 'I'll write that I shall soon be back to collect her and the little lad. I'm justified in writing that because my position's stronger than ever. And it'll be a splendid riposte to His Grace's threats.'

He rubbed his hands with glee, took out paper and pen, wrote a few words, then crossed them out. He wrote a page, tore it up. Started again. Then the telephone rang.

It was Fält, the supervisor. He announced that he intended to leave the factory at the end of the month.

'I can't hear you – I can't hear you!' Father shouted into the mouthpiece, although he could hear every word quite clearly. He needed time to think. The supervisor repeated what he had said. 'Aha!' Father thought. 'The old man has got to him.'

'Fine, Mr Fält!' he shouted into the mouthpiece. 'Go to hell! That's fine by me!'

And he hung up.

'Uncle Leonard's got to him,' Father thought. 'Or else it's Grundberg. Yes, it's bound to be Grundberg, starting to steal my people. Well, I'll teach him to let his conscience speak.'

He poured himself a whisky and went out into the storm to find his lawyer. The storm was raging, and the snow clung to his eyelashes. Father started to cough. He went into a bar and downed a whisky. Then he went to his lawyer. The two men agreed to seek a prohibition for Grundberg to sell any preparation bearing the name of Arnberg until the court's ruling was announced. Under the circumstances, the judge could surely not deny such a request.

Happy, but somewhat agitated, Father returned home. He drank one whisky, then another. He felt powerful. He had dealt a mortal blow to his enemy. He would show that an Arnberg was not to be trifled with. He felt a desire to share some of his strength with poor Sabina, languishing over there in the Bishop's Palace like a prisoner of His Grace. Father went over to the desk.

On the desk lay a letter, newly delivered. It was from Mother. She wrote that she was ill. Moreover: that the Bishop had told her what Johan was engaged in, and that she could not understand how he was prepared to pay such a price for success. Moreover: that she could no longer bear to mediate between father and husband, taking blows from both sides. Moreover: that the Bishop believed that it would be best for both of them if a divorce could be arranged amicably. In conclusion: that she had now, at long last, managed to explain the situation to Johan, delivering it into his judgement.

From all of this, Father extracted only one lucid thought: 'Yet another betrayal. Soon I shall be alone.'

He lay down on the sofa, Uncle Leonard's sofa. 'Well,' he thought, 'she's grown tired. Fine. But I haven't. I know what I want. I want money, I want seven hundred thousand kronor. I want Father's and Grandfather's estate back. The estate stolen from us by A. O. Arnfelt. That's what I want, that's my goal. Nothing else matters.'

And he thought:

'Life isn't for living, life is about reaching a goal. What goal? It doesn't matter which.'

He jumped up, took his hat, and rushed out into the storm once more. He went up and down the streets, at random to begin with.

By and by he realised what it was he wanted. And he hardened his heart.

He went to the telegram office and sent His Grace, the Bishop of W. the following:

I accept divorce. Arrange formalities.

Johan Arnberg.

He grew calmer, returned home, lay down on Uncle's sofa, drank one whisky and then another, fell asleep. He dreamed of the Bishop's Palace, calm and silent, and of Mother's gentle young face. 'Oh, such treachery,' he thought, still in the dream. 'Oh, such a little Judas.'

Months passed, half a year. Father went on working in the laboratory and in his office. Everything went tolerably well for him. The judge granted the requested prohibition. The case was approaching its conclusion and the outcome seemed in no doubt. J. W. Grundberg remained calm. There were no further desertions among the factory staff. At work, Father felt like a conquering hero. In the evenings he drank whisky.

'They can't touch you, Johan,' he would think, beating his chest. 'No, you're made of strong stuff, a man to reckon with. You're an Arnberg. You don't let anyone get the better of you.'

During the day he was very pleased with himself; in the evening, and even at night, he drank whisky.

One morning Grundberg's legal representative was announced.

'At last,' thought father, rubbing his hands together. 'This is when we see the fruits of our labour. Now the wise farmer just has to harvest them.'

He gulped down a whisky and asked for the man to be shown in.

'Well?' said Father, and smiled.

But Grundberg's legal representative was a serious man, who calmly sat down on his chair, rubbed his nose, popped a soda pastille into his mouth, and took his time.

'Well?' Father repeated, frowning.

Following his usual procedure, the lawyer pulled out a file and rifled through it before he began:

'Mr Arnberg, no doubt you have been surprised by our method of dealing with this matter? We have remained on the defensive, so to speak, indeed, sometimes barely that. That this has happened has been in no way my decision. But my client has chosen to mix emotional and business matters, and we all know what happens if one does that.'

'Grundberg – emotional!' Father laughed, clapping his hands.

But the lawyer went on:

'You have based your case upon the claim that we have made use of the Arnberg name without having any right to do so. Now, you know as well as I do that our associate and head of laboratory Mr Leonard Fält, and Leonard Arnberg, who is supposed to have died by drowning thirty years ago, are one and the same person.'

'I know nothing of the sort!' Father growled.

The lawyer smiled.

'Let us make a distinction. You know, but will not admit to knowing. Quite the right course of action, granted – as long as you have the wherewithal to defend your point of view. This, unfortunately, is no longer the case.'

'Oh, isn't it?' Father mocked. 'May I ask why not?'

'Because you have pushed us, not without skill, I might add, to the point where Mr Grundberg can no longer allow his feelings to dictate our course of action.'

'Now let's have a whisky,' exclaimed Father, 'because you're entertaining me immensely.'

But the lawyer declined, and went on:

'Allow me first to point out that we now, as you are doubtless aware, have Mr Fält-Arnberg completely at our disposal. He is prepared to retract his testimony at any time, and, in order to save his own skin, he would seek to prove that you persuaded him to give said testimony by muddling his senses with strong liquor. Well, you may rest assured, Mr Arnberg, that we do not wish to go as far as that. For us it is enough to prove that Mr Fält and Leonard Arnberg are one and the same man, third son of Dr Johan Ludvig Arnberg and his wife Claire Aurore Clémence Lebossu, and brother of your late father, owner of –dal, and of His

Eminence the Bishop of W.'

'Let us suppose that you can actually prove that,' Father interrupted. 'What do you propose?'

'We propose,' the lawyer said, rifling through his papers again, 'we propose that you abandon the case immediately, that you pay my client's costs, that you assure him in writing of his undisputed right to produce and sell certain preparations (more closely specified herein), and, finally, that you release him from a certain clause in a previous contract concerning the right of purchase to the –dal estate – '

Father went over to the cupboard, took out a bottle of whisky and two glasses.

'Now, my dear fellow, let's have a drink,' he said. 'Let's drink to your success. I've taken it to heart because you're a damned amusing fellow. Would you be so kind as to tell me why you did not present your evidence about Mr Fält-Arnberg's identity at the outset?'

The lawyer replied:

'Certainly. It was wholly a matter of sentiment. Mr Grundberg showed far too much consideration for His Eminence the Bishop, and for the honour of the Arnberg name.'

'In other words, it is Mr Grundberg who is defending the honour of the Arnberg name? Against me? Against me! No, really, let's have a drink. I tell you, let's drink to your health. You're a quite superior sort of rogue!'

The lawyer pushed the glass away.

'You will gain nothing by exciting yourself, Mr Arnberg. It appears that you are less aware of the facts of this matter than I am. Would you therefore be so good as to pay a little attention to this memorandum regarding said Fält-Arnberg.'

'Go on,' Father said, emptying his glass and sitting down.

Glancing over the paper, the lawyer read:

'Leonard Arnberg – who, at the age of twenty-three, arrived in New York with his servant, a certain Adolf Grundberg – my client's father – lived a dissolute and expensive life for a couple of years – was detained as a result of relations with persons of ill-repute – was committed for observation to a mental hospital in X.

Here Mr Arnberg remained for a little over a year; his family in Sweden was contacted for information regarding his previous circumstances. By the time the answer arrived, confirming that Arnberg had suffered from melancholy and protracted bouts of depression during his formative years, the patient had already succeeded in getting out of the establishment by unknown means.

'Between the two of us,' the lawyer added, 'I can tell you that it was my client's father who helped him to escape. As thanks, Grundberg senior received a sum of money which left him in a position to set up a small business. As you see, my client has good reason to show Mr Fält-Arnberg a certain consideration.'

'Go on!' Father said, and the lawyer continued:

'Five years later Arnberg appeared on the Pacific coast. The life that he led and the people with whom he surrounded himself led to his being arrested once more. Arnberg now asked to speak to the Swedish-Norwegian vice-consul, Mr Feurfield. To him he made a complete confession regarding a crime he is supposed to have committed prior to his departure from Sweden. His mental state was, however, such that it was once again deemed necessary to commit him for observation. At the same time, the Swedish authorities were contacted for details of the crime. At length a reply was received. The crime really had taken place, without the perpetrator ever being caught; the American authorities were asked to interrogate Arnberg, and the possibility of requesting his extradition was considered. This reply – insofar as it concerned the crime – was related to the patient, who then exclaimed: "You see! I was right!". However, the report of the doctor in charge of the observation indicated that there was no doubt that Arnberg was suffering from a specific mental disorder, for which reason it was decided to send him to the hospital in X. During the journey he succeeded in escaping a second time. It is not known whether or not he was assisted in this. One month later, the authorities and the Swedish-Norwegian consulate in F. were informed that some items of clothing, etc., belonging to Arnberg had been found in circumstances which suggested suicide by drowning. This, in fact, is the only actual evidence for Mr Arnberg's death, and, I am sure you will agree, it is singularly inconclusive.'

'It seems to have proved adequate thus far,' Father interrupted.

'Thus far, yes,' conceded the lawyer. 'But only because we have not contested its validity. From now on we consider ourselves forced to throw discretion to the winds.'

'Too late!' Father crowed. 'Too late!'

But the lawyer said:

'I hope it is not too late, Mr Arnberg. Because if you do not accept our modest proposal for settlement, we are quite determined to drag out the whole story, from the very beginning. And before you expose your family to that humiliation, you will doubtless have reason to think the matter over a few times.'

My father really did think the matter over; upon which he said:

'You see! I was right! This is, quite simply, an attempt at blackmail. Well, my dear sir, tell your client that Mr Fält-Arnberg's honour is neither more nor less of a concern to me than Mr Grundberg's. That's all I have to say. Good day!'

'It is not merely a question of his – ' began the lawyer. But Father cried: 'Good day to you! Good grief! Farewell! Farewell! And don't come back!'

The lawyer stood up, gathered his papers, and buttoned his coat. Then he said:

'Do you really not know what crime your uncle confessed to?'

'No,' said my father, 'but even if it were murder, it would be no concern of mine. We must all take responsibility for our deeds.'

The lawyer bowed and walked towards the door, but turned back:

'At any rate, surely it would be of interest to you if I told you?'

'Oh, all right then. Go ahead!' Father gave in.

The lawyer said:

'Your uncle confessed that he had taken the life of his own father, Dr J. L. Arnberg, by means of poison.'

'Yes, of course,' Father muttered. He poured out a glass and emptied it. He said:

'We'll drink to that. Tell Mr Grundberg that we drank to that.'

But suddenly he went into a rage, throwing himself at the lawyer and casting him head first out of the door.

Returning to his desk, he said:

'Yes, of course, that's the sort of old family trap that they're laying for me. Well, it won't work. You only live once, let the dead bury their dead. I know my goal; nothing else matters to me. No, not the slightest bit.'

He went back to work; working and drinking. He heard nothing from Grundberg, nor from Uncle Leonard. Then one day he received a letter from Sweden, bearing the Bishop's handwriting. It was an extremely thick letter, and he put it to one side unopened. That same day, the office boy brought in a rather soiled visiting card:

Mr Hansen jr.
of Hahn, Huhn & Co.

Father did not know a Mr Hansen; he assumed it was a matter of business, and had the man shown in. And in walked Mr Hansen, twenty-five years old, pasty-faced, with beady little eyes, like porcelain, skin like clay. He was dressed all in black, and around his top hat was a fading piece of crêpe. He bowed and said:

'Mr Arnberg, may I offer my most sincere condolences – '

'What's that?' Father muttered tiredly. 'Who are you?'

He replied:

'My name is Hansen, of Hahn, Huhn & Co. My mother has been Mr Leonard Fält's landlady for many years. My father hailed from Copenhagen, but my family has its roots in Skåne, or, to be more precise, Ystad – '

'What in God's name does this have to do with me?' Father wondered.

'Well, it has nothing to do with you,' Hansen admitted. 'But I thought I should introduce myself. I am here on delicate business. Mr Fält has sent me. He deeply regrets what has occurred. And, since he recently happened to find, in the left inside pocket of his tailcoat, this letter, which he must have picked up in a moment of distraction – '

Hansen pulled out the letter, wrapped in a handkerchief.

'– he has asked that it be delivered, along with his most sincere apologies and regrets. He asks that you take note of the fact that the envelope is unopened, and, albeit unfortunately somewhat soiled, quite intact.'

Father grabbed the letter; it was from Mother.

He said:

'Thank Mr Fält; and thank you for your trouble.'

'Not at all, please don't mention it,' said Mr Hansen, who withdrew, bowing.

Father inspected the envelope; it was unopened. He examined the post-mark; it was more than a year old. He opened it.

It was a letter that my mother had written in some happy, peaceful moment, perhaps a summer's day, as I played by the fountain at the Bishop's Palace, running time after time to her window to show her the wonderful things I had found. It was a trivial letter, with long, detailed descriptions of me and my doings. A letter without content, a letter that contained everything.

My father read it and then put it down. He said to himself:

'See the sacrifice I've made!'

And he said:

'How is possible to have faith in anyone after such a betrayal? And how is it possible to believe in happiness through love, or even the cool happiness from attachment and faithfulness? Isn't everyone doomed to be betrayed, and doomed to betray? Yes, just as she betrayed me. My little one. But it doesn't bother me. I don't care about this or anything else, as long as I reach my goal. Because the meaning of life is to reach a goal. It doesn't matter which. Here I am, putting aside my wife's last love letter in order to read my father-in-law's letter, in which the same wife admits her awakening from this foolishness.'

And he picked up the Bishop's letter.

'Talking of which,' he thought, 'how will our divorce affect the business? After all, most of the capital I've used has been Sabina's. Well, as long as I win the court case, things will work out fine. But it's a nuisance, nonetheless, and puts yet another obstacle in my path.'

He opened the letter, saying to himself:

'Anyway, I can't let it stop me. I don't intend to let anything stop me. I know what I want, and that's more than enough for me.

The honour of the family? – thank you very much! No, it's a blessed relief when your will is freed from all these sentimental impediments. Dishonour? No, I shall not submit to that or any other word, no matter how big.'

He unfolded the letter and read:

Dear Son,

Now I am writing to you. May you forget, as I have forgotten, forgive as I have forgiven. Dear son, forgive me! For I cannot alone bear what I have wrought asunder in my ignorance. Our Sabina is – '

Father closed his eyes; he put his hand over the word. He thought: 'This is something I don't understand. He's writing something – '

He started again:

'Now I am writing to you. May you forget, as I have forgotten, forgive as I have forgiven. Dear son, forgive me! For I cannot alone bear – '

Suddenly he understood. He stood up. And fell, like a broken reed.

That same evening Father took the night-train to New York. But as he was wandering the streets during the hours before departure the following happened.

A man spoke to him. It was Mr Hansen. He said:

'I see that you are looking for someone, Mr Arnberg. Dare I hope that it is Mr Fält that you seek?'

'Of course you may,' Father replied, and, looking about him now, he saw that he had chanced upon the side street where he had once met Uncle Leonard with the police constable.

'Where does he live?' Father asked.

'He lives in my mother's house,' Hansen replied. 'Be so good as to accompany me.'

Father followed him and went into a boarding-house of the very worst kind. In the corridor he bumped into a gaggle of decaying wretches, aged prostitutes, the skeletons of saucy minxes with spots of rouge and shabby curls pressed onto parchment skin. Father was not much concerned with any of this; but the poor air pained him. He began to cough, and thumped his chest with his fist.

Hansen said:

'You have a weak chest, Mr Arnberg? That is a complaint of which one cannot be too careful. Fortunately there is a cure. Arnberg's famous Tuberculin – '

Father looked askance at him; he began to stammer:

'But goodness me – I forgot – you yourself are of course – . But I also happen to be an agent for the company, and can offer the most favourable terms.'

Father stepped into a room, a dining room to judge by the smell. Around the table sat three women of indeterminate but rather high age, playing cards and drinking beer. On a black leather sofa, from whose imitation leather the horsehair stuffing was escaping, lay Uncle Leonard. On his back as usual, with his hands clasped around a glass. Father said hello.

'Oh, it's you, dear John,' Uncle Leonard said, and stood up with some difficulty. He went over to the table.

'John Arnberg,' he said, 'may I present – Mrs Feurfield, Mrs Hansen, Miss Léon.'

The three Furies opened their jaws into broad smiles, fluttered their black eye-lashes, and sighed. Father bowed, and said absent-mindedly:

'So, these are the ladies who cheat you out of all your money.'

'That's right,' Uncle Leonard replied, 'these are the three. But come with me into my room. There's something I want to ask you.'

He put his arm beneath Father's and led him through a small room, where young Fält was seated at a carpenter's bench carving a little toy boat, and into an even smaller room, whose only furnishings consisted of a table, three chairs, and a quantity of bottles. 'This is my room,' said Uncle Leonard, and invited Father to sit. 'It's a small drinking den. Of the very simplest kind, as you can see. But then, what does one want with luxury and finery? Do you want a whisky?'

Father declined.

'I understand,' said Uncle Leonard, filling a glass. 'You no longer need this sort of thing. It is only periods of waiting that need to be shortened. Yes, I really really am very sorry for both you and, even more so, brother Julius. But let us talk a little about business. Have you received a visit from Grundberg's lawyer?'

Father confirmed that he had.

'Well, what have you decided?'

Father replied:

'I don't know; I haven't decided anything. I'm going to Sweden and probably not coming back. I shall probably write to Grundberg or to my lawyer. I don't really know.'

Uncle Leonard nodded.

'No, of course not. How should you know? The main thing is that you're getting away from that job; it doesn't suit you. Now, when you meet the Bishop, be sure to give him my greetings. It's the first time I send a greeting to brother Julius. Unfortunately Grundberg has been telling tales out of school; Julius knows that my suicide was a bluff.

'Do you see,' he continued after a swig, 'I'm very fond of Julius. He's the good, the best part of us Arnbergs. Finely sieved, so to speak. The rest of us are chaff. I would gladly sacrifice my life for him. And have actually done so, or at least half done so. For God knows how many years. But you understand that a man who has done what I have done does not have much left to sacrifice.'

Father looked at the time:

'Yes, what is it that you've done?' he asked absent-mindedly. 'The lawyer told me something very peculiar. Was it true?'

'True,' said Uncle Leonard, 'in so far as it really was me who poured arsenic into Father's bottle and set the trap. True also in so far as I did so knowingly and willingly. But if I were to be charged with having done so out of ill intent, or, as the phrase goes, as a result of mental illness, I would have to protest. I acted out of the best intentions, and besides, with the full complicity of my father.'

'Oh, really?' Father muttered, looking at his watch.

'Oh yes,' the old man said, wringing whisky out of his beard. 'You see, dear John, it is a complete delusion, and a foolish one at that, to believe that one can eradicate a deed simply by not carrying it out. Deeds are not like us humans, they don't die of themselves. Each one has eternal life, and we humans are born to accomplish them, to nourish them, so to speak. With our miserable flesh, which is grass. Whether the deed is large or small, good or bad, that is something we know precious little about. Although one has one's opinions, of course.

'Regarding this specific case,' he went on, 'you know that my grandfather – Old Fält, as I usually call him, it sounds so intimate – carried out two particularly notable deeds. As far as we can judge, they were not terribly fine deeds, and we need not mention them. Well, Fält died; he even died three times: as Fält, as Fältman, and as Arnberg. But did the deed die? No. It merely changed its form. And it fell, naturally enough, to my father to maintain it in his turn. But he refused. He was half a saint, just like Julius. He did not care for such deeds. He hoped for something better for himself and his family. And he persuaded himself that the deed would die of itself if he failed to carry it out.

'But of course, dear John, he was mistaken. And when he grew older, he realised that he was mistaken. He fell to brooding. One could well divide deeds into two main types, deeds of life and deeds of death. Or as we might put it, good and evil. Because, since time immemorial, we have regarded anything connected with life as good, and the teachings of Christ have hardly changed that. Well, in his youth, when Father was strong and courageous and reckless, he decided to switch from deeds of death to deeds of life. As we know, he became a scientist. But that did not satisfy him for long; doubt gnawed away at him, and he needed proof, he needed to embody his deed. So he bought the big, old, run-down ironworks. And with thirty years of unstinting labour, he made it a model of its kind. This might well be thought a deed of life. It isn't the least bit surprising that first brother Ludvig and now you have fought to follow the same path. And it's connected to your longing for –dal as well, of course. That's not as foolish as it might seem, but it has always been doomed to come to naught.

'Because you don't have my father's strength. And not even he succeeded. The deed of life may have been carried out, granted, but the deed of death did not relinquish its hold. Father tried every way to break free, including the old tradition of paying for absolution. He took in a Frenchman, Lebossu. Well, that old man was none other than the young valet Battiste Léon, whom Old Fält incited to murder Count Arnfelt. Father took him in, and suffered ceaselessly from the old man's malice. Eventually he married Léon's daughter. It was simply an attempt to pay for absolution, but the deed can't be cheated with dodges thought up by mere mortals. That was something he had to learn.

'Try to understand his position in human terms, in worldly terms, so to speak. He had lived a long life as a thoroughly decent, competent, industrious, merciful man. He enjoyed greater than usual respect and repute. He had an honourable name, and a crowd of children to inherit it. And he knew – felt – that all of this had to be destroyed by a deed which had a claim on him. Yes, one which had him – body and soul. So what did he do? He availed himself of a human prerogative; he conjured with thoughts. That, my boy, is our famed freedom. Freedom of will, as it is called.

'He couldn't escape the deed of death. But – hey presto! – he was no longer the one who had to carry it out. On the contrary, he was to become its victim. This conjuring act can be seen in thousands and thousands of acts. I should like to call it The Conjuring Act of the Clenched Teeth. Better to be killed than kill, better to be stolen from than to steal, better to suffer than cause suffering.

'This was how my father got his famous *idée fixe*. He would be the victim of murder. That he should see his executioner in his wife shows, perhaps, the direction of his stifled thoughts. Yes, it all fits. Because a man who wishes to atone for a crime is doomed to multiply the crime.

'This also fits with what I myself saw. I was alone with Father and Mother that year. My siblings had already flown the nest: Klara was married, Ludvig was in Zürich, Julius in Göttingen, Léonie in Vevey. I was helping Father with some construction plans. He seldom spoke to me, but when the day's work was done, he used to go into my room, sit in the corner of the sofa and smoke his pipe. Lord knows, it was no pleasure for me to sit with the old man. I stayed out in the evenings, went out carousing with other youngsters. But no matter how late I came home, I would find him sitting in the corner of the sofa. Only after I had opened the window to let out the pipe-smoke would he go up to his room. Father never locked the door to his bedroom, no, he usually left it ajar. Mother, on the other hand, always slept with her door locked.

'We lived like that for months, all winter, and I didn't pay much attention to Father's eccentricities. Towards spring his mood lightened, he would invite guests and occasionally throw grand parties. Mother thought that these were good signs. And of course I was enjoying myself. Not least at the sight of Father and Mother, who had begun to touch one another like young folk do. Father had always been very polite towards Mother, but now he became so chivalrous, even romantic, that I had to hide my smiles. Goodness, I thought, they're young again. It was like a real honeymoon. Mother was delighted, but a little anxious at the same time. And when Father put his arm round her waist one beautiful evening and led her down into the park, I saw her give a start and catch her breath. But I heard them talking and laughing down in the park. It all seemed to be as good as one could have hoped.

'Then one day Mother came into my room and said: "Leonard, you have a mirror of your own, haven't you? Why do you insist on shaving in front of mine? At the very least you could stop leaving the blade after you, open as well, so that it scratches the table-top."

'The fact was that Mother had an unusually fine mirror which had once belonged to the Arnfelt family. It was a Venetian piece, in a very ornate silver frame bearing the figures of seven women. And the glass was so clear that I really did make a habit of using that mirror on occasions when I wished to look particularly fine. But on that occasion I had not done so. Well, I thought no more about it and put the blade in its case.

'That evening it was once again lying on Mother's dressing table. We couldn't understand it, neither Mother nor I. And this was repeated time after time. In the end I locked the razor away. But the following day Mother came in with another knife. She was angry. "If you don't stop spoiling my table," she said, "I'll have to tell your father." I inspected the blade and replied: "This isn't mine. Here, you can see Father's monogram." Mother went out, and I heard no more about the blade.

'But one night – at about two o'clock – she woke me up asking for my help. Father was ill. I leapt up and we both ran in our nightclothes up the stairs and along the corridor to Mother's room. You see, she lived in the room in the east gable, and Father in the west. As I came through the door, I saw Father sitting at the dressing table. He was wearing his shaving gown. On the table two candles were burning, and between them lay the blade, unfolded. In the mirror I could see Father's face. His eyes were closed. His head was resting on his right shoulder at a strange angle.

'Then I felt something very peculiar, up here at the top of my scalp. As if some devil were dripping boiling tar into my brain. It's still there, all sticky, although the heat is gone. I grew scared, you understand, I thought Father had killed himself. But Mother whispered: "I think he's sleep-walking. We must be very careful."

'At that very moment Father opened his eyes: he looked at me in the mirror. First at Mother, then at me. My dear father and I looked each other in the eye. I believe that was the very first time.

'And at that moment my suffering began, not, by any means, that I would want to compare it to that of my poor father. Oh no, mine consisted purely of obeying. He was the one who had to give the orders. Eventually we came to an agreement, or rather – eventually I understood him. Naturally enough, he never spoke in words. He would sit there in the corner of the sofa night after night, and, letter by letter, I had to decipher his silence. Finally I understood what it was that he didn't want to do. And what I had to do as a consequence. By then my dear mother was already dead. And I fulfilled my role as best I could. And, I hope, in full collusion with my father. Then I came here and lived it up a bit. Because the allotted time has to be filled one way or other. I have had one task in life – to remain dead and buried. At least as far as Julius and the better part of the family are concerned. But now that's come to an end, since Grundberg has given away my secret. It was quite a blow for Julius, which is why he ordered you to seek conciliation. Well, it's all the same to me. I drink my good whisky and shall eventually forget all about it. Sometimes I even forget what it was that I did in the half-light of that June night, as Father lay tossing and turning in his bed. But then I get worried and seek out people who know the facts. And that was why I was going to see your father, that time we met. Ah well, now the next generation can have a go. I've settled down with my memories – or rather, my friends: Mrs Feurfield, Miss Léon, and Mr Hansen – '

And he said goodbye to Father.

But in the stairwell Father met his former supervisor, J. P. Fält.

'Mr Arnberg,' he said, 'you have a son, don't you?'

Father said that he did. Fält asked him to wait a moment, disappeared, and came back with the little boat he had been carving.

'It's a toy boat,' he said, blushing. 'Well. Will you give it to Master Arnberg?'

'You're too kind,' Father replied. He put the boat under his arm and left. That was the dreamboat of my childhood, the brig *Claire Aurore*.

Chapter 3

The Bishop's Palace

I only the remember the summers at the Bishop's Palace. I remember the garden, the white poplars, the copper beech, the chestnuts (whose fruits lend themselves to all manner of applications within the smaller sort of ship-building industry), I remember the roses, the monkshood, the peonies, the wisteria that grew against the wall by my mother's window, the espaliered pears, the thicket of plum trees, the gooseberry hedge, and the poor apple trees, whose fruit never wanted to ripen. And I remember the dovecote and the doves: the arrogant white peacock doves, the puffed-up, brightly-coloured rainbow doves, the giant doves, the tumbling doves, dainty, elegant, quick, as well as a whole horde of plebeian grey pigeons.

Above all else I remember the fountain and my mother's window. The fountain was in the form of a boy with a fish. The fish squirted water: the boy laughed. I did not much care for the sculpture, but the wide pool, edged by a small-leafed, barren, tatty creeper, was the sea on which my ships sailed. Sailed to Father, because Father was far away on the other side of the sea.

I might add that Father was merely a name, nothing more. A suitable title for the otherwise unknown destination of my voyages.

Mother, on the other hand, Mother sat in the window, always. I was certain of this, and had I doubted that she was there in the alcove of the window I would not have dared stay in the garden. Because I was rather timid by nature, and often discovered suddenly threatening dangers of all kinds. Then I would run away to the window and stretch up my hand. And Mother would take it in hers. I would stand like that for a while and think. My anxiety would subside, I would forget the danger, I would get some new idea, I would twist my hand out of Mother's and dash off on my own business.

Mother's window was always open. A blue darkness framed by a dull grey curtain. I could see Mother's white hand. It would suddenly emerge from the darkness, stop, sink, disappear. Mother was sewing. Sometimes I would see her head, her sleekly combed hair. Then I knew that she was writing, and that I must not disturb her. Presumably she was writing to Father.

I did not often disturb her. Only when a new boat was to be launched would I run in to her and pull her, by hook or by crook, out into the garden. The launching was a never-changing ceremony. Mother would fill her thimble with water, and declare:

'With this clear water I christen you
To be known by day and by night too
(the name) – and Captain Jan himself shall guide you through.'

The names varied: *Hope*, *Future*, *Freebooter of the Baltic*, and so on. But the magic formula was unchanging, and was thought to protect not only against shipwreck, but also the attacks of neighbouring boys.

The boys of the neighbourhood, big and small, were my greatest fear. I had no contact with them. My only companion was my sister, Anna. In the afternoon she would come out into the garden to do her homework. She would sit on the round bench beneath the chestnut tree, pull up her long, thin, black-stockinged legs to form a sort of pulpit, rest the book on her knees, and read in a loud, monotonous voice. When she had finished, she would hit herself hard on the forehead with the book three times. Sometimes I would sneak up on her, grab her legs and pull her off the bench. But generally we got on very well. She would tell me long, long stories, in the same monotonous, rambling voice that she used to read her homework. She would tell me about my boats, and about Father. She said Father was the most learned man in the world, and that he had discovered something that could make everybody well again. I preferred to hear about my boats.

When she spoke she would hold her breath, until sometimes she ended up quite blue in the face and her voice dried up. Then Mother would call from the window and tell her to stop. I liked Anna a lot; but I think I regarded her with a certain sense of superiority. I do not know why.

After dinner Grandfather would also come out into the garden. He would walk with his hands behind his back, staring straight ahead, right past the fountain. If I was nearby, he would say: 'Well, what are you up to, my little friend?' or: 'You're not getting yourself wet, are you?' or: 'You're not frightening the doves, are you?' Questions of a purely formal nature, which neither demanded nor received replies. Grandfather always wore a long, black coat, weighed down at the back by some heavy book that threatened to tear the pocket. He always walked the same route, past the fountain, down between the poplars, to the summerhouse. After an hour or so he would return, but then usually with the book open in his hand.

Once sister Anna said to me:

'I dare you to take the book from the Bishop's pocket.' (She always called him the Bishop.)

'All right,' I replied. And I crept up behind him on tiptoe, stuck my hand in between the tails and pulled out the book. At that moment I realised what a dreadful thing I had done, and stood there stock still, staring down the path. Grandfather turned round. He looked at me and at the book and became quite bewildered. He asked what I wanted the book for. And, when I did not make a sound, he called out:

'Bina, Bina, I don't understand what's the matter with the lad!'

He crouched down in front of me and said:

'What is it you want, my little friend? Surely you can say what it is that you want.'

But because that was precisely what I could not do, I remained silent. And he left me, muttering and shaking his head.

On another occasion he trod on my favourite boat, which was lying keel up on the sea-shore. Crunch! He did not notice anything: only when he had gone some way through the poplars did he turn round, push back his thick white hair, and say:

'What was that? Did I stand on something?'

I informed him that he had trampled my best boat to pieces. I did not cry: I was convinced that he would be completely distraught, and did not wish to increase his anguish. However he took the matter lightly, saying:

'You must forgive me. I shall make you a new one at once.'

He started searching among the bushes for material, but I sullenly rejected everything he found. In the end I showed mercy and gave him a piece of wood from my own store. He sat down beneath the chestnut tree, took out his knife and began to carve. Anna and I sat on either side of him, watching him work. It went slowly and badly. I offered to help him, but he said that since he had broken the boat, then he should be the one to make a new one.

'Yes, but you can't, Grandfather!' I said.

He asked for a new piece, he broke the point of his knife, he cut himself. Mother, who was wondering what was going on, came out. She offered to help him as well, but he said:

'You would be doing me a favour if you didn't stand and watch me. I'll get the boat into shape, you'll see.'

Uncle Otto, who was my best boat-builder, came out as well, and finally so did Grandmother.

'Oh Julius,' she exclaimed, 'whatever are you doing? You're bleeding.'

Then Grandfather picked everything up and shut himself in his room. I do not know how much time he spent carving, but the following morning he gave me a boat that was the worst I had ever had. I told him this. He patted me on the head and said:

'Well, it's the best I can manage.'

I do not believe that my respect for Grandfather diminished as a result of this. It was far too great and unwavering. He resided in a room whose size I can no longer judge. To me, it seemed vast. The ceiling was low, but it was so broad and deep that its interior lay in semi-darkness. The walls were clad with book-spines, thick, black, heavy books. A pitch-black passageway led to Grandfather's room. It was full of dangers. The floorboards were worn, uneven, and full of huge knots that I would stumble over.

Along one wall ran a bench, and there was always someone sitting and waiting on it. This someone would always sigh, or cough, or sneeze, or blow their nose, or address me very suddenly. These were Grandfather's poor people; they frightened me. I never saw them, I just heard them, and noticed the smell, which was usually not good. On one occasion I was suddenly embraced by a strong pair of arms, and a hoarse voice exclaimed:

'God bless God's little angel! God bless God's little angel!'

I began to kick and lash out and shout, because the embrace was a real bear-hug. Grandfather came, and Mother came. I was carried into the room and thoroughly examined. And the more I screamed and yelled, the louder the voice in the corridor cried:

'God bless God's little angel!'

Later sister Anna told me that it was a half-mad old woman, one of the Bishop's poor, who had got hold of me. These events, and others like them, meant that I developed a terror of mad people and the poor. Indeed, I think that to a certain extent I confused the two terms. But my respect for Grandfather was based upon the fact that he dared to deal with such dangerous forces in there, in the dark.

Of course I had other reasons to respect him. Wherever I saw him, he was highest and mightiest. His face, beneath his white hair, was unusually large, and, to my mind, beautiful. The gold cross on his black outfit dazzled me. The deep bows with which he was greeted on the street and at home confirmed me in my belief that he was foremost among men.

Sometimes our garden would fill up with black-clad gentlemen. On these occasions I was forbidden to play by the fountain, and I would sit in Mother's window behind the curtain, cheek to cheek with sister Anna, who would whisper:

'They're all priests, every last one!'

They were gathered round Grandfather, who was seated among them like a duke. They were speaking amongst themselves, patting each other on the arm, bowing and smiling. I have never seen people pat each other's arms, or bow and smile as much as these priests did. Occasionally two or three would raise their voices and talk at the same time. But as soon as Grandfather uttered a few words – usually he was a man of few words – the others would all fall silent and every face would turn towards him.

'Yes, the Bishop is mightiest of them all,' sister Anna said. 'God is mightiest, then the King, and then the Bishop.'

When the priests had been talking for a while, the maids went out carrying trays. And after them went Grandmother. And as soon as Grandmother had settled into her big chair, every face would turn towards her, and she talked and laughed and all the priests began to flutter around her. But Grandfather sat alone with one or two of them. And I wondered whether Grandmother were not mightier than Grandfather.

'No, she isn't,' sister Anna replied. 'But she's so nice and jolly. She can make anyone laugh.'

Now even Mother went out, and a crowd of priests gathered around her. Then I grew reckless and exclaimed:

'Just look at Mother! She's putting them to shame!'

'Yes, she's so beautiful,' sister Anna explained. But after a little while Mother was left sitting alone and no-one spoke to her or even seemed to see her. This annoyed me.

However, I best understood how high and mighty Grandfather was when Grandmother died. She had lain ill for several weeks, and I had almost forgotten her. In any case, I used to try to keep out of her way, because she used to tease me and called me names that made me shy. Yes, she would tease everyone. Grandfather would almost always end up blushing and closing his eyes whenever Grandmother started laughing. She tormented Uncle Otto so with her remarks that he would sometimes jump up from the dining table and rush out. Only Mother was spared. And, when Mother and Grandmother were alone, it would be peaceful and quiet in the room, and they would only speak occasionally, almost whispering. But otherwise Grandmother was always surrounded by a great commotion, and I remember that whenever she went up the stairs she would puff and blow and groan; but whenever she came down, she would sing and trill like a lark. That is my clearest memory of Grandmother.

Then she became ill, lay for weeks in her bed; and I forgot her. But one morning, when I was still asleep, old Hulda,

Grandmother's maid, came into my room, pulled me out of bed, and drenched me with tears. I struggled, but she said: 'The old mistress is dying.' I stopped still, and she wrapped the blanket round me and ran with me into Grandmother's room. I did not, however, get a glimpse of the invalid, because Mother carried me out into the drawing-room at once. There were old ladies seated in every corner, black-clad old ladies whom I did not recognise. I assume they were Grandmother's friends. They were all crying. Three old gentlemen, whom I also did not recognise, were pacing up and down. And our maids and coachman were running in and out, all of them crying. Mother sat me in the lap of an old woman who was wearing a black silk dress and a large white lace-cap. I remained with her, shivering and freezing. Suddenly all the old ladies began to sob and moan loudly, and the one holding me squeezed me horribly tightly. Uncle Otto came out of the sickroom; his eyes were all swollen, and he was swaying back and forth like he sometimes did when he had drunk too much. But now it was only his tears that made him sway. He took my hands and clutched them so tightly that I started to whimper. And everyone in the room gathered around us; there was a hubbub of sobbing and whispering. But through the noise I heard Grandmother's voice. She was screaming; I could not hear what. And at that moment the room became completely silent. I craned my neck and saw Grandfather come through the door. In one hand he was carrying a book, but I could not see what he was carrying in the other. The cross was shining. I wondering if he was not going to greet all the visitors in the drawing-room. But he seemed not to see them, and walked with slow, measured steps, as he usually did, towards the sickroom. Then I understood that he had business with Grandmother.

He opened the door; and for the last time I heard Grandmother's voice. She called out:

'Julius, Julius! No, no, I don't want to!'

'What doesn't she want to do?' I asked the old woman holding me. She replied in a whisper:

'Grandmother doesn't want to die.'

The door to the sickroom was ajar. I heard Grandfather's voice.

He was reading. And as usual when Grandfather read, everything fell silent around him. The people in the drawing-room stood with their hands clasped and heads bowed.

But I whispered to the old woman:

'What's Grandfather doing?'

She replied:

'He's helping Grandmother to die.'

'Can he do that, then?' I asked. And I remember thinking of the boat which had not been particularly successful.

The old woman whispered:

'Yes, now she's calm. Now she knows that death is eternal life.'

And it was true, Grandmother was calm now. After a while Grandfather's voice fell silent, and, a while after that, Mother came out of Grandmother's room. The old woman went up to her and asked:

'Is it over?'

Mother nodded. She took me and carried me out of the drawing-room. But in the doorway I turned to look back. And I saw Grandfather return from his mission. Among all those faces, red with weeping, his was the only one that was clear and white and calm. He walked with measured steps right across the drawing-room. No-one dared approach or question him. I remember thinking that he was walking across a bridge, a high bridge, yes, across a rainbow, the heavenly bridge, high above all our heads.

That evening it occurred to me that I ought to mention Grandfather before Father in my evening prayer. Mother corrected me. I said:

'Yes, but isn't Grandfather better?'

She replied:

'No, Father is better than anyone.'

This amazed me, and I sought in vain to imagine my father, whom I had never seen.

Grandmother would almost certainly have been completely wiped from my memory had not sister Anna said to me some time after the funeral:

'My days of milk and honey are probably over now.'

And, after explaining the strange phrase, 'days of milk and honey', she told me that for some time now it had been for Grandmother's sake that she had been allowed to stay at the Bishop's Palace. In her usual long-winded way, she commenced a whole long story about Grandmother and Father and herself, and only now did I discover that she may well have been Father's daughter, but that she was not Mother's. And that Grandmother had been her fairy-godmother, and had been as wise and as powerful as one.

'Yes,' she said, 'all our days of milk and honey are over now. The Bishop may be kind, but he can't bear Father.'

There you see why I have always remembered Grandmother as a good fairy since her death. And why I have always imagined that good fairies are upright, slender old ladies wearing white lace-caps and lilac-coloured dresses, old ladies with sharp tongues, smiling eyes and booming voices.

As far as she herself was concerned, Anna's prediction proved correct. She disappeared from the Bishop's Palace, I do not remember exactly when or how. I only remember that as a parting gift she gave me her book of writing exercises, which I still possess. In it is the remarkable essay about 'God's World'.

I believe that her prediction was also true for the rest of us. For Mother, for Grandfather, for me. For Uncle Otto.

Uncle Otto was, as I have said, my best boatbuilder. He was strong, he was good with his hands, he was obedient. He obeyed everyone, and I realised soon enough that he merely needed to be given orders. He lived in a little, single-storey stone house on the other side of our garden, which was separated from his back yard by a broken fence. This fence, and the mass of rubbish in his untidy yard, provided excellent building material for my fleet.

Uncle Otto was rather short, a little bent, but very broad-shouldered. He was so strong, he could break a twelve-inch nail between his fingers as if he were breaking a sewing needle. But his hands shook. This irritated me, because the work went slowly; and I berated him. He replied, quite pleasantly:

'Well, you see, that's because I drink so valiantly.'
'So stop, then,' I commanded. But he shook his head and said:
'Oh no; you sleep so well after you've been drinking.'

Mother had forbidden me to visit him in the evenings; probably because that was when he was drunk. All the same, I remember that once he came staggering through the garden in the middle of the morning. I asked:

'What's the matter with you?'

'With me?' he muttered, staring at me from under his fringe. 'Aah, well, you see Jan, his Royal Highness has graciously appointed me a captain.'

(He was known as 'the lieutenant', but was at this point supervising poor relief, a position which he lost after the Bishop's death.)

'Have you got any soldiers, then, Uncle?' I asked.

He thought seriously for a moment, then replied:

'Well, you see Jan, I'm in a division of the army of the poor. The old men with brooms, they're my boys, they are.'

I suddenly felt afraid of him, and went and hid in Mother's room.

Another time, when I was visiting his yard, I met my mother quite unexpectedly. I was offended; I did not much like Mother leaving her room. 'What are you doing here, Mother?' I asked sullenly. She had even sat down on the pile of junk that was my lumber-yard. Uncle Otto was standing in front of her, his head hung low, eyes blinking, the corners of his mouth turned down. Mother told me to go back to the fountain, but I stayed close by and heard them talking, Mother severe, more severe than I had ever heard her, Uncle Otto muttering in monosyllables. Eventually Mother stood up, and I heard her say:

'How could I ever have expected any help from you? You tremble like a leaf if His Grace so much as looks at you.'

I do not suppose I took her words literally, but my respect for the Bishop increased still further.

And when one day I heard Grandfather say to Mother:

'Do as you will. I have no desire to force you.'

And when I heard Mother reply:

'Oh, dear Father, you must know that you are forcing me, whether you want to or not.'

Then I understood what a powerful man my grandfather was. I thought of Grandmother, whom he had helped to die, of sister Anna, whom he had made disappear, of Uncle Otto's trembling hands, of Mother, whom he could force whether or not he wanted to, and of the black passageway, Grandfather's passageway, where the coughing, sighing, groaning, mad poor hid themselves. I became afraid of Grandfather.

Despite this, on one occasion I found the courage to set myself against him and have a serious word with him. It was one winter's evening; I had just gone to bed, and Mother was sitting by the bed holding my hand. (Although I was already six years old, I could not get to sleep unless Mother was holding my hand.) Grandfather came in to us. This in itself was so unusual and astonishing that I crept beneath the covers. Grandfather said: 'There's a telegram from Johan.' And his voice sounded strange. I heard the rustle of paper. Then I heard nothing for a long time. In the end I had to peep out and take a look. Grandfather had sat down on the edge of the bed opposite Mother; he was holding her hand. I do not believe that she was crying, and I cannot recall any other signs of sorrow or pain. But I suddenly realised quite clearly that Grandfather was tormenting her. Perhaps he was nipping her hand in some sly way. And I confronted him, I knelt up in bed and cried:

'If you don't go away, you bad man, I shall ask Grandmother to come.'

He stared at me; then his face became quite red and he started to blink.

'Whatever does the lad mean?' he muttered. But Mother tucked me in under the covers, and I do not what happened after that.

Otherwise, I remember nothing of Mother's sorrow, and nothing of her illness. Only this:

I was crawling on all fours, as usual, around the fountain, when I suddenly heard the sound of a severe and prolonged attack of coughing. No-one but sister Anna could cough like that! Or so I thought. (And I knew her cough, because she had sometimes entertained me by 'coughing to order'.) 'It's Anna! It's Anna!' I cried, and rushed over to Mother's window. She looked out and shook her head. 'It's only me,' she said. But I did not believe her, and clambered in through the window – so brave had I become – and searched the whole room. Then I burst out crying. Not because Mother was coughing, but because Anna was not there.

'What's the point of fooling me!' I said to Mother.

But, after I had sulked for a while, I thought no more about it. That is all, as far as Mother's illness is concerned.

And I also remember this:

Once again, I was in the garden, and saw Grandfather coming from the summer-house, or from Uncle Otto's back yard. I grew scared, ran off to Mother's window and stretched up my hand. But Mother was not in her room. So I clambered in through the window and stood there watching from behind the curtain, waiting for Grandfather to go away. He sat down beneath the chestnut tree and sat there for a long while. Then he stood up and went in.

I returned to the fountain. That very day I had launched a big new boat, with a handkerchief sail and a silk pennant, a red one. Mother had christened it *Sabina*, and she had said:

'Now let's see you steer a course straight to Father.'

This was what I was busy with when I heard a lot of noise, and heavy, even steps from the back yard. I looked under my arm and saw Uncle Otto squeezing backwards and very slowly through the plum-tree thicket where the fence ended. I realised that he was carrying something that he was taking great care of, something he wanted to protect from the twigs. It must have been only a few days before my name-day, because I thought: 'It's a boat! It's a huge new boat!' My heart began to thump with joy but at the same time I grew so shy that I felt like sneaking away. I decided to carry on with my voyage and pretend I had not noticed.

Only when Uncle Otto had passed me, with the same heavy, even steps, did I venture to look up. I saw Mother's head. Her hair had come loose. Her face was white as chalk. Her eyes were closed and their lids dark blue. Her cheeks were white, and from her mouth, red and half-open, ran a trickle of blood.

Slowly I stood up, went over to Mother's window. I stood there for a long time. Then I heard the door being opened, I heard someone shout, I heard the maids running, I heard Uncle Otto's heavy, even steps, I heard Grandfather's voice, subdued and stammering. I heard Uncle Otto muttering softly, as if he were drunk:

'Yes, yes, that's how it goes. She'd been running. That's how it goes. She was running. Who knows where she was running. Yes, that's how it goes.'

I stayed by Mother's window. Old Hulda came and got me. She dressed me and we got into Grandfather's cabriolet. We drove to the station, we went on the train, and we rode in another cab. And I came to the parsonage in Lillhammar, to my great-aunt, Klara Rygelius. There I stayed for a week or so. Sometimes my aunt would talk about Mother; but I did not want to hear. I do not know why. When the funeral was over, I returned with Hulda to the Bishop's Palace.

One day, perhaps three weeks later, I was sitting by Mother's desk by the window. I was reading my primer. The door opened and a tall man came in. He was very tall – taller than Grandfather – and very thin. He had a dark brown beard. His coat was long and black, like Grandfather's, but of a different cut, and its cuffs shone with silk. I grew scared, but sat quite still. He sat down opposite me and took my hand, which was lying on the table. I gave a start, and tried to pull it free, but he held me tight, but not, however, hard.

He started talking about sister Anna. At that, I calmed down, and answered his questions, and we had a conversation. Then Grandfather came in as well, and sat down a little way from us. But the stranger looked only at me, and I showed him the book of essays that Anna had given me. He asked if I could read. I replied that I could only read print. Then he leafed through my sister's book, smiled, and started to read:

'We human beings must be very joyful and grateful that we are alive. The world is very beautiful and we can hardly imagine that anything could be better arranged. We only have to think of the mountains, which reach high above the clouds, and from which we have a glorious view of everything. Or we may think of the deep seas, where there are fish of all sizes and colours, such as the huge black whale, the yellow salmon, the blue trout and the red plaice, as it is known, even though it only has red spots. On the surface of the Earth live the four-footed beasts, some of which carry us, such as the elephant and the horse and the camel and the donkey, while others give us milk, such as the cow. And the sheep gives us its wool to make warm winter clothes. But cotton grows on a tree in India. But the birds are in the best position, because they can fly and quickly get to their desired destination. There are also insects and snakes which sting us, but even that is good, for we would not otherwise know how fortunate we are when we do not get stung. And some people are sick and poor, but what does that matter when they are still alive. Because wherever one turns, there is something fine and beautiful to look at. So we can never be joyful and grateful enough.'

I listened open-mouthed, astonished at sister Anna's great wisdom. But the stranger suddenly put the book down, and asked: 'Jan, do you know who I am?'

I replied that I did not.

Then he stood up and started to pace the room unhappily, occasionally beating his chest. Eventually he stopped in front of Grandfather, and said in a severe tone:

'You could at least have told him who I was.'

Grandfather beckoned me to him, and, when I was standing between his knees, he said:

'My dear little friend, this is your father.'

I almost burst into tears. I pressed myself against Grandfather, hiding my face in his thick white hair. Eventually I said:

'I like Grandfather better.'

Then the stranger burst out laughing, he threw his head back, so that his black beard pointed straight out, and I saw his thin neck.

'Excellent!' he exclaimed. 'Excellent, my dear father-in-law! Excellent, my Lord Bishop!'

Grandfather blushed and blinked, and I heard him mutter:

'My dear Johan, you know this isn't my fault.'

'Fault?' the stranger repeated. 'No, my dear father-in-law, it's to your credit! Of course it is! That the lad has a clear mind and sound judgement.'

Suddenly he took me in his arms, lifted me up, and looked me in the eyes. And he said:

'Ah well, my dear Jan. It can't be helped. I'm your father.'

Chapter 4

Arnberg's Explosives

Father and I moved in with Uncle Otto in the back yard. We lived there for two years. The Bishop lent Father some money, and he set up a laboratory. He was experimenting with a new discovery, an explosive. The entire Bishop's Palace lived in great fear of this explosive. Only Grandfather and I were not afraid. We liked to see what he was up to with our own eyes, and would walk into the laboratory hand in hand. Father would drive us out. Once, when he was out, I rushed in to Grandfather, crying: 'Come on, come on, he's gone out!' But on that occasion Grandfather did not want to. Although I believe he would have liked to.

To start with there was no woman in the house. Old Hulda cleaned the rooms and brought us food from the Bishop's kitchen. But Father ate at an inn. Sometimes he would take me with him and I was always proud to walk by his side. When I saw him in his long coat, tailored to the waist, his tall hat, as smooth as a mirror, his gloves, his cane with the band of gold around its crook, I thought him a man of real substance. People would turn on the street to look at us. Young ladies would return his greetings with the most charming smiles. I was flattered by this. But, after such a walk, to show the good people that we lived in the back yard was not to my taste at all. Instead, I would try to persuade Father to walk through the Bishop's Palace, pleading some errand with Grandfather, or saying that it was a shorter route. Sometimes I succeeded.

Otherwise I spent little time in Grandfather's garden. The Bishop's eldest daughter, a pious old spinster, had taken possession of Mother's room. She would feed the doves from Mother's window. The noisy flock of stupid, cooing, flapping,

Memoirs of a Dead Man

squabbling doves made a constant commotion around the quiet window where Mother and I had held each other by the hand. I could not bear it.

As time passed, I became reconciled with the back yard. On the other side of the kitchen lay the brewhouse, cluttered up from floor to ceiling with old furniture that Uncle Otto had brought with him from –dal. And this was where the mirror of Venetian glass, with the seven cardinal virtues engraved on its frame, hung. Father said:

'Why on earth are you hoarding all this? Some of it's valuable, you could make some money.'

'Thanks, I know – thanks – ' Uncle Otto stammered, blushing deep red. 'I'm not selling anything.'

And Father laughed at him, saying: 'You're as mad as I am. Well, one fine day, we'll take it all to –dal.'

They began to pull things out, one at a time, carefully identifying the place where each had stood, how it had been used and who had used it. They spent hours doing this; sometimes laughing, sometimes arguing, sometimes standing in silence, running their hands over some item. Meanwhile, unnoticed, I poured water into the old brewing pan, and launched my American brig, the *Claire Aurore*. I had already had time enough to suffer a shipwreck when Father suddenly took my arm and placed me in front of the mirror. He smiled at us and said:

'Do you recognise who this is, mirror? This is the future owner of –dal.'

'Absolutely,' muttered Uncle Otto, stretching his ruddy head, 'the family lives on, albeit with a noose round its neck – '

And he added:

'But the future owner looks more like a guttersnipe.'

I really did look dreadful. My clothes were too small, shabby and worn through. And on top of that, I had been rolling around in several years' worth of soot and dust. Father grew angry.

'That's no way to behave!' he growled. 'Is there no-one who can look after the boy?'

And he carried me into the bedroom at once, pulled off my clothes, rolled them into a bundle, and put them into the stove. He took out my red velvet blouse and velvet trousers.

I wrapped my arms round his neck and rubbed my nose hard against his cheek. This was my way of showing affection. Mother I used to kiss, but never Father.

The brewhouse became my habitual haunt for a while. The brewing pan, although far less grand than the pond, could still serve as one of the world's oceans. Admittedly, my brig lay like a pontoon bridge from shore to shore, but nothing could stop it from being loaded to the gunwales with gold and oranges, and nothing could stop it from rolling violently in the waves, keeling over and sinking to the bottom. After every such catastrophe I would go over to the mirror – mainly to see how much my poor Sunday blouse had suffered. But also to look at and examine myself, because I had noticed that after a shipwreck I would be pale rather than red-cheeked; I looked like a little ghost. And it amused me to see this. It fitted the game well. I had drowned and was now a ghost. Unfortunately my ghostly appearance lasted only a minute or two. Then I would once again be a rosy-cheeked captain, ready to seek out fresh misfortunes.

My poor velvet blouse, however, did not recover so easily, and would probably have become truly ghostly had not the following occurred.

One autumn evening, just as I was going down heroically with my brig, I heard footsteps in the kitchen. I was in the process of bringing back a cargo of gold from America; half would go to Father, the other half to Grandfather. And even though I knew full well that the brig's fate, and that of our riches, was already sealed, I was struggling desperately against the waves. Fought them with my right hand while my left hand was secretly creating them. But in the middle of the game I had to stop to listen to the footsteps. They were not Father's, nor Uncle Otto's. They were hardly even real footsteps, more a hasty padding back and forth. Like a rat running from wall to wall, stopping, standing up on its back legs, sniffing, turning away, padding on again.

I grew scared. I let go of the brig and crept into the corner behind the brewing pan. I heard the kitchen door open. I pressed my nose hard against the wall. But, sneaking a sideways glance, I caught sight of a black figure, searching up and down. And when the head turned in profile against the grey, dim light from the window, I could make out a little bird-like head, with a long, pointed beak. 'It's a witch,' I thought, screwing my eyes tight shut and hoping that God would make me invisible.

I was fairly well hidden in my corner, but the mirror, directly opposite, must have betrayed me. Because now I heard the witch clap her hands, and heard her come loping towards me, and I heard her ingratiating voice whine:

'God bless! God bless! God's angel!'

Then I remembered the old woman from Grandfather's passageway, and my fear was diluted with resentment. Was I about to be bear-hugged once more by that mad, impoverished woman! I cried out:

'Keep away! I'll hit you!'

But she loped towards me, crouched down in front of me, with her hands on her knees. I could see her little troll's eyes, grey as granite, peering and twinkling in the twilight.

'Don't touch me!' I screamed. 'You're poor and mad and wicked!'

But she did touch me, and pulled me out. And she turned me round and inspected me from all sides, and dried my hands on her skirt. I kicked and struggled until she was forced to let go of me. I dashed away, and hid under Father's bed. I must have lain there for at least an hour, listening to her padding about, tempting me out with her ingratiating, whining voice. In the end Father came, and I crept out. He picked me up and carried me out into the kitchen, where the woman was sitting peeling potatoes at the table. She dried her hands and took me from Father, who said:

'Hedda, my dear, this is Jan.'

She replied:

'He doesn't like me. But that'll change once he's used to me.'

And she took off my red velvet blouse and my velvet trousers at once. And she pulled out the tattered and wretched clothes that Father had put in the stove, washed them, mended them, and put them on me.

Poverty entered our home along with Hedda. In actual fact, we had been just as poor, if not more so, before, but only now did it become apparent. Father himself was forced to admit that this was the case, and to give way to it. Everything that could be called luxury was erased from our lives. The rooms were far nicer than before, because Hedda was an incomparable cleaner. But she also cleaned away the furniture. Everything became thinner and meaner. Soft mats which Father had brought with him from America disappeared, to be replaced by meagre rag-rugs. Our beautiful porcelain, with pagodas and wonderful fish on it, disappeared. Uncle Otto had to fight tooth and nail to protect the furniture in the brewhouse.

'That's all mine,' he cried. 'Johan, I really must protest.'

And Father called out from his laboratory, laughing:

'Hedda, Hedda – Otto doesn't want to make reductions. Keep your paws off!'

On that occasion she backed down. But neither Father nor I could save Mother's clothes. They were kept in the attic, and once a month old Hulda would hang them out to air in the yard. I would go from garment to garment, touching them all. I could spend the whole day silently wandering among Mother's clothes. Now Hedda put them in a rough oblong box. An old woman came with a little cart and a little pale grey horse, and collected the box. (I believe that the old woman was the one who had embraced me in Grandfather's passageway; she chattered and curtsied and laughed and cried seemingly at random. She was known as Old Mrs Gråberg. I was to see her again.)

Father raised objections, I cried. To no avail. The cart rolled away with the oblong box and Hedda was left counting a bundle of scruffy notes. She was smiling; but she always did that, whether or not she got her way. The wrinkles on her face fell into a dull, contented smile. Her eyes glittered constantly, and sometimes they would cross above the brow of her nose. I do not know if Hedda had been better-looking in her youth; as I remember her, she was a fright. Her mouth looked like it had been drawn in like a pleated hem, and bulged out beneath her huge nose. Her whole body looked squeezed and laced up. It looked as

Memoirs of a Dead Man

if she was always busy picking pins from the gaps in the floorboards. She could move with surprising speed; but in her very way of walking there was something that put one unpleasantly in mind of scampering rats.

As time passed I got used to her, and grew to like her. Father and Uncle could not have managed without her. Once, when she was away visiting sister Anna, who was ill in Gothenburg, the house fell into such disorder that Uncle and I had to move in with Grandfather. But even in the Bishop's Palace she made herself indispensable. Every day I would see her climb over the fence. Her legs, narrow as pins in their coarse grey stockings, would swing over at the same time, and the whole grey bundle would roll away through the poplars. Aunt with the doves would often come to the fence and call for Hedda. Sometimes Grandfather himself would come, red and upset (either Aunt or the maids would have annoyed him, or else he would have lost a button, or some other misfortune would have occurred).

'Where's Hedda? Jan, ask Hedda to come.'

But she would be there before I even turned round.

Grandfather showed her the greatest respect. He gave her a black silk dress that had belonged to his wife, and a gold brooch with thick swirls around a cross of garnets. Neither the dress nor the brooch suffered reductions; along with Father's elegant wardrobe, they were our only luxuries. And they were used on Sundays, when we regularly ate dinner with Grandfather. The Bishop always wanted Hedda to join us at the table. She would sit down, staring ahead of her for a while; but suddenly she would disappear, to join in with serving, or find something else to do in the kitchen. No-one seemed to notice this.

But then Grandfather celebrated his birthday; I believe it was his seventieth or seventy-fifth. It was in July. The preparations were lavish, and even I participated in them. Hulda and I gathered leaves beneath the chestnut tree. Aunt with the doves wove garlands. The coachman and Uncle erected the triumphal arch. Hedda ruled in the kitchen. Father sat in his laboratory preparing fireworks.

For Father the day was to have special significance. The whole family would be gathered, and Father intended to present his plans, which concerned the establishment of a family business to develop Father's explosives. Naturally I knew nothing of his plans; but I understood that he was worried. For several days I heard him pacing up and down in his laboratory, and every so often he would come to the window, draw deep breaths, and beat his chest with his fist. The sweat ran from his brow. His anxiety infected me. I thought that he was worried about his fireworks, and fell to my knees behind the rubbish heap and prayed to God that the firework display would be a success, for the honour of Father and me and all of us.

Early in the morning I was woken by music. I called to Hedda, leapt out of bed. The house in the back yard was deserted. In only my nightshirt I ran out into the garden and crept into the thicket of plum-trees by the fence. In Grandfather's garden was a crowd of black-coats, musicians, men in uniform, and ladies in every possible colour. (And when I saw the ladies, I thought of the fish in Anna's book, the men reminded me of the four-footed beasts, and the musicians, who were positioned on the terrace beneath the dovecote, reminded me of the birds. I agreed with Anna that the world truly was beautiful.)

As I was sitting there, Hedda came scampering past, plucking me up as she went, and scampered into the house. And, while she cleaned and did a hundred other tasks, she dressed me in my red velvet finery. She told me that Grandfather had been asking for me. This made me nervous, I did not want to go with her. But she picked me up under her arm like a parcel, and scampered off, now scurrying over the women's trains, now bending beneath the outstretched arms of the black-coats. She set me down in front of Grandfather, put her hand on my head and made me bow. Then she disappeared. Grandfather was sitting on the round bench beneath the chestnut tree, and around him sat the oldest men in black coats and uniforms, and even some old women. Grandfather drew me to him.

'This is Sabina's lad,' he said.

He waved, and up stepped two tall boys and a girl in a pink dress.

'These are your cousins, Jan,' Grandfather said. And he had us stand back to back and measured our height. The girl exclaimed:

'Oh, you're so little! You're like a doll.'

And she wanted to carry me, but I made myself heavy so that she had to let me go. The black-coats flocked around us, talking and laughing and patting us and each other.

But Grandfather called out:

'Mikael!'

At once a boy not much larger than me appeared. He bowed politely to Grandfather. I saw that he was not of the same sort as us; he resembled neither me nor my tall cousins. He was as beautiful as I imagined angels to be. And he was dressed quite differently: long black trousers, black jacket with a large white collar. I understood that he was finely dressed, and I was ashamed of my red velvet. Grandfather made the two of us stand back to back as well. And when he saw that we were almost the same size, he smiled contentedly and said:

'There! A well-matched pair of horses. You two can play together.'

The unknown boy patted me on the shoulder and said:

'I'll look after him.'

He took my arm in his and walked through the crowd with untroubled steps, skilfully avoiding either pushing or being pushed. But I followed him like a lump of wood, scarcely daring to look at him. We sat down on the edge of the pond. He crossed one leg over the other, slowly swaying to and fro in time to the music.

'Can you whistle?' he asked. And he looked sideways at me and smiled in a way that made me even more awkward.

'You!' he said, patting my knee. I drew my legs up. He suddenly became serious and said:

'Do you know what? My papa died two months ago. He was a count. He had four race-horses. He used to earn money from them. But Grandfather is immensely rich, you understand. I can have whatever I want. Which one is your father?'

I looked around and caught sight of Father, tall and dark, in a crowd of brightly clad ladies. I pointed him out.

'That one,' I said. And I felt considerably more secure. Because I saw that Father was taller and grander than all the others, and I could hear him talk and laugh merrily, and all the young ladies circled around him like people dancing round a Maypole.

But Mikael said:

'That's a very thin one.'

I found nothing to say, and merely replied:

'He's prepared a huge firework display. For tonight.'

Mikael said:

'I've seen so many fireworks. They're nothing. Have you ever seen a burning building? Now they're very fine.'

He suddenly stood up.

'Do you know what?' he said. 'This isn't much fun.'

And he walked off.

I was left sitting on the edge of the pond. The noise, the laughter, the music, it was all making me tired. I fell asleep, curled up with my head between my knees. I slept and I dozed, and eventually the noise around me grew quieter. Sometimes I sensed that Hedda was padding past, and it seemed to me that she was consciously cleaning away all these black-coats, uniforms and rainbow-coloured dresses.

The guests disappeared; in their stead the maids began running around me, under Hedda's direction. They were laying the table for dinner. A smaller table beneath the poplars was laid for me and my cousins. Mikael had left with the other guests. Now there was only the family left, along with two unknown black-coats and two men in uniform. It was to be a family dinner. Great-Aunt Klara Rygelius went from one to the other, hugging them and saying:

'What fun! Now there's just us Arnbergs left. Now we can have a good time.'

She embraced me as well, saying:

'And here we have Sabina, Sabina is here with us too.'

They gathered around me, and I wandered reluctantly, still drowsy with sleep, from one embrace to the next. Eventually I reached a young woman who was very like my mother, although she had arranged her hair in a different way, voluminous and impressive. She was the Bishop's youngest daughter. Her name was Norah, but I called her 'Aunt with the hair'. She was always at Father's side, and made me ill at ease.

There were also two men there. One was tall and broad, comfortable and slow. He was the Bishop's eldest son, a doctor, father of the two boys and the girl. His wife was small and pale and fair. Next to Father she looked like a little chicken. Laughing, they compared their heights just as we children had done. And Grandfather said:

'Helene, it's quite obvious that you are not an Arnberg.'

'No, thank heavens,' she replied, with a toss of her hair.

There was also a slim, swarthy man with thin hair. He was almost as tall as Father. He wore spectacles and had long, white teeth that snapped at the air like a horse's. He was the Bishop's youngest son, a lawyer, and was not married. It was he who first raised the subject.

'Well, Johan,' he said, rubbing his hands. 'How are things going with your explosives? Are you planning to blow up the entire family?'

Father turned his back on the ladies abruptly; he took the lawyer by the arm and pulled him after him in under the poplars. The doctor ambled slowly after them. I saw Father gesticulating. I thought he was talking about the fireworks, and, because I could not understand what he was saying, I made do with reading the expressions on his and their faces. It seemed to me that they were getting on well. Father pressed their hands; all of a sudden, he burst out laughing, ran with long strides over to Aunt with the hair, took hold of her by the waist and swung her round in the air so that I could see her petticoats flapping.

'So, Johan,' Grandfather rumbled. 'What's all this? What's all this?'

Aunt with the hair looked happy, but Helene, the little, fair, pale one, was pouting. The girl in the pink dress came up to me and said:

'Uncle Johan's so funny! Shall we dance as well?'

And she took me by the waist and swung me round, sending one of my shoes into the jasmine bush. We went over to look for it; and she put my shoe on, and tickled my leg in the gap between trousers and sock. Finally she kissed me; and we sat quietly within the jasmine bush for a while, hand in hand. But Grandfather clapped his hands, and the younger of the boys, my cousins, stepped up and said grace. So we crept out of the thicket and sat down at the little table, where old Hulda tied our napkins and exhorted us to eat nicely.

It turned out that one place too many had been set at the large table. Grandfather was placed at the head of the table, and to his right was Great-Aunt Klara. Next to her was an unfamiliar black-coat, then Aunt with the doves, then a stranger in uniform, then Dean Rygelius, Aunt Klara's son (my benefactor), then another unknown black-coat, then Helene, then Father (opposite Grandfather), then Aunt with the hair, then the lawyer, then Uncle Otto, then the doctor, then another stranger in uniform. And between him and Grandfather an empty place.

'Clear it away,' Father ordered. And old Hulda took hold of the chair. But Grandfather stretched out his arms and stood for a moment with his head bowed, as though he were pondering something.

'No,' he said, 'let it be.'

I watched Grandfather's face, and knew at once who he was thinking of. The blood rose to my head, and, although I clenched my teeth, tears began rolling from my eyes, like little peas.

'What are you crying for?' the girl asked.

I pointed to the chair and whispered:

'That's for Mother.'

She stared in horror at the chair, shaking her head. But I think everyone at the large table understood who Grandfather was thinking of. Everyone but Father. He was far too elated, far too happy. All of a sudden he said:

'But where is Hedda?'

'Hedda?' Helene repeated. 'Who's Hedda?'

Father, wide-eyed, looked from one to the other.

'Hedda! Don't you know Hedda? My Hedda?'

They did not answer. Grandfather said:

'I don't think that dear Hedda would like – '

'Goodness gracious!' Aunt Klara exclaimed. 'This is supposed to be a family dinner, is it not? Just us Arnbergs – '

'That's precisely it,' Father interrupted. And he frowned and said:

'Well, as long as you have no objection, Father-in-law?'

I could see Grandfather blush, all the way up to his white hair. He hesitated before answering.

'No,' he eventually said, slowly, 'I have no objection. If you yourself think it appropriate.'

'Well, there is a place over,' Father replied. And he turned to me and told me to fetch Hedda. I scampered off, happy to be the bearer of such an important message. Hedda was in the Bishop's kitchen, dressed in silk, looking very fine, but with her sleeves rolled up and her skirt hitched.

'You're to come to the table at once, Hedda,' I shouted.

She stared at me and her eyes crossed above her nose.

'No, Jan,' she said, 'we'll make reductions there. It's too grand. It's out of the question.'

Disappointed, I turned back. The table was silent. I repeated what Hedda had said.

'Unusually perceptive person, that Hedda,' the lawyer said. And Aunt Klara, who was deaf, cried:

'Isn't she coming? Just think, that there are still people who know their place!'

Father stood up and went to the kitchen. The table fell silent once more. But after a while the lawyer said:

'That's the strange thing with Johan. We always have to do what he wants, even when he's asking a lot. But for us to do as we want in a minor matter – no, that doesn't suit him.'

Aunt with the hair exclaimed:

'Is it really the idea that she should sit in Sabina's place?'

'Come, come,' Grandfather said, blushing badly once more. 'Sabina's place? Don't be childish, Norah dear.'

But she stood up, saying:

'If that's the case, then I'm leaving.'

'What's this? What's this?' the deaf woman complained. 'Dear Julius, this was to have been a family dinner!'

Grandfather said:

'Norah, you will sit down.'

Now the doctor pushed back his chair and put down his napkin, saying:

'I really must say that I agree with Norah – '

But Grandfather interrupted him:

'That's enough, my boy.'

And he added with a smile:

'I should have thought that this was my day. And I should prefer not to hear any more opinions. Apart from my own.'

I was standing behind his chair, listening to all of this.

Now Father came out with Hedda. She was by now badly cross-eyed, and I believe she would hardly have found her chair had Father not helped her. The Bishop reached out his hands to her, saying:

'Now what's all this, Hedda, my dear, not remembering dinner! If we were doing this properly, you'd have to eat standing up!'

He pressed her gently onto her chair, and she sat down with a thump as though she had been snapped in two. The deaf woman shouted:

'Poor little person, I can see she isn't enjoying this. But then Johan has always been a trouble-maker.'

I returned to the small table and to the girl in the pink dress. She talked non-stop and would not leave me in peace. At the large table they were all sitting in silence, apart from Grandfather and Aunt Klara: after a while I heard Father talking as well, laughing as before. And I thought that everything was alright again.

But suddenly there was absolute silence at the large table once more. And then came Father's voice, so sharp that I involuntarily straightened up and took my hands off the table:

'What do you mean?'

'Well,' the doctor replied, slowly and good-humouredly, 'I can give you greetings from your infamous tuberculin. I have the dubious honour of coming across it all over the place. You would have been a wealthy man if you hadn't let your esteemed partner lead you by the nose – '

'In any case,' said the lawyer, 'you have managed to bring our name a not inconsiderable renown. Let us hope that your explosives will be just as renowned. But in a nicer way – '

'Above all,' the doctor continued, 'we must hope that they will be more effective. Otherwise I am afraid that you might deal a new blow to the Arnberg family ark – '

'What's all this?' the deaf woman shouted. 'I can tell just by looking at Johan that something's wrong.'

I too was looking at Father, and crept over to stand behind Grandfather's chair.

'Mother, you must have heard,' Dean Rygelius shouted at his mother, 'that Johan is planning to mount another assault on our poor wallets? A new product from his famous laboratory – '

But the old woman did not hear him, and shouted:

'Well, Johan, you are an atheist! I think that was what used to trouble poor Sabina. Otherwise she would probably have been sitting where that little person is sitting now – '

'Johan isn't exactly an atheist,' the lawyer interjected, giving his spectacles a protracted polish. 'It is a well-known fact that he worships the spirits of his ancestors. Just like the Chinese. He is planning to build them a temple at –dal. The preparatory work alone has cost the family almost two hundred thousand.'

'And our good name,' the doctor said. 'For me, as a doctor, it is undeniably painful to come across that dreadful jar with its appalling drivel about ghosts and miracle cures in every other house – '

'That's always the way,' the Dean intervened in his resounding bass voice, 'atheism, superstition, ignorance and swindling. They all go together. I believe that Johan would have been a better scientist if he had been a better Christian. At least he would not have profited from other people's ignorance. And from our good natures – '

During all of this – and even my aunts added their own small straws to the heap, although I no longer remember what they said – during all of this, Father sat completely calm. But I could tell that his eyes were unseeing. Finally he raised his head and said in a quiet voice:

'I am sorry to have dishonoured the family. But a name that was borne by Fält, that great crook, and which is still borne by the criminal idiot Leonard can withstand a few knocks. Especially since His Grace the Bishop has sanctified it with his person – '

'Johan!' Grandfather cried, and I jumped back from his chair. But Father was looking at him with his unseeing eyes.

He said:

'Would Your Grace care to tell me how many pious biblical verses you had to recite in order to persuade Sabina to write that letter to me? It is said that the family has a murderous streak. It is a great shame that not even such a pious man should escape – '

At this the doctor, the lawyer and the Dean all leapt to their feet. But the Bishop pointed at them, first one, then the second, and then the third. They sat down as though he had pushed them. There was a moment's silence. Then the Bishop said:

'I'm an old man now, and will soon stand before my judge. So leave me in peace, my dear Johan. I can assure you that there is no need for you to add any more stones to my burden. What's said is said. But let us not tear into one another any further. We are too closely connected.'

'What are you saying?' the deaf woman shouted. 'Julius, this was supposed to be a family dinner. I've spent a whole year looking forward – '

Father stood up.

'It's all a mistake,' he said. 'I for my part hereby declare myself free of my beloved family. It has no need of me, and I have no need of it.'

Father left; he turned round and said:

'Otto, are you coming?'

But Uncle Otto shrank into his chair, as though he would have liked to creep under the table. Father shrugged his shoulders. The deaf woman called out:

'Johan! Can't you see that Julius is stretching out his hand to you?'

But Father neither saw nor heard. He was close to knocking me over; he took me by the arm and I had to run as fast as I could to keep up with him. We clambered over the fence. I thought that we were being pursued, but when I turned round I could see through the poplars that the Arnberg family was seated calmly at the table.

Two chairs stood empty, Father's and Hedda's.

In the hallway he let go of my arm; he brushed his hair in front of the mirror, took his cane, opened the door to the street. I followed close on his heels; he did not notice me. We stopped in front of a beautiful two-storey house. Father rang the bell. At that moment he noticed that I was there. He frowned.

'What are you doing here?'

But all of a sudden he embraced me and held me close. The door was opened by a girl with a white cap on her head. Father said something and we walked in. Into a large, light room, whose equal in elegance I had never seen.

'Is this meant to be a hallway?' I exclaimed in astonishment. The girl smiled and Father stroked me on the cheek.

'Sit down here on the boot-rack,' he said. 'And sit very still. This may take some time.'

The girl, who had gone into another room, now came back and held the door open for Father, saying:

'If you please, sir. The bank director will see you now.'

Father went in and she shut the door.

I sat on the boot-rack and looked around me curiously. But Father was gone for ages; I grew tired and fell asleep. I woke up when someone started blowing in my ear. It was the young stranger, Mikael.

'Why are you sitting here?' he asked. I rubbed my eyes and said that I was waiting for Father.

'Is he the one who's in with Grandfather?' Mikael asked. 'Then you'll be waiting a long time.'

He sat down beside me, looked me up and down, and laughed at me. Then he grew serious and said:

'When are you having the fireworks? I'll come and watch.'

When I heard mention of the fireworks, I came to think about Father leaving Grandfather's party, and about how there would surely not be any fireworks now. And I burst into tears.

'What are you crying for?' Mikael asked.

I replied:

'There aren't going to be any fireworks.'

He looked intently at me, then slowly and loftily closed his big, beautiful eyes, snorted and said:

'I might have known.'

And he went away.

After a long time, Father came out. Quickly, agitated. He snatched up his hat and cane and took my hand, squeezing it tight. Only when we had emerged onto the street did I see that his eyes were clear, that his teeth were glinting in his black beard, and that his face was radiant with joy.

He was walking so fast that I could not keep up. He lifted me up. And he whispered in my ear:

'Now, Jan! Now we shall stand on our own feet. Just you and me, Jan!'

Chapter 5

The Mirror

Father went away, and was gone all winter. Every other Sunday he would come home and visit, and would lie on the sofa all day talking to Uncle Otto. He talked about the new factory, which was being built at American speed. It was being built at Frönsan, not far from –dal. Father could see the roof of the manor-house at –dal. He was radiantly happy, but very tired. Uncle Otto told him to rest. But he would not relax until he had got the factory up and running.

That autumn I started school. We had an old teacher who seemed to have been carved out of a piece of rotting wood. He could hardly speak, but when he was angry he would thump us in the stomach. I had never encountered this sort of treatment before, and complained to Uncle Otto. I said that he was a wicked old man, and that I was thinking of doing him some harm one dark evening.

'My dear Jan,' Uncle Otto replied, 'you mustn't think badly of people. Do you know why he thumps you in the stomach? It's so you work up a better appetite. That's good. He means you well.'

The explanation satisfied me: I no longer cared about the old man's thumping, which had a benevolent, if somewhat stupid, intent. But the dull hours of eternity in the dark classroom weighed heavy on my chest, so that I would occasionally lose my breath. Sometimes I would have to yawn and gasp for air.

'You look like a roach,' said the boy sitting next to me, Karl Rygell. So I was nicknamed 'the Roach'. Rygell, who was slightly smaller than me, but heavier and twice as strong, was known as 'the Angel'. Probably because his father was known as 'the Limping Devil'. The Limping Devil was the school doctor. He was terrifying, with large, round, blue spectacles and a thick grey beard, through which his voice would rumble like thunder through a cloud. He had a club-foot. He would sit at a desk in the staff-room and we would have to step up to him in turn, naked to the waist. After every examination he would rumble a few words to the headmaster, who sat next to him. About me he said:

'Poor! The mother died of consumption. No strength. The father will probably go the same way. Hopeless!'

I hated him.

But 'the Angel' became my best friend, and taught me a great deal. He dealt in all manner of things, and made himself a lot of money. But his main business was in cats, which he would catch in back yards, slaughter and skin. He sold the skins to the furrier for half a crown a piece, and used the meat to catch crayfish. His plan was to become a trapper in Canada, but first he had to save up a thousand kronor for the necessary equipment.

The Angel could never get over how poor I was. I never had a penny. Because if I was ever given the occasional coin by Father or Grandfather or Uncle, Hedda would lure it away from me and put it in the clay piggy-bank on the dresser. And she maintained that if I broke into it, I would one day die of starvation. Whenever there was some joint expense in class, I was always left standing as the poorest of the poor.

'Roach!' Rygell once said. 'You've got to go into business. Give cats a try.'

I tried. I caught four or five cats, and shut them in the brewhouse. They started fighting; Hedda let them out. But one black and white female took a liking to me and stayed in the house. She was very affectionate. I called her Léonie after my cousin, the girl in the pink dress. The Angel wanted me to kill her.

'You have to hit her on the head with a brick, then you cut down the throat, so that there's no cross-cut. It's a good skin. You'll get seventy-five öre for that one.'

But I could not make up my mind.

'You're a fool,' the Angel said, picking up a brick and walking over to the cat, which was sitting washing itself. I threw myself at him and we fought desperately, until I lay panting and wounded on the floor. But the Angel said:

'The cat's yours. I shan't touch her. See if I don't touch her. But if she runs out into the street then she'll have abandoned you and betrayed you, and you can condemn her to death.'

This was one solution. We opened the door and Rygell began dashing around the walls of the brewhouse with an old soot-scraper. In his excitement he cracked the glass in Uncle's mirror, the Venetian one in the silver frame. We did not notice. We were too surprised at the cat, which had not moved at all, in spite of the noise. Eventually the Angel got fed up and left. After a while he came back and asked if I wanted to sell the cat for seventy-five öre. But Léonie rubbed against me, and I refused. The Angel left, came back, offered one krona, one and twenty-five, one fifty.

'No,' I replied, 'but you can always take her some time when I'm not looking, can't you. Then you can give me the money.'

'No,' he replied in turn, 'I never take a cat when I know who it belongs to. That wouldn't be right.'

There was no way we were going to agree. In the end we started fighting again, but not even that helped.

My lack of money, however, became all the more noticeable. One day an unknown old woman arrived in town, and opened up a sweet shop on the square, called 'la confiserie française'. Amongst other things, it sold a toffee of quite excellent quality. It was pale yellow and was said to consist of nothing but honey and almonds. Anyone buying ten pieces of toffee was also given a French flag made of tissue paper as a gift. Karl Rygell already had four of these flags, Mikael Arnfelt sixteen. There was only one boy in the school who did not own a single one. That was me. I felt branded.

'Do you want to swap the cat now?' the Angel asked.

I agreed. We went home together. The cat came up to me in the yard, arched its back and rubbed against my leg. I picked her up by the scruff of the neck and, looking the other way, held her out to the Angel. But just as he was about to put her inside his blouse, I suddenly changed my mind. And I offered him my American brig, the *Claire Aurore Clémence* instead. Out of sheer astonishment he let the cat go, and she ran off, God knows where, for I never saw her again. We fetched the brig and inspected it. Rygell said:

'It's worth fifteen kronor. I haven't got that much.'

I said I would be satisfied with twelve, or even ten, but the Angel was meticulous in matters of business. The brig was worth fifteen kronor, and he could not pay that much. We sat thinking about this for a while, until eventually he said:

'Come on. I know. You can sell it to Mikael. He's got money.'

It was a matter of urgency. Rumour had it that the old woman with the French toffee was about to leave town. If I wished to partake of this remarkable delicacy at all, I would have to hurry. So we set off at once for A. O. Arnfelt's house in Västra Slottsgatan. The Angel rang the bell.

'I'll wait here,' he said. 'Remember, Roach, don't let him trick you – he's sly as a fox. You're to get fifteen kronor, and you must ask to see his monkey as well.'

For Mikael had been boasting that he owned a monkey that could talk. No-one had seen it, and many doubted its existence.

The girl with the white cap let me in; Mikael came out into the hall, looking at me in an unfriendly way, and asked what I wanted. When I told him why I was there, he was at once polite, and asked me in. He showed me some toys. After a while he took the brig, inspected it, and said:

'It's nothing special. I can buy boats a hundred times better than this in the toyshop. For fifty öre.'

I grew angry, because this was obviously a lie. But I controlled myself. I told him that the boat was from America, and that Father had brought it back with him over the ocean. Then he offered me two kronor. I said I wanted fifteen, and that I also wanted to see his monkey. Mikael blushed and I realised that the monkey had been a lie as well. I felt contempt for him and was about to leave. Then he said:

'If you sell it to me for two kronor, I'll let you see my grandmother.'

'What's special about her?' I asked.

'She's completely blind. Have you ever seen anyone who's completely blind?'

Memoirs of a Dead Man

I had not. He explained that it was the most remarkable thing you could see, and he piqued my curiosity until I agreed to the sale and shook hands with him. He led me through several more beautiful rooms (and, because I still did not trust him, I was clutching the brig under my arm), until finally we came to a room whose blinds were half rolled down. The first thing I noticed in the gloomy room was a mirror. It was just like Uncle Otto's mirror in the brewhouse. And only now did it occur to me that the latter had been cracked, and that it was probably my fault. I felt heavy at heart.

The rest of the room was stuffed with old furniture. On a sofa sat a very old woman, sewing diligently. I whispered to Mikael:

'How can she sew if she's blind?'

He gestured to me to be quiet. Then he crept up to the sofa on tip-toe. There was a pile of fragments of white cloth, crumpled like used handkerchieves. He snatched at one. At that the old woman raised her head and I saw a pair of large, shining eyes, like steel-blue marbles.

'Is that you, Mikael?' the old woman asked. At once he took her hand and kissed it. He said:

'I just wanted to see how you were, Grandmother.'

'Wasn't that fun,' he asked when we came out. I replied that it was, but in my heart I was upset at having sold the brig for so little. We went out into the hall: Mikael gave me two kronor and one of the pieces of cloth his grandmother had sewn. But I did not want to let go of the boat.

'So, you're a thief,' Mikael said, and started to prise my fingers open. Just then the front door opened and an old gentleman walked in, closed the door and took off his hat. He was very like my grandfather, the Bishop. The same high forehead, large, crooked nose, broad mouth, clean-shaven, ruddy cheeks, the same thick white hair, swept back and long in the neck. But his eyes were not Grandfather's warm, brown eyes.

He looked at me.

'Who are you?' he asked, hanging up his coat and brushing his hair. Then he took my boat.

'This is a fine boat,' he said. 'Is it yours?'

I said that I had just sold it to Mikael. He gave a faint smile.
'How much did you get for it?'
'Two kronor,' I replied. 'And I got to look at a blind old woman.'
The old gentleman turned round slowly.
'Is that so? Mikael?' he said. And added:
'Go to your room, and go to bed. Do you understand?'
Mikael bowed in silence and disappeared. The old gentleman passed the boat to me, took out his purse and gave me a large gold coin, twenty kronor. He asked:
'Is that enough?'
And, when I tried to hand him the brig:
'No, you can keep the boat.'
Quite giddy with joy I rushed out of the door and told the Angel everything. He frowned, deep in thought. Then he said:
'It can't be helped, Roach. If you shook hands with Mikael, then the brig is his. We'll have to throw stones at his window and give it to him.'
Now I knew, of course, that the Angel was meticulous in matters of business. But in this instance I thought he was going too far. Mikael had tricked me with his grandmother, and I was perfectly within my rights. I galloped down the street, ran straight across the square, all the way to the old French woman's shop. Closed! There was an iron bar across the door, and shutters on the windows. I stood there with my riches, crushed. Rygell said:
'That was bound to happen, the way you're behaving. Do you think it's all right to shake hands with someone if you're going to cheat them?'
And he spat at me and walked away, angry. I trotted sadly home, sucking on my twenty-kronor coin, which did not taste of anything at all.
When I got home, I met Hedda in the porch. She said:
'Can you guess who's been here, Jan? The old French toffee woman. Look what she left for you.'
And she handed me a bag containing twenty-four toffees and an equal number of flags. My head began to spin and I did not know which leg to stand on. I ran into the parlour. Uncle Otto was

sitting there alone with his glass. He had reached the stage where he usually started to crow about his captain's licence. I stuck the bag under his nose and asked him to guess who had given it to me. He said:

'Aunt Léonie!'

'No, wrong!' I cried. 'It was the old French toffee woman herself!'

He took a gulp, then said:

'The old French toffee woman, that's Aunt Léonie, that is. That's to say, not your aunt, but mine and your father's.'

One remarkable thing after the other was tumbling on top of me, and I was feeling thoroughly confused. I sat down at the table and sucked at my toffee and tried not to think about it any more. But after a while I asked:

'Uncle, do you think I'll get more toffee from her?'

No, he did not think so. She was travelling back to her own country that evening. And, to judge by appearances, she might not be hammering much more toffee, or anything else, in this life. He laughed and said:

'Can you imagine, Jan, she travelled all this way just to have a look at the mirror in the brewhouse! That's just the sort of thing a woman would do, that is!'

I gave a start. Had they discovered that the glass was cracked? I glanced at Uncle Otto, and thought he looked sly and ill-tempered. I had to get some idea, and asked:

'Did she think it was beautiful?'

'Bah!' he snorted, and shrugged. He emptied his glass, and looked around him. And suddenly he moved his chair close to mine and, leaning his heavy body on the table, stared me right in the eye.

'Jan,' he said, 'do you want to hear a ghost story?'

Tiny flames were burning in his eyes, misty and trembling, like wills-o'-the-wisp. He smiled at me, nodding.

And he started telling me about Johan Fält, our ancestor. It was the first time I had heard about all of that. He said that Fält had been the illegitimate son of a fine gentleman – 'Illegitimate?' I asked. 'What's that?' He was furious, and shouted:

'For God's sake, stupid boy! Don't you see? Illegitimate! Like your sister Anna! She's another one of those whores' brats – '

I gasped for breath: clearly I did not understand anything, or very little. It all frightened me. He went on. He told me how Fält had been brought up on charity, despised, overlooked, abused, treated as a dog by his own father. He blustered, he shouted. He yelled:

'Now do you see? There! Just as I'm treated in the Bishop's Palace! By that hypocritical saint and his brood – '

And he went on, telling me of the general's death and how the English captain had died. In detail, not as though he were telling just anyone, more like he was giving an account to an accomplice. I sat there open-mouthed, probably doing justice to my nickname, Roach. I was so scared that it was making me feel sick. But when Hedda came to take me to bed, we were both equally cross. 'Out! Out!' Uncle Otto shouted. And I flew at her, beating her with my fists. Terrified, she withdrew. He took me by the wrist, panting:

'Damn! That's always the way! Someone comes and interrupts. You have to take that into account. Bloody hell! You have a noose around your neck and – '

He went on: it was a long story and he told it to its conclusion. We sat in silence. I heard Hedda bolt the outside door, I heard her go up the stairs to the attic. I do not recall if I wanted to, but I was in any case incapable of calling for her. I raised my left arm. He smiled at me and asked: 'Why are you doing that?'

I did not rightly know; but I replied:

'You were going to hit me, Uncle.'

He said – and his voice was thick, and he had to swallow between the words:

'How could you – what leads you to – led you, I mean – how could you think something like that – '

He looked round.

Suddenly the copper-colour left his skin, as though wiped away by a wet sponge. He stood up, his hands resting on the table top. He whispered:

'Quiet. Don't say anything. Johan's here. Keep still. I saw his face in the window. Keep still. Don't say anything.'

'Father!' I shouted, jumping up. Uncle Otto unbolted the door and we rushed out into the street. Father was standing between the parlour window and the door, leaning against the wall. Uncle Otto took hold of him round the waist. We led him into the parlour. He stood for a while, hands clutching the arm of a chair. His fingers were bluish white. Then he nodded to us.

'It's nothing,' he said slowly. 'Nothing at all. I felt giddy. I've been feeling a little under the weather recently. And worried. I thought I should come home for a while. But it will soon pass.'

Uncle Otto helped him off with his outdoor clothes. Then he put Father's coat on and ran to fetch a doctor. Father sank back onto the sofa and lay there, eyes closed. I could hear a strange bubbling sound.

'Jan,' he said after a while, 'come and stroke my brow.'

I did as he asked. He opened his eyes, and looked at me mischievously.

'I do believe we're playing the little baron here? Staying up in the evenings? What cock-and-bull stories has he been telling you? Oh yes, I was standing watching you. Well, just this once – but it mustn't become a habit.'

He grimaced and thumped his chest.

Rygell came, limping and causing a commotion as usual. I was sent out. I stood in the hallway listening, but could not make anything out. Hedda came down and started running between the parlour and the kitchen, lighting the stove and rattling pans. The doctor's voice rumbled on uninterrupted. Finally he came stomping out into the hallway. 'Hold my coat!' he roared. I stretched up to reach, but he snatched the coat from me and forced his way into it, tearing at the seams. He pressed his slouch hat over his forehead, stuck his head in through the parlour door, and shouted:

'It's your own fault, Johan! I said to you ages ago: "If you don't take some time off, then time is going to take you off." Well, here you are! Goodbye. I'll come again.'

And he left.

Father lay in bed; Uncle Otto was sitting by the bedside table reading the newspaper; and Hedda came and went with bowls of warm porridge. Father said:

'Jan, are you mad? Why don't you go to bed? Perhaps you think that I'm being ill simply so that you can stay up?'

I felt hurt, got undressed and crept beneath the covers. But I could not sleep. I lay there listening to the bubbling in Father's chest. And after a while I heard him say:

'You, Otto! It would really spoil my plans if I were to lie down and die right now.'

Uncle Otto crumpled up the newspaper and rumbled. But Father repeated:

'If I were to die! Now. I'm afraid I've got myself into a mess. And Jan too.'

'How do you mean?' asked Uncle Otto.

'I've been over-eager, as usual. The idea was that I would get shares in Arnberg's Explosives in return for the patent. But I didn't want that. A. O. Arnfelt had stipulated as a condition of his participation that the shares couldn't be sold or traded for ten years. Ten years is a long time, and you know about my contract with Grundberg, don't you? I only have eight years' grace left. I almost thought that A. O. was deliberately trying to tie my hands. But he made me a generous offer. He suggested that in return for the patent I should receive a share of the profits for the rest of my lifetime. As well as my wage as managing director. This share was to consist of the entire annual profit once the preferential shares had been allocated five percent. Can you imagine – A. O. was happy with five percent! It was generous, and I swallowed the bait. But – '

'You're not going to die,' Uncle Otto interrupted in a commanding voice. 'What sort of talk is that! A young chap – '

'Maybe,' Father conceded. 'But if! You have to admit, my dear fellow, that it would be typical of me. Wouldn't it? To be completely fooled. And by Arnfelt, of all people – '

When I heard this, I came to think about my business with Mikael, and it cheered me up. I raised myself up on my elbow and called out:

'Father! Do you know what? I've tricked Mikael Arnfelt out of two kronor.'

Memoirs of a Dead Man

Father frowned.

'Aren't you asleep yet?' he said.

'Yes,' I replied, and crept under the covers again. After a while I heard Father say:

'That would be just dandy. If A. O. Arnfelt were to reap the benefits of what I've sown. That would be a real humiliation. Wouldn't it, Otto?'

What my uncle answered, I did not hear; I fell asleep.

The following day Father had a high fever. It was pleurisy. The lame man sprang about our home for days. Uncle Otto did not leave Father's room. Aunt with the doves came and offered to look after Father, but no-one from the Bishop's Palace was allowed in. Grandfather himself came in the evening. I ran through the parlour into Father's room, and told him that Grandfather wanted to come in. Then he staggered out of bed, and, leaning on the furniture, he stumbled to the door and bolted it shut.

'It's only me,' Grandfather said from outside, and knocked. 'My dear Johan, it's me, your father-in-law.'

But Father lay down again, and did not reply. It some ways, this came at a convenient time for me. The Angel and I took the mirror to the glazier without anyone noticing. I asked for the best mirror-glass. The glazier asked if I wanted to keep the cracked glass. I declined, but the Angel, who made the most of every opportunity, asked if he could have it.

'It's good glass,' he said. 'It's worth money.'

'Yes,' the glazier agreed, 'it is unusual glass.'

That business cost me the whole of my gold coin; once again, I was poor, poorer than before, because Hedda had taken my piggy-bank. She asked if she could. She had so many expenses, and could scarcely get by. I gave it to her, but I thought it all a bit much, and complained to the Angel. He said:

'Well, Roach, it's all because you didn't give Mikael the boat. After all, you had shaken hands on it.'

I did not believe him.

One day Mikael came and rang on our door. I was ready to slam the door in his face; I thought he had come to collect the boat. But he pushed me aside.

'I have a letter from Grandfather for Mr Arnberg,' he said. 'Will you please announce that I am here.'

He was always so supercilious and calm that he made me nervous. I let him in. By that time Father was so much better that he could lie on the sofa in the parlour. Mikael bowed politely to him and asked how he was. But Father snatched the letter and tore it open. He read it, his hands shaking, and became suddenly quite red in the face.

Doctor Rygell was sitting at the table, with Uncle Otto. Uncle got worried and asked in a low voice what the matter was. But Father lay silent for a while, fingering the letter. Then he said to Mikael:

'You can tell the Count that he will be welcome tomorrow.'

Mikael bowed and left. I followed him out into the hall. He asked if I was planning to give him the boat or repay the two kronor. I replied that he would get his money back. 'When?' he asked. 'Well,' I said, in order to have something to say, 'when Father's well again.' He looked around, drew a deep breath through his nose, and snorted.

'Ugh!' he said, and went away.

I went back into the parlour. Uncle Otto was standing holding the letter. The lame doctor was stroking his beard. Father was staring at the ceiling. Suddenly he said:

'It all depends on how long I have left. I don't know what A. O. wants, but he probably means to persuade me to give up my directorship voluntarily. He thinks I'm finished. What do you think, Doctor, have I got long left?'

'How should I know?' the lame doctor rumbled. 'But your family is usually long-lived.'

'Think of Aunt Klara,' said Uncle Otto. 'Think of the Bishop, of Uncle Leonard, or Aunt Léonie.'

'Léonie?' Father repeated, turning his head a little. 'Is Aunt Léonie still alive?'

Uncle Otto explained that she had been living in town for a while. Something that brought scant joy to the Bishop, whose peace had been disturbed by the old woman's chattering. And he said:

'Well I did write to you, explaining that she wanted to speak to you. Actually, I think she left town the same evening you came home. Poor old thing, her travelling funds were running low. She made her way by selling toffee.'

Father chuckled. After a while he said:

'Well, us Arnbergs make our way as best we can. Still, it was a bad omen that she turned up. We're like crows: whenever someone's about to die, the family gathers from east and west, probably to speed up the process. Don't you remember that Uncle Leonard came back to Sweden just before Father died?'

'Coincidence,' Uncle Otto muttered.

Father turned to the lame doctor.

'Doctor, tell me something. Has Arnfelt ever spoken to you about me?'

'About you?' the doctor repeated, blinking irritably. 'How the hell should I remember? Actually, yes! I recall that he did talk about you. But that was a long time ago. Last autumn. He asked what your condition really was.'

'Do you remember roughly when it was? October?'

The lame man nodded:

'That's sounds about right.'

'Good,' Father said, and smiled. 'Now I understand his generous offer better. I had a few odd notions. I thought he had remembered a certain estate in Värmland which he had once tricked out of Father's hands. But the explanation is decidedly more sober and human. Because I assume, doctor, that you replied: "Arnberg – hopeless!"'

The lame man growled. Uncle Otto said:

'Perhaps you're doing him an injustice.'

But Father replied quietly and calmly:

'An injustice? I am doing him no injustice, and he is doing me no injustice. We are both human beings and we are trying to make our way as best we can. As the saying goes. But now, Doctor, you're going to tell me, on your honour and conscience, what condition Johan Arnberg is in. What sort of thing is this? Is this the beginning of the end?'

I was standing behind the lame doctor's back and could not see his face. Nor was there anyone who could see me. I held my breath.

Rygell hesitated for a while, and then asked, spitting out the end of his beard:

'Is this a matter of business?'

Father nodded. Rygell went on:

'Then I shall tell you that a wise man should sort out his affairs in good time.'

'Consumption?' Father asked.

He replied:

'I haven't found any tubercles. But negative results prove nothing, either good or bad. In my experience. I have never seen a case of pleurisy in a grown man where consumption was not close behind. Most often a *phtisis florida*. No, if it's a matter of business, I say: sort out your affairs, Johan Arnberg.'

'Good,' Father said. 'I shall move to the country. That should give me a few months' respite? And I could always swallow a few jars of Arnberg's Tuberculin, as prescribed by "his own grandfather".'

He laughed, and said:

'No, you can go now. I'm tired. And I must think about how best to be a human being. Tomorrow. When A. O. – another human being – comes to see me.'

He turned towards the wall and waved us away. I crept out before anyone saw me. I went and sat in the brewhouse, but felt no desire to play for a long while.

That evening Hedda scrubbed the whole house. Father was impatient and quarrelled with her. Uncle Otto drank. At last the house grew quiet and all I could hear was Uncle Otto's uneven, stumbling footsteps in the attic. He had reached the captaincy stage, and would have to roll back and forth for hours until the intoxication subsided. But so as not to disturb Father, he kept to the attic, muttering curses to its beams and uneven floorboards. I was lying in Hedda's attic room, where I had been sleeping recently. I could not sleep, I was waiting for Hedda. Eventually I heard her pad up the stairs, and I heard Uncle Otto ask where she

Memoirs of a Dead Man

had been. She replied:

'With the Bishop.'

At that I sat up, delighted at the chance to throw my weight around (and I particularly liked throwing it at Hedda).

'Hedda!' I cried sternly. 'Don't you know that you're not to go to Grandfather?'

She shone the light in my face.

'Oh, we can make reductions there,' she said, and started to undress. Disappointed, I crept beneath the covers and fell asleep.

I was woken by the sound of flapping wings, and ran to the window to see the whole back yard full of Grandfather's doves. At their centre stood Aunt with the doves and the pink girl, my cousin Léonie. I was dressed in just my nightshirt, and backed away, embarrassed. But she had already spotted me and called out:

'Little Jan! Little Jan!'

'There!' I thought. 'Now I shall have to deal with her.'

I got dressed and crept down to see Father. He was just emerging from his bedroom, dressed in his nightshirt, his cane in his hand. He walked very slowly over to the sofa and sank down with a groan. I helped lift his legs up.

'Oh Father,' I pleaded, 'can I stay in your room?'

And I told him that my cousin, the pink girl, was out in the yard with Aunt with the doves and the rest of the Bishop's household. Hedda went to fetch them last night, I said. Father blushed; he told me to fetch Hedda. But just then the door was opened without a knock, and in walked Grandfather. I had not seen him for a month or two. I ran up to him and threw my arms round him.

'How thin and small you are, Grandfather!' I cried.

'Well, my dear Jan,' he said, 'soon I shall be small enough to crawl through keyholes. And that would be very useful for someone who has trouble gaining admittance.'

He went over to Father and laid his hands on his shoulders.

'So, Johan, how are you? I heard from Hedda that you slept badly last night. You're expecting a visit.'

'I am,' Father said, 'and I must warn you – '

But Grandfather drew up a chair and sat down beside him,

putting his hand on his knee.

'Now Johan – I don't make a habit of troubling you for no reason, do I? But now you must do me a favour. You must let me be present when you settle your affairs with A. O. Arnfelt.

'I know, I know!' he went on, silencing Father with his hand. 'I know what you're going to say. You want to handle your affairs yourself. And, above all, you don't want to have anything to do with our dear family. Rather A. O. Arnfelt than that. But I have a notion that I might be useful to you. I know the bank director better than you do. And he knows me. I might go so far as to say that I believe he has – how shall I put it? – a certain respect for my humble person. In any case, it's always useful to have a witness on such an occasion as this. Very useful. And so I shall be staying, whether you permit it or not – '

'Naturally, I cannot drive out my father-in-law,' Father began. But Grandfather interrupted him, and said with a contented chuckle:

'No, you certainly can't! Your dear mother was a true woman of the world. She certainly impressed me, at any rate, as a simple country chaplain. And something of that must have passed on to her son. Do you recall how badly she was affected by our plebeian Arnberg family scenes?'

Now even Father burst out laughing. And they quarrelled no more, but chatted calmly about this and that. Eventually Grandfather pulled out a newspaper, and Father turned to the wall, dozing.

Just as the clock struck two he started from his sleep, raised himself on one elbow, and looked drowsily about him.

He said:

'Go and open the door, Jan. He's here.'

I had heard nothing, but when I looked through the window I saw a carriage pulling up at our door. I ran out into the hall and opened the door. The old gentleman who was so like Grandfather and yet not like him, was just raising his finger to the bell. He asked if it was here that Dr Arnberg lived. I opened the door wide. He stepped in, and removed his hat and coat, which I hung up with trembling hands. He pushed his hair back. Without looking at me, he said:

'Has Mikael been here today?'

'No,' I replied.

He rubbed his hands, which were blue and old and wizened.

'Does he not usually come and play with you?'

'No,' I replied. 'Never.'

'I see,' he said, giving me a sharp, clear look. And he added:

'Would you tell your father that I am here?'

I opened the door to the parlour, and saw Father quickly get up.

As soon as I had closed the door on them, Uncle Otto came out into the hallway. 'Go and play with your cousin out in the yard,' he ordered. I realised that he wanted to eavesdrop. But I knew from experience that you could only hear very badly there. I ran out into the street and clambered in through Father's bedroom window, which was always open. I had purposefully left the door between the bedroom and the parlour ajar, and could now comfortably hear every word that was spoken. I noticed now that even Arnfelt's voice resembled Grandfather's, to such an extent that at first I could not distinguish between them. There was, though, a great difference in tone.

'Not at all. On the contrary, it is a pleasure that Your Grace is present. And I understand full well the interest which has motivated Your Grace. Besides, the purpose of my visit is no secret at all. I merely wish to inform Mr Arnberg that we have been obliged to seek a replacement. Your sickness has unfortunately lasted some time, and our plans – '

'Yes, yes,' Father interrupted, 'and I have myself already suggested a replacement – '

'To be sure,' Arnfelt replied, waving a piece of paper. 'You have suggested an American Swede, a former colleague, I believe, Mr Fält. We do not know the man. But naturally we should have taken him on your recommendation if this could have been arranged without our committing ourselves for a lengthy period of time. It is particularly important to us that we hold the post open for Mr Arnberg – '

'You're too kind,' Father said with a laugh. And I gave a start. The other man continued after a moment's pause:

'Kind is, perhaps, not the right word. Clearly, we are acting in the best interests of the company and of ourselves. We consider it to be of the utmost importance that the brilliant inventor himself should lead the work – '

' – until he drops,' Father interrupted. And he added: 'assuming, of course, that this occurs within an acceptable period of time. Have you received a new report from the brilliant inventor's doctor?'

'New report?' A. O. repeated.

'Yes, because the report from last October is no longer of any use. It may have been good enough as the basis for your generous offer of a share in the profits for the lifetime of the patient. But now that is a question of estimating the length of my tenure, you have surely obtained a new report, as any cautious general would?'

There was a moment's silence, and I heard Father beat his chest. Then Arnfelt said:

'I am afraid that I do not understand you.'

'Oh, listen to that!' Father exclaimed. 'I apologise a thousand times if I am mincing my words! Father-in-law, am I expressing myself unclearly?'

Grandfather said:

'Calm yourself, Johan. You won't gain anything by getting excited.'

'No, people are always telling me that,' Father muttered. 'No matter. I shall stay calm. I apologise, Your Lordship. I am like a hen; I would prefer to be plucked after I'm dead. But, please, go on.'

A. O. rifled through his papers.

'If I am not mistaken,' he resumed, 'you were referring to our agreement regarding the right of patent. According to the settlement of 10 August last year, you were to receive one hundred ordinary shares in Arnberg's Explosives, each worth a nominal value of one thousand kronor. Was that not the case?'

'That was the first settlement,' Father said.

'Quite right. You were not entirely satisfied with it, for which reason we inserted an additional paragraph, dated 18 October, according to which you were guaranteed a share of the profits. To judge from your insinuations and agitated mood, you appear to believe that the October settlement nullified that of August. This is a misconception. You possess, as agreed, a nominal hundred thousand in ordinary shares, plus the share of the profits – '

'Shares?' Father said. 'Shares? Shares?'

'As far as I aware, they are already written in your name. At any rate, the board took the decision – '

'There you are, Johan,' Grandfather said. 'There you are! Well! Now calm yourself – '

But Father cried:

'Where's Jan? Jan!'

I put my hand on the door-handle, but before I had time to turn it I heard Father say:

'No, I don't believe you. I want to see the shares before I believe you.'

'Johan! Johan!' Grandfather scolded. But Arnfelt said:

'You'll have them this evening or tomorrow.'

There was silence. I heard someone rattle the water-jug, I heard the door to the hall open, I heard Grandfather call: 'Hedda! Otto!' in a whisper. Then it was quiet again. Eventually I heard Father's voice:

'Please excuse me. I have been ill and am a little weak. Please excuse me.'

'Don't mention it,' A. O. replied. And when I heard him say 'Don't mention it', I realised that he was a wicked man.

I opened the door and carefully crept in. Father was sitting on the sofa, Grandfather standing in front of him, mopping his brow with a damp handkerchief. A. O. was standing by the table, bent over a piece of paper that he appeared to be reading. By the door to the hall, his hand still on the door-handle, stood Uncle Otto, staring sullenly from beneath his fringe. Father said:

'Otto, everything's alright again. I have misunderstood and misjudged Count Arnfelt. I really do apologise, sir.'

'Don't mention it – ' A. O. repeated, without looking up from the sheet of paper. But suddenly he turned to Uncle Otto and said:

'Mr Arnberg, I also have some business with you – '

'With me?' Uncle Otto muttered, blushing. A. O. sat down at the table, crossed his legs, and started to swing his raised leg rapidly.

'Yes, it's rather a curious story,' he said. 'I believe it might interest Your Grace. About a month ago I received a visit from a charming and rather eccentric old lady – '

'Aunt Léonie?' Otto interrupted.

The Bishop sank onto the sofa; he looked like he had a bad taste in his mouth.

'So,' he said, 'she really did call on you then? I asked her not to – '

'For what reason?' Arnfelt asked.

'Well. As you yourself put it – she is a little eccentric. She has lived alone for many years, and has cultivated a plethora of peculiar ideas.'

'I have to say that I found her very interesting,'A. O. went on. 'And my poor wife who, as you know, is also obliged to live in isolation, was especially taken with her. She reminded me of number of half-forgotten family stories – '

'Yes, I know,' the Bishop interrupted. 'It's her hobby-horse. And certain other people's. By all means, such things may be interesting from a cultural and genealogical perspective. But I have seen instances in which they can also be dangerous. To concern oneself too much with those who have passed away.'

'That's my opinion too,' Father interjected. 'I agree with my father-in-law entirely. Let the dead rest in peace. In my will I shall ask to be spared the stupid remarks of those who come after me.'

He laughed. His face was white as chalk behind his black beard and hair, which hung on his forehead, wet with sweat. A. O. looked at him for a moment, then turned back to Grandfather:

'I don't know about that. It seems to me that it would be wise to maintain our links to the past. Modern man is exposed to far too many so-called "free impulses". He thinks that he behaves freely and according to his own good sense. But the links are there all the same. And, before you know it, he's got himself hopelessly muddled.

'But to return to business. I have in my possession – or, more correctly – my wife has in her possession – because all our family heirlooms are in her care – a very beautiful mirror from the end of the sixteenth century. North Italian craftsmanship. It is listed on an inventory of Frönsafors from the year 1668. Now, Miss Arnberg said that you have a twin piece in your possession. To be more precise, in Lieutenant Arnberg's – '

'Yes,' Uncle Otto said. 'I inherited it from Father, who in turn had it from Grandfather, Dr Arnberg of –dal, who in turn had it from Consul Arnberg of Ystad. How he came by it, I don't know. Let me just go and fetch it.'

He went out. A. O. looked at his sheet of paper. He said:

'At any rate, it's peculiar. Miss Arnberg had built an entire family theory on the two mirrors. She maintained that General Arnfelt, who died in 1792, shared them between his two sons, and that one of these brothers was the ancestor of the Arnberg family. Well, it's possible. One can find family connections like that where one least expects to. But I should have been rather sceptical, nonetheless, had I not discovered – '

He slapped his hand down on the sheet of paper.

' – in this inventory from that very year, 1792, that there existed at that time two so-called Venetian mirrors, apparently a pair. Now it is my opinion that mirror number two – let us call it the Arnberg mirror – must be an imitation – a fake.'

'I don't think so,' Uncle Otto interrupted, coming back into the parlour. 'I don't know much about the silver, but this glass can hardly be Swedish. You'll see soon enough, sir, once it's been wiped. And what would have been the point of making an imitation?'

'Yes, that's the question,' Arnfelt went on. 'I've amused myself by pondering precisely that. There is a supplement to the inventory of 1668, in which the mirror is carefully described, and at the end of which one is informed by the devoted compiler that the glass in the mirror has a remarkable property. Any man who spends a long time regarding his image in the glass will see it replaced by someone else's. And this someone will sooner or later be the cause of the viewer's death. A useful property in the somewhat bellicose seventeenth century. Well, General Arnfelt was of course a Gustavian and an Enlightenment philosopher, so it is unlikely that he attached any great significance to this story. But who can say whether there was not at Frönsafors some superstitious person who harboured malign thoughts – the General was, of course, murdered by his staff – and who was afraid of being betrayed by this wonderful mirror? Granted, this hypothesis rests upon extremely shaky ground. But nonetheless I should dearly like to know which of the two mirrors is the genuine article.'

'I understand,' Father said with a smile. 'You wish to identify the man who will cause your death!'

'In our age,' A. O. began, 'when most people die in their beds – '

But Uncle Otto interrupted:

'I'm sorry,' he said, 'but you're wrong. In our age most people are murdered.'

Grandfather objected:

'Paradoxes, Otto, paradoxes! It is quite abhorrent to me to hear such frivolous paradoxes!'

But A. O. said:

'If by murder Lieutenant Arnberg also means suicide, then I am almost inclined to think him correct. There are probably very few people who do not, to a greater or lesser extent, cause their own death.

'But I shall never get around to business at this rate. It is, as you might expect, of a mercantile nature. Plainly and simply, will you sell me the mirror?'

'No,' Uncle Otto replied. And so firmly and vehemently that we were all startled.

'No,' he repeated. 'There are things that you don't sell. But from what I understand, you have done Johan a favour. Well, if you can do us a favour, then we can do you a favour. Please. Take the mirror. I don't want it.'

'Otto!' Father cried, his face glowing with joy. 'Listen to that – Otto! Good old lad!'

Grandfather rubbed his hands. We poor Arnbergs were all feeling light at heart, and as far as I was concerned, my chest was pounding fit to burst from pride, and I was close to breaking into tears.

'Yes, there you are,' I muttered, 'there you are!'

A. O. said:

'That's really altogether too kind. But I am afraid, Lieutenant, that you do not rightly understand the purely pecuniary value – '

'I understand right enough,' Uncle Otto interrupted. 'Aunt Léonie maintained that it was worth three or four thousand kronor. What do I care? I'll wrap it up. You can take it with you – '

'Just a moment,' A. O. said, smiling for the first time. 'I'd like to tell you something, Lieutenant Arnberg. Some years ago – yes, it was the same year I sold –dal to your brother's American partner, so some ten years ago – I had a German art expert value my mirror. He estimated its value at between forty and fifty thousand marks.'

We Arnbergs gave a collective gasp, and all looked like roaches. And Grandfather's chin trembled as though he were chewing something. But Uncle Otto's redness shifted to blue; he glared furiously at A. O, until finally he said:

'Why are you talking about money? Do you think this is some sort of financial transaction? Have you done my brother a favour or not? Well, then take the mirror and let me be!'

We breathed out; Father stood up, went over to Uncle Otto, grabbed him by the collar and shook him:

'Listen to you, old boy!' he said. 'Just listen to you!'

Grandfather was smiling broadly, rubbing his hands and shaking his head so that his white locks swung. I was hopping about on one leg. To me, it seemed quite incontestable that we Arnbergs had finally shown what excellent fellows we were.

At that moment I chanced to glance at the door, which was half open, and there, in the darkness, was Hedda's long snout. She winked at me and waved me over. I understood that she had brought the mirror but was ashamed to come in. I ran out, took it from her, struggled in with the heavy object, and leant it against the wall.

A. O. Arnfelt quickly stood up. He went over to the mirror and stood right in front of it. We others formed a circle around him. He put on a pair of gold-framed spectacles, with large lenses, clear as water. He inspected the silverwork, then bent down low and exhaled. Then he took a few steps back, then stepped forward again. Then he bent the index finger of his right hand and placed the knuckle to the glass. And he stood for a long while with his knuckle pressed to the glass. Then he inspected the frame once again. Then he took several steps back. During all of this we stood breathless but smiling, watching him. Eventually he said:

'The frame is an extremely well-crafted imitation.'

'Imitation?' Uncle Otto repeated. 'Imitation?' repeated Father and Grandfather. I just stood there open-mouthed. Arnfelt said:

'Yes, an imitation. I can't understand your assertion that the glass would prove the opposite. This is a perfectly ordinary piece of mirror glass. I should almost like to say shoddy.'

Uncle Otto rushed up to the mirror, bent down and stared into his own wide, bloodshot eyes. He stood like that for a long time.

Arnfelt said:

'However, I am still willing to buy it. For curiosity's sake. As you will understand, the price – '

'The price?' Uncle Otto repeated, looking round. And all of a sudden he raised his foot and aimed a kick that shattered the glass and broke the frame. Then, without saying another word, he went out.

A. O. folded away his spectacles.

'I am sorry,' he said, 'if I have inadvertently been the cause of any disillusion or unpleasantness for you gentlemen. That was not my intention. But I have detained you far too long with my somewhat puerile business. We covered everything of true significance, did we not? Is that not the case, Mr Arnberg? No, I am forgetting. I don't think I mentioned the name of the man whom we have appointed as your replacement. Your temporary replacement, I mean, your stand-in.'

'No,' Father said, absent-mindedly. He had sunk back onto the sofa, thoroughly exhausted. A. O. went over to him.

'We assumed that he should have three characteristics. He should be an enterprising man, he should be able to devote all, or most, of his time, to our project, and he should be in such circumstances that we do not have to tie ourselves to him for any great length of time. This latter out of consideration for your welfare. Well, there is an intelligent and able man available, who is willing to continue your work *ad interim*. You will understand already who I mean – Grundberg, of –dal.'

'J. W. Grundberg?' Father repeated slowly.

'I hope you are happy with our choice,' A. O. said, patting him lightly on the shoulder. 'Now see to it that you can soon replace him.'

He turned to Grandfather and took both his hands. It was a fine sight to see these two silver-haired old men, as alike as twins. A. O. said:

'It was a great pleasure that Your Grace wished to be present. Misunderstandings are most easily avoided in the presence of a third party, someone who is simultaneously impartial and benevolently interested. And, if we are to set any store by Miss Léonie Arnberg's theories, then this was something of a family gathering. I hope, at any rate, that Your Grace has been assured of my good intentions?'

Grandfather bowed silently. A. O. disappeared into the hall. Shortly thereafter his carriage rolled away as soundlessly as it had arrived.

This was to be a terrible day for me, one that is still uncomfortable to remember. My conscience acquired its first heavy burden; a burden that I was too cowardly to throw off. For the first time, I did another person an injustice, a shameful injustice.

This is what happened:

We were seated at the dinner table, Father, Uncle Otto and I. Hedda was busy in the kitchen. Suddenly Uncle Otto reaches out his hand, points at Father and says:

'It was Hedda!'

'What do you mean?' Father says. 'What about Hedda?'

And Uncle Otto, glowering like a madman:

'It was Hedda who did it. Don't you remember, she wanted to sell my furniture? I wouldn't let her. Now she's had outgoings, large outgoings because of your illness. She didn't dare sell the mirror. But she realised the glass was the valuable part. She realised that much. She took out the glass. When Aunt Léonie was here, the old glass was still in it. The real, deep glass. Where would it have gone? She took it out. She didn't think anyone would notice.'

Suddenly his glowering gaze and threatening finger turns towards me, as I sit there in torment.

'Look at the boy!' he says. 'Look at Jan! He knows something.'

And now Father turns his feverish eyes on me as well.

'Jan – do you know something?'

'No – ' I mutter.

Uncle Otto says:

'You saw her carry the mirror off. Look how he's blushing! She's told him not to say anything.'

Father takes a firm grip of my shoulder.

'Jan!' he says, 'did you see something?'

I stammer:

'Father – I don't know – '

And burst into tears.

Father is deathly pale. The fire in his eyes has gone out.

'Otto!' he says, gets up, goes. Uncle Otto follows him into the kitchen. I dare not hear anything. I run out into the street, run bareheaded round the whole block and rush in through the door of the Bishop's Palace. I wait for a while in the big, old, silent, gloomy vestibule, catching my breath. Then I creep carefully through the dark passageway to Grandfather's room.

Grandfather is sitting at his desk, leaning back in his chair, his hands on the desk. I take a chair and tiptoe up to the desk. Grandfather does not jump, he slowly turns his head and looks at me with a soft, warm gaze. Gradually a slight smile appears.

'Is that you, Jan?' he says. 'I was just thinking about you.'

'Can I sit here?' I ask, putting the chair down next to his.

'Of course you can sit here.'

I put my right hand on the desk beside his left hand, and after a while I say:

'Can I hold your hand, Grandfather?'

'Of course you can, Jan.'

I hesitate and hesitate. Eventually I ask:

'Grandfather, what were you thinking about me for?'

His hand closes softly and with a slight tremble around mine.

'Oh, Jan,' he replies, hesitating over the words. 'I don't really know. I don't really know if I was thinking about you. Perhaps I was thinking about your mother. And then you appeared, Jan. And now I can imagine that I'm holding your mother's hand. And you can imagine that it's your mother holding your hand. Let's pretend that for a while, Jan. You and Grandfather together.'

We sit for a while, a long while, in silence. I do not look at Grandfather, and perhaps he does not look at me either. We are both pretending, of course, that we are holding my mother's hand.

But after this period of silence, there is a great commotion. The pink girl, my cousin Léonie, comes rushing in, hugs me, and starts to swing me round. She tickles me, until I'm wriggling like a worm on the floor. Then I follow her to the drawing room, where the aunts are sitting having coffee. And they stuff me full of biscuits, for I am a rare guest in the Bishop's Palace these days. All evening we play by the fountain. It is a May evening. Grandfather comes out with the spanner and turns the fountain on for the first time. Aunt with the doves is surrounded by her noisy friends. The water splashes, the pond fills, mirroring the shining, white May clouds.

But it gets late, it gets dark, I have to go home.

'Tell your father,' says Grandfather, 'that he could come and see us himself one day.'

Aunt with the hair bends down and whispers in my ear:

'Tell your father that if he doesn't come of his own accord, then I'll come and fetch him.'

And she blushes and I can hear her heart beating.

'Say hello to Hedda,' says Aunt with the doves.

'Yes, of course,' Grandfather says, 'say hello to Hedda.'

I go the usual way, through the avenue of poplars, through the plum thicket, over the fence. Our back yard is silent, our house is silent. From the kitchen window shines a faint light.

Hedda is sitting at the kitchen table under the ceiling lamp, darning my socks. Her face is yellow, with red cheeks. Father has gone to bed, Uncle Otto has gone out.

I stand for a moment by the table, then walk slowly towards the attic stairs.

'Jan!' Hedda says. I stop dead. Now it is my heart that is thudding and threatening to suffocate me.

'Jan! Do you know anything about the mirror?'

'No,' I say, 'I don't know anything.'

'Well, I just can't understand it,' Hedda mutters. 'I can't understand it. Unless the Lieutenant is mistaken. Because I know that I've never touched it.'

I stand and weigh things up, standing first on one leg, then on the other. In the end I say, meekly and shyly:

'Are you sad, Hedda?'

'You can imagine, Jan,' she replies. 'To be as good as accused of theft. If the Lieutenant doesn't believe me, then I don't wonder at it. He doesn't know me. But you'd think Arnberg would believe me.

'And how can I stay with him if he doesn't believe me?' she went on. 'And how can I leave him? The way he is now?'

She says:

'I don't know that I've ever had any other reward or thanks for my work apart from him believing me. And I've been happy with that.'

Finally she says, raising her head and shutting one eye, the better to thread her needle:

'Well, we'll just have to make reductions there, I suppose.'

I go upstairs to bed, creeping down beneath the covers. My wretched cowardice stifles me, but I am firmly resolved not to relieve my heavy conscience.

And I held fast to my decision, despite all that followed. Father made no further reproaches to her, but Uncle Otto persecuted poor Hedda. He could never forget the dirty way – as he saw it – she had frustrated his proud Arnbergian gesture. It was not the money that bothered him; he threw the silver frame into a corner of the attic, wanting neither to see nor sell it. His bitter resentment arose from the fact that his noble-mindedness had been ridiculed. He never forgave her for that, and he never left Father in peace.

'That you don't drive her out! That you can bear to have a dishonest person in your home!'

Father replied:

'Otto – if she did it – and it is possible, of course – then she isn't the one who is dishonest. It's my poverty that's dishonest, it's my illness that's dishonest, it's me that's dishonest!'

But he would not listen to reason and would not leave Father in peace. His carping had consequences. One was that we left Uncle Otto's house as early as July, and moved with all our belongings to the little cottage on the hill between –dal and the factory.

The other was that Father married Hedda.

One day – it was the same day as Grandfather's birthday – Father said to me:

'Jan, you can go in to Grandfather and tell him that Father and Hedda have asked to have the banns published. We're getting married.'

I dashed off. It was rather late; the guests had gone. Grandfather was sitting on the round bench beneath the chestnut tree; beside him sat his two daughters. My uncle, the doctor, was not there, but the lawyer was standing over by the fountain, his hand on the spanner, letting the jet of water slowly sink and disappear. I ran up to Grandfather, out of breath.

'Grandfather!' I panted. He held my waist with both hands.

'Well, Jan,' he said, smiling. 'What's the matter?'

'Grandfather! I'm to tell you from Father that he's getting married to Hedda.'

Grandfather let go of me.

The lawyer came slowly towards us, swinging the spanner between his fingers.

'Is that so?' he said. 'Our dear Johan hasn't forgotten your birthday after all, Father. He had a little surprise prepared.'

I looked from one to the other, astonished. Aunt with the doves, the pale, mild one, was blood-red, and her eyebrows had moved together in a most peculiar way, one rather lower than the other. Like a thunderbolt.

Aunt with the hair, the rosy-cheeked, lively one was pale. She carefully stood up and slowly walked over to the fountain.

Aunt with the doves said – and I could hardly recognise her voice:

'Well. What of it? Now there's one fewer in the family. One fewer to worry about. So much the better.'

Then she too stood up and walked off.

But Grandfather put his hands on my waist again.

'Jan,' he said, 'tell your father that I wish him much happiness. And tell dear Hedda that I wish her much happiness. Will you remember that, Jan?'

'Yes,' I replied.

He looked at me. And he said:

'Jan. We may not see each other for some time. But do you know what, Jan! Sometimes we shall pretend that we're holding each other by the hand.'

'Yes,' I replied.

He drew me to him and kissed me on the forehead. That was, I believe, the first time Grandfather kissed me. And it was the last time I saw him.

Chapter 6

Hitrotorp

Our new home was called Hitrotorp. It had once been the gamekeeper's cottage for Frönsafors. The house was long and low, red with sky-blue corners. The western gable leaned out dramatically; it had a broad, black door which led to an empty toolshed. The door to the house was sky-blue, like the corners; the step was extremely high and worn, a real hazard. Above the door hung a pair of yellowing elk's antlers, one with six points, the other with seven. The remnants of clusters of feathers were nailed to the outside walls.

The main room had four windows, two facing north, two facing south. The floor was new, white, fresh, and smelled strongly of resin, but the ceiling was old, smoky, covered in a thick layer of spiders' webs, as were the walls. The wallpaper showed all manner of remarkable buildings, such as castles in Stockholm, Örebro, Vadstena, Kalmar, Uppsala, Berlin, Nuremberg, Versailles, Madrid, as well as Riddarholm's Church, St. Peter's, Cologne Cathedral, Reims Cathedral, and the Colosseum, the Parthenon, the Pyramids, and Indian temples.

'Well, Jan,' Father said, 'we can learn geography from this. We've got the whole world in front of us.'

A narrow chamber ran alongside the main room, split in two by the wall of the baking oven; I was given the southern end, Hedda the northern, and the kitchen as well, which was almost as large as the main room. Father got the main room.

We arrived one August day. Hedda and I. Hedda was still wearing her wedding outfit, the black silk dress and Grandfather's gold brooch under her chin. We were travelling in a haycart, piled high with our furniture; behind us came another haycart full of furniture.

Later that day Father arrived. By then all of the furniture had been moved in and Hedda had scrubbed all the floors, walls and ceilings. Father had been at the factory; he arrived in a beautiful cabriolet, the driver was wearing livery with silver piping, and on the buttons the letters J. W. G. Father gave him two kronor. 'How much did you give him,' Hedda asked, sticking her head out as the cab rolled away. The silk had shrunk in its box, a patch of red bodice shone angrily above the top of the grey skirt. She was very ugly.

Father sat down on the bench by the door. It was grey with moss and rather ramshackle. Hedda said:

'You should be careful with those fine clothes.'

Father grew red, tugged at the sleeve of his coat, but stayed where he was, bowed, shrunken. He was tired. But within no time he raised his head, smiled so that his teeth showed, and began to sing:

'The troll it sits beside its wall – combing its silver beard – singing by the red stones – little fawn, oh do come here – I can promise true – '

'What are you singing?' I asked.

He replied:

'I'm not really sure. It's probably a nursery rhyme. It just came to me.'

He took my arm.

'Stand here, Jan. Now look beyond the copse. There's a seed-pine, do you see it? Look to the left, two spans to the left. Through those leaves. Do you see anything?'

'I can see a black roof,' I replied.

He said:

'That's where I was born. I was born under that roof. That's –dal. In the autumn, when the leaves have fallen, you'll be able to see the whole house. It's a white, two-storey building. I should think you'll be able to see the grand staircase as well. The whole of these woods, Jan, from there – all the way to there – that's the park. That's the park, Jan. You should see the paths! You should see the main path down to the summer-house! There's a fountain. Much more beautiful than Grandfather's. There's an ash tree so large, it would take six men to reach round it. Imagine – six! It's hollow at the bottom as well, but is still fine. I can see its crown; yes, I know just where it is. And the pond, Jan – now that would be something for you. There's a little island with a duck-house. I had a little dinghy – '

He fell silent, out of breath. I asked:

'Can't we go and look?'

His arm, resting on my shoulder, grew limp and heavy. His hand relaxed, tired of pointing.

'Of course, Jan,' he said at last. 'Of course we can go and look. One day. When the weather's nice.'

But the days passed, the weeks and the months.

Father would read with me. I had a leaver's certificate from the first class, and his plan was to spend the winter getting me ready for the fourth-year class. We were in a hurry. 'You see, Jan,' Father said, 'we have to work. We have to get somewhere. One fine day I shan't have time for you any more. And then you'll be left standing there.'

I do not know if I was particularly slow, or if Father was far too impatient. He often lost his temper, throwing his chair back, making it creak. He never hit me, but he would beat himself, thumping his chest with his fist. It made a terrible, thick sound which I found unbearable. In the end I asked him to stop. I said:

'It would be better if you hit me.'

He blushed and blinked.

'Oh, it's just a bad habit,' he muttered. 'I shall try to stop.'

Sometimes he would jump up and dash out, to stand in the yard with his arms outstretched, as though about to embrace someone. And he would breathe with his mouth open. It used to scare me, I would stand in the window and give a start every time his body convulsed. I was afraid that he would fall. But after a while he would turn back, calm and content, smile, and wink mischievously.

'Right, Jan! Let's go on.'

Geography was our favourite subject, or at least it was mine.

When we got to some remarkable place, we would have to find it on the wallpaper. Father would search the top rows, I the bottom. 'Here!' I would cry. 'No, here!' Father would cry. And we would roam about, searching the walls, arguing and laughing.

Or else Father would say:

'So, Captain Jan, if you were going to ship me to Hamburg, what course would you take. Imagine that we embark on the *Claire Aurore* in Gothenburg – '

That was fun; the rest went very slowly.

And even Hitrotorp had one of the world's oceans, larger, more secretive, richer than the fountain in Grandfather's garden. The cottage lay on a slope, where great boulders lay one atop the other beneath a worn, yellow-brown cover of crunchy moss. There was little grass, even fewer flowers, and no trees, apart from two enormous junipers. At the bottom of the slope, edged by the copse, was an abandoned meadow. There all manner of wild flowers bloomed; there the remnants of an old barn lay in a heap; there a spring of green water provided a refuge for toads. But even further away, beyond the rotten fence, was an old blast hole, full of water, dark, secretive. The rock was black and full of glittering particles. I thought it was silver. I thought that the water was as deep as it was black. I thought it was bottomless. There *Claire Aurore* would sail, loaded with silver. Her name, written in gold lettering, was mirrored in the still water. It was a threatening sea, so unlike Grandfather's calm and friendly pond. I was scared. I would creep there and creep back. I was scared that Father or Hedda would realise the danger and stop me from going. Yet I was just as frightened of meeting my doom alone in the dark water.

One morning the mirror of water was cloudy, grainy. It was ice. The brig had to break her way through. The next morning the *Claire Aurore* sat fast in the ice; I had to break her free. I put her in the toolshed behind the black door to hibernate.

The leaves in –dal's park began to thin. I could see the white walls, the long rows of windows. Eventually I could see the flight of steps, with its iron urns, and the roof of the summer-house in the park. I asked if we could go there yet.

'Well, now you can see it from here,' Father replied. 'Perhaps next spring. It's so beautiful in the spring. There's a large greenhouse. We must go there some time and buy flowers. Next spring.'

The evenings grew long. Father would lie on the sofa.

It started to snow. First a few flakes which sugared the yellow moss and then vanished. I climbed up into the attic to look for my sledge, a long, fine, upholstered sledge with red flowers on it, which Grandfather had given me. It was not in the attic, it was not in the toolshed. I was furious, and shouted: 'Hedda's stolen my sledge.'

'I see,' Hedda said. 'Am I to get the blame for that as well? No, I think we can make reductions there.'

I ran in to Father:

'Father, now Hedda's stolen my sledge as well.'

'As well?' Father said, sitting up. He looked at me. I blushed, standing first on one leg, then the other. In the end I said:

'Why are you looking at me, Father?'

He waved me to him. He took my head in his hands and looked me in the eye.

'Well, Jan,' he said, 'would you like to tell me what happened to Uncle Otto's mirror?'

I confessed everything.

'What are you going to do now?' Father asked. I thought for a while, squirming and wriggling. I understood full well what he wanted. But I had no desire to humble myself before Hedda, particularly as I suspected her of stealing my sledge. I thought: 'Never mind the sledge, but I'm not saying sorry.'

'Well, Jan, I'm not going to force you,' Father said, as if he had guessed what I was thinking. And he stroked my hair and added:

'Maybe one day.'

From that moment I noticed that Father spent a lot of time watching me, with a clear, attentive, observant gaze that made me awkward. Sometimes it would make me stumble or knock something over. Perhaps he had always watched me in the same observant, curious way; perhaps it was my guilty conscience which was making me awkward. But whatever it was, it could not persuade me to say sorry to Hedda.

Once a week the carriage with the silver-embroidered driver would come and take Father to the factory. The driver was a small man with a ruddy, bearded face, and peculiar little eyes. He was wall-eyed, and it was very odd to watch him and Hedda look at each other, the one cross-eyed, the other wall-eyed. The driver's name was Josef, and we became good friends. He asked if I might go with them to the factory gates. Father did not want me to. But Josef said:

'How could it harm Mr Grundberg if the young master came along? If there were any justice, Arnberg would come and Grundberg would go.'

Father and the driver had once been playmates; Father always gave him a big tip. This annoyed Hedda. She would say:

'That Josef is a fox. In the kitchen here he talks ill of Grundberg, and I daresay he talks ill of you in the kitchen at –dal.'

Sometimes, when Father had got out of the carriage and was searching in his meagre purse, Hedda would come out and start to brush the dust off him, all the while whispering:

'We can make reductions here, Arnberg! Just this once – '

Father would get angry, but could not help laughing. Josef pretended not to have heard anything. But when Father and Hedda were busy, and only I was watching him, he would make the funniest faces.

'She's a real old hag,' he would say to me. 'I can't understand why the Director wants to have anything to do with such a b--ch. She doesn't fit in with the better sort of person – '

I was too ashamed to agree with him, but deep inside I did. Everything had become poorer and more wretched and more miserable since Hedda arrived in our home. All the fine things from the Bishop's Palace and from Mother's time were gone. If Father had not been there, and if he had not still dressed well, and if the carriage from –dal had not come to take him to the factory once a week, you could easily have taken us for common crofters.

The carriage was exchanged for a sled. The drifts piled up in waves on the slope, showering the dark-red walls of the cottage with white foam. It grew silent, there were long, silent, clear moonlit nights. The bells could be heard ten minutes before Father returned from the factory. The sound would grow, grow, grow. Sometimes I grew anxious when I heard it in the distance, faint but constantly growing. Father went to the factory more and more often. There was something wrong; I do not know what. It was to have been up and running by the new year, but there was something not finished. Father would sit up long into the night, writing, calculating. 'You're going to ruin your health again,' Hedda would say, from the door to the main room. But Father would shout:

'For God's sake, let me be! Do you think I've got time to sleep?'

My lessons were neglected; I had many free days. I would crawl through snow-drifts that reached to my shoulders. It was easier to make your way through the mature forest to the north. I was on a mission. By the road was an iron cross, and Josef had told me that if you left the road by the cross and walked a couple of hundred paces into the forest, then you would come to an open space. There, many years ago, a fat ironmaster and his skinny driver had been eaten by wolves. But it was said that the ironmaster had hidden his bulging purse in a hollow tree before disaster befell them. Josef had hunted for the purse in his day, and every boy he knew, including Father, had looked for it. In vain. Now it was my turn.

I walked away from the cross several times, and eventually found the open space where the ironmaster had succumbed to the wolves. But I found no purse. Once, when I was on my way home, I heard the bell from –dal ringing through the forest. I went as fast as I could, and reached the cross and the road before the sled passed. In it sat a man whom I did not know, a fat, bluish-pale, clean-shaven man. Josef was standing behind him. I had thought I would be allowed to stand on one of the runners, as I usually did. I smiled at Josef and got ready to jump on. Suddenly I realised that Josef was different. He was not smiling at all; his face was immobile, like a wax face with artificial clumps of beard.

I quickly drew back behind the cross; I felt deeply humiliated. In spite of the white desolation, which ought to have made a flea visible, neither the fat man nor my friend Josef seemed to have noticed my existence. I had a terrible intimation of my own insignificance.

Josef tried to explain his unusual behaviour to me afterwards. He said that a driver is not allowed to greet people when he is driving his employer. He must be a creature without friends or acquaintances.

'You can imagine, Jan,' he said, caressing me with his peculiar, wind-eyed gaze, 'I'd rather drive you and your father than that American joker. But if you're employed as a driver, then you can't go giving yourself graces, as they say. So it's up to you, Jan, to get the money to buy back –dal.'

I thought a lot about this. I said that I had been looking in vain for the fat ironmaster's purse. He grinned and said:

'Yes, that's like looking for a cheese-grub in the moon. But there are plenty more purses in the world, aren't there?'

In the meantime I developed a distaste for Josef's employer. Partly because he had insulted me, and partly because I had an idea that he was Father's enemy. (It is also possible that Father might have made a few comments about Grundberg which I had only half understood. In actual fact J. W. Grundberg had by this time set in motion his final, despicable attack on Father. He maintained that Father's patent was not good enough to form the basis of large-scale and rational production. He maintained that he himself had made numerous essential improvements, that he had already sought a patent, that the company should be reorganised, etc.) I got it into my head that I should like to harm Grundberg in some way; possibly even kill him. I imagined holding him down until he was quite still and dead. These thoughts merged with others. I remembered 'the Angel's' defence when I criticised him for killing cats. 'Surely it's better that I get fifty öre than one of them goes on miaowing.' I fretted, without coming to any conclusions. As I have already mentioned, I had a lot of free time in those days. 'The Black Sea' was frozen under a layer of ice a yard thick. The *Claire Aurore* was in hibernation behind the black door. My thoughts needed something to occupy them. It was a game.

At least I realised that I was dealing with something forbidden.

Memoirs of a Dead Man

I can still recall how scared I was when Father one evening asked out of the blue:

'Jan – what are thinking about?'

I was sitting eating thin porridge; I had let go of the spoon and was staring stupidly at the slop of bluish milk. I really cannot remember what I was thinking about. But it was probably that. The blood rushed to my head, I gasped for breath.

'Oh,' I said, coming to life. 'I was thinking about Grandfather.'
Father smiled and nodded.

I was lying. I realised full well that my thoughts were wrong, quite out of order. I kept them to myself, for my isolation out in the forest and the snow-drifts. Only with Josef could I exchange one or two confidences. He was a very versatile man, I realised, a sly man. I did not like him, but I liked talking to him.

'Josef,' I said, 'if you kill someone, do you get their money?'

His strange eyes spun, making me dizzy until I had to look away.

'Well, young master, hark at you!' he mocked. 'You'd like to believe that, wouldn't you? No, it's not that easy. If you kill someone, you get your head chopped off, or at the very least a lifetime's imprisonment. Although there are those who work things out.'

He started to tell me stories of thieves. He told me about Lasse-Maja, who, in 'the old doctor's day' (J. L. Arnberg's), had broken in to –dal and remained hidden in the hollow ash tree for a whole week. I have forgotten most of the stories. He also told me how A. O. Arnfelt had tricked my grandfather. But it was too complicated for me to understand. I wanted to know how to kill a man who could ride about on his sled with such pride and disdain. And how to get hold of his money and ride about on his sled with pride and disdain. Josef's tales of thieving did not interest me.

The snow barricaded us in. One storm lasted two whole days. It was so dark in the main room that Father had to have the lamp on all day long. He sat at his desk writing. I did my homework. It was German grammar. I put my hand over the page, shut my eyes to make sure, and quietly recited what I had learned. I looked up suddenly and caught Father's gaze. I got cross. I cast the book aside and muttered bitterly:

'Why are you always looking at me, Father?'

He laughed.

'Don't you like being looked at?' he asked, waving me over to him. He said: 'Do you know why I look at you? I'm sitting and wondering if I shouldn't have left you with Grandfather. You're far too alone here; and I – well, I'm evidently not alone enough yet. Seriously, wouldn't you rather spend Christmas with your Grandfather?'

I was very happy at this, but got the impression that I ought to suppress my joy.

'Yes,' I replied, 'if you come as well.'

He took me playfully by the neck.

'Is that so?' he said. 'You're making conditions, are you? Well, we'll see.'

He went back to his work, but after a while he looked up and said:

'So you'd rather not go without me?'

'No,' I said, and blushed. In actual fact I longed to go to the Bishop's Palace. Hitrotorp struck me as unbearable now that the snow-drifts had barricaded us inside those gloomy, stuffy rooms. I hated the ingrained smell of poverty, the dark grey roof, the clumsy, treacherous steps, the dirt in the gaps in the floorboards, which not even Hedda's brush could get to grips with. And I hated Hedda. I got the idea that she had lured us away from the Bishop's Palace. She had lured us here and was holding us captive.

But now I spent weeks hoping to spend Christmas with Grandfather. The Bishop's Palace now seemed a paradise to me. I longed for the pleasant smell that would greet me in the vestibule. I longed for Mother's cool, silent room, for the window, for the garden, for Grandfather's dark passageway, for everything. I even longed for my affectionate pink cousin. Sometimes I dreamed that it was Christmas and that I was lying in Mother's room. I would wake up, but not want to wake up, and would lie under the covers crying.

One day – it was eight days before Christmas Eve – Father was standing by my bed when I woke up. He looked very secretive and was smirking.

'Jan,' he said, touching his nose with his finger, 'do you know who's coming today?'

'Grandfather!' I cried. 'Grandfather's coming to get me!'

I flew out of bed and threw my arms around Father. But he said:

'No, Jan. That was mean of me. No, it isn't Grandfather – '

I tried to work out if he was joking. He looked disappointed.

'It's your sister who's coming,' he said. 'Anna. She's coming to spend Christmas with us.'

I could hardly remember her; I had not seen her for two years. She had left teacher-training college; that autumn she had become a teacher. Oh, how boring it sounded!

'Are you upset?' Father asked.

I twisted away, went over to the commode, and dunked my head in the washbowl. I was angry and upset.

Anna was due to arrive at lunchtime; Josef had promised to collect her from the station. But we heard his bells soon after breakfast. He drove up with such speed that the runner hit the doorstep. He knocked on the window with his whip and called:

'Mr Arnberg! You have to come to –dal at once. There's a telephone call.'

Father rushed out; Hedda had to run after him with his coat and hat. And off they went –

He returned on foot. I was standing in the window watching as he emerged from the copse. He was walking very slowly. 'What now?' muttered Hedda, who was standing next to me. She went out onto the steps, holding her hand over her eyes. She called out:

'What is it, Arnberg? What's the matter?'

Father stopped; he pulled his hat off and wiped the sweat from his brow. Then he nodded in our direction and carried on walking. Hedda went to meet him. She stopped at the bottom of the slope and put her hands together. Father went up to her, she took him under the arm, and led him up the slope.

I did not dare ask anything.

Sister Anna arrived after dark. She was dressed in black and had a piece of crêpe in her hat. She was crying heavily when she greeted Father.

'Calm yourself,' he said, frowning. She embraced me.

'Do you recognise me, Jan?' she asked. I said I did not, and pulled away. I did not like her swollen, wet face. 'It's going to be a good Christmas,' I thought, 'having her here.'

As we were sitting down to supper, Father laid down his spoon all of a sudden. He rested his elbows on the table, chin on hands, and met my gaze. I leaned over my bowl. I knew that Father could read my thoughts when he watched me with that look. In the end I felt so oppressed that I slid off my chair and went to stand beside Father. He held me close to him.

'Jan,' he said, 'what made you think that Grandfather was going to come? Did you dream about him last night?'

I could not remember. Father took my hand in his, stroked it, and said:·

'Dear Jan, Grandfather died at two o'clock this morning.'

And he frowned and added:

'He was old, Jan. Over seventy-six years old. Of course it's only natural for you to be sad. But it won't do any good.'

He stood up and went out. Anna was sobbing loudly.

Father spent all of Christmas Eve at the factory. Hedda was busy as usual. Anna and I sat in the corner by the wall of the bake-oven, where it was warm. Anna told me about Grandfather's funeral. I had read the same newspapers as her, and so knew as much as her about the Bishop's last earthly journey. But when she told me, everything became a hundred times more pompous and grand. She described the priests, the servers, the marshals, how they were dressed, how they bowed. I listened eagerly. She told me about the long, black funeral procession, rippling like a train behind the carriage in which Grandfather was taken to the cathedral. She told me about the vaults of the church, ringing with the sounds of the organ and the bells above Grandfather's coffin. She spoke of the flowers. She said that the King and Queen had sent a wreath, and she described – goodness knows where she got this from! – how the King had received news of the death. The Lord Chamberlain had gone in to see him, bowed, and said with a voice trembling with emotion: 'I bring Your Majesty sad tidings. A great man has closed his eyes in eternal sleep. His Grace, Julius Arnberg, Bishop of the diocese of W– , and doctor of philosophy and theology, has this night passed away.' 'Julius Arnberg!' the King exclaimed, the colour draining from his face. 'I and the Kingdom of Sweden will never again have such a bishop.' And he ran bare-headed across the courtyard to the Queen's apartment (because they do not live in the same apartment, she informed me), and cried out as soon as he had entered the Queen's chamber: 'Your Majesty, weep, but be glad that a Servant of the Lord has found peace. Our beloved Arnberg, our Bishop, is no more – '

'Why do you say that, Anna?' I interrupted, aggrieved. 'Why do you say that he is no more?'

Tears rolled down her round, transparent, white cheeks. She took my hands and said:

'Jan, is it not a blessing that people mourn for one another? What does dying matter, as long as one is missed? I believe that the deceased remains on earth for a while; a few hours, or perhaps a few days. I believe that they stay in order to listen – '

'Yes, but what if there's no-one to miss them?' I said. 'Then it would be better to go quickly – '

She had brought some Christmas decorations with her, and we dressed the tree. Just as it was finished, and lit up, Father came back from the factory. He stood for a while looking at the tree. Then he turned to us and said:

'Dear children, you'll have to excuse me. I'm tired.'

Hedda made up the sofa; he undressed and crept in. He yawned again and again, as though he wanted to swallow all the air in the room.

'Now you're getting sick again,' Hedda sighed. 'You shouldn't spend so long at the factory.'

Father replied:

'That's all over now. I don't have to go to the factory any more.'

He turned to face the wall and for quarter of an hour did not say a word. Anna started to sing a Christmas carol, but Hedda told her

Hjalmar Bergman

to be quiet.

Father spent the whole holiday in bed. He was not sick, he was tired. Anna took her little basket and went out into the toolshed. She indicated that I should go with her. She closed the door on us and was very secretive. She opened the basket and took out a tin of Arnberg's Tuberculin. (The basket was full of similar tins, all empty, in which she kept her things.) She showed me the label and read what it said about Arnberg 'and his Grandfather'. She said:

'This is Father's invention, and it's the most remarkable invention anyone has ever made. It's saved hundreds of thousands of people. It saved me. But Father doesn't want to hear of it any longer; he has such a strange temperament. But now you and I, Jan – '

She outlined her plan. She and I were going to cure Father against his will. We would make him strong. We would mix Arnberg's Tuberculin into his food and drink. We had to be very careful; even Hedda couldn't know – she was very careful with Father's food, and would not let us spoil the taste with the bitter powder. The element of secrecy appealed to me, and Anna assured me that Father would be better in a fortnight. I agreed to help. It was usually me who carried Father's food from the kitchen; so it would not be terribly difficult to put our plan into operation.

I started with fruit cream, which was Father's favourite dish. I put a whole dessertspoonful into the bowl and stirred. When I passed the dish to him, I was so nervous that I spilled half of it.

'Clumsy!' Father said with a frown. I quickly withdrew. Father took a spoonful and swallowed it with a contented smile. But no sooner had he swallowed it than his face twisted in a grimace. He smelled the dish, took half a spoonful and tasted it. Then he sighed, pushed the dish aside, and lay down. After a while Hedda came in.

'Why aren't you eating?' she asked anxiously. 'Was there something wrong with it?'

'No, my dear Hedda,' Father said with a sigh. 'It's just me. I've got a bitter taste in my mouth.'

I hurried over, took the dish, ran out into the kitchen and rinsed it off. I felt like a poisoner. But sister Anna persuaded me to try again. I should not take so much this time, just a pinch. For a fortnight Father had a pinch of Tuberculin in all that he ate and drank. Even in his drinking water. He recognised the bitter taste, and grimaced, but made no comment.

'My appetite's gone,' he said.

Eventually the contents of the tin were gone as well. At about the same time, Father got up. Sister Anna was triumphant:

'Do you see, Jan?' she said. 'Isn't it wonderful? Now Father's saved himself; it's Father's genius that's saved him without him even realising it. Oh, there's so much that is great and wonderful in the world! If you only try to understand it.'

But Father had lost a lot of weight during the fortnight he had been in bed. His clothes hung off him like limp sacking, his neck had grown long and sallow, sticking up from his collar like a stick. He turned round and, when he saw me, burst out laughing.

'You know what, Jan?' he said. 'One of these days you'll be able to see the sun and moon through me. I shall be invisible. That's be a nuisance for you, Jan. You'll never know where I am. Before you know it, you'll be busy doing something bad, and you'll feel a hand grab you by the ear – '

That evening I told sister Anna what Father had said. It was the last evening she was staying, and I had asked if I could sit in her bed for a while, listening to stories. She told me a terribly long story about a man who had an invisible hat. As soon as he put the hat on, he became invisible. I thought for a minute, then said:

'I'd like a hat like that.'

'What would you do with it?' she asked.

I thought for a bit longer, then said:

'I'd go down to –dal one evening. And I'd hide there. And when Grundberg had gone to bed, I'd chop his head off.'

'Goodness, Jan, the way you talk!' she sighed. And she started telling me what she would do if she owned the invisibility hat. Nothing but good deeds. But I didn't want to listen, and asked her to tell another story. So she told me Andersen's story of poor Johannes whose father died. And suddenly I grew frightened. I clung to her and pressed my face against her neck.

'What is it, Jan?' she asked. I said:

'What if Father dies!'

She did not answer, and we lay there in silence until I fell asleep.

In the new year we started our lessons agin, Father and I. He had plenty of time: the factory no longer seemed to concern him. He had written to A. O. Arnfelt and was waiting for an answer. For months. Every time Josef came with the post, Hedda stuck her long snout in through the door.

'Well, Arnberg?' she would say.

Father would leaf quickly through the scant post and shrug his shoulders. Sometimes he would say:

'You know A. O. doesn't answer begging letters. It's one of his most sacred principles.'

And sometimes he would say:

'Who would write to me? I no longer exist. I'm dead.'

We studied geography, but now I had to search alone among the remarkable buildings on the wallpaper. Father did not move from the sofa. He would sit, leaning back in the corner, his arms stretched out. He would watch me with that clear, radiant, watchful gaze. I thought his eyes looked like those of some great bird, an owl or an eagle. I neglected my studies, but he did not seem to notice. When I asked something, he would usually answer with a nod or a shake of the head. His silence and his penetrating gaze sometimes made me so downcast that I would try to sneak out of the room. Then he would come to life.

Spring was slow coming, the sun ate the snow, the ground became bare, the dirty yellow covering of moss, flecked here and there by dark grey smudges of snow, came into view. Long icicles hung from the roof. I would break them off and give them to Father: he liked sucking on them.

'It's spring now,' I said one day. 'Can't we go to –dal?'

'Yes,' he said, and stood up, as though he wanted to set off at once. I hopped on one leg in delight. But he only went as far as the window, then, when he had sat looking down towards –dal for a while, he turned back to the sofa.

'Jan,' he suddenly said, 'what if I were forced to leave you?'

My heart began to pound; I blushed, and my cheeks prickled. I understood perfectly well what he meant. And I thought he could have said it straight out. I thought I was old enough for him not to have to resort to euphemisms and stories. I felt hurt. I said:

'If you have to go away, then I shall go too.'

He reached out his hand to me, and drew me to him.

'Is that what you want?' he asked.

But I understood which journey he had in mind. I looked at him in astonishment. I thought his gaze had become sharp and radiantly cruel; I thought that he was looking at me the same way Uncle Otto had looked that night when he was telling ghost stories. I twisted my arm to get away, harder and harder, pulling and tugging. In the end I got angry. I stamped my foot.

'No!' I said.

He let go of me, blinked rapidly as though he had just woken up, or as though he were upset. He nodded, and closed his eyes. After a while he said:

'I don't know why we're bothering with these studies, Jan. We don't have long, and there's a lot I should like to say. You aren't old enough to understand, but that can't be helped. Perhaps you'll remember and understand at some point in the future. Once I've gone away, there's no power on this earth that can give me a return ticket to come and visit you, Jan. So you must listen. Now. And try to understand. Or at least to remember.

'To start with, you should know that I have wasted a lot of money on behalf of you and your mother. I have wasted everything that your grandfather would have left you. And I have wasted everything that I have earned myself. And that was no small amount. And, finally, I have wasted my health. I have sacrificed everything in order to buy back –dal.'

'That?' I asked, pointing through the window.

He nodded.

'People say,' he went on, 'that it became an *idée fixe*. Well, of course it was an *idée fixe*. I've known all along – or at least half understood – that it was an *idée fixe*. And that it would probably ruin me, because I've never been a businessman, and the task was beyond my abilities. Nonetheless I regret – nothing. Or almost nothing. And I shall tell you why. You won't understand. Yet. But that can't be helped.'

He said:

'Jan, if I hadn't had this *idée fixe*, if I hadn't clung to it, body and soul, I would have been lost. I would have had no control over myself. I would have drifted about like a cockleshell, following every current. Every alien impulse which came into my path would have had more power over my actions than my own will. I would not have had any willpower. I would have had my whims, my desires, my notions. They're poor guides. Or, more accurately: they make for poor fuel. They give no impetus. With only them to power you, your ship will be wrecked. Well,' he said, with a smile: 'you might say that that has been my fate nonetheless. But that's another story.

'Jan, don't imagine that I am alone in this. Most people have an *idée fixe*. They're called goals, life goals. Yes, all of humanity, or the part of it which is called civilised, has for centuries accumulated a suitable store of this sort of 'goal'. If anyone were to examine them, they'd find that they are anything but 'goals'. They're part of the cargo. It's as hard to steer a course towards one of these 'goals' as it is for your brig to steer a course towards its own cargo. Never mind. There is no harbour for us, and we need no harbour. But what we do need is drive-power, to stop us drifting and following every current.

'And Jan! For us, for you and me – and for a lot of other people – but we must talk of you and me – for us it is of special significance. I'm not superstitious, my boy, and I hope that you aren't either. And just as I have complete faith that I shall be going to my own impending and eternal sleep, so do I believe in my forebears' eternal sleep. But there is something surrounding us, or in us, something which is always waiting for us, ready to mislead us. What it is, I don't know. It's nothing positive, nothing tangible. It's not a character trait, it's not some weakness of the soul that is passed from generation to generation. It's more like an emptiness, a great yearning to be filled with an unknown personality. A yearning to be something other than what we are. I know what I am, and what my father was before me, and my grandfather before him. Nice, well-meaning, tender, slightly foolish, vain men. Who wish everyone well, and want the best for ourselves. But in our wills there is an emptiness which longs to be filled. Our wills are birds' nests, perfectly built for cuckoos to take over.

'And Jan: this is why we, more than everyone else, need a goal, it doesn't matter what. But a goal that we ourselves have chosen and decided upon. We cannot let ourselves be fodder and nourishment for phantoms and vampires and strangers' wills. Can we? That's why I chose a goal and stuck to it. The fact that I chose this goal was no coincidence, and it wasn't the result of any outside influence. No, there really is a desire in the family, in the Arnbergs' blood, to occupy and tend that patch of soil. It was Father's desire, it was Grandfather's desire. And it has been mine. Has been, because the fire is going out and the ship is as good as wrecked. What of it? I have lived, and I have earned the right to die.

'Now, Jan! Let us be happy and content for the time we have left. I should have accompanied you for a few more years yet, but that's something that makes its own decisions. My release has arrived in the post. And neither A. O. Arnfelt or anyone else, human or superhuman, will be able to wake me up once I've put it beneath my pillow.'

Father became calmer and calmer. He was getting ready to die. Hour after hour he would lie immobile on the sofa, his hands crossed on his chest. He was not asleep; his eyes were open and clear. But he did not answer my questions, and hardly seemed to hear them. He was not concerned about anything. His mood was so tranquil that for a while Hedda thought he must be getting better. She even wondered if he might take in some pupils during the summer. She made a few suggestions; he answered neither yes or no. But he would say a few words to me now and then, which gave me an idea of what he was thinking.

He said:

'Do you know what, Jan? You just have to keep calm. It's like when you fall asleep. If you get it into your head that it's something remarkable, then your whole body comes alive with terror and resistance. No, you have to be completely calm.'

On another occasion he said:

'I've always been in a hurry. I've never had time to finish anything properly. Now I'm taking it easy, Jan.'

And on another occasion:

'I don't think it's so remarkable. I don't think the difference is so great. Here I lie, and a half-awake thought buzzes in my ear. Will it be much different? A half-awake thought, a sleeping thought, and in the end no thought at all. Or who knows? One eternal, peaceful, obstinate, whispering, sleepy thought? Oh, it's so hard to be sure.'

The turn of winter to spring was long, and I would sit day after day, hour after hour, in the main room, reading or quietly playing. It was so quiet. No-one came to visit us. Even Josef did not want to know us any more. He had stopped collecting our post. Every other day, Hedda would go to the station. I wanted to go, but she would say: 'It's better that you sit with Father.'

I cannot remember feeling down-hearted or frightened. Only when he sometimes spoke to me, I gave a start and my heart would start to pound. His voice was different, duller. But it had a beautiful, mild tone. Sometimes I got the impression that I was standing on the edge of a dark abyss. And that his voice was coming to me from the abyss. I looked around.

About a week before Easter Father received a reply from A. O. Arnfelt. Hedda came rushing into the room. 'Arnberg!' she panted. 'It's here!' Father did not move. She stopped abruptly, straightened up, and looked from Father to me, and back again. Then she crept out into the porch, took off the grey blanket that she had wrapped herself in, and returned on tip-toe, putting the letter into Father's hand. He nodded and closed his eyes, and lay for half a day without moving, the letter in his hand. Only when Hedda came in with the lamp did he sit up and break the seal.

A. O. wrote that he had done everything in his power to protect Father's interests. Unfortunately he had been ill, Grundberg had pressed his wishes upon the board, and Father's dismissal had been made definite. The question of the company's reorganisation or liquidation would be dealt with at the shareholders' meeting in June. A. O. would try to help Father once again there. However he believed that, with the support of his contract, Father could sue the company and request payment for damages. He encouraged Father to pass the matter forthwith to his brother-in-law, the district judge.

Father read the letter and passed it to Hedda. She spelled her way through a few lines.

'What are you going to do?' she asked. Father shook his head.

'Dear Hedda, if there's anything to be done, then you should do it. I have neither the time nor the inclination.'

And he smiled roguishly and said:

'I'm following your example, Hedda. I'm making reductions.'

As far as I am aware, nothing was done, by either Father or Hedda.

In May Father began to go out again. He wanted to see how far the buds had burst on the trees in –dal's park. I had long since started sailing again on 'the Black Sea', but the *Claire Aurore* had sprung a leak, which meant that she would sink in a particularly terrible and natural way. I commissioned a rescue mission with the help of some old planks, and was close to drowning myself. Surviving this threat to my life only increased my respect for myself, and I was starting to contemplate even more daring adventures. And then Father started going out, and Hedda ordered me to accompany him. We went up the slope, across the meadow, and up a little hill that grew out of the copse. From here we had a splendid view. Father sat down on a stump – he was wrapped in Hedda's old grey blanket and had a worn old fur hat on – and started pointing out all the places he had played as a child. I sighed heavily and said:

'Yes, playing is great fun.'

He looked at me, surprised. Then he burst out laughing:

'Ah, you want to play on your own,' he said, prodding me. 'Well, then, off you go – '

I ran off.

When it was time to eat I came home. 'What have you done

with Father?' Hedda asked. 'He's sitting up on the hill,' I said, 'I'll go and get him.'

But Father was no longer sitting on the hill. I shouted and searched. I tried to follow his tracks but soon lost them. In the end I had to return home and say that I could not find him. Hedda was worried. We set out to look for him. Hedda went towards the forest. She thought he might have gone to the factory. I continued my own search down towards –dal. Eventually I came to a low wall; this was the park wall, but where I stood there was a kitchen garden. There was a man ploughing, and I recognised him as my friend Josef.

'Josef!' I shouted, pulling myself up onto the wall. 'Have you seen Father anywhere, Josef?'

He looked at me in surprise, and shook his head like a horse. Then he suddenly grinned and said:

'Actually, maybe I have. He's sitting over there by the gate.'

He pointed towards the park. I followed the wall and came out on the main drive, and followed that until I came to a wrought-iron gate. And there sat Father, wrapped in his grey blanket, and scarcely visible against the wall from a distance. I was upset and angry. I thought it was disgraceful of him to be sitting there, particularly in that terrible blanket.

'What are you doing here, Father?'

He blushed.

'Oh, Jan, is that you?' he said, sly mischief creeping into the corners of his eyes. 'I thought we'd each decided to play on our own. I'm sitting and looking.'

With an authoritative grasp I took his arm and pulled him. He stood up and we walked home hand in hand. After that I realised that I should never let him out on his own again. The next day we went to the hill together. He never tired of describing in great detail every place in the park, every room in the house. I was not particularly interested, but when I realised that it made him happy, I pretended to listen with exaggerated interest.

The spring sunlight did him good. But one day in June he had a bad attack of breathlessness. He was lying on the sofa, panting and throwing his arms about. I ran into the kitchen to fetch Hedda.

Just as she went through the door, I heard him cry:
'Hedda! I don't want to! I don't want to!'
Then I remembered what had happened when Grandmother died. I thought Father's time had come. I was distraught. I ran down the track calling for help. But I soon realised how stupid it was to stand by the side of the track shouting. I crept into a ditch, crouched down, and hid. I remembered how grand and venerable Grandfather had been when he went in to Grandmother, and how quickly he had calmed her. I wondered whether God might possibly be able to send him, just for a moment, to calm father. I prayed that he might do so, and for a moment it seemed quite reasonable that my prayers would be answered. From God's point of view this was a mere bagatelle, whereas it was of great importance for Father and me.

Eventually I calmed down. I crawled out of the ditch and snuck back to the cottage. One window was open. I looked in. Father was sitting on the sofa, Hedda standing beside him, pouring something that was probably fruit soup into a cup. It all looked very calm and peaceful.

Then I heard the sound of horses' hooves and carriage wheels. This in itself was extremely unusual, because since Josef had taken his hand from us, the track had been deserted. I turned round. In the copse I could see something light shining, the pale yellow interior of a landau. Then I saw the black horses with their white blazes. I gasped. They were Grandfather's horses! It was Grandfather's landau! It was Grandfather's driver, the clean-shaven, dour driver to whom I had never dared speak. And the old gentleman who sat in one corner of the landau –

It was Grandfather!

For a moment my head spun. But I quickly regained my senses. I did not even feel surprised, just serious and very solemn. I went into the cottage on tip-toe, and said half-aloud:

'Grandfather's coming.'

They stared at me. I repeated, a little louder:

'Grandfather's coming.'

And without paying any heed to their natural surprise – they knew nothing of my prayer in the ditch, after all – I went, still on tip-toe, back to the porch and opened the sky-blue double doors as wide as I could. I made sure the porch was tidy, and quickly put away several bark boats that were cluttering the place. Then I positioned myself by the door. I wondered if I should run towards him and embrace him, but it struck me that it would be more appropriate to stay by the door and bow low and in silence.

The old gentleman had stepped down from the carriage. He walked slowly up the slope, a little crooked, supported by a cane. In his left hand he was holding a tall black hat, which caused the first faint but uncomfortable murmurings of doubt. Grandfather used to carry his hat behind his back. I leaned forward to look at the carriage. Yes, it was Grandfather's landau, his horses, his driver.

But now I saw something which immediately and mercilessly crushed me. In the back seat of the landau sat a boy; he turned his face to mine and made a recognisable, half friendly, half mocking grimace. It was Mikael. My enemy, Mikael Arnfelt.

And all at once I realised that the old man was not Grandfather, and that my prayer had not been answered. In my despair I ran up the steps and hid in the attic. After a while I heard Hedda call for me; then Father called as well. I was to play with Mikael. Perhaps I would have stayed where I was, were it not for the fear that Mikael would track down the *Claire Aurore* and take possession of her.

The first supernatural occurrence in my life had a humiliatingly simple explanation. A. O. Arnfelt had bought Grandfather's carriage at auction, had also employed Grandfather's driver and moved everything to his estate at Frönsafors. That is why Grandfather's carriage came rolling down our track! That is how my prayer was answered. I have already mentioned the similarity in appearance of the two men.

A. O. Arnfelt's visit was the last event of note in Father's life. Arnfelt encouraged him once again to try to save what could be saved. Reluctantly Father agreed. It pained him to have to step back from the final path upon which he had already embarked. His peace was broken, he grew angry and impatient. He sat at his desk for days on end, writing letters, tearing them up, writing them again. He had to travel into town for the shareholders' meeting, and returned home shattered. And all of this to no avail, in vain. It was just one final torment. Apparently meaningless.

Even for me, the visit came to have a sad significance. Mikael stayed with us. A. O. was to travel to a spa resort abroad shortly after the shareholders' meeting, and did not dare leave his grandson alone at Frönsafors. The young gentleman had already caused him enough worries. A. O., who knew of Johan Arnberg's good name as a teacher, asked him to take care of the boy for a few weeks. Father could hardly refuse.

To begin with I was glad. I had been alone with Father and Hedda for almost a whole year. I had missed my friends at school, particularly Karl Rygell, 'the Angel'. Now I could hear fresh stories about him and the others, about the school, about the old teacher who used to hit me in the stomach; perhaps also about the Bishop's Palace.

Besides, I admired Mikael. His superiority was undeniable. He was beautiful. He was well dressed. He had a wealth of things that I could only dream of, and he knew things that I could not even dream of. He was false, unreliable and insolent, true enough. But he was a reckless fighter, and, confronted with his bony knuckles and quick, bitter attacks, I had to give him the right to be false, unreliable and insolent. I could not resist him at all. Not yet.

The first days we got on well. Mikael was perfectly gracious and attentive towards Father. This in itself delighted me. But even towards me he was polite and courteous. The fear that he would demand the *Claire Aurore* once again was the one thing that spoiled my happiness. And my fears were to prove correct.

It came the very day Father travelled to town. We accompanied Father to the station; Mikael carried his knapsack, bought his ticket for him, jumped onto the train and found him a place, spread the blanket over his knees.

On the way back, we were silent for a long time; I tried to instigate a conversation about this and that, without success. Suddenly he stopped, took my arm, and said:

'Do you know why I'm here? I've come to collect that boat you sold me. Where is it?'

I had a sudden inspiration.

'It sank,' I said. 'In "the Black Sea".'

We went to look. Mikael took a stick and tested the depth. It was about a span. He undressed, jumped into the water and dived. He dived four or five times. In the end his face was swollen with the effort. I looked on, amused and content. I thought that he was welcome to search. The *Claire Aurore* was in the attic.

Eventually he clambered out onto the black stone and lay there panting. He looked at me, frowning.

'Are you sure she's here?' he asked.

'No,' I said, laughing. 'She's in the attic.'

He drew his eyebrows together in a peculiar way (the same way Uncle Otto did – one slightly higher than the other, so that they formed a thunderbolt).

'I see,' he said. He rested for a few minutes, then, before I knew it, I was on my back among the rocks, with him on top of me. He said:

'Say that the boat is mine.'

It was not long before I conceded that the *Claire Aurore* was his. But he did not let me go for all that. And he said:

'This is for telling on me.'

I cried that I had never told on him. It did not help. He put one hand on my throat and grabbed my hair with the other, and thumped my neck against the rock. Eventually he thought I had had enough.

Panting, he put his clothes on. And said:

'You don't know that you told on me, but you did anyway. Do you remember when you lived in town, and Grandfather asked if I used to play with you? You said no. But I had told him I used to go to your house. So there.'

We went home; I was miserable, puffy, tearful, bloody. Hedda asked: 'Have you been fighting?' Mikael smiled faintly and replied:

'Yes, he flew at me. I thought I ought to defend myself.'

We clambered up to the attic and inspected the brig. We spent two days mending her. When she was ready at last, Mikael said:

'Now I've got the boat, I'm going to make sure I get away from

Memoirs of a Dead Man

here pretty quickly. It's wretched here.'

After his trip to town, Father spent a couple of days in bed. Mikael tip-toed around him and was very gentle and amenable. He hushed me if I ever raised my voice, he picked flowers in the meadow and put them in a glass on Father's desk. Father was pleased.

'You're a nice lad,' he said.

Mikael smiled at him.

'Oh,' he said. 'But I'd like to ask Mr Arnberg if I can go home. I'm missing Grandmother.'

Father was worried; he could not break his promise to A. O. Mikael said:

'Of course not. But if I was to go to the station and get on a train, then you would not be responsible, Mr Arnberg.'

Father blushed and frowned. Then he burst out laughing.

'No, my lad,' he said. 'No nonsense. If you escape, I daresay I shall fetch you back.'

Mikael bowed and walked out.

The following day he lured me to the blast-hole. We had no boats. We lay on the black rock, staring at the sky. After a while Mikael said:

'Do you know what, Roach? Your mother's a thief.'

I was astonished. I did not understand what he meant.

He raised himself on one elbow and said: 'It's true. I heard it in town. She stole a mirror. Grandfather wanted to buy it, but she had already stolen it.'

'That isn't my mother. That's my step-mother.'

He was rather disappointed, lay down again and stared at the sky. After a while he said:

'Maybe. But your father's a quack.'

I did not know what he meant; but it seemed to me the worst, most shameful thing I had ever heard. It sounded lame and oily and awful. And without thinking I rolled over and clutched at his soft flaxen hair with both hands. In a second he was on top of me. He panted:

'Say it. Father is a quack.'

I clenched my teeth. All the while he was thumping my head

against the rock, and moving me inch by inch closer to the water, and suddenly he pushed my head underwater. I could not hold my breath, I swallowed a lot of water and began to choke. He pulled me up and let me rest for a while. 'Will you say it?' he asked. I would not. He pushed my head underwater again. I do not know how long we spent doing this. I was almost unconscious from fear and pain. Sometimes he let me rest for a long time – presumably he was tired as well – but as soon as I made any attempt to escape, he caught me and started again.

Eventually I did as he asked.

From that moment my resistance was completely broken. I obeyed him blindly, without thinking or arguing. When he realised this, he treated me well. He bought sweets in the shop and gave me half. And he no longer spoke ill of either Father or Hedda. About Father, he said:

'What does it matter that he's a quack? That's better than being a bank director and grand larcenist like my grandfather. I like your father. He dresses like a gentleman.'

I eagerly and gratefully swallowed the acclaim. Sometimes he would sit for a long while talking to Father. I presume he was asking to be sent home. But I do not know, because he could send me out of the room merely by batting his long eyelashes.

One day he said:

'Let's go to –dal and visit Grundberg.'

'Do you dare?' I asked. He tossed his head.

'That hired help!' he said. 'He crawls under the table if Grandfather so much as sneezes.'

We went the same way I had walked when I was looking for Father. We reached the wall and the kitchen garden, and Josef the driver, now as then, was working the soil. Mikael swung over the wall, and I followed, as obedient as a dog. Mikael walked calmly up to Josef and ordered him to show us the stables. His wall-eye shifted between us, and he grinned.

'Now I can see that you're in fine company, Jan,' he said, taking off his cap for Mikael. He accompanied us to the stables. When Mikael had inspected all the horses, he asked if Grundberg was home.

Memoirs of a Dead Man

'No,' Josef said, with another grin. 'Grundberg's away, so you young gentlemen can do as you please.'

'Come on,' Mikael said, taking my arm. We walked across the courtyard up to the flight of steps with the iron urns that I had seen from our hill. The doors were wide open. We walked in. We wandered in silence from room to room, encountering no-one. Eventually we came to a large drawing room. It was beautifully furnished (in my opinion), and I fooled about, open-mouthed, going from one table to the next. They were all loaded with beautiful and expensive ornaments. I stopped by a green marble table. On it were a dozen or more old pocket watches of silver and gold. Mikael asked if I had a watch. No, I did not.

'Take this one, then,' he said, pointing at a gold watch.

I took it.

'Put it under your blouse,' he said.

I put it under my blouse.

When we had had a thorough look around, we went back out into the park. Josef came up to us, cap in hand. Mikael pulled out a coin and gave it to him.

'That's for being so beautifully wall-eyed,' he said. 'Now bring the bay out; I want to ride.'

He rode around the park for a while (as I watched, full of admiration). When he was tired of that, he jumped off, giving the bay a slap so that she raced off across the lawns and flowerbeds.

'Goodbye, Wall-eye,' he said, taking my arm and leaving. Once we were back on the slope at home, I caught sight of Father sitting on the bench watching us. 'Where have you been?' he called.

Mikael took off his cap and said:

'We've been to –dal.'

'What were you doing there?' Father went on.

Mikael turned to me and laughed.

'Ask Jan what he did,' he said. And to me: 'Show Mr Arnberg your watch, Jan.'

My heart leapt. I had forgotten the watch. I did not want to show it. But Mikael looked at me, and I obeyed.

'Where – ' Father began, gasping for breath, 'where – Jan –

where – '

Mikael said:

'He took it from a table in Mr Grundberg's drawing room. There was no-one home, so we could do as we pleased.'

I stood holding the watch, staring at Father. He was pale but completely calm. After a while he said to Mikael:

'I think you're right, lad. You don't belong here.'

Mikael bowed.

'Thank you,' he said, suppressing a smile.

The following morning Mikael left, taking with him the *Claire Aurore* as bounty. He was collected by Grandfather's carriage.

Father spent much of the day lying down; at one o'clock he got up, dressed carefully and ordered Hedda to dress me in my Sunday best. He took my hand and we walked down towards –dal. Father had not said a cross word to me, but when we reached the main road and could see the wrought-iron gates, he said:

'Well Jan, here we are at –dal after all, you and me.'

I burst into tears and clung to his arm. He held me tight for a moment. But when I started sobbing even more loudly, my whole body shaking, he said sharply:

'Now calm down. I shall explain everything.'

He opened the gate and went into the park. Then he stopped. He was looking around. I could not stop looking at his face. And I saw his sour expression lift, his eyes started to shine, his lips parted and his sparkling blue-white teeth peeped through a smile –

'Do you know what, Jan?' he said. 'I've just remembered something. This is where Otto and I used to – '

He broke off abruptly. The smile disappeared. He took my hand once more and walked slowly, one step at a time, up the drive. By the fountain he stopped once again. And now he could not help himself.

'Look, Jan!' he cried. 'Now you must admit that this is more impressive than Grandfather's? And look at the elms, and the ash! Can you believe that there was room for Otto and me inside that ash-tree? – '

Just as he was about to relate his adventures in the ash-tree, I heard rapid steps behind us. It was Josef. He stepped up to Father, touched two fingers to his cap, and asked sullenly:

'Are you looking for someone?'

Father got confused; he stammered:

'Yes – dear Josef – of course – '

Josef squinted at Father, then at me, then suddenly he grinned so that his whole face cracked in a thousand wrinkles and creases:

'I see that you're here to see the master,' he said. 'I shall inform him – '

And he strode ahead of us towards the house.

Father and I waited in the vestibule; a maid came and asked us to step into the drawing room. Father pressed my hand so hard that my nails dug into my palm. I clenched my teeth.

In the drawing room, with his back to the window, stood a tall, broad-shouldered, fat man; he was clean-shaven, his face was bluish-red, stiff and expressionless. He bowed half an inch –

Father explained everything, calmly and without once raising his voice. And he held out the watch. The stranger took it and inspected it.

'It was here?' he turned to me, pointing at the green marble table. I whispered that it was. He went up to the table, and seemed to be counting the watches. Then he turned to Father.

'I am sorry that my staff are so lax about the doors. It is highly inappropriate to lead people into temptation. But there's no damage done.'

Father said nothing. The stranger said:

'Was there anything else – ?'

Father swallowed, and said:

'Jan, go and say you're sorry.'

I took an unsteady step forward towards the stranger. But he suddenly lifted his hands, a pair of fat hands with large, thick fingers, and said impatiently:

'No, please! I don't like scenes! The boy has given back the watch – that is all that interests me – '

Father said nothing. The stranger said:

'Well, I don't think we have anything else to discuss.'

Father said – and his voice was suddenly shrill and harsh –

'If you will not permit the lad to apologise, I shall be obliged to beat him in your presence. You understand?'

'Really!' the stranger shouted, and the whole of his great body seemed to dance before my tear-filled eyes. 'Well, I recognise your impudence, Mr Arnberg! Really! It isn't enough that I am robbed, I must also be discomfited. I have a weak heart, Mr Arnberg, I cannot stomach such performances. Remarkable! Do I really have to educate your wretched children? No, I have had quite enough of you yourself, Mr Arnberg. Quite enough.'

And he walked out of the room with thundering steps. Father stood staring ahead of him for a moment. Then he took my hand, stroking it gently. 'Come on, Jan,' he whispered.

We returned the same way we had come.

And I could not help thinking:

'Oh, what a relief that that's over! Thank you, Lord, that I did not have to apologise! Oh, what a relief!'

Father closed the wrought-iron gate behind us. I ran out into the road. Father stopped for a moment, holding two of the gate poles, then leaned over as though he wanted to see the building. Suddenly he shouted:

'Jan! Jan!'

I gave a start and looked back in terror. Father was walking towards me, hand outstretched, and took hold of my shoulder. His face was calm and he was not looking at me. But his voice had a slack, breathless, panting tone.

'Jan,' he said, one corner of his mouth twisting into a crooked smile, 'this really was the crowning glory. Don't you think? The crowning glory. Finally, I made it to –dal. And you too, Jan.'

He screamed.

'Jan!'

I looked up. His eyes were bulging out of his head as though he were suffocating. Something resembling white foam was running from his nostrils. His teeth were grinding. He let go of my shoulder and his fist shot past my right eye. Then I felt a blow to my left temple. I tried to stay upright, but the wall and the trees and the white road spun round and disappeared into a grey haze.

When I came to again, I was met by Josef's wall-eyed gaze, which made me even more giddy.

Beside me was the carriage that used to take Father to the factory. Father was sitting slumped in one corner. He was holding his handkerchief to his mouth. It was dark red and blood was dripping from its corner.

Josef lifted me up beside Father, climbed up into the driver's seat himself, and drove us home. Still holding the handkerchief to his nose, Father fumbled for a two-kronor coin for the driver. But Hedda, Josef and I had to help carry him inside the cottage.

For two silent weeks Father lay in a constant half-doze, waking up sometimes once or twice a day, sometimes several times an hour, but dozing off again after a few minutes. Hedda fed him. He did not say a word, either to her or to me. Only once did he wave me over and say:

'I never hear you running, Jan. Don't you play any more? Where's your brig?'

I explained that Mikael had taken the brig. Father shook his head in sympathy – the way adults do when they want to show their sorrow at children's worries.

'Don't be sad, Jan,' he whispered (his voice had become completely hoarse). 'Soon we shan't need a brig, neither you nor I. Soon we shall have a chariot of fire. Like the prophet Elijah. I was just thinking about its design.'

This gave me a lot to worry about, and in the end I told Hedda what Father had said. She put her hands together.

'Yes, I can well believe that,' she said. 'He's lying there raving. I thought as much. From all the strange things he whispers right through the night.'

His dozing became deeper and calmer by the day. Sometimes he would cough, but less than before, and less violently and protractedly.

At the beginning of July sister Anna came to visit. I hardly recognised her. She had arranged her hair differently, in waves over her temples, not combed straight as before. There was something different about the way she dressed as well. It was because she had spent three weeks abroad. She had been given a grant of two hundred kronor; she had been in Copenhagen, in Berlin and in Hamburg. All that she had seen had almost crushed her with its grandness and beauty. She could not even talk about it, as she would once have done. She would sit in silence for long periods, her hands clasped in her lap, her head slightly askew. She would look up at the sky (or the ceiling), and smile a smile of melancholy, astonishment and happiness.

One day, when she was sitting looking up at the ceiling from the end of Father's bed (and we all thought that he was asleep), he suddenly raised himself onto his elbow and started laughing, quietly but properly, so that he had to hold his chest. Anna blushed and looked rather taken aback. She asked why he was laughing. He whispered:

'I thought that you could tell us about the different types of towns and villages, and how well they are constructed and furnished; and about the different types of men and women, and how finely proportioned and dressed they are, and about the different kinds of lakes and rivers and seas and railways and machines and department stores and churches and museums and how finely organised everything is. But you're saying something entirely different. Oh Anna – dear Anna!'

And he wagged his index finger at her. But she crossed her arms and leaned over, as though she were trying to hide something. She whimpered pathetically and squeaked like a mouse. But Father said:

'For God's, dear Anna, tell us! This could be dangerous! You'll explode if you don't tell us!'

She told us.

In Copenhagen she had stayed in a simple little hotel. There she had met a young man. He was Swedish by descent, but was from America, and, having visited friends in Skåne, he was going to Hamburg. But for sister Anna's sake, he made a detour to Berlin. He was very well-bred, and could speak seven languages (American, English, Swedish, Norwegian, Danish, High German, Low German, as well as some French and a few words of Italian, Russian and Greek). His manner was pleasant, courteous, respectful. He was generous; when they shared expenses, he paid not only for his own share, but for half of Anna's as well. But so that she should not feel embarrassed by his generosity, he allowed her to give him an hour or so's lesson of Swedish spelling each day. His linguistic skills were of great help to Anna, but even more so his experience of people. He could tell what women were like just by looking at them. He had worked for a while as a missionary among fallen women in Chicago and had told her remarkable things; always, however, in such a way as would not offend even the most sensitive listener. He had said that the lives of fallen women are generally less oppressed than one might imagine. He had suggested that many poor seamstresses or teachers might have good cause to envy them – naturally, not including the moral side of the matter. And even if one were to take that into account, a comparison might give surprising results. Was the charming folly of these creatures more morally despicable than the dull bitterness and hatred of those worn out through toil and troubles? Was not Mary Magdalene a fallen woman? Do we not see in numerous immortal works, modern as well as classical, fallen women depicted as a more noble type than the virtuous? The issue certainly has its complexities, and is worthy of discussion.

He had discussed this with sister Anna; in a considerate way. And her large, bright, blue eyes had seemed to discern something else that was fine and well organised here in this world. But only for as long as he spoke. When, in order to demonstrate his thesis, he had taken her to the strangest places, she felt such repulsion that she had almost been sick. He had quickly had to take her away. He had said that she was the noblest woman he had ever met; albeit perhaps a little self-righteous. He had given her a large bouquet of flowers, whose silk ribbon was fastened by a needle adorned with agate. The agate had once been part of a signet ring, and depicted the letter A beneath a crown. This was why he had chosen it.

'It is the crown of innocence,' he had said, 'it is the halo about your brow. And, who knows – perhaps it might become the crown of a duchess, or a countess, or a baroness; something noble, at any rate. Because you are beautiful.'

'Do you still have the piece?' Father asked.

Obediently, she unbuttoned her blouse and took it out. Father inspected the monogram.

'This is a ducal crown,' he said. 'Well, Anna, tell us the end.'

As usual, she had told her tale in great detail, and I have only repeated one hundredth of her tirade. Now, however, she became taciturn, reluctant, stammering and wriggling, lacing her long fingers together so hard that you could hear her knuckles crack.

'You funny thing,' Father smiled. 'Let me help you. He made you a proposal – '

No, he had not made her any proposal. But on one occasion, when he was going to show her the Elbe Tunnel –

'Ah,' Father said, 'he became rather forward – '

No, he had not been forward, but he had kissed her. And that evening he had come into her room –

'You don't need to tell us that,' Father said. 'Just tell us what you said in reply.'

She was very reluctant.

'Dear Father,' she said eventually, 'you mustn't be angry with me. He liked me, Father; and I liked him. But I knew, of course, that we could not belong to one another. I said as much to him. I said – that I had a weak chest, and that there was tuberculosis in the family.'

She looked very unhappy, she was afraid that she had hurt Father. But he nodded to her and said:

'You're a very sensible girl! I should have advised you to say precisely that. So tell us, how did he take it. My dear friend, Mr Hansen – '

She straightened up, her mouth falling open.

'Father!' she gasped, 'Father – '

'Well, was that not his name? He resembles a Mr Hansen whom I once knew. Well, it doesn't matter. What did he do?'

She thought for a moment. Then she stood up and bowed deeply to Father, took a few steps backwards, bowed once more, took some more steps, and bowed for a third time.

'Not a word, Father,' she said, and her pale, round, girlish face shone with rapture. 'He just bowed. Low, Father, low. Three times. To me! Wasn't that lovely!'

Father held out his hand to her.

'Well,' he said, 'maybe it was lovely. In any case, it was lovely that you responded so sensibly. All things considered, you gained more from Mr Hansen than he gained from you. That is as good as an examination, and you passed with honours.'

The praise lightened her heart once again, and she started to babble. She said:

'Just think, Father! My trip was so cheap. I had almost eighty kronor left at the end.'

Hedda stuck her long nose in at once.

'What have you done with them?' she asked anxiously.

Anna replied with a secretive grimace. Suddenly she threw herself down on her knees beside the sofa, and took Father by the hand.

'Will you promise me something?' she asked. He nodded. She stood up and ran out. After a while she came back, her arms full – of four great jars of Arnberg's Tuberculin. Father stared at them, and his jaw dropped in utter astonishment. Anna said:

'Remember, now, Father! You promised! You must take it properly – '

'Is that what you spent your eighty kronor on?' Father asked.

She blushed.

'My eighty kronor?' she said. 'In a way, I got them from him. Well, at first I was going to buy a souvenir. But I already have the pin. And I didn't think I could find a better use for them than this – '

'Well,' Father muttered, 'I suppose this is just another greeting from Mr Hansen.'

He nodded, closed his eyes, and said:

'Thank you, dear Anna. And I promise. Properly – '

Sister Anna took over Father's care. She sat with him day and night; I never saw her rest. When Father did not want her in the room, she would take a chair and sit in the porch, or outside the open window. She would sit there with her hands clasped in her lap, her head a little askew, staring at the ceiling or sky. And, regular as clockwork, at certain times she would go in to Father and give him some tuberculin. He would make faces and twist his head to avoid it, but he made no objections. Sometimes he would burst out laughing.

After three days he was able to sit up on the sofa, after five he could cross the floor to the open window.

'That's bloody good powder,' he said. 'And it's called Arnberg's Tuberculin. *Haben wir das alles gethan?*'

Anna was jubilant.

But when I asked Hedda if Father would soon be well again, she replied:

'Yes, as good as you can be when all your pains are behind you.'

And on another occasion she said:

'I'm writing to your uncle. I'm not allowed to call for a priest. He's never been able to stand priests. But no-one shall say that he died without a doctor.'

She dictated the letter to Anna, and I took it to the post. Father knew nothing. My uncle replied by return. He wrote that he could not leave his practice at once, but that he would take the day off on the coming Sunday. He added:

'I shall bring Léonie with me. She's longing to see Jan.'

Léonie was my cousin, the pink girl.

When I heard that, I became distraught. I looked around, thinking: 'Isn't it enough that Mikael has seen how wretchedly we live?'

I started surreptitiously to make whatever improvements and changes were possible; I stuck down peeled wallpaper, I planed the step, I spread sand in front of the door in an attempt to create a courtyard like the one at –dal. But it was a Sisyphean labour! And the worst thing of all, my own shabby appearance, my outgrown, patched, bleached clothes – nothing could help that.

Now Hedda had to confess what she had done to Father. He got angry. His hoarse voice became so shrill that I stuck my head through the door, terrified. He was standing in front of Hedda waving his fist at her; she had hidden her hands under her apron and was staring at the floor. Suddenly Father noticed me, and

Memoirs of a Dead Man

fell silent. And eventually that roguish look came into his eyes and he waved me to him.

'Jan,' he said, panting with the exertion, 'do you understand what the woman is thinking? She won't let us be in peace. When we've got so much to think about!

'I'll tell you one thing, Hedda,' he went on, pointing right at her nose. 'I'm going to play a trick on you. Yes, I am. You're going to pay for this. Well, let him come, let the whole of my dear family come. But I have no intention of receiving him like a pauper. I intend to receive him as a gentleman, as a wealthy and respected gentleman. Now listen. I shall dictate the menu. Make sure you don't lose a single letter of it, my dear Hedda – '

And he started to list the dishes, each one more expensive and extravagant than the previous one, and he named all manner of wines and liqueurs, he talked about silver, table cloths, flowers, all sorts of things. He took great delight in it all, and every time poor Hedda made to withdraw he would point at her nose and gasp: 'No, stay a little longer. Let me think. There's so much more. I'd almost forgotten that. It's going to be great fun – '

In the end he ran out of things to say. Then he noticed me, took me by the shoulders and spun me round.

'And this young fellow,' he said. 'Do you expect him to receive his beautiful cousin dressed like this? You're to take him to town and make sure he looks handsome. No objections. No reductions.'

Hedda gave a deep sigh.

'Where am I to get the money from?' she asked.

Father clapped his hands.

'That doesn't concern me in the slightest. That's up to you. You've got money. You must have money. What do you do with all your money? How much did you get for the mirror, for instance? Confess! Jan, how much do you think she got for the mirror?'

I blushed and hung my head.

'Father, you know – ' I stammered, 'I told you – it was me who took the mirror – '

And there I stood, between Hedda, who was staring at me,

open-mouthed, and Father, who was watching me with feverish eyes. I twisted and turned, but in the end I walked over to Hedda and asked her to forgive me.

'At last,' Father said, with a faint smile. Then he turned towards Hedda once more, his face stern:

'I have spoken. No objections, no reductions! For God's sake, my dear Hedda, this is as good as my last wish.'

She thought for a moment, then said:

'Well, Arnberg, you shall have your way.'

We really did go to town, and she went into all manner of shops, buying baskets full of the goods Father had listed, not neglecting a single one.

My outfit, however, was not entirely new. She bought it from a clothing stall, from the same half-mad woman who had once embraced me in Grandfather's dark passageway. And once again, she took me in her arms and exclaimed:

'God bless God's little angel!'

Early on Sunday morning I went down to the station to meet my uncle and cousin. Uncle was even fatter than before, and was breathing heavily when he embraced me. The pink girl merely offered me her hand. She was different; she had a few spots on her forehead which upset me. Perhaps they upset her as well, because she barely answered my questions, and made no attempt to kiss me.

Father was in a splendid mood all day, and everything went as well as it could have done. I ate so much of the wonderful food that I felt ill. Léonie looked askance at me and hissed:

'Usch, how greedy you are!'

But I was thinking: 'I shall never eat such fine food again, and besides, she's got spots. Why should I care what she thinks?'

And I ate a good deal more.

My uncle, who was quite red from wine and food, squinted in our direction and said:

'Look at them sitting there whispering! Léonie is quite mad about Jan. She doesn't give me a moment's peace. She wants to marry him. But I say no. As a doctor, you understand, Johan. I

Memoirs of a Dead Man

won't hear of cousins marrying. We've already had one too many in the family.'

'My own?' Father asked.

'Wh... What – ?' Uncle stammered, rolling his eyes. 'No, good Lord, my dear Johan, what on earth am I saying? It's your own fault – you're encouraging me to drink – '

Father laughed and filled his glass.

'Don't worry,' he said. 'I'm not as easily offended as I once was. Not even a tenth as sensitive. But if Léonie wants to marry Jan, she'll have to hurry.'

'Why?' Uncle asked.

Father looked at me.

'Well,' he said. 'We're thinking about going away, Jan and I.'

'Wh... Wh... What do you mean?' Uncle muttered, clearly the worse for drink. Then he raised his glass and said:

'Well, my dear Johan, I am delighted to find you – very well, very well, Johan – very well, under the circumstances. But you shouldn't be thinking of making any journeys. No. But you're very well. You're an Arnberg, after all. We're made of stern stuff. Yes, yes, it's a miracle that you're alive. But you're very well. Just don't lose heart, old boy. Under the circumstances, very well. It's most peculiar, almost unnatural. But you're in any case very well. That's all I wanted to say – hold your head high, old friend – '

Father interrupted him.

'Do you know what? Come again next Sunday. Hedda, we've enough wine for another dinner, haven't we?'

'Come again next Sunday?' Uncle muttered. Suddenly he took hold of Father's hand, pressed it hard, and held it for a long time. He said:

'I understand, Johan. I shall come. I shall come with the midday train.'

'Better to catch the morning train,' Father said, and smiled. 'And bring Léonie with you. Jan can show her the park at –dal.'

'Johan!' my uncle exclaimed, putting his arm round Father's shoulders. 'We're still both Arnbergs. I'm glad you wrote to me. But you felt that you had to write to me. Didn't you? You felt that I had to come, that you had to see me – '

'Perhaps,' Father said, glowering at Hedda and me.

After the meal I accompanied them to the train. Uncle went ahead, wheezing and puffing. Léonie and I followed him. Léonie asked if I knew that Grandfather had left me ten thousand in his will. I did not know.

'No,' she said in a serious tone, 'you're not to know until you're of age. He wrote a letter to you as well, but you're not to know about that either until you're of age.'

'But now I know,' I pointed out. She pursed her lips and gave me a stern look:

'Well,' she said, 'I thought you might be grateful to Grandfather. You never think of him otherwise. He told me that before he died. "Jan never thinks of me", he said.'

I felt ashamed and did not reply.

When I returned home, Father had gone to bed, but was still awake. He was very happy. He said to Hedda:

'You can do magic, you can! That was an excellent dinner, and everything was good. It's a relief that it's over. The family has had what it wanted.'

Nothing happened on Monday. Father lay in bed all day, but did not sleep. Hedda and Anna sat with him. We were all silent.

On Tuesday nothing happened. Hedda aired Father's wardrobe and Anna helped her. I sat inside with Father. He asked if I would rather be outside playing. 'No,' I replied. Then he said:

'Do you know what, Jan? On Sunday you must entertain your cousin properly. You can show her –dal, but you're not to go inside the wall. You understand?'

'What do you think?' I said, blushing. He stroked my hand.

'You're not to worry about that business with the watch,' he said. 'Do you remember when I spoke to you about your will? Well, I was right. Your will is a tender plant, and can be broken by anyone. Like most wills. But I think I know how to help you. I've managed to accumulate a bit of will as I've got older. And do you know what it is I want, Jan?

'Well,' he said after a while, letting go of my hand, 'it's a secret. For the time being. There are one or two things I should tell you. But it's best that I concentrate. On the only important thing.'

After a while he asked what was flapping outside the window. I said it was his clothes. He sat up. Hedda and Anna had started to take the clothes off the line, and were walking past with the outfits, holding them carefully in front of them. Father watched as they went past. When it was over, he turned to me, his face glowing with roguish and surprised delight.

'Well I never, Jan!' he said, sinking back into the pillows. 'Was I really such a fine fellow? Well I'm glad, I'm glad. That was almost as good as an obituary.'

On Wednesday Hedda did the washing, and Anna had to help her. I sat with Father. He was asleep, or at least was lying completely still and with his eyes closed, all day. Sometimes he seemed to have trouble swallowing. I sat watching his throat, and noticed that he had a scar running about an inch below his chin. I knew how he had got it. When they were boys, he and Uncle Otto had been playing and had climbed the wrought-iron gate at –dal. For some reason they started arguing, Otto shoved Father and he lost his grip and ended up hanging by the neck between two poles, which are shaped like arrowheads at the top. That's where the ugly scar on his throat came from.

On Thursday Anna sat with Father. I was to help Hedda by chopping wood for the washing. But before I knew it Anna came out and said:

'Father wants to know if Jan is chopping wood?'

Hedda thought I was big enough to chop wood; since Josef had stopped helping us with things like that, she and I had shared them between us. But she thought again and said:

'You'd best go in, Jan. I'll do it myself, otherwise he won't settle down.'

When I went in, father was leaning on his elbow.

'Jan,' he said. 'Go down to Josef. Tell him from me that he's to come up at once and chop wood for the wash. You understand? Don't ask him. Just say: Father says that you should come – '

I ran down to –dal as fast as I could. Josef was busy in the garden. I hung over the wall and panted out Father's order. He brushed the soil from his hands, came slowly over to me, and swung over the wall.

'So, is it the shroud that needs washing?'

I did not understand what he meant. But I got cross and snapped:

'It's none of your business. Just do as Father says.'

He grinned.

'Well,' he said, 'seeing as he's the son of my old master, and seeing as he was my master when I was young, I don't suppose I should betray him the same night, as it says in the good book.'

And he gave a deep sigh, and the grin vanished from his face.

'Yes, the time is coming,' he muttered. 'May the Lord help us.'

Josef chopped wood, and I sat with Father. When the wood was all chopped, Father opened his eyes and said:

'Ask him to come in.'

I did so; he stopped and stood by the door.

'Come in,' Father said. He pushed off his clogs and padded over to the sofa.

'Josef,' Father said, 'do you remember the last years when my father lived at –dal?'

He remembered. Father said:

'Do you know who kept Arnfelt informed about everything that happened at –dal?'

He took a step back, but remained standing. Suddenly he grinned:

'Oh yes,' he replied, 'that would have been old Grundberg, and me too. The little I knew.'

'Here you are,' Father said, handing him two kronor. 'Grundberg has already has his reward. And I think you'll find that you've had your thirty pieces of silver if you count them up. Now go, Josef. I want nothing more from you.'

He bowed and padded back towards the door.

'Close it after him,' Father said.

Memoirs of a Dead Man

On Friday Father lay quite still. We took turns sitting with him.

On Saturday there was a strong wind blowing. It whined around the corners, and the attic hatch was banging. I hurried up the stairs and shut it, but at once something else began to bang. Father slept all morning, albeit fitfully. Anna and I took turns sitting with him. At about six o'clock I heard wheels on the road. I crept over to the window.

'Who's that coming?' Father asked.

'It's an old woman in a cart,' I said. 'Shall I ask who she is?'

'No,' Father said, 'it doesn't matter. Come and sit here.' But I could not help listening to the wheels, which came ever closer and eventually stopped right outside. I could see the head of the little grey horse through the window.

Then I heard a voice call:

'Go' bless! Go' Bless! Is there anybody home?'

I jumped and wanted to run out; but Father held my hand.

After a while the door opened and the old woman stepped in. It was Old Mrs Gråberg, who kept the clothes stall. She closed the door behind her, gave a deep curtsy, and whispered: 'God bless! God bless!'

Then she crept up to the sofa, stopped a couple of steps away, and crossed her hands over her stomach.

'Ah, here he is,' she said in a sweet, sympathetic voice.

Father opened his eyes.

'Yes, here he is,' he replied.

At that the old woman became very agitated, bowing and curtsying, clapping her hands together and lifting them up in the air, but all in complete silence.

'Why are you doing that?' Father asked.

She found her tongue again:

'That's the strangest thing I've ever seen,' she said. 'He's alive, God bless, God bless. It's the funniest thing I've ever been part of. Just think, how funny that he's alive.'

'What is it you actually want?' Father asked.

'Well,' she said, tearing her hair, 'that's just it. Go' bless, but I see I've come too early. I should have come next month, see.

183

But I was passing and thought I might take a look – '

'What were going to take a look at?' Father asked.

'Ah, well, you see, Hedda spoke to me about some clothes. I gave her an advance, see, and I was going to collect them next month – '

'My clothes?' Father asked.

'Well, of course,' she said, half smiling. 'You're known for your clothes, see. You're known as a fine gentleman, and particularly for your clothes – '

'Tell Hedda to come in here!' Father ordered.

I rushed out, knotting my fingers and clenching my teeth so as not to scream in rage. I ran down to the well, where Hedda and Anna had lit a fire under the cauldron. Without saying a word I started beating Hedda with my fists. Eventually I said:

'She's here! The old woman who's getting Father's clothes. She's in with Father.'

She did not understand me at first. Then her whole body began to tremble.

'Oh, dear Lord,' she muttered. 'Oh, sweet Jesus, why should this happen to me? Oh, dear Lord, what's he going to think? Oh, dear Lord, dear Lord, I daren't go in to him. Anna, Anna, you must come with me.'

I was moved to sympathy by her terror.

'Just come,' I said, taking her hand and pulling her up the slope. But she stopped at the step, refusing to go any further.

'Hedda,' Father said, and she jumped over the step as though she had been pushed from behind.

'Have you sold my clothes to this old woman?' Father asked.

She nodded and put her hands together.

'What in the Lord's name do you think you're doing?' Father said. 'Give the woman the clothes. I don't want any more blessings from her.'

Hedda scuttled over to the old woman, grabbed her arm and dragged her out with such speed that she only had time to shout 'Go' bless!' a couple of times.

'Women,' Father muttered, and turned to face the wall. I was crying and sobbing. After a while Anna came in and sat by

Father's feet, crying and sobbing. Eventually Hedda came in. She stood by the stove, put her hands over her face, and wept. Father seemed not to notice anything. He was probably asleep. But after an hour or so – we had finally stopped crying – he turned around. His whole body was shaking, and finally he raised his head a little, and we could see that he was laughing.

'Hedda,' he said, 'that was a stroke of genius, that business with the clothes. You sly devil. You thought I should pay for my farewell dinner. Myself. Well, you were quite right.'

He stroked her hand on the blanket, raised his finger and wagged it at her.

'But now, dear Hedda,' he said, 'now I lie here with nothing. Please, no further reductions.'

On Sunday morning I was woken by Anna; she helped me to dress and saw to it that I looked really fine. I asked how Father was. I had a vague memory of having heard hustle and bustle in my sleep.

'Ah,' Anna said, hesitating. 'It's not worth you going in to him. He wants to sleep.'

I was content with that, but just as I was about to leave for the station to meet my uncle and Léonie, Anna came out of Father's room. He wanted to talk to me.

Father was sitting up, leaning against a pile of pillows. I could not see any difference in his appearance from the day before, except that his left eyelid was hanging down over his eye. He was also having more trouble talking. He made several attempts before he got going.

'Jan,' he said, 'I've been thinking of something. There's a fountain at –dal. You know. If you stand at the gate and look along the drive, you can see the water falling. Not the fountain itself, just the water. And when the sun is at a certain angle, you can see the whole rainbow in the water. I've been wondering what time of day that might be. I think it's between one and two o'clock, but I'm not sure. I'd like you to go and check. Take Léonie with you, and go straight from the train. The fountain will probably be switched on today. As it's Sunday. Wait by the gate and see if you can see the rainbow. Then come and tell me.

Take my watch, so that you know the time – '

I took Father's watch and left.

Uncle and my cousin were on the train. We separated at the crossroads, and Léonie and I continued towards –dal. She was very friendly towards me this time, and as beautiful as before. The spots on her forehead had disappeared. We sat down on the meadow on the other side of the road, opposite the gates. It was only just after ten o'clock, so we had plenty of time. We played all sorts of games, and I was the one who decided what they should be. She did everything I wanted. And she gave me sweets. Every now and then I looked at the watch, partly to see how time was passing, and partly to show off.

'Oh look!' she said. 'Have you got a watch?'

I did not reply, but told her about the rainbow that we were there to see instead. She found that so funny that she burst out laughing.

'Uncle Johan has always been funny!' she said.

I looked at her and wondered if she was going to kiss me. I was not really bothered, but seeing as she was supposed to be so fond of me, surely she ought to kiss me. But she did not, and eventually I got rather cross. I could not stop thinking about it. Every time she caught me in our games, I closed my eyes. Because in the Bishop's Palace I had always closed my eyes when she kissed me. I kept closing them – but no. In the end I lay down and pretended to sleep. But not even that helped.

It annoyed me. Admittedly, I was not really bothered, but I could not understand the reason why she was not kissing me. It worried me. I thought: 'Perhaps there's something wrong with me.'

I could hardly ask her.

But I could do something else, I could kiss her instead. That way I could find out if she liked me or not, and if there was anything wrong with me.

And I did all manner of silly things, trying to find excuses to get close to her. I did not really know what to do, and thought it probably best to take her by surprise.

We played and played, and we stood at the gates for long

periods, staring at the water from the fountain, which hung in a veil across the vault of the trees. But all the while I kept my goal in mind, and did not let it out of my mind for a moment.

At last a suitable moment arose. We were both standing at the gate; she was pressing her nose flat against one of the railings, and I was pressing mine against the next railing. I just had to turn my head to reach her cheek with my lips. I did so. And she turned to me and smiled.

'We can't,' she said. 'Father's said so.'

But we kissed each other. And when she looked up at the avenue again, she kissed me on the cheek once more.

Then she cried:

'Jan! Look at the rainbow!'

I took out the watch and noted that it was a quarter to two.

'Let's go home to Father now,' I said.

We walked arm in arm.

Anna came towards us on the slope. Father had just died. I wanted to run in to him, but she held me back. And no matter how I begged and pleaded, they would not let me into the room. Father himself had decreed that I was not to see him after his death.

MEMOIRS OF A DEAD MAN
II

LÉONIE
AN INTERMEZZO

In the autumn of 1907 a collection was made in the diocese of W.; the proceeds were to be used to erect a memorial to the late Bishop, Julius Arnberg. The appeal was signed by the Governor of W., by Count A. O. Arnfelt the bank director, as well as a score of priests, with Dean Rygelius at their head. However the current Bishop's name was not to be found beneath the appeal. This was the cause of much gossip and anger. Some criticised the Bishop, while others maintained that Dean Rygelius had deliberately excluded Julius Arnberg's successor. In my opinion the latter were correct, but the Dean himself soon believed the former, and complained far and wide about the Bishop's lack of tact and piety.

Dean David Rygelius the Younger, my father's cousin, and my guardian, was a very hot-tempered man. After Julius Arnberg's death, he became the older clergy's candidate for the bishopric. An academic from Lund with far greater scholarly merits was appointed; Rygelius could never forgive that. On one occasion, when the new Bishop exhorted him not to incite dissent in the diocese through his impetuosity, he is said to have replied:

'What hast thou to do to declare my statutes, or that thou shouldest take my covenant in thy mouth? The man who stole my bishopric had best not come and talk to me about dissent!'

A large crowd of clergymen was present when this remark was made. But the usual black-coats who had once smiled and bowed and patted each other in Grandfather's garden were prepared to dismiss the scandal immediately with a flutter of their handkerchiefs. And Rygelius still had his supporters.

In his day, Julius Arnberg had been one of the most High-Church and conservative clergymen in the country. He hated all forms of sectarianism and once in a pastoral letter described the Free Church movement as the 'half-sister of anarchism' – a word which could cause a great stir in those days. After his death his nephew, Rygelius, assumed the leadership of the High Church and conservative party within the diocese – and with it also the editorship of *The Diocesan News* – and for seven years he had missed no opportunity to attack or criticise his more fortunate rival for the crozier and mitre. As a consequence, the new Bishop had been proclaimed leader of the liberal wing of the church, and was allied with the Free Church organisations. Countless attempts had been made to reconcile the Bishop and the Dean, but without success. Finally it looked as though a reconciliation might take place, as a result of something quite insignificant. The insignificant reason was – superficially, at least – closely connected with one Jan Arnberg, my own humble person.

When my guardian came to town – an occurrence which took place two or three times a month – he would stay with his cousins, the Misses Arnberg. After Grandfather's death they bought a little one-storey house at the end of Västra Trädgårdsgatan. The gable faced the cemetery, and the little garden was protected by the cemetery wall. Sometimes this garden, like Grandfather's before it, teemed with black-coats – when the Dean summoned his sympathisers to some important conference. And daily it was filled with Aunt Amelie's cooing friends, the doves from the Bishop's Palace. They were known in the town as 'the Bishop's doves', and my aunts were still called 'the Bishop's young ladies'. Wags would switch the names, calling the doves the Bishop's young ladies, and the ladies the Bishop's doves. The house was known as The Dovecote. Apart from this, I was very satisfied with the respect that was shown to them. On special occasions there was always someone, a constable, doorman, parish clerk or priest, who would officiously clear a path for 'the Bishop's young ladies' – and for me! – and secure us a good and prominent position.

They had aged, my aunts. Amelie was already an old woman, tall, thin, sallow, bent, with sunken breasts, quite hard of hearing, and very suspicious. She lived for her doves, her poor, her priests.

Norah's hair was snow-white, just like Grandfather's, but thick and bushy. She had also inherited Grandfather's healthy, ruddy complexion and his cheerful disposition. For six years I was her faithful escort and attendant. She used to joke about being a spinster, swearing that she could not let me go until Léonie, my cousin, was old enough to marry. She would tease me about Léonie. To begin with I took this badly; but the older I got, the more these insinuations pleased me. Sometimes we would talk about Father, and I understood that she had been fond of him. It was for his sake that she worried about me and my future. She used to say to the Dean:

'We're not letting go of Jan until he's Bishop of W.'

And he would laugh and say:

'Just what I was thinking! Jan must recapture the Arnbergian crozier. One could almost call it *successio apostolica*.'

In consultation with my aunts he had decided that I should go into the clergy. Personally, I was more inclined towards the sea, but Rygelius was my guardian, and it seemed natural to obey him. When my friends Mikael Arnfelt and Karl Rygell, known as 'the Angel', made fun of me for my choice of profession, I would reply:

'I'm not the one going into the clergy. It's the Dean's wallet.'

I took the matter no more seriously than that. The fact that Léonie sometimes stayed with the Bishop's young ladies was far more important to me. And the fact that Rygelius was her guardian as well as mine made me more submissive and obedient than any debt of gratitude would have done. If my guardian had given me Léonie's garter as a collar, he could have led me wherever he pleased. But he preferred to combat my recalcitrance – because he imagined that I was recalcitrant by nature – with long sermons. He once wrote the following to me, and I still have it:

'The duty of the Christian priest, now as ever, is to fight, tirelessly and courageously, against demons.

'The Church is no longer attacked by the spirits of faithlessness, but by those of false belief. The people of the new century are seeking their own gods. Wheresoever they find something signifying power, they fall down and pray. Thus in our time has Mammon found worshippers not merely in deed and emotion – this has sadly always been the case – but even in thought and word.

'Others fashion their idols out of their lust for power; and still others make fetishes of their erotic fantasies, sometimes in attractive and artistic guise, sometimes disgusting and raw; and they keep these as household gods throughout their lives, sacrificing body and soul on their altar. I could continue *ad infinitum* to list for you the shifting shapes of demons, some created out of lust and sensual longing, some out of repugnance and fear. They are legion. But they may all be known by their desire to take precedence over the living God.

'Our guiding principal is the First Commandment, which takes precedence over all others:

'"Thou shalt have no other gods before me.

'"Whosoever breaks this Commandment, he breaks them all."

'He opens the door to the demons. And, however "enlightened" and "righteous" he may seem, you shall soon see him sink into the darkest superstition. He shall hold his excrement holy, and worship his decaying flesh.

'For God alone is salvation from death, and what is not in God is decay. It is of the Devil. But the priest or layman (here he meant the Bishop!) who has never escaped the conjuror's booth of modern scholarship, he considers the Devil to be a flight of fancy, or merely a symbol. Isaiah speaks of these priests when he says:

'"His watchmen are blind: they are all ignorant, they are all dumb dogs, they cannot bark; sleeping, lying down, loving to slumber."

'And to them Ezekiel's words:

'"Thus saith the Lord God; Behold, I am against the shepherds; and I will require my flock at their hand, and cause them to cease from feeding the flock; neither shall the shepherds feed themselves any more; for I will deliver my flock from their mouth – "'

He wrote this, and more of the same, to me. If only he had woven in Léonie's name at some appropriate – or inappropriate – point!

In a red, two-storey, ramshackle wooden building out to the north my stepmother Hedda had opened a private hostel. It was very run down. With the exception of the main room upstairs, in which Hedda had gathered Father's old furniture from –dal, the rooms were bare and unwelcoming. But quite a lot of country-folk would stay there anyway. Farmers with carpet-bags, even one or two country squires of the thriftier sort. This ramshackle establishment was not exactly a credit to the family. Sometimes people of very dubious repute would find refuge there. This was, however, not Hedda's fault. She was cook to the whole town, and the hotel business was managed in the main by sister Anna, who had been obliged to stop teaching because of her weak chest. But the poor dear could not distinguish between different types of people. I was constantly having to tell her. I used to eat Sunday lunch at Hedda's, and would eat enough to see me through half the week. She offered well-prepared, good, rich food; although Dr Rygell alleged that she bought rotten ingredients. In the Rygell household where I lived, hardly any ingredients at all were bought.

So poor Hedda did not lend any increased lustre to the name of Arnberg; unfortunately there was one person who, to put it bluntly, brought disgrace to the name. Otto Arnberg, my father's elder brother. On the corner of Kyrkogårdsgatan and Lilla Bruksgränd is a tavern known as 'The Ship'. The tavern itself lies in the inner courtyard. This is where he spent his time; where he actually lived I do not know. He had fallen through the ice altogether. As soon as Grandfather died people began to gossip about the way Otto managed the poor relief. The street-sweepers let their brooms lie, drinking and playing cards; the old women slurped coffee and fought among themselves. All day, every day, was a party. In spite of this, it is just possible that the Bishop's name might have saved Otto Arnberg if only he had promised to mend his ways. But, challenged by those concerned either to perform his duties or to relinquish them, he replied: 'I perform my duties according to my own conscience, and not yours. Damn it, my old men and women have never had any fun before, so why not let them now that they're old? Soon enough they'll be as quiet as any of you gentlemen could wish – '

He was dismissed. The accounts were in impeccable order; but the organisation's expenses had so shamelessly exceeded the allotted funds that the Misses Arnberg had to make a considerable contribution in order to keep the matter quiet. And that was only the start of it. Every year, every six months, almost every month, they had to buy their way out of some new scandal. In the end, Rygelius advised them to leave the town and the surrounding district. But to them this was an insufferable notion, that the Arnberg name should be sullied in W., in the Bishop's town. And mutual friends who sought to persuade Uncle Otto to move on to pastures new would be told:

'No, I'm not that stupid. I'm known here, and people like me here. Damn it, the Bishop's nephew! I can live off that until my dying day.'

He also alleged that the family owed him money. Sometimes it was the Bishop who had withheld some of his patrimony, and sometimes it was his own brother, my father, who had cheated him out of money. And, as he believed that I should defray my father's debts, he sued my guardian and demanded the money that Grandfather had left me. The lawsuit lasted several years and judgement was not pronounced until just after New Year, 1908.

Otherwise he was in splendid spirits. His total ruin had freed him from grief and melancholy. He was fat as a barrel, ruddy-faced, cheerful and good-natured. And he really was well-liked. The habitués of the tavern would listen devoutly to his chatter and nonsense. Damn it! He was the Bishop's nephew, after all! Cousin to the Bishop's doves! And he was no toothless lion, and could give as good as he got. He was implacably bitter about Arnfelt. He would openly insult the venerable, white-haired old man in the street, and commanded street urchins and longshoremen to throw mud at the Arnfelt carriage (which had once been Grandfather's). Then one night he almost killed the old man by frightening his horses into a gallop. The police intervened, but A. O. stepped in and he was released without even the slightest rebuke. In actual fact, it was A. O. who supported him financially, albeit in secret. Every quarter he would send him a sum of money, a sum which was not entrusted to the postal service or any servant. No, it was entrusted to Mikael. Perhaps Mikael had asked for the job. He was entertained by the drunkard's talk, and would sometimes accompany him to the roughest taverns.

I avoided him like the plague. If we met, I would pretend not to see him. And, oddly enough, he would do the same, and never troubled me with a greeting. Only once, when Léonie and I were strolling down the main street with some other boys and girls, did he come staggering after us, calling:

'Jan! Léonie! My dear little children!'

We hid in a doorway. When we dared to emerge, he was standing squarely in front of the door, thinking. He looked furtively at us, turned around, and stumbled away.

But he proved all the more difficult to shake off for the Bishop's young ladies. He haunted them. And if I ever saw them with pale faces, a fixed stare in their eyes, jaws clenched, hurrying along the street, I would know that Uncle Otto was sailing along in their wake. All the town knew this, and people would stop and watch to see how the race ended. But so great was the respect commanded by the Bishop's young ladies that I rarely saw anyone even smile at their flight. My friends often made fun of the old man in my presence, but never alluded to the fact that we were related. I belonged to the other branch of the Arnberg family, the better one, the finer one, the Bishop's branch, whose reputation was still high in W.

For the duration of my education, six years, I lived with Dr Rygell, sharing a garret, a long, narrow, rather dark room with a sloping ceiling, with the Angel. The furnishings consisted of a rib-backed sofa, a camp-bed, two wooden chairs, a table, and a washstand. A black-framed mirror, with cracked glass, the same glass that had once been part of Uncle Otto's renowned treasure, was my property, and was much used, as I was rather particular about my appearance, especially on the occasions when Léonie was in town. On each side of the garret stood a wardrobe. In one we kept our clothes, and the other was the Angel's storeroom. He was still trading, for the past year mostly in schoolbooks that he bought from friends in financial difficulties – not least Mikael – and sold on at a good profit.

The attic was pitch-black, its floor consisted of loose planks that we would stumble over. The attic-stairs creaked terribly, giving Dr Rygell a firm foundation for the fabrication of various accusations. It was his *idée fixe* that we spent our nights out of the house. His bearded, rumbling mouth would overflow with maxims and paradoxes. And with every word of wisdom he would scrape the floor with his club-foot, like an old goat. He kept careful accounts of the expenses his sons occasioned. The Angel's account had reached thirty thousand – he would round the figures up to his own advantage – and he used to say:

'You should know how much is invested in you. And remember! Until you pay the interest and repay the capital, every last bit of food is stolen!'

He held me in deep contempt, partly because I was rather delicate, and partly because I was poor. He would say:

'Sickness is more a just punishment than an undeserved misfortune. Healthcare should be the preserve of the doctor, care of the sick that of the executioner. Poverty is undeniably a misfortune, but it is just as undeniably a disgrace. A family that serves and protects is a family that deserves to be protected.'

When A. O. celebrated his eightieth birthday, Rygell published a pamphlet, 'What is health?', in which he extolled the old man's strength and wealth. (In return, according to the Angel, he was supposed to have procured a bank loan on favourable terms. For he himself was rather poor.) Dean Rygelius reviewed the pamphlet in *The Diocesan News* with the words: 'yet another of the Antichrist's innumerable Symbolic Books, an apotheosis of Mammon-worship, a new book in the *Biblia Diabolicorum*!'

On a personal level, however, the two gentlemen got on very well together, and the Dean would often drink his toddy at the doctor's. Occasionally they would summon me before them and scrutinise me. Both had large, red, bearded faces with staring, glassy eyes enlarged by spectacles. I felt like a little roach between two sea-monsters. The doctor would spit:

'Pah! Poor stock. Never get anywhere!'
But the Dean would say:
'Ah well, I think we've already helped him to get a fair way.'

The Angel hated all authority. Perhaps it was his premature experience of business that made him feel so bitterly the pressure of laws and regulations. But above all else he hated his father. This is why:

Dr Rygell had five sons; the second youngest was called Rutger, and was four years older than the Angel. The same spring that he was to have taken his school leaving certificate, he drew upon himself a secret illness. His fear that his father would discover the secret worried him to death. He killed himself.

I remember the evening they brought him home. He had a gunshot wound beneath his right temple. A bloody lump clung to his cheek: his eye. I met them in the alley beneath our window. I stopped and heard them go up the back stairs. I heard the doctor's rumbling voice, and the scraping sound as he dragged his club-foot across the floor in his consulting room. Then I heard him bellow something, then I heard a roar, a long, howling cry. Then I heard nothing. But when I dared to return several hours later, he was sitting on the stairs in the hall, his legs crossed, hands on his knees, eyes closed, mouth hanging open, tongue hanging out over his lower lip as though he were mentally subnormal. This was Dr Rygell, the cocksure author of 'What is health?'

But of course he soon recovered, and all that remained was an implacable hatred of loose women, and the *idée fixe* that the Angel and I slipped out at night. As far as the Angel was concerned, there was some truth in this. He and Mikael spent several nights at The Ship and other similar dens. There were also girls. One called Sonja, Rygell's friend, and her sister, who was Mikael's. Mikael tried to persuade me to meet them. But I had other things on my mind.

I had Léonie and our future to think about. Things did not look very bright. I had worked out that if I became a priest, I would be able to marry in six years' time. A ridiculously, impossibly long time! I was already eighteen. But if I chose another profession, the Dean, Léonie's and my guardian, would be against me. Of course we could defy him, but in that case I would need to be a man of independent position and some fortune. I had no desire to marry Léonie to a pauper. Many projects suggested themselves to me, and I began to put a number of them into effect.

For instance, I spent all my free time that autumn shooting squirrels. My intention was to buy myself a real hunting-rifle with the money I made from the skins, whereupon I would devote myself to shooting foxes. But of course I had no intention of remaining a hunter. The fox-skins would merely provide me with the capital necessary to open a magnificent furrier's shop. At school I applied myself particularly to learning English and French, so that I could establish direct contacts with North America and Siberia as soon as possible. My choice of this particular trade had been influenced by the town's furrier, a relatively young man who had become wealthy in a very short time. All the same, I could demonstrate that the man had made impractical purchases, with far too many middle-men. I would have suggested that we go into partnership had I not found him so disagreeable. He refused to buy my squirrel-skins, saying that they had been skinned wrongly. I had to sell them for a song to the Angel.

I also had other plans. The Angel, partly because he was so worried about his exams, and partly because he wanted to play a trick on his father, had decided to run away the week before the exams. He was planning to go to Hamburg, where one of his brothers lived. He maintained that we would have plenty of opportunities in a city like Hamburg. Mikael, who also had useful contacts there, had promised to help us. But we needed money for the journey, and some capital to start us off. Mikael suggested that I should somehow get hold of the money I had inherited from Grandfather – the inheritance would not be mine until I had reached my majority – but I refused. Our plan ran aground on this point. Besides, we also fell out with one another. This is what happened:

I have already mentioned that Mikael and the Angel each had a girlfriend, two sisters. One day the doctor got wind of this and involved the police, and it became necessary to find the girls a temporary refuge. The Angel suggested that we relinquish our garret to Sonja, one of the sisters. The idea of hiding her in Dr Rygell's house was audacious and appealed to me. The girl came, she was small and pretty, pale and scared. We treated her like a princess, we bought her clothes and food, we slept on the floor and took turns standing watch on the staircase, around which we set so many traps that the doctor could hardly have penetrated our lair alive. After a couple of days she left us; Mikael had found a new, safe abode for the girls. And I thought no more about it. It was just before Christmas, and Léonie was expected in town. I found as many excuses as I could to go to The Dovecote. Aunt Norah, who could see me coming down the street in the window-mirror, would open the window and call:

'Don't trouble yourself, Jan dear. Not yet.'

Aunt Amelie would pull annoyed faces. Then I would go to visit sister Anna, so that at least I could talk about Léonie –

One evening as I was sitting in Anna's little room – a sort of porter's lodge – and leafing through the visitors' book, I caught sight of two names:

Sonja and Klara Arnberg.

'Who in God's name are they?' I asked. Instead of answering, Anna blushed deeply and burst into tears. I could see from the book that the girls were staying in the best room, 'Father's room'. I ran upstairs and opened the door without knocking. On the sofa, half-dressed and sleeping peacefully, lay Sonja, and her sister, Mikael's friend, was in bed. I ran back down to Anna and opened the interrogation. Who had brought them? Mikael Arnfelt. How long had they been there? A week. Did Hedda know? No. Did Anna know what sort of girls were living in Father's room? Yes, but Christ himself had –

'Oh, shut up!' I cried, so furious that I pushed her in the chest. Why had they taken the name Arnberg? Because they could not use their real name; because wicked people wanted to harm them. (The police!) The name Arnberg had been chosen specifically to fool the wicked people completely. Whose idea had that been? Mikael's.

I did not know what to do. I ran home to get my gun, and loaded it. And went off to the Arnfelt house on Västra Trädgårdsgatan. Mikael saw me from the window and came to open the door himself. As soon as we were in his room, behind closed doors, I said:

'If you don't make sure that they're gone by this evening, I'll shoot you.'

He understood what I meant at once, and tried to make excuses; I repeated what I had said. Then he smiled at me and asked to see the gun. And he said:

'I really am sorry, Roach. It was thoughtless of me, but I didn't know that you were so particular. They'll be gone by this evening, I promise you.'

And he stroked his chin, a gesture he had inherited from his grandfather. Then he held out his hand:

'Well, do you forgive me?'

I turned my back on him and left, still furious.

To see whether or not he intended to keep his promise, I went back to the old house and waited with Anna all evening. She cried, but would not admit that she had done anything wrong. In the end I was obliged to kiss and console her. Above our heads, the girls spent the evening singing like nightingales.

At about ten o'clock Mikael and the Angel finally appeared, accompanied by a town porter. I did not make myself known. After an hour or so, the whole company moved off. First the Angel, peering to right and left, stopping at every street corner, then the girls, tripping elegantly along, arm in arm, and then Mikael, also looking around carefully, and finally the porter. I had to laugh, it was such a ridiculous procession.

And it was not my fault – as the Angel later alleged – that matters took a turn for the worse.

The ridiculous procession had reached the castle bridge. They were making their way to Uncle Otto, who had promised to get them some rooms. But by the bridge Sonja stops and explains that she dare not walk through the park in the dark. She has experienced supernatural occurrences in W.; a drowned sailor has

Memoirs of a Dead Man

been pursuing her, and she is terribly afraid of the dark. So Rygell turns and offers her his arm. At that very moment, a terrible figure steps out of the darkness of the shadow of the castle. It is no ghost, but Dr Rygell. Furious at finding his son in such company, he raises his cane and begins to give the pair a sound thrashing. The Angel was quite taken aback; the girl kept quiet to start with. But when she caught a glimpse of the ugly bearded face and the club-foot as well in the light of the bridge lamp, she became terrified and screamed:

'It's the very devil himself!'

And, screaming for help, she ran up the main street, straight into the arms of the police. Mikael and the Angel had followed her. The street was otherwise deserted; the Angel threw himself at the constable, Mikael helping him. And they did actually manage to free their friend, but were themselves dragged off to the police station by the embittered constable, where they were obliged to give their names.

'We'll end up in prison!' Mikael explained. 'And it's your fault.'

I said:

'It's entirely your own fault. And I say again, Mikael, that if you hadn't got rid of them, I would have shot you. Like a dog. Now you know where I stand.'

I went to bed, leaving them to think and say what they liked.

A. O. intervened and hushed up the trouble with the police. But Dr Rygell reported his son and Mikael Arnfelt to the headmaster, and an inquiry had to be held at the school. Perhaps this could have had a satisfactory outcome – the desire was certainly there – had not the headmaster hit upon the idea of asking, *pro forma*, what Arnfelt's intentions had been toward the women in question. The question had amused Mikael so much that he burst out laughing (he was, in spite of his impudence, very nervous). And before the teaching staff had had time to collect themselves after this insult, he replied:

'Gentlemen, do you not think that we might draw a veil over my intentions for the sake of decency?'

In the face of such unalloyed cynicism, the teachers were no longer able to make any allowances to the school's generous patron, A. O. Arnfelt. It was the first time in ten years that a pupil in the final year had been expelled. People began to speculate, whisper, and suspect. There was something very suspicious. The Bishop's wife, chair of the Society for the Clothing of Poor Children, made a public pronouncement. She said that poverty and suffering, like baptism, could often wash people clean and offer new life; whereas vice thrives in the hothouse atmosphere of wealth. While this remark was perhaps merely intended as a consolation for the poor, it was generally understood to be an attack on the house of Arnfelt. A. O. was angry, and that Christmas the S.C.P.C. was only able to clothe forty children, instead of the hundred clothed the previous year. To the Bishop's wife's supposition A. O. is said to have responded:

'No, no. I have no desire to stop them washing.'

More cynicism! People started to understand. A gloomy future was predicted for Mikael. Riches may be powerful, but they are not all-powerful. People were affronted that Mikael had the impudence to remain in town, as though nothing had happened. Dr Rygell, of course, could not afford to send his son away, but A. O. could! Therein lay something of a challenge. The Bishop himself hinted that there was something unrepentant in Mikael's behaviour. And Rygell, A. O.'s faithful admirer, exclaimed:

'Pah! There's something rotten about this. It stinks!'

He was also furious that his son had been expelled. It meant that he had lost money. And he was even more annoyed that the hussies had not been caught. He wrote a biting article in the W. newspaper demanding a razzia and the closure of certain small hotels and taverns. Hedda's hostel was not named, but was certainly implied. Fear reigned in The Dovecote; Norah said: 'Now we're for it again!' (Spoken like a true Arnberg!) And Amelie took to her bed. The Dean came rushing from the station, swinging his black bag like a missile. He threw it into my arms and cried: 'Idiot! You did the right thing, but you're a blockhead.' And he flung off his fur-coat and sat down, his hat still on, at Norah's secretaire, and wrote an article for *The Diocesan News*. He said:

'Just wait! I'm going to crush him this time!'

And by 'him' he meant the Bishop, because he had got it into his head that it was His Grace who, somehow or other, was behind the whole affair. The Bishop wanted to sully the Arnberg name by dragging the benighted Hedda before a court. Norah sought to calm him, but in vain. He read out his article: 'The Mote and the Beam: a Reflection upon Modern Pharisaism within Church and Society.' As he was doing so, old Hulda, Grandfather's faithful old servant, came padding in and announced that the Bishop's driver was waiting in the kitchen. He brought a message from His Grace, who wished to speak with Jan Arnberg. We looked at one another in silence. Eventually the Dean took off his hat, mopped his brow, nodded, and said:

'Well, Jan. Off you go.'

His Grace received me in Grandfather's old room. He was seated at the desk and, as he gestured towards a chair on the other side of the desk, I could make out barely half of his mutterings. He spoke very softly, and with long pauses. All I understood was that it was a matter of a clerical scholarship. After another pause, he went on:

'You have conducted yourself in a most worthy and commendable fashion, my dear Arnberg. From what I have heard, first you admonished your unfortunate friends in the strongest terms. This shows that you possess the appropriate prerequisites for the responsibilities of your chosen career. You bring honour to the Arnberg name. I should like to consult your guardian regarding your future. Would you tell him that?'

And he sighed, as though he lacked the energy to say more, and held out a small, yellow, wrinkled hand, soft as cotton.

The following day the Dean made his way to the Bishop's Palace. And the day after that the first article to bear the Bishop's initials appeared in *The Diocesan News*. Amusingly, this too bore the title: 'The Mote and the Beam'; it was temperate and serious and warned against allowing pious zealotry to go too far. There was a risk that the innocent might be punished along with the guilty.

The article caused a stir; that the Bishop was writing in *The Diocesan News* indicated a rapprochement between the two parties. One month later the reconciliation was complete.

During that month the praise heaped upon me became unbearable. I do not know who was spreading rumours about my part in the affair. I myself spoke as little as possible about the matter, because I was ashamed. The story went that first I had patiently admonished and warned my friends, that I went on to threaten them, and that finally, in despair, I had forced my way in to the charming couples and, revolver in hand, had turned them out onto the street. And had called the police. This last claim I found particularly annoying. But I could do nothing about it. I was being turned into a hero, and precisely the sort of hero people wanted. The headmaster congratulated me on my courageous behaviour. The younger masters approached me in confidence and wanted to hear the details. But I was sparing with the details. Rygell said:

'Pah, Jan! I'd never have thought it. So, there's a bit of backbone in you. I'd never of expected that of your father's son.'

And my old teacher, the rotten plank from the first year, who had not seen fit to recognise me in six years, now stopped in the middle of the square, prodding me with his umbrella, and muttering:

'So. You. Really.'

Rygelius said:

'Jan, you acted like a blockhead, but it was good nonetheless. You can't sweep blackguards under the carpet. If you're going to mess with muck, you need a pitch-fork, not a silver spoon. Now I know I can rely on you. In cases like this – '

And there was no end to the cooing of the Bishop's old doves. They saw in me a crusader for virtue, a slayer of vice. Norah said: 'Yes, your father was just the same.' And Amelie said: 'Thank the Lord that you take after your mother and grandfather.' But they both agreed that I had rescued the family honour, which the lamentable offshoot of Hedda and Anna had threatened to drag into the gutter.

The Bishop's doves knew what my reward should be. One day

when I stepped into the dark little drawing room – where Norah's secretaire stood – I saw a girl's head in the window recess behind the net curtain. And a hand hastily pulling the curtain.

Léonie!

I said:

'Oh, I can see you! So you're here?'

I felt honoured, and, in a peculiar way, I began to feel at home in town. I felt I had been given a share in the streets and squares, in the parks, the town hall, castle and cathedral. I had done something for the good of society, although it was difficult to determine precisely what – but something, anyway. I guided Léonie about my town, people watching us, smiling at us –

Unfortunately we were never allowed to be alone. Usually we had Norah or Amelie with us, sometimes old Hulda.

One day, as we were walking back and forth along the main street – Norah was in a shop just then – Mikael Arnfelt crossed the street to greet Léonie. He had already taken off his hat. But Léonie blushed, turned her back on him and went into the shop.

I could see that he was annoyed. He tried to laugh, but could only manage a grimace, lips curled, revealing his teeth.

'How sad,' he said, sighing pathetically, 'to see virtue flee when vice approaches. The opposite ought to be the case.'

He offered me his hand, and we stood in silence for a moment. Then he said:

'Well, Roach, are you coming to Hamburg with me and the Angel?'

I laughed, and could not resist saying:

'No! Do you know what? I've never had less inclination to run away – '

He blinked understandingly:

'I can well imagine. Well, there's no hurry.'

And he nodded and walked off.

That evening, as we were seated at the little table in the window recess, Léonie asked me how I could wish to speak to Mikael Arnfelt –

And she said:

'He should be ashamed to show himself. Why doesn't he go away somewhere?'

I replied, very earnestly:

'He's waiting for me. We agreed to travel together.'

She became quite rigid and breathless and stared at me. But then she realised that I was joking. And she took me by the hair and pulled my head to hers, so that our foreheads and noses were touching.

'What are you doing?' asked Norah, who was sitting writing at the drop-leaf of the secretaire. We started moving the chess pieces once more, and Léonie replied resentfully: 'That silly Jan has put me in mate.'

Norah turned round and looked at us.

'You can't see properly over there,' she said. 'Come and sit here by the secretaire.'

Sighing, we got up –

After a while Norah went out; the Amelie came in, talking about her doves. Léonie asked: 'Have you shut them up, Aunt? I thought I saw the hatch open.' And I suggested that we go and shut it. But she said: 'No, no, my dear children, I'll go myself – '

Scarcely had she shut the door when Hulda came shuffling in. She went over to the secretaire, glancing at us and muttering: 'Hmm, I wonder what it was I came in for – '

Léonie said: 'You wouldn't happen to know where Jan's letter is, Hulda?'

'Jan's letter,' the old woman muttered. 'You must mean the Bishop's letter to Jan. Yes, it should be here – '

And she turned her back on us and started searching through the drawers.

'Jan,' Léonie whispered, 'can you see the rainbow?'

Our foreheads met, then our noses, and, after we had looked into each other's eyes, our lips.

We called this 'playing rainbows'. It was a childhood memory, a memory from the day Father died which had taken on a new meaning.

'So, have you found the letter?' Léonie asked.

And the old woman replied:

Memoirs of a Dead Man

'Well, it should be here, in the third drawer down on the left. In a grey envelope with the late Bishop's own handwriting on it – '

'No, imagine! The things you know!' Léonie said flatteringly.

But there were short periods, moments that merely made me more anxious.

One day, when I was helping Norah and Léonie to arrange flowers on Grandfather's grave, I suggested that we pay Hedda a Christmas visit in her old house on our way back from the cemetery. I was counting on the fact that Norah, who could not abide my stepmother, would leave us alone. But the plan failed; Norah agreed to pay Hedda a Christmas visit, and so all three of us walked up Kyrkogatan; I walked a little behind the others, because I was having difficulty concealing my disappointment.

When we came to the corner of Lilla Bruksgränd, where The Ship tavern is situated, we could hear screaming and swearing. Someone was calling for help. Norah turned round, pale, mouth agape. She had recognised Otto Arnberg's voice. She took Léonie by the arm and began practically to run down the street. I hesitated. Norah and Léonie turned off towards the square. I stepped into the passageway. The courtyard was full of people, mostly women. They were running about in the slushy snow, their skirts pulled up, screaming and kicking. I moved closer.

In the centre of the courtyard, right in front of the tavern door, stood a ramshackle old haycart. Beside the haycart, on his front, his face buried in the snow, lay Uncle Otto. He was dressed in a shabby frock-coat and greyish-yellow homespun trousers, with a large green patch across his behind. Mikael Arnfelt was riding on his broad shoulders, holding the old man by the ears and rubbing his face in the snow. And round the combatants danced the innkeeper's wife, an old hag with bare, wrinkled arms, a red bodice and a thin plait that bounced like a whip –

She was clapping her hands and shrieking:

'Now you're going to get it, Arnberg! Now you're going to get it!'

Everyone in the yard was shouting:

'Hit him! Hit him!'

But I wanted to help him. I grabbed Mikael by the shoulder in order to throw him off. Without letting go of Otto's ears, he turned to me, laughing so much he was almost choking. And he yelled:

'Good, Jan! Come and help me! Now he's going to get it! I've got him by the ears. Take off your belt.'

I put my hand to my waist. Everyone in the yard was shouting: 'Hit him! Hit him!'

And Mikael was yelling:

'Good, Jan! Hurry up! Hurry up!'

I loosened my belt, holding it in my hand. I did not know what to do. A boy snatched the belt and swung it above his head. I cast him aside. Someone shoved me in the back, and I half fell, half threw myself on the prostrate figure. I was sitting astride him. Everyone in the yard was shouting: 'Hit him! Hit him! Give him what for!' I hit him once, then began to pound him. I really did hate him, for all the suffering he had caused me and my family. He was an oaf and a disgrace to all of us. And the more I hit him, the more I hated him. I felt perfectly happy when they all shouted 'That's right! Now he's getting his just desserts! Harder! Give him what for!'

And I pummelled him.

But in the midst of the agitated, panting, screaming, jostling crowd, completely calm and silent, stood a man I had never seen before. Yet he was a head taller than anyone else in the crowd, and was wrapped in a full-length black oilskin, like the ones sailors usually wear. The collar was turned up. Naturally enough, he was looking at me, and our eyes met.

At that moment I had a feeling that Léonie was waiting for me. Perhaps at Hedda's, perhaps at home. Perhaps she had found a pretext to go to a certain confectioner's, or else there were other possibilities –

And here I was, sitting astride my Uncle Otto, while old hags and ruffians yelled:

'That's right! Give it to him! Go on!'

In the meantime the boy who had snatched the belt began lashing at Otto's legs, bare right up to the knee. The belt was made of leather. And, as though we were a pair of kittens clinging to his back, Otto Arnberg stood up, throwing me in the dirt, and Mikael into the haycart. The innkeeper's wife crept back into her hole –

Mikael called out:

'Run, Jan! He'll kill you! He's mad!'

Otto ran around the walls bellowing, knocking over empty crates, crushing empty barrels. He grabbed the pump handle. I stood up. Fortunately the boy had dropped the belt; I dried it and fastened my trousers. 'Are you mad!' yelled Mikael, who was lying spread-eagled in the haycart. 'Run! Run!'

But I was trying to work out where I was most likely to meet Léonie, and could think of nothing else. I took out my handkerchief and wiped my dirty clothes, because the way I looked now I could hardly show myself in respectable company. There were now only three of us left in the courtyard, Mikael, Otto and me. The man in the oilskin had also disappeared. A cry could be heard from the street: 'It'll end in murder! Police!'

And now he rushed at me, holding the pump handle before him like a soldier clutching his bayonet for a charge. His frock-coat had split across his bulging back, hanging in two fluttering halves. His face was dirty and bloody.

I took a step to the side. He fell with all his weight and momentum against the cart, which overturned with a crash and broke apart. There he lay, and there Mikael lay, and there lay the pump handle, planks, spokes, wreckage. I was obliged to help them up, first Mikael, who could hardly stand for laughter and injuries. Then the old man. When I held out my hand to him, he recognised me, and his dirty, violet-blue face lit up:

'So, it's Johan's lad,' he said. 'Well, who the hell would help me if not Johan's lad – '

We led him into the tavern and the old innkeeper's wife fussed about him, wrapping him in a yellow and red blanket, and bandaging his head with a nightcap. He ordered cognac for himself, and punch for us. Then he went on to drink beer and whisky, and we drank more punch. I was quite unused to drink. We laughed and talked: Mikael explained how the fight had started.

An unknown sailor – the one I had noticed – had walked into the tavern and sat down in 'the snug', to which Uncle Otto did not allow strangers access. All the same, he had taken such an instant liking to the stranger that he had gone up to him and politely introduced himself, saying: 'I am Lieutenant Arnberg.' The stranger had turned his back on him. The old man had taken offence: but still polite, he had encouraged the stranger to give his name. Whereupon he had received this mocking reply:

'If you're a lieutenant, Arnberg, then I'm a captain.'

Now this was the old man's Achilles heel and a constant source of irritation to him, that his military career had been ignominiously curtailed. He lost his temper, accused the stranger of bragging, called him a damned bath-tub sailor, pursued him right out into the courtyard and took aim with his fist. At the last moment, Mikael tripped him up –

'Ha, yes. Ha, yes,' the old man muttered. 'He was a mean piece of work, a nasty fellow. But what does that matter? Now Johan's lad is here, and we're going to have a drink. Just the one, so that we'll be merry. Did you see he had a tattoo round his neck? He had a rope round his neck. Bloody hell! No, let's drink a toast to Léonie now. Right, Johan's lad, tell me! I've seen you both. Youngsters. The resurrection of the family. But you mustn't let anyone mess you about. You, Johan's lad. Jan, that's your name. You mustn't let the hypocrites mess you about. You've got money! Did you know that? It's in Norah's secretaire, in a grey envelope with the Bishop's seal. I've seen it with my own eyes. You ought to take the money, Jan, and the girl – '

Mikael was half lying across the table; his face was right next to mine. He smiled at me, his beautiful eyes twinkling. He said:

'Of course, Jan! And you'll come to Hamburg with me – or wherever you like. Wouldn't you like that?'

I pushed him away from me.

'Stop making fun of me!' I said. 'If only you knew what it's like! We're not allowed to be alone for a minute – '

'Drink, lads!' urged Uncle Otto.

And he said:

'No, you can't stay here. Us Arnbergs become either sinners or ghosts. The sinner, that's me, that is. Hah! I'll admit it, I've abused my privileges. Hah! But the rest are ghosts. Just like that nasty fellow. The captain, I mean. Dangling on strings. Now we pull the dutiful string; arms out straight! Now we pull the happiness string; knees bend, hop and jump! Now the sadness string; head back, eyes shut, open mouth – waaaah – we all wail! Yes, they're ghosts – the devil only knows how to make them dance. But you, Jan, and Léonie – '

Mikael said:

'Why didn't you tell me? I can help you. I know a way, a really good way – '

'Drink, lads!' urged Uncle Otto. 'See, I do as I like. I'm cheerful and happy. I don't harm anyone. No-one is my slave, and I'm no-one else's slave. Authority is my spittoon, and the Church my bedpan. I pay my taxes in kind, and I have a quite particular use for the statute book. If an old man can be respectable, well, that's for the ladies to decide, but I've an idea I know what goes on between the sheets. I've never stolen, and the fact that I've been stolen from wasn't my fault. I've never harmed a soul, and if God wishes me to die as I have lived – well, it will be a pleasure.'

'Shut up and drink!' Mikael commanded.

The two of us conferred. And, being already half drunk, I confided all my hopes and desires to Mikael.

He asked: 'Are you so in love?'

And I replied: 'What sort of stupid question is that? And why do you ask? Are you making fun of me? Aren't you in love?'

'Me?' he said. 'That's a different matter entirely. I suppose.'

I said: 'Suppose all you like! But help me!'

And I was drunk.

The old man, who had been listening on and off, said:

'You, Mikael! A. O.'s son or grandson or whatever sort of bloody brat you are. Are you thinking of taking the girl from him? Well I can tell you, in my own name, and my brother Johan's, and the whole family's: Lay not thine hand upon the lad – '

'Shut up and drink!' Mikael commanded. We drank.

And Mikael said:

'I'm not the one who shall lay my hand upon the lad. No, he shall lay his upon me. As it says in the Bible, you old drunkard.'

'Then I'm content,' Otto declared, and urged us to drink.

Léonie and the Dean left two days before Christmas Eve. It had been decided that she should be sent to a finishing school in Switzerland in April. But in the middle of March a monument commemorating Grandfather was to be unveiled in the cemetery. Léonie would be coming to town for this, but only for a week.

We had christened this week 'Arnberg Week'. The headstone was to be unveiled with great ceremony. All the priests in the diocese, certainly the foremost among them, were expected to come to town. It was said that the duke of the province would also be there. The Bishop had agreed to make a speech. And I had been given the task of reading some poems written by the Dean. They were so long and difficult to read that I almost choked; I spent longer learning them than I did on all of my schoolwork. The Angel tested me once a week, and on each occasion I forgot something. Moreover, the Dean kept adding new verses. In the end it was veritable epic in honour of Julius Arnberg. The family did not go entirely without credit either; the Bishop's father, Dr Johan Arnberg of –dal, received his share of the acclaim.

The Bishop's young ladies, who were to give a dinner in The Dovecote, spent months in a state of extreme anxiety. I advised them to ask Hedda for help, and, after much indecision, they decided to call on her. She wept with gratitude. It was at least a way of playing a small part in the posthumous Arnberg ceremony.

But the Bishop's young ladies had another worry, a far greater one. Would Uncle Otto put in an appearance by the graveside? And how could he be stopped? To reassure them, I said:

'Oh, I could probably arrange things so that he doesn't come – '

Their eyes opened wide and they asked:

'Do you see him?'

I blushed and said no. But that was a gross falsehood. I saw him almost every day.

I had no-one but Mikael. He was my confidant. He had promised to stand by us one way or other during 'Arnberg Week'.

Memoirs of a Dead Man

Besides, he helped us exchange letters. Léonie addressed hers to the old Countess, Mikael's grandmother, and he intercepted them in the letter box. And he placed at my disposal a number of envelopes bearing the old woman's coronated stamp.

Most of the time we met at The Ship, where we could sit undisturbed in the snug; Uncle Otto's prattle did not worry us. Besides, I enjoyed having a drink. I was in low spirits. At home, in the Rygellian household, the Doctor was on the rampage day and night, never leaving us in peace. He had recently heard that the Angel was still trying to find the girl, Sonja. Sometimes he would stand in front me, staring at me through his spectacles, then suddenly grab me by the shoulders and shake me:

'You know something!' he would shriek. 'Even if you're not involved in this filth, you know something!'

And I could not help teasing him, replying:

'He that keepeth his mouth keepeth his life: but he that openeth wide his lips shall have destruction.'

Then he would rush off to track down the Angel. Or else he would hover about Hedda's old hostel. On one occasion he burst in on Anna, shouting:

'My son is here with a whore!' And, unconcerned by Anna's terror, he limped through all the rooms, vacant and occupied alike, and finally came tumbling down the stairs, thrown out by some hot-tempered guest.

He had also begun writing in the papers again, complaining about the laxity of the authorities, and talking obliquely about the great and honourable name that was being dragged through the mud. – But people were starting to find him ridiculous, and the only people distressed by him were the Bishop's poor young ladies. I tried to console them, but Amelie said:

'I know precisely what is going to happen. In the same edition of the newspaper as the reports of the festivities, the Arnberg name will feature in the columns detailing the activities of the police and the courts. It's all because your father married that creature. I shall never forgive him.'

And she went on complaining about Father. In the end I grew angry and said:

'You make such a fuss about Saint Julius the Bishop. Is it too much to ask that the other branch of the family be allowed a share of the attention – ?'

They thought I had gone mad.

The closer it got to Arnberg Week, the more uneasy I felt. It was not the festivities that worried me, or that terrible epic poem. I could only think of Léonie and of how I could get to see her alone. Every spare moment – I made sure I had a lot of these – I would seek out Mikael and consult with him. He would laugh and smile at me.

'Now Jan,' he said tenderly, pouting. 'Now that you're in a bit of a fix – do you want to come with me when I shake the dust of this town from my boots?'

His silliness annoyed me, but I had to be polite. So I said:

'Try to be sensible! What's that got to do with anything?'

He smiled and nodded knowingly:

'It has everything to do with it. You'll see – '

At that moment the door opened – we were sitting in the snug of The Ship – and the man in the black oilskin walked in. Without looking round, and without loosening either hat or coat, he sat down at the far end of the table. He tapped on the table with a silver coin and ordered a drink. Mikael nudged me in the side and whispered:

'There's Otto's ghost. The ghost with the rope.'

I looked at him; he looked like a sailor; a weather-beaten, severe yet cheerful face. His features were actually so indistinct and commonplace that they were soon forgotten.

The old woman in the red bodice put a glass of beer in front of him. He poured it slowly into his mouth. 'He's right!' Mikael exclaimed, half audibly. 'He really has got a tattoo – there on his neck. Look!'

I could see that the stranger had a tattoo, but I could not see what it depicted. It looked like a long, broad, blue-black plaster right across his neck, just above the larynx.

We turned our backs on him in order to talk about Léonie without disturbance. After a while Uncle Otto arrived. He was shouting and blustering in the main room; we could hear that he was in a bad mood. And he came in, snorting and snarling, his shoulders more hunched than usual, his head down, ready to charge.

'Ah, here you are!' he shouted. 'Listen to this! The liberties that damned Dean has taken. Rygelius! Writing. To me, Lieutenant Arnberg. That I should not be so bold – so bold as to make an appearance by the graveside. Beside the grave of my uncle, the Bishop. Because it would be a disgrace for the family. Do you hear, Jan! A disgrace to the family – '

He fell silent, cocked his head and stared at the stranger. And he stood like that, not moving, silent but scowling, until the stranger eventually ordered more beer in a loud voice. Then he started, shook his head, shrugged.

'Ugh!' he snorted. 'Ugh!'

He came over to us and began again, snorting and spluttering:

'Me! He forbids me! Me, from whom they've stolen a hundred thousand kronor! Because that's what the Bishop's crowd have done. You know that, Jan. Or perhaps you don't. But I know. A great injustice has taken place in this family. That sort of thing ends up being avenged.'

'Don't talk such rubbish!' Mikael interrupted. 'You're getting it all mixed up. It was A. O. who tricked you out of the hundred thousand – '

'A. O. – yes!' the old man growled. 'Yes, of course. But the others are no better. No, I'm going to tell you how things stand in this family. I'm going to explain everything. First and foremost, I'm going to explain how they behaved towards my brother. Towards your father, Jan. Towards Johan. Towards their own flesh and blood. Now you're going to find out, lads – '

But we found out nothing. The stranger stood up and came over to us. The three of fell silent and stared at him, a little surprised. He sat on the edge of the table, an arm's length from Otto Arnberg. He leaned towards him and said, half whispering, in a friendly but firm way:

'Lieutenant Arnberg ought not to speak of family affairs in taverns. Most people are tricked at some time or other, but the best of them bear it with a certain dignity.'

Mikael grabbed me by the wrist and winked, indicating that we were about to see something entertaining. But the choleric old man merely shrugged his shoulders, shivered like a wet dog, and snorted:

'Ugh!'

After a while Mikael said:

'Well, Otto, are you going to make a speech by the grave?'

The old man sized up his enemy with his eyes, then turned towards us.

'Boys,' he said, 'look at me! I'm an old fighter. I'm happy and cheerful and I don't harm anyone. Have I so much as killed a fly or stolen a pin in my whole life? But if people mess with me, threaten me, make fun of me, then I shall speak, for – '

'For,' the stranger interrupted, prodding the old man in the stomach slowly and playfully with his finger; 'for I am full of matter, the spirit within me constraineth me. Behold, it is as wine which hath no vent, it is ready to burst like new bottles. I will speak, that I may be refreshed. Let me not, I pray you, accept any man's person, neither let me give flattering titles unto man. For I know not to give flattering titles; in so doing my maker would soon take me away.'

And he prodded the old man in the stomach and laughed, throwing his head back. Mikael prodded me in the side and whispered:

'He's teasing him. You'll see, this'll be fun – '

Uncle Otto really did get up, but slowly, hesitantly, clumsily. His eyes were wide as saucers. He lifted his hand and touched the stranger's neck with his fingertips, then quickly withdrew his hand, wiping it on his coat –

'Ugh!' he snorted, and shivered. 'Ugh!'

'Is that a tattoo?' Mikael asked. 'What design is it?'

'A – a – rope,' Uncle Otto stammered. 'Ugh! He's got a rope round his neck.'

Mikael asked:

'What does it mean? Or perhaps it doesn't mean anything?'

The stranger turned to him and smiled:

Memoirs of a Dead Man

'Oh yes,' he replied, 'everything has a meaning – if you only choose to give it a meaning. Wouldn't you say, Lieutenant Arnberg? The ox is free so long as he doesn't feel the yoke. And then the yoke has no meaning. Wouldn't you say, Lieutenant Arnberg? But when the rope is tightened, the rope assumes a new and quite particular meaning. Wouldn't you say, Lieutenant Arnberg?

'As far as my rope is concerned,' he went on, turning to me, 'it means, quite simply: I am subject unto my Lord.

'Do you understand that, Lieutenant Arnberg?'

And he touched Otto's shoulder with his fingertips. But the old man pushed himself back, so that his stomach rose like a rampart between him and the stranger.

'Ugh!' he snorted, and shivered. 'Ugh!'

The stranger turned up the collar of his coat, nodded to us, and went towards the door, tossing a silver coin onto the bar.

At the beginning of March the following advertisement was published in *The Diocesan News* and several other newspapers:

Friends of ecclesiastical
and Christian social work who wish to honour the memory of the late Bishop of the Diocese of W. and Dr of Divinity and Theology, JULIUS ARNBERG, are hereby called to a meeting in the Town Hotel of W. (the Assembly Rooms) on Saturday 12 March at 1 pm. The intention of the hosts, if such should prove appropriate, is to establish a society for the protection and promotion of Christian social interests within the diocese, in commemoration of Julius Arnberg's life and works.

X. X.	*Y.Y.*	*A. O. Arnfelt.*
Bishop.	Governor.	Count, Bank Director.
Z. Z.	*C. O. Rygell.*	*David Rygelius, jr.*
Headmaster	Mun. M. O., Chairman, Town Council	Dean

The next day, the following stood in the W. newspaper:

Friends of ecclesiastical
and Christian social peace and pleasure who wish to honour the memory of the late philanthropist JULIUS ARNBERG, are hereby called to a meeting at the licensed premises (no. 19) named 'The Ship' (the snug) on Saturday, 12 March, whenever is convenient. The intention of the host, in all simplicity and without ridiculous or sanctimonious affectation, is to down a few drinks in memory of the good old fellow.

Otto Arnberg
Lieut. (ret.), Manager, Poor Relief (ret.).
The Bishop's Nephew.

This second advertisement was the cause of great confusion in The Dovecote, in the Bishop's Palace, throughout the town, and in the entire diocese. 'Arnberg Week' had assumed ever greater significance. It was regarded as a reconciliation, a conclusion of peace between the Bishop's party and the Dean's. The hand of friendship had finally been extended in the name of Julius Arnberg. The High Church and highly conservative Julius Arnberg had been, as *The Diocesan News* remarked, a truly evangelical personality, a conciliator, *arbiter concordiae pacisque civium*. It was indeed no coincidence that it was in his name that a long-awaited reconciliation had been achieved.

And now these fine festivities were threatened by a scandal that could only be avoided with great difficulty. Because after the publication of the advertisement it could not be denied that Otto Arnberg intended to cause some scandal or other. And there was no getting away from him. However insignificant he might be, he still bore the name, the name of reconciliation. (To find a new one with the same power would, of course, be impossible at such short notice.) Otto Arnberg also enjoyed a certain shameful, ridiculous, but not inconsiderable popularity among the town's lower strata. The town's two or three gossip writers would not miss a chance to make capital out of his words and deeds. The scandal – people were already talking of it without knowing what form it would take – would find its way to certain newspapers in Stockholm, and from there would be spread throughout the realm. Everyone was at a complete loss as to what to do.

Dr Rygell said:

'Ha! Because the world is governed by stupidity, vermin are allowed to crawl in the face of decent people! Pah! Insecticide! I could sort this out in five minutes. Painlessly and to the satisfaction of all concerned.'

And his son, the Angel, suggested:

'We could get him drunk and lock him up – '

Perhaps he was harbouring a certain hope that his father would entrust him with the task and the necessary means. But the Doctor screamed:

'Oh yes! You're marked with same stamp! Drinking! And other things! You're good at that! Just you wait! One day I'll catch you in the act – '

And in his fury over the private Rygellian scandal, he forgot the more general scandal, and began once again to prowl around certain districts, particularly in the vicinity of Hedda's hostel, about which he still harboured suspicions. He had already lost one son to that district, and had no wish to lose his Benjamin.

For my part, I was not really bothered by the scandal, the festivities, or Arnberg Week. But with a great deal of effort I did manage to learn the Dean's ever-expanding epic poem. (When he heard that the Duke would be in attendance, he revised it so thoroughly that it was practically a new work!) This was partly because I was afraid of him, and partly because I believed my performance ought to raise me in Léonie's estimation.

On March 10, at about six o'clock, I went off to The Ship, encountering Dean Rygelius on the way. I was obliged to accompany him some distance. The Dean walked with great strides: his heavy wolfskin coat, unbuttoned, flapped in the wind like a snowy grey rotunda, a monument of cloud. His beard was thick and ice-grey, like God the Father's. I ventured to ask what day Léonie would be coming to town, but he did not hear me. Suddenly he stopped short, took hold of the collar of my coat, and tugged at it as though he were ringing a churchbell.

'Jan,' he began, 'I should like to ask you something in confidence. Do you know how things really are over there – with your stepmother – with Hedda?'

I replied that things were in a bad way. Anna had been bedridden for several days, and Hedda thought it was serious.

'I see, she thinks so, does she?' the Dean muttered. Then he tugged at my collar even more impatiently and said: 'Well, that's unfortunate, but it is a matter for the Almighty, not us. You see Jan, I meant something else. You know, of course, what Rygell is saying. He alleges that incidents like that are still occurring – at Hedda's – '

'He's mad,' I interrupted. 'It's all lies.'

The Dean looked at me, then quickly went on:

'That's what I think as well. It would be far too dreadful. We have enough to deal with with that wretch Otto. Well, you understand me. You are a sensible lad, and I trust you.'

He placed his heavy hands on my shoulders and made me sway like a reed in the wind.

'Thank the Lord, Jan, that I have got you this far! There was something unstable in you before that I didn't like. A man shouldn't flit hither and thither like a will-o'-the-wisp, but should walk tall. But I trust you now. By the way, have you learned those verses? I've added a couple of stanzas – But that wasn't what I was about to say. Rather, praise the Lord, that I have got you this far! It has been difficult at times. For I am no Croecus. But enough of that! I've received interest on my pennies, and interest on the interest. And for that I thank you, Jan.'

And he made me sway like a reed in the wind.

As we parted, I asked once more:

'When is Léonie coming?'

He stared at me over his shoulder, absent-mindedly. Then he suddenly lit up in a benevolent smile.

'Oh, Léonie! She's coming on Sunday morning. On the eight o'clock train. I hereby authorise you to meet her at the station, take good care of the child, and deliver her unharmed to The Dovecote.'

He nodded and winked. We parted.

At The Ship I first encountered the Angel. He was half lying across the table, his face buried in his arms. I slapped him on the shoulder. 'No, leave me alone,' he muttered. 'I want to sleep.'

Mikael came in.

'Yes, let him be. He's finally made a momentous decision. Tomorrow, or the day after, or some other day, he's going to flee the paternal nest and run away with Sonja. They just lack the financial wherewithal. As do I. Grandfather has sent me on a grand mission to Lieutenant Arnberg, scourge of Christendom, to redeem the freedom of Christendom with two thousand kronor. At a secret briefing, I was authorised to go as high as five thousand, but then he would have to leave town. As far as I can see, there's nothing to stop me from taking possession of the surplus three thousand in order to fund our mutual travels. But human wisdom is vain. There is one immense obstacle. The honourable old man refuses to be bribed. He maintains that it would be dishonourable. Perhaps you, being of the same lineage, but of a younger and more refined vintage, can convert him to a more sound opinion – '

I asked: 'Have you heard anything from Léonie?'

But he brushed me aside impatiently. And now Uncle Otto came in, already puffed up and emboldened with drink, although not yet drunk. On his head he sported a green smoking cap, his white waistcoat was yellow with egg stains, and his frock-coat, tacked together across the back, was decorated with mould and damp like an old wall. His arms rested securely across his stomach, and he was snapping his thick, yellowing fingers disdainfully to left and right. He stopped in front of me. And said:

'Me, I mean, me! Otto Arnberg. He offers me money. You, Jan, you remember what I did with the mirror Hedda stole from me, don't you? You remember that? Well, tell the junior devil there what I chose to do with that mirror in the eminent presence of the senior devil himself. A mirror worth a hundred thousand kronor. Tell him about that! Ha, what I did was – '

And with admirable agility, he took a great leap, kicked like a dancer in mid-air, and snapped his heels together with a click.

'That's what I did. In the presence of that sanctimonious hypocrite, that master criminal, A. O. Arnfelt. The very same man who is now offering me two thousand. To me! Who smashed the mirror into pieces as though it were a chamber pot. All the same, it was proof of our family's distinguished origins. But two thousand, to act dishonourably? To quit the field and abandon the sacred memory of the Bishop to those hypocrites? Never! Tell him – never! Tell him Otto Arnberg will speak by the grave, loud and clear. Tell him I don't care for his money. I'm an old warrior; I can die, but I can't disgrace myself. I would sooner steal my daily bread than accept his blood-money. It's dripping with my own brother's blood. And plenty of other people's. Tell him that. Tell him to send the money to his father, the very devil, whence it came – '

'Your quarterly allowance as well?' Mikael asked.

The old man walked up and down a few times in a dignified manner. Then he stopped in front of me once more and said:

'You, Johan's lad, tell him – the quarterly allowance as well! If he dare! But I shall squeeze his fine name until there's nothing left of it. But let him do it! I have resources. I shall no longer make false allowances for other people. I have been a lamb, but shall become a tiger. For I must live. Isn't that so, Jan, even a lamb must live? My gracious ladies, I shall say, there in that secretaire lies a fortune. I am taking it because it belongs to the family, of which I am now head. I can break open a lock, but I can't act dishonourably. That's the difference! I shall speak at the grave. I shall unveil the memorial! I shall say: *Hic jacet* – an Arnberg, a saint, the best of all of us, the only one upon whom the Lord chose to have mercy – '

He began to sob; a sure sign that the drink was having its effect. I said: 'So there's going to be a scandal?' Mikael shrugged his shoulders.

The old man sank onto the table.

'You, young Rygell,' he said, 'little Angel. Why are you crying? Why am I crying? And all of us. Yes, children. We have the rope round our necks. One, two, three, pull! Ugh! But I don't believe in nonsense. An old soldier like me should die with his sword in his hand. In any case, I'm still young, and if anyone threatens me, I react without concern for the consequences.

Remember that. But what a mean piece of work, a nasty fellow. He's following me about. "Aaah!" Sonja cries when she hears him. As though someone were tickling her feet. "Now he's here, now he's turning the handle." Women know more than us men. Ah, but she's pretty! Well then! I like girls! In the poor house there was one girl who was a little – you know – But make me act dishonourably? – never! The head of the Arnberg family would sooner step into his grave. No, ugh, young Rygell. Don't talk to me about ropes in a hanged man's house! Yesterday he was in Trädgårdsgatan. A crafty fellow! What a bloody idea, having a rope tattooed on him! And it's a real rope. No, act dishonourably, never! Should Johan's lad see me act dishonourably? No, brother Johan, sleep soundly in your grave. I'm keeping watch. A. O., that's A and O – ha! Money, in other words. A very crafty fellow! He stops right in front of The Dovecote. Looks in through the window. Damned bath-tub sailor – shameless. "Why are you looking at the secretaire?" I ask. "Are you perhaps a little less than honest, sir?" Honesty has always been one of the fundamental features of an Arnberg's character, gentlemen. We have our faults, large ones at that, but we aren't hypocrites. Not to our fellows, or God, or even ourselves. So I shall permit myself, as the Bishop's nephew and current head of the family, to say as I unveil the memorial: *Hic hacet – jacet –* '

'Quite,' said Mikael, pressing the old man's snoring nose to the table. '*Hic jacet –* '

And he said:

'Come on, Angel, let's go home to Sonja and Klara – '

I wanted to go with them, but he said:

'No, we're going home to pack.'

When he saw that I was getting annoyed, he put his arm round my neck and whispered:

'I've got a surprise for you! And what a surprise!'

It was rumoured in town that A. O. Arnfelt had paid Otto Arnberg a considerable amount for him to stay away from the festivities. This helped calm things down, and the Bishop's young ladies themselves began to hope that the memorial festival in honour of their father would be untroubled and beautiful. But on the evening of the tenth, they received the following letter:

To the Misses Amelie and Norah Arnberg.
   My dear cousins! I herewith wish to announce
   1) that I shall attend the ceremonial unveiling of the memorial, and that I, as current head of the family, intend to say a few words in honour of the deceased,
   2) that if the Misses Arnberg, Dean Rygelius, Bank Director Arnfelt and others persist in wishing to deny me my means of sustenance, I shall make full use of my rights as a warrior and a human being (for I must live!) and
   3) that if a certain crafty individual who is in the pay of the above-mentioned confederacy does not leave me in peace, I am prepared to use arms to defend myself.
Otto Arnberg.

On Saturday morning, at about half past eight, just as I was about to go out, the telephone rang. It was Mikael; he said:
   'Are you listening? You're to go down to the station. Today. Do you understand? – today. For the two o'clock train.'
   And he hung up. Rygell came rushing out of his bedroom, half-dressed, and asked who had telephoned. I put the receiver down and walked towards the door.
   'So!' he cried, throwing something at me. 'So you're in on the conspiracy. Well, I've a shrewd idea! It was Karl! He's been out all night. I've got my eye on you! Watch out! Soon I shall sweep this house clean, that's what I shall do.'
   I paid no heed to his words.
   It was eight o'clock. I had six hours to wait. I walked and wandered and waited. The shops opened, small boys trailed to school in long black lines. The mayor took his morning constitutional, hands behind his back. In the Bishop's Palace the coachman polished a pair of boots. Two maids cleaned the windows. It was the first day of Arnberg Week, and His Grace was expecting a large number of guests. I was also expecting a guest.
   And I thought:

Memoirs of a Dead Man

'How is it possible? What did she say in the deanery? What has she managed to come up with? And how does she dare?'

A crowd of teachers was crossing the bridge by the castle; they were talking animatedly to each other. I heard one of them say: 'At least he was a true Christian. You can't say that of all prelates – '

Just behind them came the Angel, dark rings under his eyes, exhausted through lack of sleep. He asked: 'Has Father been looking for me?'

And I was thinking: 'How will we be able to hide? Where shall we stay? Where will she sleep tonight? How will she be able to pretend that she's arriving on the eight o'clock train tomorrow morning?'

I ran into Hedda.

'Oh, what a bother it all is.' I stopped and asked if Anna was worse.

'Oh no, not exactly. But today of all days, just when so many people are coming to town, we have to stay closed. Anna's in bed, of course; and I've promised to help the ladies.'

'There?' I thought. 'With Anna? Indeed, why shouldn't she sleep in Father's room? At least that's nice.'

The half past nine train arrived, bringing with it a few black-coats. I knew most of them, and greeted them. One of them, an old parish priest, embraced me, saying:

'Yes, dear Jan, it's a great joy to all of us who were close to him when he was alive.'

And I was thinking:

'What if there as many priests on the two o'clock train? There's bound to be someone who recognises her. And who will say to the Dean: "I saw your ward" – That she dare, that she dare, that she dare – '

Above the black mansard roof of The Dovecote the flag was being raised. And the doves, scared by the fluttering cloth, flew downward in ever decreasing circles. And I was thinking: 'For me! For me alone, for me!'

I went up to the cemetery. The stone was standing there already, covered with a grey cloth. A couple of men were working on a lintel, digging at the ground. One reminded me of Josef, the labourer from –dal. I said: 'You haven't had to move the coffin, have you?' And the false Josef grinned and said: 'Oh no, we're not going to disturb the Bishop's peace and quiet.'

And I was thinking: 'For me!'

At eleven o'clock I went to find Mikael. He was not at home. I went down for the 11.15, the 11.40 and the 11.56. More priests, more black-coats. Still about two hours to go. And I was getting nervous. What if he had tricked me? I went to The Ship. Nothing. I ran home, rushed upstairs, across the attic, pulled the door open. Mikael – no. Only the Angel, half buried in a piles of books that he was sorting through and putting in a clothes-basket. 'Help me carry these to the second-hand bookshop, would you?' he asked. 'I'm getting two hundred for them – half what I was – '

I rushed downstairs, ran along Slottsgatan and the main street; the square, Trädgårdsgatan, I rang, rang, rang the bell. 'Is Mikael home yet?' No.

'This is ridiculous,' I thought, and laughed at myself. The 1.05 arrived with more black-coats, but the 1.20 was free of them. I remembered that the meeting was to have opened at one o'clock. So my concern was premature –

And the train arrived. I went from carriage to carriage, from window to window. Nothing. It was a lie. He had lied. The carriages emptied. The conductor began shutting doors and gates. But there were other trains, of course. She had missed the train. Or else he had been lying. As simple as that.

Someone touched me on the shoulder. It was him, the sailor, the man in the oilskin. He was carrying a small case. He asked for directions to a hotel. I replied: 'What in the name of the God has that got to do with me?' Or perhaps something else. Because he said: 'No, that's too expensive.' We exchanged a few more words.

Then she arrived.

She found half a horseshoe; she put it in my pocket. And when we had climbed to the top of Prästberget, she found a few magpie's feathers under the tall pine-tree, and fastened them to my hat. But I did not know what I could find to give her. But in the end I found the very best thing possible. I clambered up into the pine and

Memoirs of a Dead Man

pulled down the magpie's nest. And when we looked through the twigs, I found a little silver ring. I put it on her finger, and now we were engaged.

From the hill we could see the Bishop's Palace and its garden. I pointed out the jasmine bush where we had looked for my shoe together. She maintained that I had kissed her, but I maintained that I had not kissed her until that time when we saw the rainbow in the park at –dal. We squabbled about that and got quite heated and almost had an argument. But we started laughing.

We went into the woods. There was snow on the ground.

Towards evening, as twilight was falling, I came to think about the approaching night. I said: 'Where are you going to sleep?' She took offence and said: 'Oh, why do we have to talk about that? I don't need to sleep. Early tomorrow morning I'll collect my bag from the station and go to our Aunts' and sleep all day.'

I suggested that she could sleep at Anna's. To begin with she was reluctant; nor did I try to persuade her. But after a while she said: 'Perhaps I could get a little food at Anna's?'

Then I realised that she had not had anything to eat. And we went down to the tavern; I went first to reconnoitre. I ordered all the food they had. And we ate. But when I came to pay, I did not have a penny on me. I wanted to leave Father's watch as a pledge, but she would not let me, and paid herself. 'You'll have to pay me back tomorrow,' she said, 'because now I don't have a penny either.' And we laughed.

When we went to fetch her bag from the station it was already too late. She said: 'Just look at that! My toilette! And my nightdress. Now I haven't got a nightdress!'

Tired as she was, she began to sob. I had no good idea of what we should do. We both sat thinking for a while in the waiting room, in very low spirits. But that was our only concern that day. And before we knew it, we were both laughing again.

Anna let us in; we had thought that she would be surprised, but Mikael had been there and booked a room for Léonie.

'And now I can make up the bed,' Anna said, but was so tired that she could hardly drag herself up the stairs. We sent her to bed, and I helped Léonie to make up Father's bed. I did so badly. And

I'm going to write – '

He picked up the pen again, dipped it, smoothed the paper, put his head to one side, screwed up his eyes. And wrote in large, uneven, halting letters: Johan Arnberg, the brig *Claire Aurore*.

He passed the book to me; I lay a sheet of blotting-paper over the writing, and shut the book.

I was woken by a noise, I was woken by someone on the stairs. My heart was pounding and for a moment I thought that was the sound I had heard. I could not move, could not open my eyes; but I could listen. And I heard steps on the stairs, belonging not to one but to several people. And I heard voices.

Finally I managed to sit up. I took Léonie's hand and put it back on the covers.

The voices fell silent, and the steps on the stairs stopped. I slid out of bed and crept over to the door. After a moment, they started talking again, first in a whisper, then louder. I recognised Hedda's voice, then Dr Rygell's. And two unfamiliar male voices. I thought: 'Who can save me now?' I ran over to the bed on tip-toe and began searching for my clothes. I dared not turn on the lamp. They were still moving on the staircase, which seemed so long that it must have been a real Jacob's Ladder. I heard Dr Rygell's voice again. I thought: 'Who can save me now?' I grabbed my clothes and quickly put them on.

And I thought:

'No, I don't want to. This can't happen. We haven't done anything wrong. We haven't hurt anyone.'

Then, from the other side of the room, I heard the sailor's voice. He said:

'What do you have to fear?'

'Hah,' I thought, 'what a foolish man. The whole town will fall on us, that's what. It's the shame of it all – '

And I thought: 'Who can save me now?'

He replied:

'You have nothing to fear.'

And I thought: 'It's a death sentence, it's the end. It's everything mortal dying. It's the disgrace. It's Léonie. It's everything.'

He replied:

'You have nothing to fear but your fear.'

I jumped up and tried to gather my thoughts. If I woke Léonie, perhaps we would still have time to hide, to escape through the window –

But they opened the door. The light shone in my eyes. I heard Rygell's triumphant roar. They came towards us, one by one. One by one, as though they wanted to torment me for ever. Eventually the Dean, my guardian, raised his great fist and struck me across the brow.

And in the end:

The next day, Sunday 13 March, the day before the Arnberg festivities, I left the Rygell household just as the cathedral bells were ringing for vespers. I had chosen the time with care. Amelie had gone to church, Norah, from what Mikael had told me, was with the old Countess. Léonie lay sick in the little room facing the yard, and Hulda, who was looking after her, would be no problem to me. Deaf and half-blind, she hardly knew what was going on. Besides, I had the keys.

I could do no other than what I was doing. I could not wish other than I wished. I had no choice. I must live, and I could not live among people whose trust I had betrayed. I was planning to run away, to go with Mikael and the Angel to Hamburg. There I would sign up as an ordinary seaman on some ship.

To get to The Dovecote I had to walk right across town. I took the back streets. I went past the garden gate of the Bishop's Palace, and the little house where Father and I had lived. I stopped for a moment by the parlour window. I could not see anything; the house was abandoned.

So, in order to have travelling money, and funds to set myself up, I had decided to take possession of the money which Grandfather had left me, and which would be mine when I came of age. The money was divided between a savings book (some four or five thousand), and four shares in A. O.'s bank. The book was of no use to me; but Mikael believed he could exchange the shares for cash. Their value on the stock exchange, about 1,600 at the time of Grandfather's death, had risen to 2,350. In total, almost ten thousand kronor. This sum belonged to Jan Arnberg, and no-one but Jan Arnberg. If this was theft, then I was stealing from myself.

And in the end:

When I came to the cathedral on Sunday 13 March, the day before the Arnberg festivities, the sailor approached me. The bells were ringing, the chancel windows were shining like three tall blue phosphorus flames in the darkness of the wall, and the crescent moon was hanging above the top of the roof, and there were a good many stars.

He put his hand on my shoulder, so that his finger tips were touching my neck.

I said: 'I have to get away from here. I have no other choice if I wish to live. I have to get away from here. You can't possibly understand what it means to have done what I have done. I can hardly understand it myself. All I know is that I have betrayed people who trusted me. And that, to me, is unbearable. I must get away, at any cost. Because I must.'

He replied: 'Think carefully, Jan. "Must" is a bad advisor.'

I could have said that if 'must' is a bad advisor, it is also often a very persuasive one.

But I could no longer feel his fingers on my neck.

And now I was there.

The Dovecote was in complete darkness. The hall door was open. This surprised me. I went into the drawing room and turned the lamp on. The leaf of the secretaire was folded down, all its drawers pulled open, the contents in a mess. On the table I found the grey envelope with my name and Grandfather's seal on it. But the large envelope with the book and the shares was not there; instead, a note fastened to the secretaire with a drawing-pin. I read:

The Misses Amelie and Norah Arnberg.

Dear cousins! Since my letter of yesterday has not had the desired effect, and since people will not leave an inoffensive man such as myself in peace, I must take certain measures. *For I must live.* In my capacity as the head of the family, I am herewith taking certain valuable documents into my possession. People have tried to force me to commit a dishonourable act. This will not succeed. I know how to defend myself. For I must live. At least for the great day, ladies! You understand. Au revoir! I shall defend my life and my honour with arms if necessary.

Your true and affectionate cousin
Otto Arnberg.

The sailor was reading the letter over my shoulder and I heard him laugh – that roguish, arrogant laugh I knew so well. He said: 'You see, Jan? Someone else who must live!'

I replied: 'Yes, "must"! He must live! And in order to live, he must have money. And since he could not get it anywhere else, he must try his luck here. Three musts, in other words. Bad advisors, maybe, but persuasive.'

Again, he laughed, and said:

'So you think, my dear Jan, that he took the money because he must live?'

I did not bother to reply, and walked away.

I set off for The Ship at a jog. Because I thought that the old man ought at least to share the money. (And I took some pleasure in the fact that it was he and not I who had committed the theft.)

When I arrived at the tavern, the courtyard was full of people. The innkeeper was standing in the door, blocking the way, but when I said who I was, he let me in. In the bar sat the old woman, the one with bare arms, her plait hanging like a whip over her red bodice. She was weeping. I asked what had happened. She said: 'See for yourself!' And pointed at the table.

There, under a sheet, lay Otto's great body. I lifted a corner of the sheet, but let go of it immediately. I looked around. The dark window-panes were shining with wide eyes, their whites shimmering like fish-bellies in an aquarium.

'When did it happen?' I asked. She replied:

'Feel him! He's hardly cold. The police cut him down quarter of an hour ago. They're sitting in there going through his papers.'

I thought for a moment. And, since the windows were all full of eyes, I kept quite calm and made sure my appearance did not reveal that I was scared.

He whispered in my ear: 'Well, Jan? What was it? "He must live?" Can you read the signs, Jan, or do you need more?'

And he smiled and said: 'Alas – more!'

I hurried to Mikael and told him what had happened. He and the Angel were putting the finishing touches to their packing. There was scarcely an hour before the night train left. Without letting himself be distracted, Mikael said:

'That's a shame, Roach. You'll have to stay, then.'

But now, when it dawned on me that I only had an hour left at my disposal, and that in that hour I had to find a means of salvation or be ruined, I lost all control. And I pleaded and begged him, ending up on my knees, to take me with him.

He allowed himself to be persuaded. In the end he embraced me and swore that would have taken me with him, whether I liked it or not –

We travelled to Copenhagen on the night train, and then on to Hamburg, where, after a few days, we split up. I went to sea.

As far as the Arnberg festivities were concerned, they passed off as worthily and as beautifully as anyone had hoped. To be sure, only the Dean and the lawyer were present from the Arnberg family, and neither he nor anyone else read out that long epic poem. But in the newspaper report of the festivities – I read it more than a year later – there stood not a word about Otto Arnberg's suicide. Perhaps they were sensitively holding back the news until the following day's edition. Bishop Julius was the only one who bore the name that day, and bore it with honour.

No, not quite the only one – because, in a little paragraph of three lines, it was announced that the former primary school teacher Anna Arnberg had passed away peacefully on the night between the twelfth and thirteenth. No biographical details, as was only natural.

The Bishop's commemorative speech in Julius Arnberg's

honour was printed in full. Even that was beautiful and worthy. And I was sure that it comforted the Bishop's doves in their manifold sorrows and anguish.

My grandfather's letter, the only thing Otto left me, consisted of only a few lines. These:

To my dear grandson Jan, whom I have not seen for so long, and shall never see again! It is probably the duty of an old priest and grandfather at this moment to gather and sort through all his experience and wisdom in order to find a pearl of wisdom for his grandson. But Jan, my wisdom, if it ever existed, is gone, and in my memory is only chaff, not grain. I only wish I could hold your hand in mine. And that I could forget that I have lived almost eighty years among people who have hated me and whom I have not been able to love, not been capable of loving. Yes, I should like to hold your hand and take you with me to the place where all is security, peace and silence. Where the human voice can no longer be heard, and where no human word is spoken or thought. But these are just the fantasies of a tired old man, my dear Jan. For you, life, and people, will be quite different. And I pray – although it will happen without my prayer – that you might soon forget your old grandfather

Julius Arnberg.

I kept his letter in my coat-pocket for a long time. But at some point it must have got soaked with water; the writing became illegible. So I tore it up and threw it away.

THE INHERITANCE AND THE PROMISE

> 'When now the boy learned that he was not of this world – '
> (From the family archive at Frönsafors.)

Chapter 1

Arnberg's Transatlantic

N. M. B. W. Nothing Must Be Wasted, that is a free but reasonable interpretation of Mr Hansen's motto, N. T. S. Nothing Too Small.

We also have M. M. L., meaning Man Must Live. *Oder Man Muss Lieben.*

After two years at sea I tired of the ocean, and one autumn decided to stay in Hamburg. You can call it jumping ship if you will. My conscience was untroubled by it. Hamburg is a good place, a springboard from one continent to another. I met Karl Rygell, who helped me find work in an office with Swedish connections. (Among others, with the firm of Arnfelt and Grundberg.) The work was monotonous; I soon tired of it. I spent a year and four months working for a German-American shipping company. That was where I got to know J. P. Fält, who at that time was not yet employed by HAPAG. I suggested getting into the scrap business with him; it came to nothing, and Fält lost a few hundred marks, but that was the beginning of our friendship. He took me with him to the Rossbacher Keller and introduced me to his friends Kugel, Steintheel, Rygell and the rest. And to Eline. (I seem to recall that Fält and Eline were engaged.) In moments of dire need he would advance small sums of money to me against promissory notes. On Sundays we would travel out to Cuxhaven and take a look at the docks, and criticise them. Large, but still too small. We were both foreigners but spoke of Hamburg as if it were our city. Our dreams travelled the seas, and when we returned to the canals we felt the warmth of a small, old and hard-working home. In which Eline was the housewife. I liked Fält a lot, a serious, calculating man in his forties.

He often spoke about my father. He had known him in America

and had admired him. He said:

'He was the most remarkable man I have ever met. A man of will-power, you see. Pure will-power. I'll tell you something. I had an excellent position over there. Then your father wrote and asked me to come over to Sweden. He was planning to start up a munitions factory, and he needed me. "No," I thought, and wrote and said no. After a few weeks I wrote another letter and explained the reason why I couldn't come. I received no answer, and in fact never heard from him again. But after several more weeks I wrote again, explaining myself and declining the offer. All in all I wrote five letters of refusal in six months. And no sooner had I posted the last of them than I went and resigned, sold my belongings and bought a ticket to Sweden. That was the sort of man your father was. But I when I arrived, he'd gone and – well, he'd died.'

He had admired my father, but the fact that he had died was something he would never forgive him for. I protested that it was hardly Father's fault. But he said:

'Well, that all depends on how you look at it. I imagine that if Johan Arnberg had really wanted to live then he would still be alive today. But I'm not complaining. I started a munitions factory myself at Remscheid. And that would have been a great success if I hadn't had a scoundrel for a partner. But I can still show you something that might amuse you.'

He pulled out a black, oblong metal box. On the lid was written in white letters:

Arnberg's Explosives
Hahn, Huhn & Company.
Remscheid   Hamburg

I opened the lid; the box contained fifty revolver cartridges. Fält giggled; his long, thin, yellow-brown face had settled into deep laughter-lines. He said:

'When you were a baby, Master Arnberg, I gave you a toy boat. Now you're a young man. Just wait a moment.'

From the breast-pocket of his jacket he pulled out a black case, opened it and took out a revolver. He had made it himself, and it was a fine piece of workmanship. On the butt my name was engraved: Jan Arnberg.

'Take it!' he said. 'It's yours. You must learn to shoot. A man with no weapon is like a bee with no sting. Man must defend himself. (M. M. D. H!) Even the good Lord Himself has to defend Himself. Against Satan.'

He was a versatile man, Fält, like most Americans. Chemist, mechanic, businessman. And a preacher as well – baptist or mormon or something like that. He had also made his way as a printer, waiter, guide and barber. In this last profession he was so proficient that I would entrust my chin to his razorblade whenever I wanted to look my best.

As far as the revolver was concerned, I thanked him and took it, carrying it on my person at all times in a special leather-lined pocket that I asked Eline to make.

Meanwhile, I fell in love with Eline Eikmeier. It happened all of a sudden. One evening we were sitting at our usual table; Kugel had been promoted that day and we were celebrating. We downed tankards of beer with a vengeance, smoked still worse, and talked a very great deal, and perhaps rather loudly. Old Pappa Eikmeier strode up to our table, solemn and not unlike a penguin with his curved black back, large white stomach and swinging flippers on either side of his belly. He bowed as well as he could, and asked us to be less noisy. I took offence, because it had actually been me doing most of the talking. In my agitation I managed to knock over several tankards.

'Eline!' Pappa Eikmeier called, from the depths of both his stomach and his authority, 'Eline! This needs cleaning up.'

And Eline, to whom I had not paid any attention at all up to that point – I did not even know that she was engaged to Fält – stood before me, head bowed in humility and with her busy, red, darting, lively hands guiding the cloth. She took a sidelong look at me, serious and thoughtful. Then it hit me, the way a wave hits the unprepared swimmer, picking me up violently only to drop me with dizzying speed, lashing my brow and filling my eyes and ears with stinging, hissing, singing foam. I quickly stood up, took my hat and left. But after a while I returned, soaked through by the Hamburg fog. I took her busy hands in mine and drew her away from the others. I told her that she was so tiny, tiny, tiny, that I could easily have put her in my pocket. I said I was a wolf and she a lamb, *weiss und weich*. I do not recall whether or not she replied; that was not really the point. I returned to my surprised friends, bestowing a deep bow on Pappa Eikmeier as I passed. My friends teased me and Fält warned me against strong liquor, saying:

'Your father had that particular bad habit. He drank far too much. It's in the family. Your great-uncle Leonard drank himself to death. He died in my arms; and it was awful. We were related, by the way. To put it bluntly, he was my father. But I am, of course, illegitimate, as they say.'

Eventually, when I remained silent and sat with my eyes following Eline, he got annoyed and said:

'Do you know what the prophet Hosea says in his fourth chapter, verse eleven? "Whoredom and wine and new wine take away the heart." That's what he says.'

And he went on to quote other prophets, because he was, as I said, also a preacher. But that evening I did not utter another word, quiet or noisy.

At the same time I began to construct my grand Transatlantic Project; a relatively quick line to America, intended exclusively for emigrants, with a democratic standard price for the transportation of people and with the present luxury tonnage exploited for mercantile ends. My Transatlantic would become a *Bon-Marché*, where the emigrant could be supplied with the equipment necessary for his future business by knowledgeable salesmen.

My project was comprehensive; it demanded my full attention. I quit the office. The work there had long seemed monotonous to me. It was, after all, only a small Elbe shipping company, without any possibility of development. Wasting time and energy on a company like that was ridiculous. Fält shared my view; he resigned as well and went to work for HAPAG. I told him, Kugel,

Memoirs of a Dead Man

Steintheel and a few others a little about my project.

My business would primarily work with living material. Offices would be set up in Canada, the States and in South America to help the emigrants find work and land. Our offices in Europe's larger cities would not content themselves with selling tickets. Their business would be to use carefully controlled amounts of credit to buy the emigrant. The capable, skillful, honourable man – he would be our material! Our raw material! The emigrant would be entered in the books, his physical, mental and social qualities would be tested, his skill at his trade would be evaluated, and his plans for the future would be influenced to take a suitable direction.

'Slave trade!' Rygell exclaimed. And there were those who laughed. But Fält expressed approval. Could there be any greater triumph just then than to have Fält listen and believe? The soberminded Fält! The miserly Fält, who kept an account of his thoughts and demanded a promissory note for a loan of ten marks! I felt I was on solid ground. I told Eline at once that I was now on solid ground –

Furthermore – as soon as the emigrant signed the contract for his ticket in Europe, our apparatus across the ocean would whirr into motion to help this specific individual to find the plot of land or the machinery or the spiritual or physical work that would be right and rewarding for him. As soon as he set foot on deck, he would be our man, and his future would lie before him as firmly fixed as a railway track. Once he had been assessed and deemed suitable, we had no intention of letting him go. We would bind him with elastic credit, in direct proportion to his development capacity. Bind him with help. (B. W. H.) Farmer or factory worker, tradesman or journalist, he would be a footsoldier in our army of agents. And whatever advertisement, whatever massproduced item, whatever social or political truth we saw fit to throw to the New World would be taken from home to home, from the Atlantic to the Pacific, from the North to the South Pole, by this secret, unstoppable army.

'Slave trade!' Rygell exclaimed.

This was the outline of my project. As you can see, three

cornerstones. 1) A floating *Bon-Marché*, which would suck up and administer the emigrant's capital, 2) the employment agency, which would suck up and direct his labour, and 3) the mass agency, which would organise part of this workforce for our specific aims.

The fourth cornerstone, working capital, was absent thus far. But there was no reason why this should delay work on the details of the plan. One fine day I would find the fourth cornerstone – and was I supposed to stand there like some lazy toad with an unfinished plan? I worked like a slave, day and night, mostly at night. I bought a neat, strong briefcase with a patent lock in which I kept my calculations. I never left my room without the briefcase under my arm. Wherever I sat down, I would open it and start work with one red and one blue pen. Once Kugel managed to splash beer on my papers. He could not have insulted me more deeply. I reverted to the primitive habits of boyhood and gave him a beating. Pappa Eikmeier had to broker a truce –

I worked so hard that my health suffered. I grew thin and pale, my back became bent, and I developed a cough. My clothes were in a terrible state. Fält was critical of my slovenly appearance and reminded me that my father had always been impeccably dressed. But that did not worry me. Fripperies! In any case, Eline removed the worst stains every Saturday evening with benzine and turpentine. Fripperies! If I ever took a walk along the Jungfernstieg or around the Alster, I was not the least embarrassed to unbutton my coat like the other bucks and show my waistcoat and trousers, which were in a dreadful state. Fripperies! On one such occasion I encountered an exceedingly elegant car. It was a beautiful Sunday and there were a lot of people about. The car slowed down, and then stopped. In the back-seat sat a very beautiful woman, and at the wheel a dandy. And who was that? Mikael Arnfelt, my friend and comrade in misfortune, Sonja's brother-in-law, if I may express myself so loosely. 'Aha,' I thought, 'the fop probably won't even recognise me.' But I was wrong; he raised his eyebrows, smiled, nodded, even held out his hand. I waved, raised my hat out of politeness to the lady, and walked on.

But my favourite place was beside Eline's sewing-table in the tap-room. There I found peace, that was the best place to work. Especially as she would often stand behind me with her warm little paw on my shoulder, next to my cheek. Sometimes she would blow in my ear to make me look up. Then I would have to interrupt my work.

One day I received a letter containing 200 marks from my benefactor, Dean Rygelius. Had the sum been larger I could have paid off my debts to Fält. As it was, it still came in useful. It was Eline's nineteenth birthday! I decided to hold a party at the Two Hares, down by the bank of the Elbe. The lads were all invited, and Pappa Eikmeier. Rygell thought the old man should be excluded for being altogether too fat and troublesome. But I said: 'Of course he must come! And anyone not wanting his company can stay at home!'

Because I was angry. Was I to invite Eline to join a company of young men without a chaperone? That might have suited lesser gentlemen who kept mistresses. I for my part intended to marry Eline, and in all propriety. I had already picked out the villa by the Alster where we would live. And I had given some thought to the two Siberian dogs she would have. And I had christened our son and elevated him to the nobility, and our grandson to a dukedom. I could go no further if I intended to stick to the realm of the plausible.

On the morning of the sixth of May we set off. We made slow progress, because Pappa Eikmeier was fat and unsteady, the boys were constantly picking flowers for Eline, and Eline and I kept leaping across a ditch until in the end we fell into each other's arms. And Pappa Eikmeier would grunt at regular intervals:

'*Kinder, aber Kinder!* This needs cleaning up.'

For the state of the road was appalling; it had been raining for a month. But not that day! Now I remember – Mikael was with us as well. He was the only one of the men not to roll up his trousers to the knee. What did a pair of trousers matter to him? He was courteous and charming, but Eline did not like him. The boys, on the other hand, were enchanted; and when they found out that he really was a duke there was an unending stream of 'your Lordships' and 'your Graces'. Worst was Fält, the American, of course. Once we had drunk a few bottles of wine, Pappa Eikmeier pointed at Eline and me and said:

'Your Lordship, those two are engaged!'

Mikael put his head to one side, smiled, and said:

'I congratulate my old friend on having such an enchanting fiancée.'

I replied:

'Thank you. But it's really no concern of yours.'

Because I could see that all of this was tormenting poor Fält. But apart from that the party was a success. Pappa Eikmeier defamed the landlord of the Two Hares as mercilessly and factually as only a rival could. Mikael and the boys played skittles. Eline and I took care of ourselves.

Eventually we drove home by charabanc. Pappa Eikmeier was so big that there was room for only Mikael beside him. Eline had to sit on my lap up on the driver's seat. Every so often she would turn to look at her father. He was reclining with his stomach in the air, splendidly plump with food and Rhenish wine. Now and then a large gilded button would fly from his waistcoat, arcing like a falling star. And the street-urchins following us would pick up the buttons and cheer. A proper procession! By the end Eline was tired and cold, and had crept inside my coat to fall asleep.

That was the sixth of May, 1912, about a month before my first meeting with Mr Hansen.

One day, while I was busy working on my Transatlantic Project, it suddenly dawned on me that to all intents and purposes I lacked the means to support myself. I could expect nothing from Sweden, and my purse contained four silver marks, a five-mark note, and a little small change. The matter was made worse by the fact that I had already made extensive use of my friends' helpfulness. I owed Fält more than eight hundred marks, and his claim was supported by the necessary documentation. And Pappa Eikmeier had been giving me food on credit for two or three months. I even owed money to my landlady.

Thus there was good reason to devote some attention to this minor but immediate problem. I decided to spend my last note on a advertisement in H. N. N. It would run twice, two days apart, and read as follows:

Young Swede
seeks t e m p o r a r y well-remunerated employment.

A successful composition, succinct and to the point. The word 'temporary' was spaced out as I obviously did not wish to commit myself to any trivial occupation for any length of time.

Fält, however, maintained that it was a poor advertisement. His unbearable condescension irritated me. I had not attached much significance to this attempt until then, but was now forced to do so. Success became a point of honour. I stayed in my room all day to make sure I did not miss any visitors. But none came; the attic stairs did not creak once. In spite of this I was certainly not bored, nor did I feel hungry. I lay on the bed commanding my transatlantic army.

On the fifth day I went to the Rossbacher Keller, where I met Fält on his own with Eline. I asked him for a loan, I wanted to run the advertisement again. He immediately wrote out a promissory note for twenty marks, but insisted on drafting the advertisement himself. He maintained that I was in dire straits and that this should be hinted at in the advertisement. What a fool! But I controlled myself and merely said that from that moment on I considered all ties between us broken as a result of his incredible pettiness. This upset him. I went in to Eline; when she saw me thin, pale and dishevelled, she burst into tears. This provoked me. I went out to Fält once more and demanded that he give me fifty marks. Against a promissory note, naturally. At that moment it struck me that the advertisement had lacked a certain critical something. It had not been imperative enough.

What had been lacking in the advertisement were the words 'without delay'. Give me the money, Shylock, ten per cent and my head as the stake.

It was a quarter to five, quarter of hour to place the advertisement. I took a cab and was standing in the office by two minutes to five. A greyish woman, her hat and coat already on, refused to accept the advertisement. Her watch said it was already five. But I showed her my watch and told her that my father had given it to me on his deathbed, and that under such circumstances one would not give one's son an unreliable watch. She certainly appreciated that, and relented.

The advertisement took the following form:

Young Swede
seeks t e m p o r a r y well-remunerated employment
w i t h o u t d e l a y.

I thought it excellent, vigorous but polite, without being obsequious.

The following morning I received a visit from Mr Hansen, he tumbled over on the stairs, where a couple of steps were missing, so I leapt out of bed to give him a helping hand. He did not let go of it until I had hauled him up from the darkness. He said:

'A colossally poor staircase, scarcely usable. My name is Hansen, of Hahn, Huhn & Co. Yes, I am Mr Hansen himself. That must please you, because I am a genuine Scandinavian. You know of Hahn, Huhn & Co., of course – the large employment bureau? It's a witty name, I wouldn't sell it for a hundred thousand marks. It's not the sort of witticism that makes people laugh out loud, oh no. But you feel it, you get the sense that there's something behind it, the hand of fate, so to speak. Your esteemed advertisement of 6/6 was noted, but in today's newspaper we see that you are seeking employment without delay. A very good phrase, that, without delay, very good. Now let's see – '

He moved my clothes aside and sat down on the chair. When he came in he had already had in his hand a Leporello list of hectographed addresses. And as I slowly finished dressing, he reeled off a list of names half-audibly. Eventually he said:

'I stumbled over your extremely poor staircase. One might see that as a coincidence, but perhaps it was something more. Because look here – I tore a hole in this sheet. Might this not be the hand of fate? Let's see. Madame de Montsousonge, St. George, Hôtel de Montsousonge, one footman, one parlour-maid, one secretary, one reader. This last post would be the one, I think – ?'

He looked me up and down thoughtfully.

'I shall now give you some information which cannot but please you. Our firm has the best reputation of such companies in Hamburg. Our methods are necessarily extremely sensitive, since flesh and blood are our raw materials. Our goal is to find everyone the job that really suits them. We examine and take into account each and every one of our clients' capabilities. Our fee is 10% of the first month's wages. Colossally cheap, wouldn't you say? But our primary motivation is best expressed in our renowned and respected motto: *Nothing Too Small*.'

I found his words rather offensive, and said:

'If you would keep quiet for a moment, I should like to ask if you have already assessed and evaluated my capabilities?'

To which he replied, with incredible impudence:

'I have. Documents such as your two esteemed advertisements of 6/6 and 12/6 reveal a number of things. *Nota bene* – to the seasoned professional. It is possible that I may have to complement my knowledge of your resources. But that can come later. We never let our clients out of our sight. It's one of our main business principles – C. C. C., Chase, Capture, Contain. Of course, it's only a slogan. Regarding Madame de Montsousonge of St. George, I know her colossally well. I have provided her with a colossal number of staff, including numerous Swedes. I have great respect for Swedes. They – or should I say "we" – think big, sir, sometimes altogether too big. But this does command respect and goodwill.'

I indicated that Mr Hansen's respect or lack thereof was of little import to me. But he went on:

'Sooner or later, all my clients learn to appreciate me. Madame de Montsousonge too. She is a lady of the very finest quality, young, beautiful, educated, talented. She is the widow of a man who died. You see! That fact alone! There are many, many widows, a colossal number, but I should say that a first-class widow is one whose husband is authentically dead. Monsieur Montsousonge was, just between the two of us, a rogue. Farmed rubber and negroes in the Congo. It's colossally sad to have to say it, but that's the way of it. And so now he is authentically dead. However, her aged mother is still alive. And it is colossally touching to see the tenderness and care she lavishes on her mother, Mrs Feurfield.'

Mr Hansen's face, however, showed no sign of being touched, and his rusty hoarse voice remained the same. I gave him to understand that the qualities of the Montsousonge family interested me far less than the remuneration I would receive. Mr Hansen consulted his list.

'Your wage will be one hundred marks a month, which cannot be said to be much. But I would ask you to consider a couple of things. Madame de Montsousonge runs a large household. You can eat all of your meals at her table without any special invitation. Moreover, you could take up residence in the Hôtel without hesitation. There are plenty of rooms. By doing so you would save at least one hundred and fifty marks a month, which could be used for – well, for whatever you like.'

He cast a quick glance at my attire, which was now complete. And it must be admitted that I could not be counted among Hamburg's more elegant citizens.

'Good,' I said. 'What about my duties?'

We were sitting opposite one another; I on the table by the window and he on the chair. Mr Hansen has no neck at all, his head is sunken and screwed into his shoulders. To avoid my gaze he had to turn the whole of his round, swollen trunk a full ninety degrees. I watched him intently. Because I imagined I could discern certain signs of unease and embarrassment in his behaviour. And now I could make out a faint red glow beneath the corpse-blue skin of his face.

'Your duties,' he said hurriedly, 'will probably not be exacting. But at this moment I cannot be more specific about them. Madame de Montsousonge is a lady who plays an extensive rôle in society. By that I do not mean the society specific to Hamburg, but rather the international *grand monde*. You understand. Her house is a focal point for a number of distinguished foreigners. Of varying qualities, of course, but all of value. It is a question of neither over nor underestimating this value. Perhaps – and I say perhaps – it will be your duty to assist her with this in some way. In any case, you will doubtless receive full instructions. And now – '

He stood up, delved about in the pockets of his waistcoat, and pulled out a card.

'I have the honour of giving you Madame de Montsousonge's address.'

I said:

'Fine, but I haven't decided – '

Mr Hansen stood up, put the Leporello list in his pocket, buttoned his coat, pulled on a pair of dirty yellow gloves, all with exasperating slowness. I turned, thumbing the card: for some reason I felt timid. Mr Hansen performed a measured bow. I bowed. I was thinking of saying that I would contact him or something similar; but I could not utter a sound. Mr Hansen hypnotised me: Mr Hansen's corpse-blue, round, swollen, unpleasant face hypnotised me. I could have gone up to him and kissed him, or spat at him, it would have made no difference, because I was powerless. – Fortunately I remained where I was, merely bowing now and then. And he bowed in turn –

Eventually I noticed that Mr Hansen's gloved right hand was resting on the arm of the chair, palm uppermost. Its fingers in the air like a dung-beetle on its back. And the fingers were performing an almost imperceptible grasping motion. I understood and became thoroughly confused and diffident. I pulled out my purse and searched through all its pockets. Eventually I managed to scrape together ten marks in silver and nickel – 10% of my first month's wages. I handed them to him.

Mr Hansen smiled and said:

'You must by no means imagine that I would refuse you credit for ten measly marks. On the contrary, it is always a pleasure to be of assistance. But this is an assurance that you really have accepted the post. And now – '

His face suddenly assumed an expression of saccharine familiarity which made me put my hands behind my back.

'Now that these formalities have been dealt with, you must permit me one question. How is your dear sister? I believe her name is Anna – '

'Aha,' I thought. Only then did it dawn on me that he was that Hansen, Anna's Hansen. I replied curtly that she was dead. He gestured to his chest with his hat. I nodded. But I cannot comprehend how I could stand there talking to that man about my sister. Even if it was only in sign language –

He gave a deep sigh; then he stretched out his hand to me, and I took it. He said:

'If you would care to visit me at my office, it would please me colossally. I was fond of your father, and I loved your sister. But enough said. You may have absolute confidence in me. – '

He put his hat to his chest again and bowed.

I was walking towards the HAPAG building when I bumped into Fält and Rygell coming the other way at the corner of Dammthorstrasse and Gänsemarkt. The Angel pretended not to see me and trod heavily on my toes and, feigning indignant surprise, exclaimed:

'Oh, so it's you, is it?'

Upon which he took a firm grip of my coat-collar and, in front of everyone in the Botanical Gardens, dragged me off, screaming:

'No nonsense, sir! You're the very man we've been looking for. Come along quietly with us to the police station.'

I laughed and put up a struggle. A crowd was gathering. Steintheel ran up with his notebook in his hand. A couple of constables got mixed up in it all –

Finally we settled down on a bench. And the Angel said:

'Well, sir, is it still your intention to break all contact with J. P. Fält esquire?'

I said: 'What in God's name is going on?'

Whereupon the Angel embraced me and cried out:

'Your future is made, my boy. Hurrah!'

The idiots! And Fält began, in his long-winded way:

'It's obvious, Jan Arnberg, that friendship carries with it certain obligations. It is as important to help one's friends as to help oneself. We have come to understand that we must do something to help you. Well, sir. J. P. Fält has made a modest attempt. He has obtained for you a temporary position as a copy-writer at HAPAG.'

Tel bruit –

I said nothing. He went on:

'The wage is not large, eight Taler a week. But it's a start. Isn't that right, Rygell, it's a start – '

I said nothing. He repeated:

'It's a start. And you'll be working under me. I'll decide your hours. And I guarantee you six hours a day for day-dreaming and speculation.'

Ha! Was that how it was now? Day-dreams and speculation? But I said nothing. And he repeated impatiently:

'You do understand, don't you, Arnberg? It's not much, but it's a start. And you don't even have to thank me. I'm doing it as much for Eline's sake as for yours – '

I said – quite calmly – :

'So you think I should pin my future on HAPAG?'

All three of them started at me. Astonished. The Angel blushed like a young girl. Steintheel turned away, put the notebook in his pocket and walked off. Fält leaned over so far that his thin neck was at the same level as his knobbly knees.

'But of course,' he said, 'you were thinking of setting up in competition with HAPAG. I had almost forgotten that. But it'll be a good twenty-five years before you get your outfit up and running. And what could be more advantageous than having fought for the enemy – '

Hypocrite. Plain and simple. I determined to get to the bottom of the matter. I asked them politely but firmly to divulge their honest opinions of my Transatlantic Project.

The Angel shrugged, stood up and walked off.

Fält said:

'Honest?'

Then he too stood up and walked off, shaking his head. But after a few steps he turned round and came back.

'Jan Arnberg,' he said, sitting down beside me. 'There's one thing I will say to you. The idea of a floating *Bon-Marché* is not entirely without merit. If the scheme has any real value in and of itself, I don't know. But I believe that you could use it as a bluff. For instance: you work with two or three hundred lads and you're as alike as berries. One day you go to the head of department and outline your plan. He laughs and tells you to go to hell. Well, sir. But another day there'll be a question of promotion. One of the two hundred berries is to be separated from the others and put on the next shelf up. But which one? They're all the same. Then a faint memory surfaces in the boss's tired mind. "That lad Fält," he thinks, "he's got a brain. He's alert, he's got a brain, he's got ideas. Why not take him?" And so the project might be worth a monthly increase of three hundred marks – '

And thus he revealed himself. As a spectacle, it was priceless to hear his unconscious confession. He had revealed his own wretchedness by replacing my name with his. And demonstrated plain and simple that he intended to steal, or perhaps had already stolen, my project in order to gain advantage for himself. And what a feeble advantage! Three hundred marks. And so the gold of the fairy tale is transformed into rotting leaves –

However I contained myself completely and said politely but firmly that I would ask him to spare me his goodwill in future. He should keep his copy-writing jobs for his friends, amongst whom I did not wish to count myself. If I needed employment, then I would find it myself. And that was precisely what I had done.

He swallowed his anger and began to ask me questions. And when he heard that Mr Hansen of Hahn, Huhn & Co. had secured the position for me, he warned me that the same Mr Hansen had once been his partner.

I put in:

'Just because he was once your partner doesn't necessarily mean that he's a rogue. He has at least found me a decent, well-paid job.'

He retorted:

'Then perhaps the time has come for you to settle our account.'

And he tapped his breast pocket. I said:

'Your wish is granted. There are certain people to whom one would rather not be in debt.'

I wandered about aimlessly. I went to the Haupt-Bahnhof and strolled up and down the platform for a while. I read the signs indicating the trains' destinations as they were put up. I thought about buying a ticket to Malmö or Stockholm. Or to W.

But I had no money. I was hungry, but did not have enough to buy a meal. A tankard of dark ale was all I could afford. I happened to walk into the Catholic church. I sat down in a pew and fell asleep. Some time later I was woken by two young priests. They took me under the arms and led me carefully but resolutely towards the exit. I apologised and they smiled; not, however, towards me, but each other.

I was, in actual fact, at a complete loss.

On the one hand: gaining a foothold, however small, within HAPAG – and on the other: committing myself –

But of course it did not mean committing myself.

And why had I insulted Fält? Meaningless.

Moreover: Hansen and his widow? Dubious.

Finally: my project. So what I had shared with my friends they had secretly been laughing at, or using for the feeblest of motives. Such disloyalty is neither meaningless nor dubious. It is low.

I read the address on Mr Hansen's card and set off. To begin with, I wanted to have a look at the house. If I found it appealing, that might be as good a sign as any. That I ought to go in.

But I did not find it appealing. I had been expecting an Alster villa, and found something more like a warehouse. If the house had not been surrounded by a well-tended garden and enclosed by wrought-iron railings, I would have taken it to be a warehouse for short-term storage. The thick, cold, blue-grey stucco reminded me of Mr Hansen's unpleasant face.

For an hour or more – dusk was falling – I wandered around Madame de Montsousonge's property, which made up half of a small block. If the house did not quite resemble a warehouse, it looked like a prison or a hospital or a school for delinquents. And the windows were equipped with bars. The stable-door was open, a horse whinnied, a man walked across the yard, a lantern in his hand. Otherwise I saw no sign of life.

A job at HAPAG was something tangible, something which would please Eline and dazzle Pappa Eikmeier.

A job with Madame de Montsousonge, on the other hand –

I stopped by the gate. It was almost dark. I took a couple of steps into the garden. Then someone took a firm grip of my right wrist, and a tall, dark figure stepped right up to me. It was the gatekeeper. Presumably. I thought: 'Now I'll be taken as a burglar – '

He asked: 'What do you want?'

In my confusion I replied:

'That's precisely what I don't know.'

And I pulled free.

HAPAG or Montsousonge? The question was more a matter for Eline than me. Because it was merely a question of immediate advantage, of what was right for the moment. Fripperies! My future was not at stake. I was the person who needed to decide that, and I had already done so. My will was to realise my project. And that was as unshakeable as Father's will to realise his project. It did not matter that I might fail. The will itself was the important thing, a strong will, unflinching in the face of passing fancies, transitory needs, transitory desires.

HAPAG or Montsousonge – Eline could decide. It would please her to be entrusted with the decision. It would show how much I liked her.

I went off to the Rossbacher Keller. It was half past nine, but the boys had not yet appeared; the room was almost empty. Pappa Eikmeier was leaning on the bar, asleep. Eline was sitting in the taproom spelling her way through a Swedish newspaper. She waved me over.

'Come and look at this!' she cried. 'Come and look at this!'

I leaned over her; she searched the columns, but when she felt my breath on her cheek she stopped. I took her index-finger and moved it up and down the columns.

Memoirs of a Dead Man

And as we looked, my eyes fixed upon an announcement. Married. Mikael Arnfelt and Léonie Arnberg, Hamburg, W. –

I pretended not to see it; but that was precisely what she had wanted to show me. She asked: 'Isn't that your friend?'

I replied:

'That's my cousin.'

And I started to tell her about Léonie. But I broke off and said: 'What about us? When are we going to get married?'

She threw her arms round my neck and pulled me down to her. But that was not the reason for my visit, which was to make a decision in a serious yet rather trivial matter. We discussed it. Pappa Eikmeier came in, and all three of us discussed it. He said:

'HAPAG – now there's a job with prospects. For God's sake, Herr Arnberg, think of Eline! HAPAG – now there's a job with prospects.'

'Then we'll take HAPAG,' I said, and the matter seemed to have been settled.

At about ten o'clock the boys arrived. The wind had got up and doors and window-shutters were banging. I went out into the saloon and announced that I had decided on HAPAG. They began to cheer (they did this whenever they had the chance, appropriate or not), they carried me in their arms and demanded I buy everyone a drink. This I did. Steintheel, the journalist, told us what he knew of Madame de Montsousonge. She occasionally appeared in the society columns. She received visits from remarkable tourists. A dollar-king had once been her guest.

'But – but – ' he concluded, wrinkling his nose, 'there's something fishy – '

I said:

'You understand, lads, that if I had been considering that job, then I had my reasons. I have, as you know, plans for the future. You may laugh at them, but I intend to realise them. Sooner or later. What I lack is any contact with capital. Not all roads lead to Rome, but some of them do. And this could have been one of them. But HAPAG is, of course, more secure. For the moment. And one must live. Especially if one is thinking of getting married – '

They started cheering again for me and Eline, they drank and laughed. It was a noisy evening. Mostly because of the wind outside. As soon as a door was opened, the tablecloths billowed from the tables, glasses were smashed, shutters slammed. All of this simultaneously unsettled and encouraged me. Eline said:

'Calm yourself – calm yourself – '

A thought occurred to me: presumably Mikael had told Léonie that I was engaged.

'Calm yourself,' Eline pleaded.

In order to calm the lads down, I took out the cards. We played, and I won. Rygell was sitting opposite me. I asked:

'Have you heard that Mikael's got married?'

He was caught up in the game. 'It's none of my business,' he said. After a while he asked: 'What was that you said? Who's he married?'

But I pretended not to hear. I already had the information I needed. Rygell, who had friends in W., ought to have heard about the engagement or the plans for the wedding if they were long-standing. Mikael had left Hamburg on 7 May, the day after the party at the Two Hares. And it was now 12 June.

In the meantime I was winning a considerable sum, more than two hundred marks. We were all excited, and I became a little hot-headed. Eline called across the room: 'Please, Jan! Calm down!' This irritated me. I said:

'I have no reason not to be calm, and I am absolutely and completely calm. Anyone who suggests otherwise is lying.'

'What's got into you?' Rygell asked. 'Why did you say that? She's crying – '

And he got up from the table; but I said: 'I can't help that.'

I dealt, we played, I won. Just as I was raking in my winnings, there was another burst of banging and crashing. (It had been quiet for a while and I had begun to calm down.) The cards blew across the floor, a tankard was upset, a glass was smashed. It was Fält who had opened the door on the storm. He looked as though he had been in a fight. His coat was dishevelled and his hat was battered – it must have blown off. The boys invited him to sit down, but he came and stood in front of me and asked in a loud voice:

'Arnberg, tell me truthfully – why have you accepted the job?'

I replied:

'Because it amuses me.'

But at that very moment a thought struck me, making me absolutely furious. Who was in a position to force me to accept either of these jobs? Who was forcing me to commit myself to either of these paltry occupations? Was it not J. P. Fält himself? With his eight hundred marks, his wretched promissory notes!

I said:

'I shall take whatever bloody job I please to be free of your extortion. Hypocrite! First you steal my project to gain a feeble advantage – '

I felt someone tug at my coat-tail, jerking and twitching like a fish on a hook. It was Eline. Pappa Eikmeier padded over to us. Steintheel leaned back and stared at us, wide-eyed. Little Kugel cowered like a rat –

Rygell said:

'But this is all a misunderstanding. The matter's settled. He's decided on HAPAG.'

But I interrupted him.

I said:

'How do you know it's settled? Am I supposed to commit myself to a halfwit's job just because Mr J. P. Fält has lent me eight hundred marks?'

Fält walked up to the table; he unbuttoned his coat and took out some sheets of paper that I easily recognised. My promissory notes.

'Look,' he said, 'this is what you owe me. Eight hundred and forty marks. I never had any intention of using your I.O.U.s, but this morning I happened to let slip a remark that could be taken as meaning that I did intend to use them. And so now – '

He tore up the whole bundle and threw the fragments onto the table. He said:

'Now you're all witnesses to the fact that I'm not the one driving him into Mr Hansen's arms.'

'Hansen? Hansen?' Steintheel cried, and breathlessly began

telling a story about Mr Hansen. But I pushed him aside and walked up to Fält.

'Why did you do that?' I asked, pointing at the I.O.U.s. He replied:

'If I'm not doing it for your sake, then perhaps I'm doing it for Eline's.'

I saw right through him then, as though he were made of the clearest crystal. Yes, I saw his heart.

And I said:

'So it's a way of winning back Eline. Don't trouble yourself, dear friend. It would have been more honest to cut my throat. I understand you completely. I've taken Eline away from you. And one must have one's revenge, isn't that so? It's almost the only thing one really must have. Dear friend, if only you knew how well I understand you – '

And I sat down at the table and started to count my winnings. One by one they left the inn. I heard the door slam, and every time the wind hit me in the face. In the end I was alone with Eline. She asked what was going to happen now. I replied:

'Dear child. It doesn't matter.'

She sat down at the table right next to me. She caressed my hair and forehead. Eventually she asked:

'Don't I matter to you either?'

I was tired and lay my head on her lap. I told her about Léonie. Half the night passed. The storm subsided and I started to feel calmer. Half the night passed, but I did not tire of telling her. Eline listened; perhaps she did not listen. She caressed me, and did not tire of caressing me.

Chapter 2

The Hôtel de Montsousonge

Father Johannes, the gatekeeper of the Hôtel de Montsousonge, has a motto that I have appropriated. Better a live dog than a dead lion. And if I have not adopted this motto, then it has adopted me.

In the Hôtel de Montsousonge I am a dog, or the equivalent of a dog. I have all the duties of a dog, and some of its privileges. It is my task to stand guard and observe. I must distinguish between the friends and enemies of the house by their smell, or by whatever means I choose, as long as it is not by their words or deeds. Because in words and deeds they are all alike. Uniform. I can be present for hours without anyone noticing me. And suddenly I become the focal point of everyone's gaze, people talk to me, praise me, have me perform tricks. I have lost my name, my family name. I am merely Jan. A nice short name for a dog.

When people talk to me, I have to guess rather than understand, much as a dog does. It is not difficult. The words are many, the thoughts few. A young woman talks to me, and I understand at once that it is a question of the simplest of my tricks: fetching and retrieving. For instance, I might have to carry a small note from one place to another, from one person to another. A nice trick, but one of the basics of the canine repertoire. Sometimes it is made more difficult by some slight twist that demands a little ingenuity to work out. I am not rewarded with sugar-lumps, but with pieces of gold, and they are not placed on my nose but slid into my pocket unnoticed. Because people have got the impression that I am a sensitive dog.

For a while I thought that traffic in letters was the speciality of the house, indeed, its very purpose. But no. It is not in the Hôtel de Montsousonge that Cupid celebrates his triumphs. Those men who seek their mistresses in the entresol of the grey house, and those women who allow themselves to be sought there, have long since ceased to regard love as a triumph. It is merely a habit that that they have not found a reason to give up. It is an exercise, a system, an arcanum with which to retain their youth and happiness. Do people believe in this? No. But people do not believe in anything else instead.

Mrs Feurfield reigns supreme in the entresol. It is in her stern presence that glances are exchanged, words muttered, whispers breathed, letters slid from hand to hand. If she did not exist, then nor would the game. She has the head of a vulture, the eyes of a vulture, the beak of a vulture. I presume that she also has the claws of a vulture, although she seldom shows them. The doves that flock around the Hôtel de Montsousonge have chosen the vulture as the guardian of tradition. She inhabits her rôle as a strict *grande dame* of puritanical Anglo-Saxon blood. There is not a single paragraph in the strictest codex of respectability of which she is unaware. Any dove that allows itself to be caught she will seize, claw, brand, tear away the feathered disguise of innocence and reveal the bleeding flesh. Once or twice a year there is a great scandal in the entresol. There is no need for them more often than this. This engenders sufficient tension. And it is the game that gives love its spice. In the Hôtel de Montsousonge.

But when a man whispers: 'Jan, dear Jan – ' and then draws me aside, smiling or – if he can no longer smile – with his lips pulled back, and speaks to me in short, breathless sentences or in long, serpentine sentences, then I know that what he requires of me is a more complex trick. Not the pup conveying caresses, but the bloodhound who must sniff out its prey.

People play in the Hôtel de Montsousonge. In two senses. Every Thursday at 10 pm music is played in the white salon. At the same time the lamps are lit in the round chamber two floors up. This is a large, cold room without windows. And this is where the card-tables are. Why playing strings and playing for gold should be combined, I do not know. Presumably the former is supposed to explain why the whole of St. George resounds all evening with the sound of car horns and horses' hooves. Perhaps the sound of strings eggs them on.

My task is not easy, and it is significant. The survival of the Hôtel de Montsousonge depends upon none but gamblers finding their way from one playing-room to the other. I have to read people's eyes. And when I imagine that I have read correctly, I have to utter a few words. And when I imagine that the words have fallen on fertile ground, I have to wait patiently for them to germinate and take root, to grow and mature until they are ripe. For I am also a sower of seed.

But I am also a bloodhound. Because our clients, the regulars, come to us neither to win nor to lose. They come to hunt. And not every man in patent-leather shoes is suitable prey. It is neither the quality of his attire nor that of his wallet that makes him suitable prey. It is his body and soul, his blood and bile, his heart and head, the stamina of his will, the speed of his thought, his strength of feeling. He must be a worthy opponent. That is what makes the game a pleasure. In order to satisfy our clients, the regulars, and to provide them with this sort of prey, I have to summon forth all my powers of deduction, divulgence, discovery and entrapment. I have made this art my own, and take pleasure in it.

At the same time I have to fulfil my duties as a watchdog. As I climb the spiral staircase that links the white salon to the gaming room, with that evening's unfamiliar guest close on my heels, I have to deliberate and evaluate with care. I must examine my words and his in my mind, I must conjure up his appearance, his face, expression, glances. When did he understand and how did he understand? Is he a player, or can he become a player? The indifferent are dangerous. And there is an even greater danger. He might be a spy, a police agent.

The staircase lies in pitch blackness; it has forty-eight steps, and I hesitate on each and every one. Sometimes he gets impatient, the man following me. 'Hurry up!' he whispers. Ah, my dear sir, if you only knew how much I have to think about! And what I am thinking about.

Should I actually come to the conclusion that he is a spy,

Maurette has given me orders to make short work of him. To that end she has provided me with a little knife, no larger than a penknife, but with excellent qualities. I have told her: 'No, I won't do that. Thus far and no further.'

She laughs and says:

'My poor Jan, don't you know that there are only two things worth experiencing? Killing, and dying. Why deny yourself one of them?'

She always says 'poor Jan'. Well, it's a good term of endearment for a dog. But I could reply with words from the Bible – and from Father Johannes – :

'Thou hast a name that thou livest, and art dead.'

My beautiful mistress, Maurette de Montsousonge.

For a while – two years in total – I lived in the belief that the round salon was the core of the Hôtel de Montsousonge, the card-tables the seeds of this fair fruit.

The gaming room was for me at least the most rewarding. In the entresol the coins fell as rarely as stars from the heavens. In the round room my takings in a single night could exceed a thousand marks. But it surprised me that, of all the gold changing hands at the tables, none seemed to go to the mistress of the house. It was always one of the guests who held the bank, and neither Madame de Montsousonge nor her mother would ever show themselves in the gaming room.

But who would run a gambling house with no thought of profit? And where did she get her money? That Monsieur de Montsousonge had not left any great riches was certain enough, because Monsieur de Montsousonge had, according to Maurette's own admission, never existed. So where did it come from, and how?

I made one observation.

The estimable Mrs Feurfield took part in all public parties – charity occasions and the like – to which members of the expatriate community and passing tourists were invited. Madame de Montsousonge did not, however; she seldom left her Hôtel at all. Every summer Mrs Feurfield would visit one of the larger seaside resorts, and in the winter she would spend two months on the Riviera, in Switzerland or in Italy. It was acquaintances from these trips whom she received in her entresol.

Moreover:

The guests in the entresol almost all became guests in Madame de Montsousonge's music room sooner or later. From there I would guide suitable guests, ladies as well as gentlemen, up the spiral staircase. Some became regular clients and seldom missed an evening's play; others disappeared after they had visited us once or twice.

Still others – and this third group was exclusively male – soon stopped playing, but continued to visit us. Far from disappearing, they appeared almost every day. And Madame, who rarely exchanged more than a greeting, if that, with the others, would receive them like intimate friends.

As far as I could make out, these men were a selection of our wealthiest guests (with a very few exceptions). I drew the conclusion that it was these chosen few who maintained Madame de Montsousonge, paid for her extravagences and kept up this house, which must surely have devoured large sums of money.

And I could not help but draw a further conclusion. She was selling herself, she was their mistress. Mistress of one or all, at the same time or in turn – it was all the same to me.

In my fury – and I had good reason to be furious! – I one day let her know what I thought of her. She did not get angry, was not even offended. She merely replied:

'No, my poor Jan, you've got that wrong.'

And she went on, smiling:

'My virtue is my only luxury.'

She did not appease me with this, but only made me more annoyed. So I countered:

'I thought, Madame, that luxury was your only virtue.'

She burst out laughing and said:

'I've said the same words to a hundred men, and ninety-nine of them have managed to turn them round in that same, spiritual way. But one mustn't expect variety.'

'And the hundredth?' I asked.

'The hundredth said nothing, dear Jan. But there was a reason for that. He was deaf.'

But she could not fob me off with that sort of mockery.

I had more free time than I desired, and I should have liked to have looked up my friends from the Rossbacher Keller. To begin with they pretended not to know me. They did not respond to my greetings, did not seem to realise that I still existed. But that soon changed. Steintheel renewed our acquaintanceship, Eline our friendship.

It had happened that a young couple – I forget what their nationality was – who had been introduced to one another in Mrs Feurfield's salon had both committed suicide. The matter was to be settled in court, and the estimable old lady was called as a witness. But she had produced a medical certificate stating that as the result of a serious heart complaint she could not leave her bed. The public scandal had been avoided, the silent scandal flourished. And it was part of the house's system of advertisement to permit silent scandals to flourish.

Now Steintheel, the journalist, could no longer resist the temptation. He recognised me in the street, embraced me and swore that our friendship was as strong as it had ever been. This pleased me, and in return I stuffed him so full of invented scandals that he was obliged to take me off to Pappa Eikmeier's to organise his material in peace and quiet. Eline received me as though nothing had happened; yes, she tweaked my ears and admonished me for my long absence. Fält, who had just finished his dinner, showed signs of wishing to leave the party, however. But when I took him by the collar and pushed him down on the bench, he let it pass, and soon we were back in the old routine. Almost –

At any rate, I had someone to talk to during my time off. I had Eline. There was not a trace of embarrassment between us. I helped to furnish her new home, and it cost me considerably more than the eight hundred marks I owed her husband. I was also one of the witnesses at their wedding, and their first-born was named after me – Jan Leonard. When Fält saw so many signs of selfless friendship, he said:

'Thine own friend, and thy father's friend, forsake not; for a friend sticketh closer than a brother.'

And he went on quoting biblical verses, until eventually Eline got angry and asked him to keep quiet –

But I did favours for the others as well. I lent Kugel money; I found work for Rygell, who had lost his job, with Mr Hansen; I ran countless errands for them and gave them all manner of gifts. In short: I fawned on them and begged for their friendship as humbly as only a dog can do. All the same, in reality they were pretty unimportant to me.

The only one whose company I still sought of my own volition, and for my own pleasure, was Eline. I would spend all of Friday – I had the whole of Friday off – in her company, first at the Rossbacher Keller, then in her own home. We would talk about my home country. She asked if it was dark and silent, if it was cold and lonely living there, whether one only rarely met other living beings, if the snow lay deep and white in an unbroken soft blanket, darkening under the polar night. The more childish her questions became, the more homesick I grew. I should have liked to take her there. Or someone else. And live a quiet life.

Once she said:

'Your friend has come back to Hamburg.'

'Who?' I asked.

'Mikael Arnfelt.'

After a while I asked:

'Alone?'

She replied:

'How should I know?'

She blushed and turned away. She was beautiful then, Eline, and Fält took her in his arms and said:

'Let her be as the loving hind and pleasant roe. She will do me good and not evil all the days of her life.'

On the whole, he quoted far too many biblical verses; a habit from his days as a preacher. This used to annoy Eline.

Following his lead, I wrote the following on the gates of the Hôtel de Montsousonge:

'Let not thine heart decline to her ways, go not astray in her paths.

'For she hath cast down many wounded: yea, many strong men have been slain by her.

'Her house is the way to hell, going down to the chambers of death.'

But Father Johannes, the gatekeeper, wiped away the inscription.

I wanted to know who visited Maurette when I was not there. To this end I plagued the old man with devious questions. He lived like a hermit in the little gatehouse, whose single room measured little more than a few square metres. During the day you never saw him; only his hand, reaching out to pull the lever of the lock on the gate. But when he made his nightly round of the garden, I would follow him, and in the course of conversation pretend to ask by chance to whom he had opened the gate that day. He claimed not to remember.

I said:

'What do you do all day, if you don't know anything?'

He replied: 'I invoke the Lord.' And I joked with him, suggesting that he must be a Muslim since he was invoking the Lord on a Friday. 'Yes,' he said, 'on Friday I am a Muslim, on Saturday a Jew, and on Sunday Christian. And on the other days of the week there are certain alternatives.' 'Alternatives?' I repeated. 'So that you need not see anything, nor know anything?'

I do not remember what he replied. I was more agitated than usual that day.

I determined to put an end to my uncertainty. If Maurette had one lover or several was no concern of mine. But what did concern me was that she was making fun of me. I would put a stop to that.

Among our guests was a young Polish aristocrat. For a while he was one of the most avid players, losing and winning large amounts. Then he stopped playing: I never saw him again in the round room. Instead I would meet him on the narrow staircase leading to Maurette's room. Once I stopped him, taking hold of his shoulders and turning him round, saying: 'You've no business here.' His face turned white as chalk, and I felt him trembling beneath my hands. He did not utter a word in response to my coarse behaviour, and crept down the stairs. I spent a long time watching him, and found him so timid that I would easily be able to scare him into doing anything. Luring him to my room and forcing a confession out of him would not have been difficult. I decided to do precisely that, but never had time to put my plan into action. One day – when I was with Eline – he had an accident. On his way up the main staircase he tripped and tumbled backwards, breaking his neck. Once again there was a great fuss, and Steintheel clung to me for more than a week. The police concluded, however, that it was simply an accident.

An American succeeded the Pole, a large, coarse, stocky man, sandy-haired, with sleepy, watery blue eyes. He had arrived in Hamburg on board his own yacht, and was said to be immensely wealthy. He was not a player, nor did he seek out gallant adventures in Mrs Feurfield's salons. To begin with Maurette wanted nothing to do with him. She ordered Father Johannes not to let him through the gate. So he turned to me. He sought me out at the Rossbacher Keller and offered me money in return for my persuading Maurette to receive him. That made me angry and I turned him down.

But afterwards I realised that here was a chance to interest someone with a lot of capital in my project. I had made numerous alterations and modifications to my original plan; it no longer seemed so impracticable. Besides, just then I would gladly have accepted any job, no matter what, if it meant I could break free from the Hôtel de Montsousonge.

So now it was my turn to seek out the American. He received me politely, and listened so patiently that I began to feel hopeful. We ate dinner on board his yacht, and I drank a lot of wine. In the end he renewed his offer. I replied, after some thought, that I would do as he desired if he did not offer me money. He claimed to be distantly related to Mrs Feurfield and her daughter, and that he had been deeply hurt at not being received in their salons. I pretended to believe him and we shook on it.

The following day I asked Maurette if she would repeal the

ban. She replied absent-mindedly: 'As you will, Jan – '

After a week the American was a daily visitor to the Hôtel de Montsousonge, and after another week he was the one I met on Maurette's staircase. I made no attempt to stop him, partly because he was a giant, and partly because I was still counting on his help. But I needed to be sure. And since Father Johannes refused to give me any information, I turned to Steintheel. I led him to understand that something was brewing, and advised him to shadow the American. That way I was able to find out which days and at what times he had visited Maurette. I could have shadowed him myself. But Maurette had forbidden me to spy.

I remained in the garden until midnight. On the stroke of midnight Father Johannes disappeared into his hermitage and I opened the little door, Maurette's door. I went slowly up the stairs, not making any attempt to soften the sound of my footsteps. I wanted to surprise them, but could not even be bothered to walk on tip-toe. On the third landing there is a small opening looking onto the gaming room. I stopped for a moment. It was a 'quiet evening', *cercle des amis*, twenty or so gentlemen. Among them Mikael Arnfelt. He held the bank and was winning. I knew that he had played several nights in succession. He was very pale, and looked ill. Despite the fact that he was from time to time one of our most faithful visitors, I never met him. To be more precise, I avoided him. I also knew that Léonie was in Hamburg, I even knew which villa they were staying in, and in which window she usually sat. But that was something which did not concern me.

I did not stop to listen at Maurette's door – she had forbidden me to do that – but rapped hard on the door as soon as I reached it. Then I pushed the handle. The door opened.

At that moment she switched on the lamp. I shut the door behind me but remained standing beside it. This was the first time I had entered Maurette's room. It was oval in shape, the ceiling vaulted and very low. I could see no trace of a door other than the one through which I had entered. The walls were hung with a light-grey fabric; there were two chairs clad in the same material. There was also a marble-topped washstand, a mirror set into the wall, a little rococo table, its top damaged by water. And the bed.

When I saw her bed, I could not help but smile. It was dark brown, probably stained pine, and consisted of four posts and a rather small mattress. As a child I had slept in a bed just like it, albeit somewhat shorter. Hedda had bought it at the autumn market in W. when they were in fashion (in W.); they were known as 'maid's beds', and replaced the old truckle beds used by servants.

In just such a bed lay Maurette; the bedspread was a dark grey blanket, the sheets and pillowcases had no embroidery or lacework. There was no trace of luxury at all, and the only things that stood out in the whole room were Maurette's blood-red, gold-red, sun-red hair and her skin.

She gave a stretch under the blanket, yawning and rubbing the sleep from her eyes; then she raised her head and stared at me, wide-eyed.

'What are you doing here?' she asked. 'You're standing there laughing. In the middle of the night you come into my room and laugh. But one can't expect common sense from you. What exactly do you want?'

I did not trouble to reply; first and foremost I wanted to make sure there was only one way out of the room. So I examined the walls; I found nothing and returned to my position by the door. Her eyes followed me the whole time; she said:

'So you didn't find anything, poor Jan. Was it a secret door you were looking for? Whatever must you think of me?'

I replied:

'That you sell yourself.'

She nodded, and made a face, as if to say: 'You're smart, Jan. There's no fooling you.' She smoothed her pillow and pulled the blanket up under her chin –

'Well,' she said, 'what do you want me to do? One must live, after all. And in order to live, you must have something to sell. Something. I have only myself; that is all I possess. And not even that is entirely my own. Mr Hansen has a certain stake; it is also he who manages the sale.'

I said:

'So it's the American?'

She replied:

'The American is a speculator, but the deal is far from concluded. He thinks the price too high; and it is high. Of course, I am the most beautiful woman in the world, but there are thousands of those. So that circumstance alone is not enough to justify the unique price. But I also possess other qualities – of which he has a notion and which he will get to know in the course of time. But not today, not tomorrow. Today I drove him away; tomorrow he is leaving Hamburg. In a week he will be back, or in a month or two. It is a matter of who has the greater staying power, him or me. If the deal is concluded, Mr Hansen will have made a successful speculation. If it comes to nothing, then this house of cards will tumble, like so many others. But why are you standing by the door, Jan?'

I replied:

'Because that is my place.'

She smiled and said:

'At the moment. If the house of cards falls, I will be so cheap that even you could be a speculator. I assume that you've been lining your pockets while you've been in my service. My value really only arises from the fact that I am as yet unsold, that Mr Hansen has set a fantastic price on me, and that there is a speculator who is furious that the price is so high. Is there anything else you want to know?'

I shook my head; she nodded and stretched her naked arm to turn off the light. The switch clicked; it was dark. I heard her shake the pillow and turn over in bed. And silence fell, I could not even hear her breathing.

But after a while she said:

'Jan! When I consider how high a price a connoisseur like Mr Hansen has set on me, and the even higher price I shall force the American to pay – and when I feel my body between my hands – and when I consider that I also possess an immortal soul, which is supposed to be the most precious of all precious things – then I get a preposterous urge to give it all to some poor wretch. I would go out onto the street and give it all to some beggar. As alms. "It's not much, but it's all that I have – "

'Jan, when I consider that I could give away with one word what I must sell to the highest bidder, because I must live, then I get a preposterous urge to play a trick on all the "musts" in the world. I would give myself to a beggar, a madman, who had so little appreciation of my worth that he would take me, cast me aside, and forget me.

'If I did that, I think that "must" would release its hold for a moment, drop its reins and whip, and that I should be free for a moment. What do you think, Jan?'

And she said:

'Jan, you haven't even got the sense to praise my generosity. I could have claimed a stammered thank you or a sigh that might burst your chest, or, still better, a cry of joy. I have called you by your name, I have called you a beggar and a madman, how much longer do I have to wait? My arms will go numb in a minute. Do you have to have light to see that they're reaching out for you?'

I fell asleep and dreamed that someone was pulling her away from me. And I woke with a start, crying: 'No! No! No!' She teased me, saying:

'He believes in magic. "No, no, no!" Hey presto, and the world is transformed. But what use does your "no" do, poor Jan? Now listen. I shall tell you once more – in a week or a month or two, we shall have him here again. The deal must be concluded then. Sooner or later we must; you must and I must.'

We lay silent for a long while.

Eventually I said:

'Must? Who's forcing us?'

She replied:

'You poor thing! If no-one else forced us, we would force ourselves. Necessity forces us, the price forces us. I have him and I cannot let him go. It's a game, and we must win. Doesn't that sound like a truism? It's nothing to worry about. Let us just find the best way, the means – '

I interrupted her:

'If that's the case, Maurette – then there's no way and no means that won't tear me to pieces. Command, and I shall obey you.'

She said:

'If you suffered as I suffer, you would soon find a way out.'

I understood then how false she was, and that she wanted to use my suffering to gain something. But I pretended I had not realised, and drew her to me, pressing my brow and eyes to her skin. To test her, I whispered:

'Maurette, you want me to – '

I put my ear to her chest and listened. Her heart was beating quickly, hard and unevenly, as though she were frightened or greatly agitated. I was forcing her to speak. She said:

'When he was here today, he wanted to give me a string of pearls. It was beautiful, worth perhaps twenty thousand. I took it as a reason to show him the door. I know my business –

'But if I had been for sale at that price, or found it sufficient as pocket-money, I would have replied: "tomorrow". And he would have left the necklace here and returned to his pleasure yacht. You know where it's berthed, Jan? Yes. And where his dinghy is moored? And he would have been satisfied with the deal, probably very happy, and entirely unsuspecting – '

I said: 'No – what would he have been suspicious of?'

'No, Jan, what would he have been suspicious of? You would accompany him down to the harbour, perhaps you would have a torch with you to light the way down to the dinghy. And his men would row him out to the yacht. Or perhaps you would do it. And he would climb aboard and sleep soundly and dream of the following day.

'But Jan, I could tell you an old story about a man who was far too credulous in similar circumstances, and fell into an ambush. He too had left some valuables ashore, and was planning to return to collect them. But he had not left them with a woman, and it was not the woman's lover who took his life. Apart from that, there is a lot in the story that matches our own. I heard it as a child from my father, and he had heard it from his.

'Shall I tell it to you? No. Because you know it as well as I do. And your father heard it from his father. And you know that you are my property not only because I have bought you with my kisses and my body and my heart.'

I wrapped the blanket around her naked body, which was shaking with cold. But she disentangled herself and laughed at me, saying:

'No, Jan, I'd rather freeze if that's all the warmth you can offer me.'

But when I held her to me, she whispered: 'I want the person who desires me to die. Anyone who desires me shall die. A wedding march with muffled drums and a heavy, insidious beat would suit me well. Melancholy souls know me and grasp after my body, seeking it like blind worms seek their nests. But I want anyone who desires me to die. That's why I'm as chaste as an oriental queen guarded by black eunuchs, because death keeps watch over my heart and waits in my court.'

Once more I woke with a start, crying: 'No! No! No!'

She laughed at me, saying: 'Poor Jan! Let us believe in dreams, in ghosts and spirits. Let us believe that the world is governed by fate or by God, or, even less likely, that it governs itself. But let's not believe that our "yes" or our "no" can alter the unalterable.'

After several days, or weeks, or perhaps months, Maurette started treating me like a dog again. I had to guard her door, but it was closed to me. If my obedience wavered, she would threaten to throw me out. But that was only a matter of small things, minor issues of service. She uttered not a word about the big thing, the great service. Nor did she need to.

I had thought that I merely required certainty, certainty as to her identity, in order to be free. That was a mistake. I had thought that I merely needed to possess her in order to be rid of her. That was also a mistake. I now knew whom I served – it merely made me more wretched, weaker, more apathetic. I could no longer delude myself about my own worth. And when I missed her and longed for her, I could not even delude myself about the nature of my longing.

Everything began to seem meaningless, worthless, unreal to me. As far as reality was concerned, nothing in the whole world seemed able to compete with my great Transatlantic Project. And now I understood why I had allowed myself to become obsessed with my chimaera with such childlike stupidity. In all its absurdity it had at least been a goal; and a goal, whether distant or close, is, at the very least, a small piece of reality. Now it had withered, and now I had nothing.

I found no remedy within myself, nor in others. I sought out my friends from the Rossbacher Keller. But the people had changed and we no longer had anything in common. Each of them had realised something, small plans, small dreams, small hopes. Something. I alone had not.

Kugel, for instance, short, plump and indolent, with a wife, short, plump and indolent. He showed me round his home, which was furnished throughout according to the same rule: short, plump and indolent. 'Look here, look here, look here!' Yes – a home. It lasts for a while and then fades. But its passage is recorded in time.

My life is timeless. Father's watch has lost its hands. The numbers are there, and the mechanism ticks, but I do not know if it is morning or evening, day or night.

Rygell, green with bile, his eyes burnt dark with rage at the injustices and evils of the world. Always worn out, from his balding pate to his battered shoes, but always alert, always ready to attack or defend.

What do the injustices and evils of this world matter to me? If it were only a question of another world. Which I could imagine for myself.

Or Steintheel! He has reached his goal and become a reference book of Hamburg. In vellum binding. But a book which people are constantly consulting. When I stand, holding on to his coat button, I imagine that perhaps I still exist for him, the news-hound, or that one day I will exist for him. And I do not release him until he says:

'My dear Jan, one fine day you'll pull that button off!'

Pappa Eikmeier has paid his debt to nature. We carried him to the grave in a large oak coffin with a convex lid. It all went very well, well ordered, well polished. Thus ended his life. And he had lived.

That was the last time I saw Eline.

But long after that I bumped into J. P. Fält on Thorgasse. He was just the same and had aged as little as I had. But he had a timekeeper in the boy, my godson, whose hand he was holding. He straightened up, swallowed, and I imagined the biblical quotations lining themselves up before his eyes. And so he began, at great length and in great detail.

The content, in short, was that Eline had left him. She had gone after Mikael Arnfelt. Somewhere, I forget exactly where. Mikael had returned to Hamburg, but not Eline.

For a moment I thought of Léonie.

Everything was unreal, except for the fact that she had given me an order. And the more worthless my life became, the fewer my scruples. If she desired it, why should I refuse? She had a will, I did not. Should I not be thankful that there was still an ounce of reality?

My scruples dissolved to nothing. Eventually it became a mere question of feasibility, a question of ways and means. On the occasions when the American was in the city, I did all that I could to get close to him and win his trust. I crawled, flattered, played the fool. Sometimes this amused him, because he was as simple as a child in many ways, and it was not hard to make him laugh helplessly. Every now and then I had to pluck other strings, but not the emotional ones – for there was no resonance in those. Instead I would have to try to scare him, by being secretive, hinting at some mysterious danger from Maurette that threatened him. Then he would cling to me and not let go. And although he was sometimes coarse and threw his mistrust in my face, I realised that in the end he would entrust his precious life to my hands.

All the same, I made attempt after attempt to break away. But to no avail. There was nothing within me, there was nothing within other people. In the end I latched onto Father Johannes. At least we had one thing in common; our nights were more wakeful than our days. And his life at the gate could hardly have been any more real than mine. Once, when I was walking past the gatehouse and saw the old man's hand and arm in the window as usual, I came to think of Mother's window, and how, when someone had frightened me, I would run to the window and hold her hand. It woke a peculiar longing within me. And I called out:

'Hello, Father Johannes! Here's an old friend who wants to shake your hand.'

He stretched out his hand to me, and I held it in mine for a moment. This was repeated several times, under various pretexts. But it was just childishness, and was in any case of no help.

But we did speak about it, he and I. In hints and paraphrases. How much he guessed I do not know. I said:

'When you are in love, Father Johannes, you don't have a will of your own. Isn't that right, Father Johannes?'

He replied:

'Do you think that you're in love?'

On another occasion I said:

'There are many things one is forced to do. Not nice things, either. But a man must live, of course.'

He replied:

'Are you sure that you're alive?'

I said:

'If you had asked me a year ago, I would have said yes. Now I'm less sure. But if I'm neither alive nor in love, then it doesn't really matter what I do.'

He replied:

'We'll see. Perhaps you'll have other thoughts.'

I liked this sort of answer. There was, I thought, a glimpse of hope in them. Perhaps because they were so vague –

But on other occasions he would ruin everything by giving me quotations and biblical verses. Just like Fält. –

Love thy neighbour, love God, etc.

By all means, but none of this concerns a person who does not love and does not even hate. It might be true for the living. –

For me neither true nor untrue, neither good nor bad.

And of any help? No.

However, a source of temporary respite did appear at the eleventh hour.

In the end I had prepared so thoroughly that nothing was missing. I had procured a suitable rowing boat, thin as eggshell, easy to overturn. I had positioned it at the very spot on the quay where his dinghy usually landed. I had gained the confidence of his men and could easily arrange for the dinghy not to meet him at the quay on any given day. He would be forced to entrust himself to me.

That was one aspect of it. The second aspect was just as well prepared. The deal might be struck any day now: Maurette was just waiting for a signal from me. And I was to have given it that evening.

The third aspect of the matter – the consequences for me, worried me least. Maurette had promised me the moon. Or love and eternal happiness. It mattered not which.

But the matter in and of itself was not meaningless; on the contrary, it was the only thing which had any meaning.

It was pouring with rain, such a fog of rain that the street-lamps looked as if they were wrapped in cotton-wool. Only when I had entered the gates could I make out the illuminated windows of the Hôtel de Montsousonge. The cars were bellowing like fog-horns. It was to be a grand evening of play; moreover, Mrs Feurfield was receiving guests in the entresol. A pair of horses reared up; the coupé pressed me up against the gatehouse. I was left standing there. Father Johannes's window was lit up, there was a lantern on the sill. I asked if there were any letters for me. He passed one to me. The envelope bore the stamp of Mr Hansen's company. I thought it might contain something important and was about to open it. But now the rain really began to pour down and I put the letter in my pocket. I said to Father Johannes:

'What do you think? Is this the Flood at last?'

He replied:

'Do you know so little, Jan, and have you forgotten so much? Don't you know that the Lord has set his bow in the cloud, as a sign to us.'

I said:

'Of course, as comfort for the fearful.'

He repeated:

'As comfort for the fearful.'

I said:

'Right, old man. But there are no rainbows tonight, unless you count the ones round the street-lamps.'

He replied:

'Couldn't that be enough for you, Jan? It used to be enough to show you God's bow in the water of a fountain.'

At that moment the column of cars and carriages moved, and the coupé that had squeezed me against the gatehouse wall started to roll slowly forwards. I took the opportunity and followed it, walking between the rear wheels. When it stopped by the steps I saw that a solitary woman was seated in the carriage, so I opened the door and offered her my hand as support.

She stood up and stepped down onto the footboard, one hand clutching her coat, the other resting on my shoulder. Suddenly she cried: 'Jan!' And then again, lower: 'Jan – '

I stared at her; I said:

'What do you want here?'

The carriage rolled away, the next one forced us up the steps.

I said:

'You've no business here.'

And I wanted to call back her carriage. But she stepped into the hall and a lackey took her coat. I heard her ask if Mrs Feurfield was receiving visitors. And she turned to me and said with a smile:

'Do you know why I've come, Jan? To see if I could possibly meet my husband.'

I said:

'Léonie, Léonie, Léonie. – '

And I said:

'Léonie, I forbid you – '

She replied:

'Then you're forgetting your position altogether, Jan. The only person who can forbid me to visit Mrs Feurfield is Mikael. And he is hardly likely to do so.'

I could not stop her from walking up the stairs towards the entresol. But that Léonie should become one of the guests at the

Hôtel de Montsousonge seemed so incredible to me that I decided to postpone everything else for the time being in order to try to find some satisfactory solution to Léonie's case. So important and devoid of indifference did the matter seem to me.

And this alone, the fact that something seemed important to me and not indifferent, was a help and a wonder. For he who cleaveth to harlots will become impudent. Moths and worms shall have him to heritage, and a bold man shall be taken away.

I followed her, keeping a distance of three steps. She pretended not to notice, but I could tell by her walk and way of moving that she was aware of my presence.

In the anteroom, leaning over a table awash with visiting cards, stood a young Catholic priest, possibly one of those who had led me out of the church. When he heard the rustling of skirts, he quickly turned round; he drew his cassock to him, pressed his arms tight to his sides, pursed his lips and mournfully lowered his gaze. He looked like a martyr in a saint's alcove. The room was half in darkness.

Léonie gave a mischievous glance over her shoulder; she said in Swedish:

'No, look Jan, a priest! So this must be a respectable house.'

And she added:

'Well, Mikael's always had a weakness for priests.'

She handed her card to the servant. He stepped forward to the door, his thin, pale face with its dark blue stubble reflected a red glow, as though he had turned towards a furnace.

'Madame la Comtesse Arnfelt – '

Now the light from Mrs Feurfield's pink lamps fell across Léonie's hair and cheeks and neck and shoulders. I heard the old woman's harsh, slippery, breathless voice:

'My dear child, this really is too kind – I hardly dared hope – '

And Léonie's girlish voice, still rather shy, still with an undertone of a girl's awkward pleasure: –

'Oh, Madame, it is I who hope – '

Whispers, the rustle of skirts, footsteps on soft mats; a gentleman and a lady start talking of the Hamburg fog, and about an accident, a sailing accident in the harbour. They speak calmly, fluently, the strength of their voices well-matched, with the sort of natural intonation that one only hears on stage. Surprise, regret, sympathy, deep sorrow that such an accident should befall a fellow human being, fear, indignation at poor procedures, resignation, hope of improvement, lighter tones, a loose digression, an anecdote, discreet laughter. All of it utterly natural and with such well-measured strength of voice that the sound of whispering fades, as does the sound of footsteps on soft mats.

My first impulse was to seek out Mikael, who was most likely in the gaming room. But the thought was too abhorrent. So I decided to turn to Maurette instead. Particularly as I had another task.

In the white salon that evening a young violinist with a growing reputation was performing. The guests numbered above a hundred, and were of higher quality than usual. Predominantly women. Maurette herself was seated at the grand piano, dressed in a coarse, pearl-grey fabric with an irregular dark pattern, like wine stains or smears of dark red clay. Beside her stood a one-eyed gentleman, talking, reciting, describing. This was the young musician's father. For the time being he himself was imprisoned in a window-bay, casting long, impatient glances across women's naked shoulders towards the grand, or Maurette.

Maurette asked with her eyes and a slight frown: 'What do you want?' I did not reply, but positioned myself opposite the one-eyed man, and listened politely. He was in the middle of describing his accident, how during a car journey in the south of France he had driven into a road barrier, been thrown out of the car, and lost an eye.

And Maurette's eyes commanded: 'Go.' But that evening I was not obedient, and stayed. And when the one-eyed man drew me into the conversation with a '*n'est-ce pas, monsieur?*', I agreed and disagreed for a while. After which I turned to Maurette and said:

'Madame, what was to have taken place tomorrow evening must be postponed.'

Her skin grew so translucent that I could clearly see the fine tracery of veins around her eyes. But at once she calmly asked:

'How is that, Jan? Does our great American suspect something?'

I replied:

'No, but now I have other things to consider.'

The one-eyed man directed his gaze at the ceiling, or at the window-bay where his son was held captive; and he had already left us with half a pace when Maurette held him back.

'One moment, Mr Spaulding! You must act as judge between me and this poor boy. Listen. We have a mutual enemy, and I have ordered the boy to kill him. I have already paid and rewarded him handsomely, yet here he is, trying to get out of it. Can that be right?'

'Oh, Madame, what a question!' the one-eyed man groaned; and, to me:

'What are you thinking of, young man? Hurry up and sharpen the knife! For I assume that it is John's head in a charger that Salome desires?'

She shrugged her shoulders:

'I give my champion free rein with the detail. As long as he obeys me.'

The one-eyed man laughed and cackled. But I said:

'Your audacity no longer has any effect on me, Maurette.'

The one-eyed ape was suddenly silent, hung like a weather-vane for a few moments, then vanished. I leaned over and whispered; she said:

'I forbid you to whisper; speak out loud! What's happened?'

But even if I had been able to tell her, in front of all these listening people, that she was a harlot whose mercenary had tired of his duties, I had no desire whatever to mention Léonie by name. Thus I was unable to explain what had happened, and felt a sudden desire to tear the Hôtel de Montsousonge apart, stone by stone.

I had no choice but to seek out Mikael and, if he was in the gaming room, force him to take Léonie away from Mrs Feurfield's pink salons at once. I climbed slowly up the forty-eight steep steps of the spiral staircase; and with every step my fervour diminished further.

I was thinking: 'What if he refuses? If he just shrugs his shoulders? If he smiles that same smile, his top lip scornfully curled? If he says: "So? Why stop her? It's up to Léonie – "'

I grew scared; I could hear steps behind me. I had climbed these stairs so often followed by some stranger to whose steps I would listen. Now I could hear them again, and I thought:

'You're ridiculous, thinking Léonie's welfare is any of your business. Why right do you have to be worried about Léonie? It's not as if you're an honourable man, or even half-honourable. Or even a man with a good heart. No. And so now you're going to break with Maurette and relinquish Maurette and abandon Maurette to someone else merely in order to save Léonie? If you search your heart and soul, you'll find that you no longer love Léonie, who abandoned you. After you'd abandoned her.

'But Mikael, who took her from you once you had cast her aside, you hate him. And now you're creeping about in the dark like a dog, trying to find a chance to attack him and bite at his throat.

'For it is good will that drives you. You will remain the same, whether you obey Maurette's will or your own.

'So stop this hypocrisy! Being honest is still like a drop of fresh water, some refreshment in purgatory. So cling on to the fact that Léonie is a matter of indifference to you, and don't forget it. Especially when Maurette can still be yours. And if you are not completely indifferent to Léonie, it is only because you hate Mikael – '

And suddenly my fear intensified to terror. I felt like a vagrant, vicious, wild dog, one which every right-thinking and sensible person has a duty to render harmless. I felt terror for myself, for Maurette, for Mikael, for all the people I had hurt or wanted to hurt. I did not feel repugnance or regret. But terror.

The pink lamps in Mrs Feurfield's salons had gone out, as had the blinding light in the white salon. The garden lay silent and the courtyard was empty; the latch on the gate clicked one last time and Father Johannes' lamp slid away into the darkness. I no longer had anything to hold my gaze.

I turned round to light the lamp. Then I heard a whisper from inside the room:

'Herr Arnberg – for God's sake – it's only me – don't be scared – don't call out – '

I turned the lamp on; in front of me, on the edge of the bed, sat Mr Hansen, hunched up, his shoulders pulled up above his ears, hands knotted and clasped between his trembling knees; his mouth stretched into a humble smile, or a tearful grimace. And his gaze directed at the heights. Like a toad.

He said:

'I am colossally pleased that you didn't cry out. I am myself very nervous. I wrote to you this morning, and sent it by express delivery. But since you did not come, I myself had to – '

He fell silent, and such a deep sigh swelled his chest that I thought the toad was going to explode before my very eyes. But he merely collapsed into himself even further, his pale blue face became even paler, and there was no longer any doubt that it was sobbing and not laughter that framed his mouth.

I asked what he wanted. He muttered something about being the most unfortunate man on earth. And I began to undress. I put my purse, wallet, watch and revolver on the bedside table. I took my jacket off and was about to hang it in the wardrobe when I caught sight of Mr Hansen's reflection in the mirror as he quickly snatched the revolver. I thought: 'Maurette has sent him! She wants to get rid of me, have her revenge – '

I screamed –

He threw down the revolver, and clapped his hand to his mouth as though he had burned himself. I put the revolver in my trouser pocket. I was a little ashamed of being scared, I slapped him on the shoulder and said:

'Not that I don't trust you; but, between the two of us, you can never be too careful.' He agreed. – And explained his behaviour:

'I took your revolver because I recognised it. It's J. P. Fält's handiwork, isn't it? Poor man! Have you heard that he's gone to the dogs completely now? Yes, started drinking, and had to leave

HAPAG. I have him here on my list. Seeking employment. In four categories: engineer, waiter, preacher and barber. Valet would also do for such a multi-talented man. It was his wife, of course, a bad woman – '

And he went on in the same breath, but in a different tone, huffing and puffing with indignation, either simulated or real.

Chapter 3

Mr Hansen Explains and Reconnects

'Now listen, young man! What sort of fancies have you got into your head? What do you take Maurette for? Do you really imagine that she's some petty criminal? The shame of it! That she's trying to induce you to commit a heinous crime? You should be ashamed! Explain yourself! What on earth are you thinking?'

I replied:

'Please calm down. Perhaps you imagine that I have discovered some scruples, that I might warn the American, or even report Madame to the police? Well, this is not the case. You can't buy scruples for love nor money these days. I don't know where I'd get them from – '

His indignation subsided into a calm, lofty dignity, and we carried on in the factual manner that suited him best:

'What you have just said indicates that you misunderstand and misjudge Madame de Montsousonge. This ought not to be the case. She is a mystery to most people; but you ought to see clearly in this matter.

'People believe that the Hôtel de Montsousonge is a gaming house. Wrong. Others are of the opinion that it is a *maison de gaîté*. Also wrong. Gaming goes on here, granted; and naturally the wingéd god cannot be completely excluded from a place where young men and women meet. But you cannot but have noticed the extremely formal etiquette that is observed in Mrs Feurfield's salons? The house is in actual fact a quite colossally special *spécialité*. In order to understand it correctly, one must understand Madame de Montsousonge correctly. Or rather, let us say – Miss Feurfield. The other is, as you already know, merely a *nom de guerre*.

'Maurette belongs to what was once a colossally respectable family. For three centuries her forefathers have given the British Crown steadfast service as naval officers. The remarkable profits which were part and parcel of naval service in those days secured the family a fairly solid financial position. Everything was going splendidly. They had an estate, they made good marriages, they had a family tradition – within the navy – in short: they had a secure position within society. But at some point at the beginning of the last century a catastrophe occurred. The head of the family, Captain Mogens Feurfield, was killed in a robbery. You have doubtless heard the story. However, there are two different versions. The family maintains that it was robbery and murder. But according to the other version, Captain Feurfield is said to have taken his own life after he had embezzled the war-chest. The authorities preferred this latter version and sequestered the late Captain's property. As a result, the family's solid financial position was destroyed.

'But, more importantly, Herr Arnberg, colossally more importantly – the good, solid family tradition was broken. A thief and a suicide had infiltrated the long line of dashing, honest, faithful sailors. Had the matter been fully evident, it might have been less damaging. The family's social reputation would have been lost, but could have been regained. However the matter was anything but evident. Sir Mogens' descendants saw themselves as the victims of a glaring injustice. His son became a typically querulous litigant, pouring the last of his assets into all manner of impossible lawsuits. His grandson tried hard to make a new start, moving to America and trying his luck in various professions. All without success. He was altogether too eager, never stopping for breath, just rushing on regardless. He also laboured under the unfortunate belief that people did not trust him. He and his family quickly went downhill. As far as Maurette's father is concerned, he ended up just as Sir Mogens is said to have done – as a thief and a suicide. Well, that's the way things go sometimes.

'I have known Maurette since she was a child, yes, I even carried her at her christening. And when the time came, Mrs Feurfield entrusted me with the task of finding the girl a position in life. And I dare say that I approached my task with the greatest care and reflection. She was not lacking in talents, but above all else she possessed a piquant and enticing appearance. She was as though created to appeal and delight. On a grand scale. And by that, Herr Arnberg, I do not mean anything indecent, because naturally a woman can appeal and delight on a grand scale in an entirely respectable way. For instance as a theatrical performer. And that was what I decided upon. I took her to an old gentleman in the business who had the finest reputation. After much scrutiny, he declared that she had the makings of a great tragic artiste. That was not quite what I had anticipated, but, as always, I gave way to empirical knowledge.

'After six months or so the old gentleman came to me and said: "Hansen, I don't know if your protégée is going to be a great tragic artiste; but it is patently obvious that she is going to be the cause of a tragedy among my pupils. Please take her away at once. Immediately. I am old, but I am not at all tired of life – "

'Quite horrified, I asked what she had said or done. He replied: "Said? Done? That I don't know. Had she said or done anything that I deemed unsuitable, I would have laid her over my knee. That wouldn't worry me. No, she's neither said nor done anything. But ask her what she intends to do. Hypnotise her, beat her, force her to confess, then you'll find out! What she intends to do? She intends to cut my throat, that's what she intends to do! I'd sooner be hanged by law – "

'And although I tried to reason with the old man, I could not persuade him to keep the girl on. It distressed me colossally. Mrs Feurfield, her mother, took the matter far more lightly, because she assumed that a girl with Maurette's looks would always get on. But for a professional man such as myself, it was hard to see something of such extraordinary quality being sold off as if it were any old thing. I brooded over that for a long time; but I could not work out what went to make up Maurette's peculiar powers of attraction. Still less, naturally, what they could be used for. It took more than a decade – and both Maurette and I had undergone many dreadful experiences and twists of fate – before I saw what the answer was.

'This is what happened. Some years ago I made a study tour of the Continent. In Paris I made the acquaintance of Monsieur Lebossu, who had just opened his so-called *maison des morts*. I found the establishment rather naïve and banal. One would drink red wine from skulls, lie down in coffins, play with bones, and so on. The staff were dressed as highwaymen, the guests were treated brutally and threateningly, and a few all too transparent tricks were supposed to hint at hidden dangers. As I said, I found it all rather naïve. The patrons seemed to me to be more harmlessly amused than impressed. But J. P. Fält, who was accompanying me on my journey, was deeply affected. And he said: "Which of us that liveth does not think of death?"

'Then it struck me that there really must be something valuable in the reasoning behind this new enterprise. What, Herr Arnberg, is the *raison d'être* of a place of entertainment? Might it not be that the public finds stimulation and gratification of certain tendencies there? The desires of the palate are certainly a powerful factor in the entertainment business. I need only hint at the rôle played by certain other urges. Well, then, could one not talk of a death wish? People talk about cheating death. Well, people cheat love as well. How many sports do not have as their driving force this death wish? Well. Might this not be something to cultivate? In a hothouse, so to speak –

'This thought lies behind the activities of the Hôtel de Montsousonge. We do not entice our guests with nothing more than a few altogether too obvious symbols of death. On the contrary, we avoid them. One does not give credence to poisoned wine by serving it in skulls. The means we use are ambiguous, suspect, disconcerting, stimulating. Our method is thoroughly individual, one must be born a master of it. Maurette is a master of it. And I shall tell you why.

'She was begotten by a dead man and born of a dead woman. She belongs to a family for which an act of death – if I might so express myself – has had decisive importance for generations. Her thoughts are with death, her emotions and will are with death, and not with life. She is in the fortunate position of not needing to play a rôle in order to fulfil her task. Her imagination is constantly working in one single direction, and everyone who comes near her is enmeshed in a spider's web of sombre unease. She is, quite simply, a real find.

'Yes, Herr Arnberg, from the point of view of this establishment, she is an invaluable find. The charm she exerts on certain people, those who have long since tired of banal Venus-worship and who do not even notice their pulse at a gaming-table, is colossal. And please note, Herr Arnberg, this passion, which I should like to call the death wish, and which is strongest and most final of all – even though it is often manifest in very young people – this passion is colossally lucrative. Oh, people do so wish to be driven close to the portals of death –

'But, naturally, not within those portals! No, no, no, Herr Arnberg. You're mistaken there, and have entered a train of thought, under the pressure of Maurette's lugubrious imagination, which I must vehemently regret. Our method is quite respectable. What we offer our clients is stimulation. Nothing more. And we should think ourselves dishonoured the moment a real accident occurred.'

I said:

'Then you're pretty close to being dishonoured, Mr Hansen. Maurette has been playing with her mouse so long that she can no longer let go of it.'

He looked up at the ceiling again and, when I looked at him more closely, I saw tears as big as peas rolling down his cheeks, so profusely that my bedsheet was getting wet.

After a while he said:

'Herr Arnberg, do you believe that I have a conscience? No, you don't. But if I were to tell you that I have not slept a wink for four nights, you have to believe that I am suffering. And in the end I decided to ask you for help.

'Herr Arnberg, I, Anton Hansen, am the one who has been making use of Maurette's unusual gift – or, if I might say so – her fertile and lugubrious imagination. I understand, I feel the weight of responsibility. I have always understood the risk that I and she and the third party were running. I have always been on my guard, and always intervened at the right moment. This is the first time that I have been negligent to even a small extent. Because, Herr Arnberg, I had not correctly judged the extent of Maurette's influence over you. I did not think that the time was right.

'But now I am begging you, appealing to you! I appeal to the memory of your noble father – '

I said:

'Be quiet and let me think.'

And we were silent for a while.

Then I said:

'Well, Mr Hansen, I can't see why I shouldn't do as Maurette wishes. But nor do I see why I shouldn't do as you wish. It's fairly evenly balanced. A feather added to one side of the scales or the other would be decisive.'

He was attentive.

'And what sort of feather would that be?'

I said:

'Mrs Feurfield received a new guest today in her salon. A young lady – '

And I forced myself to say:

'Léonie Arnberg.'

'Léonie Arnberg?' he repeated. 'Isn't that Countess Arnfelt?'

I nodded. And after a while I said.

'Well, Mr Hansen, there you have the feather. I have got it into my head that the young lady is not suitable for the entresol. If you arrange for the visit not to be repeated, then I should feel obliged to do as you wish.'

He closed his eyes and sighed.

'Sadly, Herr Arnberg, I cannot do that. I cannot forbid Mrs Feurfield from receiving whomsoever she wishes. And of course I have even less influence over the gracious Countess. Why not turn to her husband? I believe he visits the gaming room every day.'

To change the subject, I replied:

'No, Mikael Arnfelt has stopped playing.'

He opened his eyes wide and looked at me. He said:

'What? Really? Has he stopped playing?'

And we fell silent. Each of us pondering his own worries, I suppose.

But Mr Hansen was quicker than I was:

'Jan Arnberg,' he began, stretching out his hands as though wanting to take hold of mine, 'you would not be your father's son nor your dear sister's brother if you did not have a good heart. You say you have no scruples, no conscience. That may be the case. Because, to be truthful, conscience is something most people lay aside at some point or other. But the heart! We have to drag that with us all our lives. Believe me, I know.

'So now your heart is playing tricks on you. You care a great deal for your little cousin, Léonie?'

I said:

'Take not her name into your lips, for you are unclean.'

His horrible mouth flapped open and a silent laugh emerged, like bubbles from murky water.

'J. P. Fält might have said that; it sounded just like him. But if you will not permit me to speak of your cousin Léonie, you may come to regret it. I am more familiar with her present circumstances than you. If she leaves her beautiful villa to spend a few hours with Mrs Feurfield, I can assure you that she does not lose anything in the exchange. From the point of view of morals. On the contrary. It isn't Mrs Feurfield who will corrupt her – if that isn't already done and dusted – '

As I watched him now, the toad, hearing his horrible mouth talk about Léonie, I pulled out my revolver, quite unconsciously, as it happens. His response was instantaneous:

'Quite right! The revolver! But you don't want to point it at me. Not if you want to save Léonie.'

I realised then the direction in which he was aiming me, or wanted to aim me. And I understood that he had seen through me, and that his gaze had penetrated right into the stony little capsule that lay like a seed and an eternal torment and a constant threat in my head.

I said:

'No! Stop it!'

He was transformed at once and was once more good-natured and trustworthy and factual. He said:

'Yes, well, I'm sure you must think me an ugly customer. But do you really know who I am? If I were to lay myself open before you, you might perhaps find that we have a certain amount in common. And I've a good mind to do just that.

'My parents are completely unknown. And that's as bad a start as you can get. You have nothing to stand on, nothing to hold on to, and have to cling to first one person, then the other. When I was young Mrs Feurfield took care of me, she became a sort of foster-mother. But when she saw that I was getting less, not more, attractive with age, until eventually I developed into the hideous monster you see before you today, she withdrew her support. For a few years I lived as a street urchin, until by a twist of fate I gained a foster-father instead of a foster-mother. And he was a kind-hearted old gentleman, none other than your great-uncle, Leonard Arnberg, or Leonard Fält as he called himself.

'But he was mad! Quite authentically mad, he had a doctor's certificate to prove it. He had a most peculiar way of looking at God's wonderful world; he thought he was dead and living in hell. But that wasn't his greatest delusion. He thought that he himself was innocent, and that he was suffering for the misdeeds of his forefathers, and that his and his family's punishment was that the same crime had to be repeated generation after generation. And regarding me, Mrs Feurfield and various other people, he gathered us about him in the belief that we were the victims of his family's crimes. My father or grandfather – I don't recall which – was supposed to be the servant who murdered Mr Feurfield and was then himself murdered.

'Well, when I realised he was mad, there was nothing I could do, given my circumstances at the time, but try to gain the greatest possible advantage from his madness. And that I did. But you're mistaken if you think it was pleasant or profitable or even tolerable for a young man to live like a parasite off the sick mind of an old man. But that's precisely what I did. And, on the whole, I felt perfectly inclined to share my benefactor's view of hell.

'But if I somehow succeeded in protecting myself from his

mad ideas, it was because I am by nature practical, industrious and sensible. I had my motto: Nothing Too Small, and I floated on that like a cork-mat, crawling from one small deal to the next. When your uncle died, I had fairly firm ground beneath my feet, and, although I had to provide for both Mrs Feurfield and Maurette, I managed pretty well. By then Maurette was already my betrothed. And still is to this day.'

'Your betrothed!' I exclaimed. And even though I did not feel the slightest inclination to laugh, I burst out laughing.

If Mr Hansen had said: 'Maurette is my wife', it would not have surprised me. But that she was his betrothed –

He said:

'Yes, you laugh, you find it incredible. But if you knew Maurette, you would understand me. I have never had any reason to trust people's promises, women's least of all. But I trust Maurette.'

I said:

'I'm sorry, Mr Hansen, I didn't mean to interrupt.'

And he went on:

'We could have been married; but before I bound her to my foul personage, I wanted to be sure of providing her with a home worthy of her, a comfortable life. I must get rich. Must – you understand.

'For some time I had been working as an agent for Grundberg's Chemical Laboratory, the company that was later renamed after your father. That was during the days when Arnberg's famous Tuberculin was spreading round the world. I admired your father, I believed in his Tuberculin. You must not forget that I was completely uneducated. I believed every word of that boastful advertisement. I thought: "This is magnificent! And this is your chance."

'Your father left America, and Grundberg was also hoping to withdraw, having reaped his millions. He suggested that I buy the Tuberculin. He showed me his books, he showed me the orders on hand. It was immense! The whole world was his customer, America, Europe, Japan. I worked like a dog, I was quite beside myself. He threatened me with other speculators. I did what I had to do under the circumstances. I entered into a little deal which I have no desire to describe in detail. Suffice to say that it was a little beyond the pale of the law. But it succeeded, and I acquired the Tuberculin.

'I said to Maurette: "One more year!"

'How stupid! Month by month, week by week, day by day the sales dropped off, dried up, and finally stopped. I couldn't understand it. I thought it was down to advertising, and threw away my last reserves. Impossible. It was infernal – I had seen the accounts, I'd seen the order book, I'd seen authentic written orders from America, Europe, Japan! Orders were cancelled, consignments returned. I couldn't understand it. I thought I'd landed up in hell. And it was a hell, Jan Arnberg, a hell, a hell! I shall never forget those days.

'Well, eventually I realised what was at the bottom of it, I realised that Arnberg's Tuberculin was a humbug. And realised that although the humbug genus is immortal, each individual humbug is relatively short-lived.

'"Goodnight, Herr Hansen," I thought. "Goodnight."

'And Herr Hansen would have dearly liked to take his leave. But Maurette? No. Maurette? No, no, no.

'So we started afresh – a hundred rungs lower down, of course. Minor deals that I don't wish to go into.

'But I fretted. I thought: "Can't we learn something from all of this? The Tuberculin may have been a humbug, but it was a humbug that brought in two million dollars net profit in three years. And two million dollars don't start dancing on their own, unless some living force sets them moving. It wasn't the Tuberculin that did it; was it the advertising? Pah! Advertising is a wheel one sets in motion, it isn't a living force –

'And I thought: "Who bought it, and why?" And suddenly I saw them before me – thousands, hundreds of thousands, millions! The endless, swarming horde of crooked, shrunken, emaciated, staggering, coughing, shuffling, fumbling invalids, who must, must, must. Who must recover, who must grasp at every chance of recovery, who must stumble after every tiny glimpse of hope, who must believe in the incredible, no matter how absurd the form in which it is offered to them.

'And who must buy Arnberg's Tuberculin.

'Herr Arnberg! I am no philosopher, I am a businessman. I thought: "The living force in this business was a 'must'. A very powerful must, and, just at the moment, too powerful for you. But there must be more of them, and perhaps some of them are smaller. Nothing Too Small."

'I made observations, I collected them, I examined them.

'And I discovered that a swarm of gnats just before a storm on a summer's evening is nowhere near as numerous and furious and inescapable as the swarm of "musts" that assaults us on a daily basis.

'From the greatest: must live, down through countless gradations: must love, must hate, must have revenge, must be honourable, must be attractive, must have fun, must be polite, must keep up with the times, down to the tiniest and most ridiculous, albeit not the least insistent: must have a drink, must hear music, must shower in cold water, must have yellow shoes, must have a certain sort of wallpaper, must get out of bed on the right foot – *ad infinitum*, Herr Arnberg, for, as I say, it is easier to count the stars in the heavens that the "musts" that rule our lives.

'And when I examined these insects more closely, I found that if you discount the greatest of these – must live, for instance – then the differences in their force and power are largely insignificant. Often it is the smallest of them that rule us most absolutely. And I also found that when evaluating their power one cannot use any logical formulae, nor indeed any formulae at all. For instance, if one were to seek a logical basis for the very greatest of them – must live – one would be quite lost.

'And even the less, and least, significant ones have nothing to do with logic or common sense. Sometimes they strike us as eternal, and, as such, ought to have taught us to think in such a way that there can be no doubt as to their legitimacy. But this is not the case. Not even the very greatest of them – must live – is always raised beyond all doubt, and is still doubted in some quarters even to this day. And others – must reproduce, for instance – a "must" which I have taken as the basis for my highly regarded matrimonial agency – have occasionally been so weakened that their absolute opposite appears to be the only source of salvation.'

'Well, Herr Arnberg, I am no philosopher, I am a businessman. I no longer let all these musts worry me (although at times they seem to me to be the only living forces on earth, and we human beings their dead play-things), but I make use of them. I have based my activities on them. Not on the greatest of them – I leave those to men with greater capital. No, I use the smaller ones. Hahn, Huhn & Co. has taken on the task of nurturing, so to speak, the dominant "must" in every individual who puts his faith in us. Because it is this "must" which is his motive force, and by purifying it and freeing him from other less important "musts" we are able to produce a serviceable tool for some task or other from even quite insignificant men. Our enterprise is extremely extensive – in spite of the fact that it is only concerned with lesser matters, or perhaps precisely because of that. All the same, we've taken the time to pay particular attention to you. And I'd like to tell you why.'

He stood up and bowed, and put his hand on his heart.

'First and foremost, of course, you know the reasons for my personal attachment to you. Your father! Your sister! And, I might add, your great-uncle! But that's a different story entirely.

'Your sister was a remarkable person, in light of what I have just been saying. She was unusually free of all manner of "musts". She did not even feel a compulsion to live. And how she lived was a matter of complete indifference to her. She had, if I might express it thus, merely a theoretical interest. One might almost say it was immoral – with due respect to her memory.

'Your father, on the other hand – '

He sank down onto the bed once more.

'Yes, your father. I never did make him out. I say that to my great professional shame. I never understood what it was he was aiming for. He had his "must", there's no doubting that. Well, you know all about his *idée fixe*. But there was a semblance of free will in his compulsion that often puzzled me.

'However, he's dead now; some might say that he should be allowed to rest in peace.'

Mr Hansen shut his eyes in reflection. But my whole body was trembling, because I knew what was coming, and that there was no avoiding it. At last he said:

'Jan Arnberg, you know full well what you must do. You know that the state of apathy in which you find yourself is the result of your having withdrawn in the most cowardly way. You know that your father didn't die of his illness, but was strangled by a pair of miserable wretches. Yes, murdered in the most merciless way, for there is no deed worse than stealing the fruits of a man's lifetime of work and toil. You watched your father sink into a state of shameful misery. And yet so far you haven't lifted a finger to avenge him.'

And he said:

'Come, come – calm yourself. Wailing and gnashing of teeth are music to the ears of demons. But that isn't the sort of music you should be offering them. Let us be calm and think about this. You're far too upset to think clearly. But you can listen.'

I said:

'Why are you staring at me? Stop it.'

He replied:

'If my eyes leave you, then your ears will leave me. But you know that you must listen.

'You know that J. W. Grundberg and A. O. Arnfelt stole your father's invention, Arnberg's Explosive. You know that your father died in extreme poverty and humiliation while these two gentlemen were reaping the rewards of his labour. And you know that the current proprietor of the company Arnfelt & Grundberg, Mikael Arnfelt, is still reaping what your father sowed, while poverty has driven Johan Arnberg's son to the brink of crime –

'That is your position, isn't it?

'Now I want to tell you something. Listen carefully – because it's important. Your father had two true friends. One was J. P. Fält. Before your father died, he asked Fält for help. Fält came – but too late. Johan Arnberg was beyond help.

'But he left a son. Was there any hope of restoring justice? To rescue for the son at least part of what had been stolen from the father? Yes. Fält, a chemist and for many years your father's right-hand man, was well acquainted with the discovery that had been stolen from him. He decided to commence production without the protection of a patent, and in spite of this fact. He turned to me. I was prepared. Not just because I admired your father, but – and I say this quite openly – because I hoped to profit by it. We set up 'Arnberg's Explosives' in Remscheid. We have had a great many obstacles to deal with, and Fält grew tired. But not me. And we pledged to pay you, your father's heir, the commission that was rightly his. I say this not to win your gratitude, but so that you can see that there is a practical side to the matter. We have had great obstacles to deal with, and Fält grew tired. Not me. I have carried the burden alone up to now, when I have reached the point where I – and you as well – can begin to make a small profit.

'Well, the proprietor of Arnfelt & Grundberg, Mikael Arnfelt, is threatening to take us to court. He wishes to do to me and to you what his grandfather did to your father. I have invested a good deal of capital in this, and am now faced with ruin for the second time – '

As he related all these details, all these calculations, all these deals, it felt as though my chest were expanding, as though the heaviness in my eyelids and the pressure on my brow were lifting. It felt as though I were just on the point of waking from a deep sleep and about to be rid of a terrible nightmare. And I smiled to myself and thought:

'No, there's nothing forcing you – '

No sooner had he seen my smile than he came right up to me. And I heard his voice as if it were my own. He said:

'You know what you must do. Or do you imagine that your will has vanished without leaving a gap for something else? Or do you imagine that you've sold your honour and your conscience to serve an unknown woman? Do you imagine that you've opened the portals of death and yourself become a shadow and a ghost purely in order to kill a stranger? Would that not be meaningless, Jan Arnberg? Do you not have a prey for which you have been chosen?

'There is no need to worry about it, your poor wretch, because you must do it.

'But perhaps you don't know that what he did to your father – which is worth neither hatred nor revenge – and what he has done to you – which is worth neither hatred nor revenge – he is now doing to her. He has stolen from her and made her a beggar. Were you fond of her? He has made her a beggar, and so nauseatingly poor that she begs crumbs from the table of a harlot.'

And once again I was standing in the darkness by my window, which was fitted with firm iron bars. A fury like red-hot iron held me captive. Hatred – a nightmare from which one cannot wake – held me captive.

I could see Father Johannes' lantern gliding through the darkness. Silent as a night-bird. I hoped he would come up to my window. And no matter how indifferent it might seem, it was nonetheless a hope. And my only one.

It happened. He came up to my window, and, holding the lantern above his head so I could only vaguely make out a tall, dark figure and the pale oval of his face, he said:

'Jan, do you remember how afraid you were of being left alone when you were small? And how desperate you were to hold your mother's hand, or someone else's?'

I remembered.

He laughed and said:

'Perhaps you imagined that some terrible killer was lying in wait for you in Grandfather's jasmine hedge? Or that a thief had gone to ground in the plum-tree thicket? Or some other cruel and evil person was hiding behind the dovecote?'

And he said, as he lowered the lantern and went on his way:

'Ah, dear Jan, in Grandfather's garden there was only one evil and cruel person, only one thief and killer, and in the whole world there is only one evil and cruel person, only one thief and killer. You yourself.'

Chapter 4

The Four-Fold Reduction

The next day I was due to meet the American at the Rossbacher Keller; we were going to eat there, and – above all – drink, after which I was to take him to Maurette, and from Maurette to the St. Paul jetty, where my rowing-boat was moored. That was Maurette's plan; Mr Hansen had suggested another, or at least hinted at it.

But if I was finally to settle my account with Mikael Arnfelt, and that of the Arnberg family with the Arnfelt family, it really ought not to happen at the behest of Mr Hansen. I had fallen into a tangle of various people's wills, and was having difficulty telling them apart. In order to appreciate the problem I must reduce its various elements to their proper proportions.

Reduce – that was a word I had been given. Father Johannes handed me a letter through his hatch; it was from Hedda. It read:

Dear Jan!

I hope you haven't got a cold, although it's probably raining just as much there as it is here. It's been a dreary autumn. Otherwise things are much the same here. But I never meet any of the family, so cannot tell you how they are. But Miss Amelie is said to have been ill, and she looks it. But she doesn't acknowledge me, and I'd sooner avoid her. And perhaps you know more about Léonie than I do. Well, we knew well enough what sort of person he was, so I can't understand why the Dean gave his consent. But I daresay it would have made no difference if he'd refused.

Dear Jan, I've managed to get into debt this quarter, although I've got a breathing space until 1 Nov. I can see no way out. So I thought I would ask if you could lend me 200 kronor for six months? But I'm only asking, dear boy – don't give it a moment's thought if it would be a problem. Without it, we can always make it up through reductions. An old woman will always get by, you know, Jan. You know that I remain your affectionate

Hedda.

Jan, you mustn't put yourself out – we'd rather make reductions.

Quite so, dear Hedda – reductions! Change your magnificent, ramshackle old hostel for the poorhouse! It's true – for someone who knows how to make reductions, there's always a way out.

There were four elements to my problem that needed to be reduced to more reasonable and more easily managed proportions: the American, Maurette, Mr Hansen, and Léonie. And a fifth: myself. But that reduction would come of itself as a result of the others.

I began at the beginning:

1) The American. A simple operation. After we had eaten and drunk a good deal, I said: 'Monsieur, what exactly is it about Maurette that you cannot resist? What is it that's so unique and enticing that you must pay a fortune for it?'

He growled and blinked, shrugged and turned away. But I said: 'You think little Maurette is a rattlesnake who's still got her fangs. A mistake, my dear sir! Only the rattle is left, the fangs are gone. Maurette is harmless as *le favori du dompteur* usually is. If you imagine that you're playing with death, you're making a fool of yourself. And the price is quite unreasonable. Have you visited Monsieur Lebossu's establishment? *La maison des morts*? The same sensations, I assure you – but for five *louis d'or*, including champagne. Maurette is a pupil of Lebossu – perhaps the very best – but nothing more.'

When he heard what banal happiness awaited him in Maurette's embrace, he became furious at first, and for a moment it looked as though he wanted to experience tragedy at any cost. But after a while he calmed down, and only one last shred of doubt troubled him. Why had I betrayed the secret of the Hôtel de

Montsousonge? I replied:

'Because I am scandalously poorly paid, monsieur. Just think – one hundred marks a month! I must live, after all.'

And, working out what Hedda's rent would be in German currency, I asked whether the information might not be worth 230 marks. The paltriness of the sum took him aback to begin with; but I have no doubt that he later thought it too high. A sensible fellow of around a hundred kilos, not counting his soul or his millions. We parted – not as friends, because I had quickly been reduced from a comrade in an adventure to a lackey in a brothel. But nor did we part as enemies.

2) Maurette. Rather more difficult. When I went in to see her, she received me with a friendly, sad smile.

'Poor Jan,' she said, 'I'm inconsolable, but I have to give you your notice. You can't stay at the Hôtel de Montsousonge.'

I asked if my disobedience had angered her. She frowned and replied: 'Childish nonsense!'

And, smiling once more, she said:

'No, Jan, it's your own fault. You are said to have behaved badly towards one of Mrs Feurfield's beautiful protegées. Countess Arnfelt. How could you be so impudent? Poor Jan.'

I was quite taken aback, and blushed. My heart suddenly began to pound the way it used to. With indignation and fear.

I stammered:

'Was it the Countess – ?'

'No,' Maurette replied, enjoying my confused state, 'it was the Count who complained. And you know how strictly Mrs Feurfield stands on convention. I really can't help you, poor Jan. You'll have to go.'

She turned her back on me; and, picking up a photograph of a young musician tuning his violin from the table – we were in the small salon – she said:

'People say that the Countess is very fond of music. That would explain why Mrs Feurfield received another visit today. From both parties. Oh, how people talk!'

She put the photograph down, nodded and said:

'Well, dear Jan – farewell.'

I replied – tersely and abruptly, like an unfairly dismissed servant or an embittered lover – :

'As you wish, Madame. But you will forgive me for reminding you of what you owe me before I go.'

She had been expecting that. And she turned to face me, as quickly and lithely as only an animal could. When hunting. Ah, Maurette. What a magnificent performance. And how completely unnecessary.

'Owe you?' she repeated. 'Owe you?'

I replied:

'Quite so, Madame. You owe me two months' wages and another thirty marks for diverse expenses. In total, two hundred and thirty marks.'

This she had not been expecting. And as luck would have it, in her confusion she did not think to question my demand. Instead she paid me what I had asked for, and I counted the notes twice, wrote a receipt, thanked her and left.

A well accomplished reduction, it seemed to me.

3) Léonie. It occurred to me that I ought to change my clothes. I went through my wardrobe and found a suit from my Transatlantic days, an outfit that still held a faint odour of Eline's turpentine and benzine. I put it on and ended up looking rather shabby. So dressed, I headed off towards the Lombard Bridge, and walked slowly back and forth along the shore of the Alster. When I saw Mikael's car drive across the bridge towards St. George, I walked in through the gates and rang the bell. The maid made me wait in the hall. It was a long time before Léonie appeared. I was hanging about, leaning against an umbrella stand. I wiped my hand on my coat, stepped forward, took her hand, bowed. She asked me in.

Once inside, I noticed that she was dressed in black, pale, and looked as though she had been crying. I guessed and said:

'I was so sorry to hear about Aunt Amelie.'

She nodded. I asked why she had not returned for the funeral. She looked up and said very calmly:

'I can't leave Mikael.'

I made a gesture which I imagine Hedda might have made; gave a little shiver, shook my head, sighed, pressed my knees together, rocked a little on the edge of my chair, and stared at the floor. And said:

'Yes, it's terribly sad.'

After a while:

'Dear Léonie, I'm worried that I might have upset you the other day. I didn't mean to. I have no right to forbid you doing anything, or even to advise against it. It was just so strange, seeing you at the Hôtel de Montsousonge. – '

She said:

'Jan, I can't just walk about here with my eyes closed. I can't watch him changing day by day, little by little – sitting here with my arms folded. I have to know, at the very least! – '

And suddenly she was standing right next to me, her hands on my shoulders, her lips close to my cheek. Just like that time, long ago, when the rainbow appeared in the park at –dal.

She wanted information about Maurette.

It was a while before I could answer. But that was quite natural, of course – that I was reflecting upon it.

'Maurette – ' I said. 'Yes, what can I tell you about Maurette? Without being too severe or too generous. Naturally she is not what one might call a fine lady. But, on the other hand, she is really rather *chic*. I imagine you would find her a little shocking. Of course she's nowhere near as particular as Mrs Feurfield. No, I'd sooner say that she is a little too liberal in her ways – '

I sat there alone and reeled off my words. Léonie had taken up her position by the window once more. The light was in my eyes; the room was grey and hazy, it could have been any room. I saw only the dark silhouette.

Léonie said:

'Maurette – yes, I know her name is Maurette.'

I went on:

'But I think it would be a shame if people started to talk about you. You can't imagine what a hotbed of gossip Hamburg is. Of course, it doesn't really matter what people say here. But imagine

Memoirs of a Dead Man

if it were to get back to W. Imagine if the Dean were to hear something. Or Aunt Norah! I should be very glad if you would be more careful, Léonie. Perhaps you think I'm being impudent – but we are cousins, after all, and childhood friends besides – '

I could have gone on like that for hours, because the tongue is an organ one can safely leave to itself. And all the while I am like a drowned man in my own stream of words, and only my eyes are alive.

But as I was sitting there, secure in my lifelessness, I was surprised to feel my heart start beating like a living organ. And my eyes were transformed, as though a wind had blown across them, and I seemed to be seeing her for the first time. At that very moment she said:

'My dear Jan, it isn't working. You're no good at deception. So please stop! You mean to torment me, but you must help me. Why would you have come otherwise?'

And she repeated this time after time, each time more assured and triumphant:

'You've come here to help me. Why would you have come otherwise? You can help me, Jan, and that's why you're here.'

My system of reductions was sorely tested by this, but I withstood the test nonetheless, saying:

'My dear Léonie, I am afraid I am the one who must ask for help. Mikael has seen to it that I have lost my position with Madame de Montsousonge. Unless you can lend me two hundred and thirty marks, I shall be out on the streets. I am quite destitute.'

She left the room, and after I had stood for a while staring at the floor, I quickly turned and went out into the hall, because my courage had deserted me. But my eyes were blinded by the light from the windows and I could not immediately find the door. Then I heard her call my name, and I stopped. She came out to me and handed me a thousand mark note. I said: 'No, no more than two hundred and thirty. That's all I need.' And in my confusion I took out my wallet and my purse and counted out seven hundred and thirty marks in notes and gold coins, which I gave her as change for her charitable donation. This, naturally, meant that I was betraying my rôle of penniless beggar. What she made of this I do not know. I did not look at her but went on my way.

4) Mr Hansen. Caused me few problems. I decided to free myself from him the same way I had freed myself from Maurette. *Mutatis mutandis*. I sought him out in his office, in an old, red, gabled building, really rather fine, although it smelled of old junk. His car – a ridiculous contraption with a body that was far too small and a chassis so large that it looked like a cranefly with its legs spread out – was parked outside the door. So Mr Hansen was in, but I had to wait almost two hours among the clerks in the anteroom. And would perhaps have had to wait even longer had the door to Mr Hansen's room not suddenly flown open and Rygell burst out. He was laughing shrilly and bitterly, and rushed across the room without noticing me. I asked one of the clerks: 'What's up with him?' He shook his head, smiled and whispered: 'Maybe he's got St. Vitus's dance – '

'Fine,' I thought, 'then I shall make Mr Hansen dance for a change.'

And without further ceremony I marched into the office, closing and bolting the door behind me. Mr Hansen, who was sitting at his desk writing, glanced at me and growled:

'So who's this, then? What do you want?'

I pulled up a chair and sat down. I also pulled out my revolver and placed it within reach. Eventually I said:

'Mr Hansen, I'm sure you haven't forgotten our conversation of the thirteenth, and the agreement we reached – '

'Agreement?' he muttered, staring at the revolver.

I went on:

'Yes, you remember that your fiancée, Miss Feurfield, had a relationship with a certain American gentleman – '

'Excuse me!' he exclaimed, the colour of his skin turning from blue to violet. 'A relationship! I will thank you not to use that word! You should be ashamed of yourself!'

I said:

'I don't mean to hurt your feelings. "Relationship" was too

strong a word. Rather, an unhealthy inclination. At any rate, you expressed a wish that I might persuade the American to leave Hamburg. I have done as you asked, and now I expect you to fulfil your part of the bargain – '

He gestured towards the revolver and said: 'Put that away.' And when I did not comply, he looked towards the door, which was bolted. He subsided into quiet deliberation, and only his heavy breathing and the movement of his eyelids indicated that he was still alive. I did not disturb him, and finally he came round again:

'Herr Arnberg,' he began, gesturing with his hand as though inviting me to sit down. 'I am sure that you recall the fact that I was extremely nervous that night. Miss Feurfield has a temperament that would make even the calmest man nervous. I was looking on the dark side of things, and I may have exaggerated somewhat. I seem to recall that we spoke about Arnberg's Explosives. In Remscheid. Was that not so? And that I hinted at certain possibilities in relation to that.

'But I could not possibly have given you a firm promise, Herr Arnberg. Because the whole business was far from being decided at that point. Since then, thank goodness, it has assumed more solid form. I mentioned to you that we were being threatened with court action. That danger has thankfully receded. A quite colossally satisfactory agreement has been reached between Arnfelt & Grundberg on the one side and Arnberg's Explosives in Remscheid on the other. The future now looks much brighter for us. We believe we are heading for a boom in business, and our risks are relatively small now that we have such an affluent and respected company as Arnfelt & Grundberg behind us. It is all colossally gratifying. And I am not flattering Miss Feurfield if I say that she played a successful and considerable part in our negotiations. Count Arnfelt is a highly educated man in matters of aesthetics, and he has the best possible qualifications for understanding and appreciating Miss Feurfield's remarkable personality. For her part, Maurette fully appreciates the advantages of having Count Arnfelt as our friend. So if you wish to avoid a breach with Miss Feurfield, you would be wise to regard him as worthy of the greatest respect. Which, of course, he is.'

I said: 'You don't know that Maurette has dismissed me?'

He put his hand to his chest and leaned forward in a bow.

'Yes, I know. And I am sorry. But it was necessary. The Count expressed a wish which, under our present circumstances, we could hardly refuse. The Count could not be reckoned among your friends, Herr Arnberg. And that was precisely what I wanted to talk to you about. I seem to recall that in my confused state that night I mentioned something about a commission? That was not a commitment, merely a hope. Unfortunately it has come to naught. You understand, Count Arnfelt could not possibly acknowledge that you have any such right or privilege. He is morally impeded from doing so. Because that would be tantamount to admitting that his honourable grandfather had committed a crime against your own esteemed father. So you must give up – '

I saw that my moment had come; I leapt up, snatching the revolver, and banged the butt hard on the desk. Then, the revolver still in my hand, I began to pace up and down the room, swinging my arms and steadily letting my voice grow louder.

'So!' I said, 'you mean to cheat me again. First you do me out of a job where I was happy and could make a small income. And now this! Don't you see, Mr Hansen, that it might all get too much for me? Don't you think a man like me might get desperate? Don't you think I could avenge myself? Take a look at this revolver, Mr Hansen! It's loaded with Arnberg's Explosive! Might that not be regarded as a twist of fate? – '

And I paced back and forth, and, just as I had with Léonie, I let my tongue look after itself while I gathered my thoughts. Mr Hansen had positioned himself in front of the door, arms outstretched, as though hoping to block my voice and stop my words from seeping out to the listening clerks. Finally I threw myself down in Mr Hansen's chair – I was genuinely tired – and laid my head and arms on the desk. I heard Mr Hansen padding about me uneasily, like a cat round hot porridge; then he stroked my back, my shoulder, my arm. His hand worked its way down to mine, and carefully his fingers began to loosen my grip on the

Memoirs of a Dead Man

revolver. I let him have his way. He took it and locked it in the side-drawer of the desk. I muttered: 'What are you doing? Are you taking my gun away?' Eventually I sat up, rubbed my temples and sighed. I said:

'What are you going to do with me, Mr Hansen? Have you no suggestions for me?'

He leaned his elbows on the desk and looked searchingly at me for a long while, perhaps a little suspiciously. His voice was now calm, steady and factual once more:

'Yes, Herr Arnberg, I do have a suggestion for you. You must give up, that's my advice. I'm afraid you've been harbouring far too high an opinion of yourself. You've imagined yourself to be an unusual person, and have been hoping for an unusual fate. Your so-called Transatlantic Project illustrates best how ridiculously you have over-estimated yourself. And then when that bubble burst, your megalomania found expression elsewhere, and you believed yourself capable of committing all manner of audacious crimes. But there again you over-estimate yourself. Believe me; I am a expert. I admit that I over-estimated you to start with. But my observations during the last half an hour have confirmed my opinion.

'You must give up, Herr Arnberg; that would be your best option, all things considered. You have lost a position where you really could – as you said – earn a tidy little income. But there's no reason why you should go without your daily bread. Our firm does not abandon its clients. It may occasionally make a mistake, but in such cases it always makes good its mistake. We shall take steps to procure for you a suitable and respectable position straight away. You will be quite satisfied with us, and I hope we shall be satisfied with you. And now I would ask you to detain me no longer.'

I stood up, my movements unsteady, as though I had just woken up. I pushed my hair back, buttoned my stained coat and sighed. Then I said, giving Mr Hansen a pleading, troubled look:

'And the commission, Mr Hansen? Do you really mean to say that I won't get a penny?'

He shook his head.

I held out my hands to him and said: 'A thousand marks, Mr Hansen, a paltry thousand marks! A thousand marks and I'll give you a signed agreement to relinquish all claims – '

He closed his eyes, shook his head. I took my time, examining him, evaluating him, weighing him up. Eventually I said – my tone revealing that this was my final proposal – :

'Mr Hansen, I'm in dire straits. I need two hundred and thirty marks. You, who were a friend to both my father and my sister, will you refuse me two hundred and thirty marks?'

Thirty seconds – then he opened one eye.

'In return for an agreement?' he asked. I sighed and made a feeble, desperate gesture with my hands.

'Why not? I must – '

He sat down and began to write. Once he looked up and our eyes met for a second, but I lowered my gaze immediately. He passed me the receipt and I signed without reading it. Then he took out his wallet and counted out two hundred and thirty marks in small notes. I counted the money in turn and put it away. Mr Hansen said:

'And now, Herr Arnberg, once and for all, I would ask that you do not seek credit against my affection for your father and sister. It is scarcely honourable to profiteer like that from a sacred memory. One must have a career of one's own, no matter how modest – '

I listened quietly and patiently, then made a deep bow to Mr Hansen and left.

With my 4 x 230 marks in my pocket, I made my way to the nearest post-office and wrote out a money order for 800 kronor, and wrote in the margin: 'Procured without inconvenience through four reductions, Jan.'

I felt calm and light-hearted. The American dollar-man had left my world, and with him went the last hope of ever realising my project. I had sold the rights and honour of my youth to Maurette for 230 marks, and for the same sum I had got rid of the rights and honour of my heart. And finally I had sold The Great Injustice, my inheritance from my father, the family heirloom, to Hahn, Huhn

& Co. for 230 marks, or three months' rent on Hedda's hostel.

Four elements of my problem had been erased or reduced as far as possible. The fifth, myself, had assumed more manageable proportions. The sixth, Mikael Arnfelt, remained – with undiminished powers of attraction.

I paused by the window of the gatehouse and told Father Johannes everything. (Nowadays he was my confidant in all things, but he gave no advice, and I had to act as I myself thought best.) He held out his hand to me, and I heard him laugh – the roguish laugh I have never been able to forget. He said:

'You've become quite the mendicant friar, Jan! You humble yourself at the door for the sake of Christ, but still hope that something will fall into your sack. Well, what did you get?'

I thought for a moment, and replied:

'Well, I didn't get anything. I've given or thrown away my last ounce of pride, my last mote of self-respect. I have thrown away myself, down to the bare essentials. The will, Father. Have I understood you correctly?'

And I felt free and calm and light-hearted.

Nothing concerned me. I felt I did not even need to look out for my chance. On the contrary, it amused me to avoid everything connected to Mikael Arnfelt. It was a sort of affected gallows' humour. I could have said, like a man sentenced to death: 'The gallows will just have to wait until I arrive.' – I made no attempt to hurry.

Mr Hansen offered me a position in his office. I accepted the job and eagerly applied myself to it. My task was to compile a multi-faceted advertising campaign for Hahn & Huhn's matrimonial agency. I engaged Fält to help me, and approached the faithful with a pamphlet in which we quoted 84 biblical passages, beginning with Genesis 1:27. The patriot's duty was emphasised in a series of alarmist articles written by Steintheel. The hygienic aspect of the subject was illuminated in the pamphlet 'Why must you?', in the journal *The Decline of the Species*, as well as in a score of brochures for more mature young people. We published a famous didactic novel, *Sarai or Hagar?*

Nor did we neglect occult societies; a hand-written message, 'Message from a Mormon preacher to his favourite surviving wife' (written by an expert in spiritualism), was distributed to certain groups. In it 'the prominent Mormon preacher J. P. Fält, deceased as a result of an accident' addresses his beloved and inconsolable wife Eline – confirming that the doctrine concerning the longing of unborn spirits for life was the kernel of truth which facilitated God's support for the activities of Smith and his apostles. It was Fält himself who composed the pamphlet; it was full of intimate details of his life with Eline, and afforded him such satisfaction that he was constantly quoting from it, as he had once quoted from Scripture. And in an enormous advertisement, beneath the heading 'Build your own home! Free!' we offered '2,000 hand-tinted and absolutely authentic plans for your own home. Free! A rich man may be homeless, but a home makes a poor man rich! Free, from Hahn, Huhn & Co. – advice and support for all who seek their fortune with us.'

I had also released a triptych of postcards: 'Father's Grave', 'Mother's Grave' and 'The Single Person's Grave'; and I was just about to follow that with a series of sentimental and comical cards 'From the Bachelor's Den and the Nursery' when Mr Hansen came in to see me and asked whether I had been using any population statistics. I replied that I had used a great many figures in the pamphlet 'The Treasures of the Earth – Who Shall Inherit Them?' This was evidently to his satisfaction, and he said:

'Arnberg, you'll have to stop this. I need you elsewhere.'

But I had become so attached to the nursery project that I had no desire at all to stop. Only when he had hinted at an increase in my wages of 25 marks a month did I relent and ask what I was to be used for. Mr Hansen shifted from one foot to the other, and appeared quite absent-minded. Eventually he said:

'Arnberg, it's a colossally important matter. It really lies entirely outside our field of operations. Thus far we have only been concerned with minor things that we could imprint on the public consciousness with one or two short, clear slogans. But this – this, my dear Arnberg, must, so to speak, be introduced by circuitous means, by the back door. It is really a matter for the larger companies. And if Hahn, Huhn & Co. is to join them, then it must happen in the humble but optimistic realisation that even the slightest detail – hmm – has its importance.

'In short, my dear Arnberg, it's a question of pointing out and imprinting upon the public consciousness the dangers that threaten Europe as a result of over-population. The problem is – I have been told – both real and imminent. At least it could be made to be imminent, if it were introduced to the agenda in a suitable way. If it became one of today's "musts", if I might put it like that. At the moment I cannot give you detailed instructions, for I am myself awaiting certain advice and suggestions. But you should be prepared, you should improve your knowledge of the relevant fields, and, above all else, you should establish connections with Steintheel and others of his ilk. And as of today you will cease working for Department IV – '

I said:

'As you wish. And which department will I belong to now? – '

He paced back and forth, rubbing his frozen blue cheeks, giggling self-consciously, uneasily, almost roguishly –

'My dear Arnberg,' he said finally, 'I tell you this in confidence. Because it will please you. For reasons of piety alone, it will please you colossally. You will be working in Department XIX – '

And he leaned close to my ear and whispered, smugly and giggling:

'Arnberg's Explosives – you see – '

But I did not last long in Department XIX.

When I left the Hôtel de Montsousonge in the middle of October, I moved in with Kugel. The indolent little man had followed the advice and suggestions of Department IV so faithfully that his family had started to get out of control. He needed my hundred and twenty marks a month all too well. I for my part needed him, his wife, his children, his home and his life. It would have been impossible for me to wait and watch if I had not had his life to inhabit. I was a parasite. I assumed my host's shape and colouring so completely that we were like a pair of twins. I cradled his children, I gave his wife money for the housekeeping, I kept him company to the beer-halls and bowling alleys, even to political meetings. For the indolent little man was a great politician – I do not remember of what particular hue, but I recall that he hated Rygell, who was a socialist, or possibly an anarchist. We lived a very happy life; and when the youngest Kugel died that Christmas, I did not simply wear a black armband, but also cried as bitterly as if it were my own life I were grieving for. And Mrs Kugel took me in her arms and said:

'Jan – you've a good heart, all the same.'

On New Year's Day itself I received a first reminder. Steintheel came to me with his notebook, saying as he sharpened his pen:

'Jan, can you give me some personalia? About Countess Arnfelt?'

I asked if she had died. But it was only the latest Montsousonge scandal, still in its infancy, which had set him in motion. He must be prepared. Certain rumours were circulating. Had I not heard?

I told him what he wanted to know, but avoided asking anything –

All the same, I could not rid myself of my curiosity. I turned to J. P. Fält, but I could not bring myself to ask any direct questions, and so received no answers. Then I looked up Rygell, who was working in Hahn & Huhn's Department VIII – private detective assignments. He said:

'It's this season's scandal for Mrs Feurfield. But it's not ripe yet and isn't due for a few weeks. It's probably some sort of publicity for the carnival, which by all accounts will be magnificent this year. Among other things, Madame is preparing a grand masked ball. I presume it will be in her usual genre – with tragic masks. As far as the scandal goes, it concerns the Countess and a priest. They've already tried with a musician, but the Countess didn't take the bait. Fält is saying that the Count himself is behind it all. He wants rid of her. Ask Fält!'

So I turned back to Fält. He had taken a job with Madame; not my superior position as privileged dog, though – he's a menial lackey. I asked him straight out, but he knew nothing. He thinks only of Eline, and speaks only of Eline. He has found her again and resurrected their marriage. He insists that everything is as it used to be. But when he is drunk he becomes more open-hearted, saying:

'She's the same, Jan. But I'm not. I'm the one who needs the washing of regeneration.'

The second reminder came from Rygell. We met one evening at the Rossbacher Keller, and were drinking and singing as we used to do. We ended up playing cards, and it got late. When the clock struck two Rygell started and stood up. Then he threw himself back in the chair and said with a laugh:

'No. Why should I work like a dog for Mr Hansen? Sweet dreams, Mr Hansen, Rygell is keeping watch.'

I asked what assignment he was on. He replied:

'I'm watching Maurette. Maurette and Mikael. Maurette held Mikael dear, and Mikael, Maurette. That sounds like the refrain of an old ballad. But Hansen doesn't like old ballads. The Count has sued for divorce from the Countess, and has moved into the Hôtel de Montsousonge. Mr Hansen thinks that this is too much. It's introduced an unnecessary touch of realism to the comedy. So I have to keep watch. But I know the way of a man, and can quite easily write freehand reports about Maurette and Mikael.'

And we carried on playing, but after half an hour he stood up, threw down his cards, and left without saying goodbye. I followed him and saw that he was heading for the Hôtel de Montsousonge.

The third reminder came from Steintheel again. He asked a favour of me.

'I'm going to Spain and Morocco at the end of February. But before I leave I must write a few lines about the masked ball at the Hôtel de Montsousonge in March. Would you mind writing them for me?'

I replied that I had not thought of attending the masked ball. He put pen and paper in front of me and said:

'That doesn't matter. I already know the sort of thing that's required. The Hôtel de Montsousonge is no longer so unpredictable, not since Mr Hansen let it go – '

'Let it go!' I exclaimed.

'What, haven't you heard? Mr Hansen has released the establishment, including Maurette, into the hands of Monsieur Lebossu from Paris. You know – *maison des morts*. So we can no longer expect any surprises. It'll be skeletons, sheets and pistol shots. The new regime is being heralded by an historical masquerade: the death of Gustav III. Check the story, if you have a copy of it, and work out what the best masks are. Count Arnfelt will be the King, Maurette a prophetess. You can identify the other masks as you see fit, it doesn't matter. Please say you'll do it – '

I agreed. I was thinking: 'Is this masquerade Maurette's idea, or Monsieur Lebossu's? If it's Maurette's, then there may not being any time to lose.'

But I was confident in my plan, and as arrogant as the man who kept the gallows waiting.

I had such confidence in my plan and in myself that I could afford to do a good deed. From Rygell I got hold of Léonie's new address, a pension some five minutes' walk from the Hôtel de Montsousonge. I made my way there, handed over my card, and was told in reply that the Countess was not receiving visitors. I pushed the girl aside, opened the door and walked in. Léonie was sitting at a table by the window writing letters. Like last time, I could only see her as a dark silhouette against the hazy grey glass. I did not bother with introductions but asked her to go home, or somewhere else, just as long as she left Hamburg. I said:

'Why do you stay here? Only to torment yourself. And what good does that do?'

But to all my questions, justifications and pleas she replied unerringly:

'I can't leave Mikael.'

And she said:

'I know something is going to happen to him. And I can't leave him.'

I asked what she would be able to do to help him. Hadn't he denied her any possibility of helping him? Did she know of any way of liberating him from Maurette? Did she have even the

Memoirs of a Dead Man

slightest chance of visiting him in the Hôtel de Montsousonge?'

But to everything I said, explained and pleaded she had but one response: 'I can't leave Mikael.'

So I had to go further than I had anticipated, so much further that I was in danger of falling into my own pit. I said:

'Léonie, that's an *idée fixe*. But I'll make you see sense. You yourself admit that you can do nothing for Mikael? Well. If you promise to leave Hamburg tomorrow, I in turn will promise to watch over Mikael. I know Maurette, I know the Hôtel de Montsousonge. Who do you think will be more use to him – you or me?'

And to convince her – because she doubted me – I said:

'If you believe that I've ever cared for you, Léonie – '

She believed.

And so I was able to remove Léonie from the arena.

Only a few days later people began to talk about the masked ball. Even Kugel had heard something. And Rygell said: 'We'll see if Mr Hansen doesn't play some trick on the young Count. He loves Arnberg's Explosives and as a consequence even the Count. But he still loves Maurette more.'

Steintheel postponed his trip.

But I was sure of my plan. I decided not even to attend the masked ball. I bet ten to one that it would go off in true Lebossu-style, gruesome and inoffensive.

The evening before the masked ball I sat down to write a letter to Léonie. I post-dated it by two days, pretended that the masked ball was over, and described it. I did so out of defiance and to pass the time. I did not even know if I was going to send the letter –

As I was writing there was a knock at the door. It was J. P. Fält. But at first I did not recognise him. He was dressed in black livery with knee-breeches and silk stockings. Poor Fält! He had legs like knitting-needles and looked quite ridiculous. I asked who had dressed him up like that. He muttered sullenly:

'Oh, it's on Monsieur Lebossu's orders. I have to dress like this.'

He handed me a note. I recognised Mikael's writing at once

and felt no desire to open the envelope. But Fält, silent and sullen, was waiting for a reply. Eventually, when Fält refused to leave without an answer, I broke the seal and read:

Dear Jan.

I have just received a letter from Léonie. She is concerned for my safety and writes that I should turn to you if I am in need of help. You are said to have placed yourself at my disposal. If she has not misunderstood you, I would ask that you visit me, tomorrow at the latest –

I tore up the note, throwing the pieces in the stove. I replied that I would come. –

And the letter to Léonie – I tore it up.

Chapter 5

Le Maschere da Capo

Monday, 31 March was to be the day of the masked ball in the Hôtel de Montsousonge, now Monsieur Lebossu's establishment.

I got up at half past ten, dressed, had breakfast on a tray, wrote two letters, one to Hedda, the other to the Dean. After that I did not know what to do. I drank a shot of whisky, lay down on the sofa and fell asleep. But after half an hour Mrs Kugel came in with her eldest son. She showed me his right foot; there was a swelling under the heel, as big as my thumb. The boy had probably got a splinter in his foot, and it had festered, allowing pus to build up. The boy screamed terribly if I so much as touched the swelling. I made a decision; it must be lanced at once. Little Kugel ran out of the room screaming, and his mother asked me to reflect on what I was about to do. I said:

'It's unpleasant, but it can't be helped. The swelling must be lanced. It will be done in an instant. Wash the lad's foot and put something in his mouth.'

I ran down to the chemist's, bought a gauze bandage, cotton-wool and disinfectant, and asked the chemist for advice as to the best way of making such an incision. He advised me to use my razor-blade. I returned, fairly confident about what I was about to do; I said to Mrs Kugel: 'We'll take him by surprise; he won't notice anything if only you can stay calm. Get him lying face-down on the drawing-room table and play with him. It will be done in an instant.'

She did as I asked. I went out to the kitchen and sterilised the blade over the gas-flame. Then, humming softly, I walked straight up to the drawing-room table, took a firm grip of the boy's ankle, lifted the foot towards the daylight, and, before the child could catch his breath, I had lanced the boil, cleaned the wound and bandaged it. Naturally the boy screamed, but it was all over in three minutes. I was really rather pleased with myself, and Mrs Kugel did not know how she would ever be able to thank me.

But it was still no later than two o'clock.

I was struck by the notion of eating at the Rossbacher Keller. But that was a mistake; I turned round at the door. I walked all the way down to the Two Hares; but even that turned out to be a mistake. I got home at six o'clock; I was quite ravenous, and Mrs Kugel had to fix me something. I fetched a bottle of fortified wine, but drank just a couple of glasses. Mrs Kugel passed me a package which had arrived by express delivery at about four o'clock. I opened it and found my revolver, which I had left behind in Mr Hansen's office a few months earlier. Kugel stared, and for some obscure reason started talking about the masked ball. I went into my room.

I wondered: 'Is this just a coincidence, or a deliberate coincidence?' By this time I was thoroughly familiar with Mr Hansen's methods. And I determined not to use the revolver under any circumstances. I would not tolerate that sort of pressure. I thought: 'I can take my razor-blade or something else with me. I'll know what to do when the time comes.' It was half past seven.

Kugel rapped on my door.

'I almost forgot,' he said. 'Fält was here looking for you. Count Arnfelt wants to speak to you.'

And he stared at me, wide-eyed; so I shrugged my shoulders and replied: 'The Count will have to wait.'

'Ah, of course,' Kugel said. He started to make fun of poor Fält, running about the streets in his lackey's uniform. I said:

'Whatever do you mean, my dear Kugel? It's the way of the world that we should all wear our insignia sometimes.'

He laughed and said:

'Yes, you're right. Fält has always had the soul of a lackey. I remember that time at the Two Hares! You were sitting there with his fiancée in your lap – we made such fun of poor Fält! I for one was almost ashamed. He was far too easy a target. – '

I conceded that he was right, and that his feelings did him credit. And I guided him out of the room.

It was only half past seven. I gulped a large whisky, quickly checked my outfit, lay down on the sofa and fell asleep. –

I woke up. – It was five minutes past eleven. I leapt up, changed from top to toe, stropped my knife, shaved, washed, got dressed. I took a cab in the street and drove to the Hôtel de Montsousonge.

It struck me at once that the Hôtel looked more like a public building. The courtyard was harshly lit up. A number of lackeys in black and silver were standing on the steps. Above the door grinned a death's head, blue flames burning in its eye-sockets. The guests were beginning to arrive.

When I took out my purse to pay the driver I noticed that the revolver was in my pocket. In my haste, and out of habit, I must have picked it up; but it was of no consequence. I also had the knife on me, and – in any case – I had not decided upon anything in particular. I was entrusting the details to the hand of fate.

Beside the gatehouse, close to its window, stood Steintheel, notebook and pen at the ready, noting down the more significant guests. This annoyed me, as I had been hoping to have a few words with Father Johannes. I shook Steintheel by the hand and asked in jest:

'Well, have you worked out who's going to do it?'

He shrugged his shoulders:

'Do you know what?' he said. 'I ought to be ashamed at feeling disappointed. I've let myself be fooled. Just look at that death's head! This is just another *bal macabre à la Lebossu*. Why on earth didn't I go to Morocco!'

I consoled him, saying:

'Morocco remains, but Montsousonge will fall.'

As I was about to walk in, I realised how much the character of the place had changed. The lackey asked to see my ticket! Tickets for the Hôtel de Montsousonge. Satan will be selling tickets next! I told him to go to hell.

In the hall I spotted Rygell; he was standing talking to a

gentleman who resembled the head waiter of one of the better restaurants. I must admit that it was mainly his costume that gave that impression; but he seemed to be nothing more than costume.

I came up with an excuse to talk to Rygell, and found out from him that Mikael's rooms were on the first floor, next to the gaming room. We talked about guests and masks, and eventually I asked:

'Well, Rygell, have you found out anything?'

He looked at me with his fiery, defiant schoolboy's eyes.

'What do you know?'

I laughed and said:

'Well at least I now know where to find His Lordship.'

Rygell reflected.

'Yes,' he said, 'one can always draw certain conclusions. Or guess. I have orders from Mr Hansen to watch Maurette, whom he supposes to be suffering badly from her lugubrious melancholy. But I also have orders from Maurette to watch Mr Hansen, whom she supposes to be suffering badly from jealousy. From this I deduce that neither Maurette nor Hansen is the right person. But if I had to guess – '

He gestured with his head.

' – well, then I'd guess at him there. Him.'

'Who?' I asked, looking round wide-eyed.

'That one. The man himself. Monsieur Lebossu.'

I looked at the man; but there was not much to look at. Almost only clothes, and, under a jet-black wig, a pointed, wizened, yellow face, adorned with several obvious touches of rouge. I said: 'Well, my dear Rygell, you've clearly got your suspicions.'

I climbed the spiral staircase and crossed the gaming room, which was in darkness. I did not bother to switch the lights on, and so do not know if there was anyone in the room. Next to the gaming room lay a smaller room which was used by the most intimate guests of the house on special occasions. The rooms were linked by a jib-door; against expectation, I found it locked. So I had to fumble along the corridor, which was also in darkness. Just as I put my hand to the doorknob, I heard Mikael's voice, sharp and dry: 'Who's there?' I opened the door and stepped in.

The small gaming room was the counterpart of Maurette's oval room, but was slightly larger as it had an alcove – and in that alcove was the door to the large gaming room. The walls were clad in inlaid mirrors and old Genoese silk. There used to be a card-table in the alcove, but now in the gloom I saw that there was a large bed there. The other card-tables had also been removed. In their place, at the other end of the oval from the door, stood a writing desk. At the centre of the long wall stood a dressing table, groaning under the weight of the toiletries upon it, and above the table – in spite of all the wall-mirrors – hung the family heirloom, the mirror with the Seven Virtues and the Arnfelt coat of arms on its silver frame.

Mikael was standing in the middle of the floor; he was dressed in a light-blue silk gown that reached all the way to his slippers. On his head he was wearing a skull-cap of a similar hue, and over his eyes a shade that made me think of his blind grandmother. At the desk a young man was writing. Mikael said: 'One moment, Jan.' And he dictated some closing phrases from which I understood that it was a business letter. The young man stood up when he had finished writing, and now that I saw him standing there, arms pressed hard to his sides, head humbly and piously inclined to one side, I suddenly recognised him. It was the same priest Léonie and I had met in Mrs Feurfield's anteroom, although he was now dressed in layman's clothing. It seemed likely to me that this was the priest with whom Mikael had sought to compromise Léonie.

Once the young man had left the room, with a bow to the Count and a somewhat slighter one to me, Mikael said:

'Hah, that one! He's an ugly customer. *Sacrebleu*, how he disappoints me! But his handwriting is quite charming.'

Suddenly he approached me with his arms raised, as though about to embrace me. But he contented himself with shaking my hand.

'My dear Jan, it's been a long time! But don't you think we could leave out the pleasantries? What time is it?'

The clock had just struck midnight.

'Well,' he went on, 'we have a couple of hours. Sit down. I'm already a little tired.'

He sat down at the dressing table and absent-mindedly began to arrange the objects upon it. He pulled off the skull-cap. His hair was thinner, he was almost bald; his neck was thin and the colour of his skin had a yellowish tint; his ears were white as chalk, possibly powdered, because I could see traces of powder on his shoulders. His posture was slovenly, his shoulders hanging, the right somewhat lower than the left. I noticed a slight but constant trembling in his hands. His whole frame seemed to falter a little in the chair, as though seeking support and rest.

I had just had time to notice all of this when I suddenly realised that he was watching me in the mirror. I gave a start, and could not help blushing. He raised an eyebrow. Then he pulled off the shade and said with a smile:

'You were looking at me, my dear Jan? Well, I've got older. And just as well, I was about to say.

'But now there's the matter of this puerile masquerade. It's Maurette's idea, as you will appreciate. And, seeing as I need Maurette, I do as Maurette wishes. You know her, don't you? That's as may be, but you can hardly be aware of just what a find she is, as Mr Hansen would say. She is an arcanum, worthy of Doctor Faust or his friend, Satan. I can imagine finding her like as a mistress, but not as an enemy. She is quite extraordinarily underhand, deceitful and ruthless. Any man who holds her in his arms cannot but feel like a hero. And Jan – that's a valuable feeling. An elixir of youth. She is a game – a game of life and death. Well – one imagines that she is. And that, of course, is enough.

'But, to stick to matter in hand: Maurette is amused by old stories in the vein of, let us say, Bulwer. In order to satisfy this innocent passion, I have been leafing through some old documents – these here – our family chronicle, which offers one or two episodes along those lines. Above all one glorious episode – my dear great-great-grandfather's participation in the ultimate tragedy: what is known as the Opera Masquerade. In order to impress my little friend, I gave my ancestor a far more important rôle than the relatively obscure one he actually played. I cast him in the part of Anckarström himself, and stole for our family a certain hallowed glory – in Maurette's eyes. Well, she thought the story charming – particularly as the basis for an entertaining masked ball. It's just to her taste, arranging a fictitious murder of such highly tragic piquancy. So you can see why the ruler of the Hôtel de Montsousonge is arranging *tableaux vivants* of motifs taken from the histories of our old friend Odhner.

'What's more, she wants me to take on the rôle of His Late Majesty. It's altogether too flattering. I should have declined, had the little minx not put it like this: "Mikael – dare you play the king?" And, with that, the little schemer's feline claws were in me; and the old game was afoot again. It's a strange word, "dare". As a boy, one regards it almost as the touchstone of masculine morality and masculine worth. And God only knows if we are any the wiser with age. In any event, the word retains its power over the Arnfelt heart. *Quia leo* – that's our motto. I don't think I've ever been able to translate such heroic and heraldic Latin. But I have tried.

'So now we have reached the point where the woman asks: "Dare you?" To which the man naturally replies: "Of course I dare!" And that may be regarded as an end to such a matter as this, where the dare concerns a masked ball in the year 1913 in the good city of Hamburg. But Jan! Something has changed. Something quite fatal. Something which is bound to make me blush – just as you blushed a moment ago –

'Jan. Something's frightened me. I'm frightened.'

'Yes, I really am frightened. Of course, it's a proper Montsousonge fear, the quivering of over-excited nerves. Weakness of the heart. But – I can't help it – my brain is also playing its part in this absurdity. And there are good reasons for concern.

'First and foremost: my demise would benefit the former protector both of the house and of Maurette, Mr Hansen. *Titulus* Hansen has connections with my business, but Mr Hansen is as sanguine as he is unreliable. He has lived in the happy belief that the cat would collect chestnuts for the monkey. But the cat – if I might so degrade our proud family crest – is too sly for the monkey. And Mr Hansen is beginning to realise that. Moreover, Maurette claims that he is mortally jealous. Well, I don't set much store by that. What sort of nonsense is that? Mr Hansen's motivations must surely be more concrete than that.

'But Maurette's? Is she purely and simply a *comedienne*, flaunting borrowed plumage? Do you remember, Jan, a young Pole who was her lover, or at least her admirer for a time. That young man confided to me that he would die at Maurette's beautiful hand. He didn't, of course. But he did die in Maurette's house. An accident. Of course. But it is just such an accident that I am afraid of.

'I really am frightened, Jan. Yes, properly frightened. And now I shall tell you what really did it. An invisible hand from the past has – '

I interrupted him, saying:

'There's no need to try to make jokes, my dear Mikael. I find you neither cowardly nor ridiculous.'

He made a grimace, one that I recognised, curling his lips so that his teeth showed.

'Thank you,' he said. 'But you must permit me to joke a little. Because this really is ridiculous. It's the result of reading the family chronicle. It's a coincidence, a quirk of fate, but it's frightened me to such an extent that my mouth is quite dry. A week or so ago Mr Hansen transferred the Hôtel de Montsousonge – without my knowledge – to a certain Monsieur Lebossu of Paris. Well and good. A fortnight after the Opera Masquerade my grandfather's grandfather, General Arnfelt, was murdered. The instigator of the murder is said to have been his illegitimate son, by the name of Fält. But the man who performed the deed was the General's valet, a Frenchman, Lebossu.'

I poured him a glass of water, but he pushed it aside.

'No, I don't need that. Now, this coincidence has made a

certain impression on me. But I'd still rather stick to the facts; an accident that cost me my life would be welcomed by certain less than scrupulous individuals; moreover, at least *one* extremely odd accident has already occurred in the Hôtel de Montsousonge. And lastly: this carnivalesque nonsense offers the perfect opportunity. A shot is to be fired – that is part of the performance – and mistakes are easily made – . No, nothing could be more simple.

'Under the circumstances, I have at least taken one precautionary measure. I have reserved for myself the task of appointing the interpreter of Anckarström's rôle. There are not many people I can trust. I have chosen you, my dear Jan. Do you think me very ridiculous?'

I replied:

'No. Especially as I genuinely believe that a trap has been laid for you. Yes, my dear Mikael, I would go so far as to say that I am convinced that you will die tonight.'

I caught his eye in the mirror; but neither he nor I altered our expression. And after a few moments I went on:

'But won't you first tell me why you trust me so implicitly? As far as I know, I have no earthly reason to be your friend.'

He replied – and, although his expression was quite calm and restrained, I could hear his teeth chattering between the words –

'I trust you, Jan, because Léonie trusts you. As I wrote to you, it was Léonie who suggested I turn to you.'

I leaned forward, resting my arms on the back of his chair – that way I could better watch his face in the mirror. I said:

'And have you any reason to trust Léonie?'

He looked down and smiled, his hands moving over the items on the table.

'Léonie,' he repeated, curling his lips around the name. 'Yes, Jan, there you have hit upon another irrational aspect lurking beneath my oh so sound reasoning. If there is anyone on this earth whom I trust unconditionally, then it is Léonie. But I can't say why. If I were very conceited, I might say that I love her in spite of everything, and that that is why I trust her. But I have no illusions in that way. Love is something quite alien to me, the very word is too large for my mouth. I do not even love myself. If I have ever loved anyone, it would have been my grandmother. Do you remember the blind old lady I let you look at? At a price, I seem to recall.'

He laughed.

'No, that's really not my strongest side. If I say that I'm fond of Léonie, then that's saying a lot. Yes, I'm fond of her, but in the end her jealousy became too oppressive. I was watched day and night. Of course, it was just another illustration of her good heart. And however hard you try, my dear Jan, you won't shake my faith – '

I straightened up, nodded at him in the mirror and said:

'Good. Now I know why you're honouring me with your confidence. Now do you want to give me the necessary instructions?'

He did so, adding:

'If you wait a few minutes, I'll ask the valet to lay out the costume. In the meantime you can go into the next room and select one of my guns – '

I said:

'That's not necessary; I've got my revolver on me.'

He asked to see it, and when he saw my name engraved on the butt, joked and said:

'Now that's really rather careless, my dear assassin. Besides, the revolver hardly matches the costume.'

I replied that a detail like that was of no consequence; he made no further objections. He looked at the clock and said:

'We've plenty of time. It's one o'clock, but His Majesty doesn't intend to show himself before two. I want to make it as short as possible. And I also intend to devote the entire night to the demon of superstition – if there is such a thing. And two o'clock is said to be an ominous time for us Arnfelts. Again, according to this reliable chronicle – '

He leafed through the pages, and we were silent for a while.

He looked towards the alcove.

'I really can't understand what's taking him so long. The valet.

I have to be shaved and powdered and all that. That'll take an hour or so. This mirror – do you remember it? It used to hang in Grandmother's room. She maintained that Lieutenant Arnberg possessed a companion piece, but I don't know if that was true. But it's quite possible, because there really was a matching piece. Only a copy, but so skilfully done that it was impossible to tell apart from the original. It's quite an odd story –

'Our reliable chronicle tells us, you see, that the original mirror, which came to the family during the seventeenth century, possessed such a peculiar and valuable characteristic that the head of the family made it an entailed possession, and, moreover, decreed that the head of the family should take it with him wherever he went. As you see, I am a dutiful descendant.

'The valuable characteristic was that by looking long and hard in the mirror, one could discern one's mortal enemy. Similar properties have been attributed to other mirrors. But for us the legend has a particular significance. I mentioned that the Gustavian General Arnfelt had an illegitimate son. The General, who had perhaps been reading Jean Jacques, had the illegitimate child raised alongside the legitimate one, making no distinction between them. Because he wished to find out – through an experiment very much in keeping with the spirit of the age – the extent to which legitimate birth really mattered. To the soul, I should imagine. The chronicler does not reveal what conclusion he reached, but he does tell of how the illegitimate child, upon being told the truth at the age of seventeen – I believe it was – underwent a terrible transformation. Well, I'm not surprised. The chronicle says: "When now the boy learned that he was not of this world – "

'An odd phrase, don't you think? The boy decided to avenge himself, and is said to have brooded over his revenge from his seventeenth to his thirty-fourth year. That was really taking it to heart. And what is said to have held him back was a healthy respect for the mirror, in which his unacknowledged father would be able to discover his mortal enemy. Eventually he hit upon the idea of having a copy made, so that he could lull his victim into a false sense of security.

'Well, be that as it may. But do you know what I've been thinking? I think that my venerable ancestor, the one who burdened us with this mirror, was more of a philosopher than an obscurant. I have spent many solitary hours with my mirror. And after a while I came to the conclusion that my ancestor was right. In the end you do see your mortal enemy. As long as you're a child, my dear Jan, you won't see him, and perhaps not during the first years of your youth. But then it begins. And each time he grins back at us a little less disguised. I can sit watching him for hours. The seven stern ladies watch me, and I watch him. And it seems to me that we are both alone, not just in the room, but in the whole world.

'Sometimes it makes me frightened. *Quia leo*. I'm not ashamed of that. Because I see him as a test of manhood, as good as any other. It almost seems to me that I should be spared other tests of manhood. But – Mikael Arnfelt. *Quia leo*! Try translating that. "Can't you even translate your forefathers' motto?" old Sundblad used to say. Do you remember him? In the lower sixth?'

He stood up and, putting his hands on my shoulders, said:

'Jan! If you see Léonie – it's not impossible, after all – then tell her that I looked at myself in the mirror right to the end. Because I was such a peacock. And seeing as you were Sundblad's blue-eyed boy, I'm sure you could say something nice in Latin. For instance:

'*Quia leo, ultimus sic mortuus est comes Arnfelt.*'

He stamped on the floor and shouted:

'Well! At last! How long do I have to wait? I assume that you have at least got my costume ready?'

I turned round. In the opening of the alcove stood Fält, a silk outfit hanging over his arm.

'And Mr Arnberg's costume?' Mikael went on. 'Where have you got that? Do you know what time it is? I suppose you think you can behave as you like just because you've got a beautiful wife!'

Fält replied:

'I've laid out Mr Arnberg's costume in his old room.'

Mikael pressed my hand.

'Good,' he said, guiding me to the door. 'We'll meet in an hour. Play the assassin with bravura, but don't forget to take out the bullets. For it is written: Better a live dog than a dead lion.'

The corridor and staircase were now full of noise from the white salon, where the masked ball was in full swing. I was hurrying to my room when a thought suddenly struck me: the revolver! When I left it with Mr Hansen, it had not been loaded.

I pulled it out, pulled back the safety catch and spun the cylinder. My anxiety was unfounded. Mr Hansen had returned the revolver loaded with six bullets. I leaned against the wall and rested for a while. I was breathless, my heart pounding.

Just as I was about to continue on my way, the door to Maurette's room opened and a stream of light hit me right in the eyes. I shut them for a second; when I looked up again, Father Johannes was standing beside me. As usual, he was wearing his long black coat, but his head was uncovered. He took my hand and led me into Maurette's room. We stopped by the door.

Maurette was sitting on the bed; she had not yet put on her costume. At the little table sat Mr Hansen, also without his mask. And between them, at the end of the bed, his back to the wall, stood Monsieur Lebossu, twirling his goatee beard with his fingers and staring at the floor.

I did not greet them; and no-one seemed to notice me. I turned to Father Johannes for an explanation, but even he was staring stubbornly at the floor. And so we remained, in silence, I do not know for how long.

Eventually Mr Hansen said:

'I, for my part, have no choice. I am faced with ruin. I now know that he has knowingly and willingly, methodically and without a moment's hesitation lured me to the brink. There is only one thing that can save my business, and that is me, or rather, my life. It goes against the grain, but I must do it. Because I believe that my life has just as much justification as his. And so I must do it. What do you say, Monsieur Lebossu?'

The scarecrow at the end of the bed suddenly crumpled. But it was merely a bow, repeated several times as he croaked:

'I submit, I submit, monsieur.'

The Maurette stretched her lithe body, sublimely indolent and supple. And she yawned and said:

'Your ruin, poor little Hansen, is something which may possibly interest you, but no-one else. Anyway, you know it's all lies, this talk of your ruin. You're just being kicked down the staircase of life one more time, that's all. But when haven't you crawled back up again? Even higher up. No, poor little Hansen, you're jealous. And I can appreciate that. And I could whisper things in your ear, little Hansen. Things that would turn you into a real hero. No, I have no objections to the deed itself, but I would ask that we be honest. Am I not right, Lebossu?'

The scarecrow bowed as before and croaked:

'I submit, I submit, madame.'

Then I asked Father Johannes what they were talking about. And he turned to the scarecrow and asked:

'Do you hear, Lebossu? My son is asking what you are talking about.'

The scarecrow raised his right arm, and his sleeve was so long that only the yellow end of his index finger was visible. He pointed at me and said:

'What we're talking about, monsieur? We're not talking at all, we're thinking. But if you are asking what we are thinking about, then I would have a little difficulty explaining. Because explaining oneself is very difficult, monsieur, and we are not far from being nothing but thoughts. Very old thoughts, monsieur. *Enfin*, one has come into the world, and one must live. This is something a human being has in common with his thoughts. But I, for my part, I submit, I submit, monsieur.'

Now Maurette spoke, showing her teeth:

'Stupid Jan, asking what we're thinking. We're thinking of revenge, and nothing else. The fat gentleman may say what he likes – '

Mr Hansen interrupted:

'That's extremely illogical, my poor Maurette. Why should

you wish to be avenged on a person who hasn't done you any harm? Can revenge float about in the air like that, merely striking the first dove that comes into range? No, that's childish, it's gratuitous. In contrast, a business deal is never gratuitous. It must be nurtured in just the right way. Only such and such a method may be used. That's what I call having your papers in order – '

I said:

'How ridiculous the three of you are. So you want the same thing, but are wasting time squabbling about the reasons. Well, then, look at me. I want the same thing too. But I've got enough sense to leave all my reasons and justifications at home. I know that my revolver is loaded, that's enough. I know what I want, and that's enough. I am acting, because it is my duty. It is an obligation placed on me by someone. Who? That doesn't concern me. Why? That doesn't concern me. Am I not right, Lebossu?'

He replied:

'Certainly, monsieur. For that is the difference between the human being and his thoughts. He has obligations that he must fulfil. Thoughts do not. No, thoughts are free, as they say – heh, heh, heh – but human beings are not. But I submit, monsieur.'

I said:

'Yes, you may laugh, monsieur. But the difference between us is that you are a scruffy Methuselah who seems to have centuries ahead of him yet. Whereas I have fifteen minutes or half an hour. So farewell, madame and messieurs.'

And I turned to hurry out. But Maurette stopped me.

'Listen, Jan,' she said. 'A serious word. What do you actually intend to do? This really has nothing to do with you.'

'What do you mean?' I asked. 'Since when has this had nothing to do with me? I should have thought the very opposite was true, that I have nothing to do with anything but this.'

Mr Hansen shrugged his shoulders disdainfully, Monsieur Lebossu smiled, revealing a pair of yellow fangs beneath his moustache, and twirled his beard. Maurette said:

'Poor little Jan! So you don't remember a promise you made to a certain young lady named Léonie?'

I blushed and felt embarrassed. But I said:

'I remember that promise very well. But to show you just what sort of a man I am, I can tell you that when I made that promise, I promised myself that I would break it. Now you see how much that promise constrains me. Now let me go.'

But she laughed. And she stretched out her arms to me and said:

'Poor little Jan. You're a child, and as such quite enchanting to my old heart. So, that was the nature of your promise? How clever you are! But there's one thing you must still explain. What was it that drove you to make that promise? I don't know that anyone forced you, or even asked you to do it. And voluntary promises, poor Jan – oh, they're very dangerous.'

And she laughed right in my face; but soon turned back to the others.

I said:

'Why I made the promise? That's natural enough. I didn't want Léonie – it was for Léonie's sake – after all, one must bear in mind – it seemed quite obvious to me, that when I could spare her in such a simple way – I don't see why I shouldn't have – to the best of my knowledge, Léonie has never done me any harm – and if I could – Good Lord, my so-called honour had already been sacrificed – what would a broken promise signify to me – if I could spare Léonie by making it – '

And I sought to explain myself as best I could. But suddenly I realised that the three of them were not listening to my words at all. They had turned to face each other again and were conversing in an undertone. First Mr Hansen spoke; then the scarecrow crumpled, whining: 'I submit, I submit.' Then Maurette spoke, and was answered the same way. But I listened with growing astonishment and terror, because they they were repeating the same words each time, and were no longer talking like human beings, but machines.

And I tugged Father Johannes by the sleeve and whispered:
'Father, I don't want – '
He asked:
'What is it you don't want? – '

'I don't want them to – they're masks, they're ghosts, they're mannequins – I don't want – it's my business – we're both the same, after all – I mean Mikael and me – I can do it – but I don't want them to – and if I am bound by my promise – to Léonie – then I don't want – '

And I tugged at his sleeve. He said:

'Yes, Jan, but what is it you don't want?'

But I could only say:

'I don't want – I don't want – '

Then I felt Father start. And I saw the three by the wall start and listen. But I could only hear a clock striking two o'clock.

And several minutes passed.

Father Johannes said in a whisper:

'My learned friend, Lebossu, you who know the difference between human will and thought – can you also tell us the difference between human beings and God?'

But the scarecrow bowed silently and did not answer.

Father Johannes put his hand to his ear and listened.

Then he said, raising his voice somewhat:

'I see the difference in the fact that human beings cannot change the unchangeable with either their will or their thought. So neither you with your thoughts nor my son with his will have managed to add or subtract a second either to or from the allotted time. So let us humbly admit that our thoughts and our will merely flutter like moths around a flame. And it is precisely this that constitutes our power and our security – that we are powerless.

'The clock has struck two. Now our mutual enemy, Mikael Arnfelt, is breathing his last. And it was neither us, nor any of God's creatures, who scorched him. Instead, he fell into the fire and was consumed.'

As he said this, he opened the door and I caught a fleeting glimpse of a figure caught mid-flight, one arm and one leg raised, as though he were hanging from strings. And, as he flew past the door, he threw into the room the knife he had used.

But when I came to the mirrored chamber, it was packed full of motley masked figures. I forced my way through to the chair and saw Mikael sitting there, his head leaning back, his right cheek lathered with soap, his eyelids half closed so that, in the mirror, I could only see the whites and the lower part of the rainbow-tinted irises.

Rygell was standing to one side of him, with his hand on Mikael's chest. On the other side stood Steintheel, frantically writing in his notebook.

And now I heard someone shout:

'Lock all the doors! No-one must get out!'

I grew frightened then. And I clung to Father Johannes. I heard Maurette cry out; and I saw how two men grabbed Mr Hansen by the shoulders, pushed him up against the wall and put handcuffs around his wrists. And, lastly, I saw Lebossu's hideous powdered face in the alcove. He was screaming and invoking the devil, his mouth gaping open as though his innards were burning and suffocating him.

And he screamed:

'I'm innocent! I'm innocent! They tricked me. It was Fält who did it.'

And masks and people began shouting and screaming and protesting. And in the whole room, only Mikael was silent.

But I realised that I had found my way into a nest of criminals. And I clung to Father Johannes. He said:

'What is it that you want now, Jan, that's making you frightened?'

I indicated that it was the people who were frightening me. But he smiled at me and whispered close to my ear:

'You have nothing to fear from people. Have you not yet understood that you and I are not of this world?'

And we left the room and the house.

We were standing under the open sky once more. And he said:

'Not everyone who lives is alive; nor is death a portal that only opens in one direction. The Unchangeable forms life as He pleases, and of death He makes a plaything. Our thoughts are wills-o'-the-wisp that amuse Him with their flitting play. But our wills rest in His hand. And when you feel yourself condemned by your will, you shall know that it rests in His hand, who has given you the bow in the cloud as a sign. So do not fear your will, for it is not your tool, but His who guides you.'

So speaking, he left me.

AFTERWORD

Karin Petherick

In the decade preceding Hjalmar Bergman's birth in 1883, the distinguished Danish literary historian Georg Brandes maintained that the criterion for a literature's vitality was that it debated current issues. He cited amongst others the Naturalist works of Flaubert and Zola, thereby presciently approving the coming Naturalistic plays of August Strindberg. But ultimately committed social realism leads to an appetite for poetic imagination and a measure of romance, which swiftly blossomed in Sweden with the neo-romantic revival of the 1890s. The pendulum swung back again early in the 1900s with a group of young writers with a background in journalism and a lively interest in modernity, fired by an optimistic belief in free will and progress; they included Elin Wägner, Gustaf Hellström, and Ludvig Nordström, who wrote lively novels with sharp observation of industrialisation and social change. Their contemporary Hjalmar Bergman's work was of a different order; he was, as *Memoirs of a Dead Man* proves, a determinist seeking to express a tenable belief within a transcendental framework. His first novel *Solivro* (1906), is a stylised symbolist story set in a fictive far-away country, about forbidden passions, guilt, and the death of illusions. He moved on to novels with realistic components but with many dream-like elements. Apart from a powerful novel set entirely in Florence about the Franciscan monk *Savonarola* (1909), burnt at the stake in 1497, he came in succeeding works to mark out a territory in Sweden as uniquely his own. Initially he does not name the town which is its hub (namely Örebro with its moated, medieval castle), but calls it W. in *Memoirs of a Dead Man*, and Wadköping in the novel published the following year, *Markurells i Wadköping* (1919, literal title *The Markurells of Wadköping* but published in English as *God's Orchid*), and in all his subsequent works.

Bergman's concerns are deeply and personally existential. He and Pär Lagerkvist are arguably Sweden's greatest twentieth-century writers. He commands that old black magic which fills readers with the joy that comes from recognizing the voice of a master narrator. When in 1918 at the age of thirty-four he embarked on writing *Memoirs of a Dead Man* he must have felt it time to revive memories (with, to use a Freudian term, many dream displacements) and to tackle problems of the will. In terms of his work this was a watershed, for he subsequently embarked on three novels in 1919-1921, *God's Orchid*, *Herr von Hancken*, and *Farmor och Vår Herre* (literal title: *Grandma and The Lord*, published in English as *Thy Rod and Thy Staff*), which won him acclaim and wide readership in Sweden. They are often wildly humorous but at heart tragic, about the necessity of coming to terms with the truth about oneself.

Bergman's father was a dominating and explosive personality who demonstrated contempt for his chubby and clumsy son until the boy at around the age of eleven proved to be exceptionally gifted. Hjalmar described to his wife in a letter assumed to have been written in 1914, known to researchers as the 'Confession' (*Biktbrevet*), that as a small child, knowing that the Lord had created the world, he (Hjalmar) created no less than seven imaginary worlds of his own, where *he* was sovereign and commanded over all that he had created. 'And *what* was I in reality? A small, awkward, abnormally fat and clumsy child. Adults laughed at me, kids persecuted me. Have you any idea of how many humiliations I swallowed during my first decade? My heart had no shield. A look and a laugh penetrated quivering flesh. That was when I had to learn my art: that of parrying. Parry, parry, parry. Never meet anyone without thinking of defence.'

Bergman enrolled at Uppsala university at the age of seventeen (where the only thing which interested him was his private lessons with the philosopher Hans Larsson, who became a benign and wise correspondent for the rest of Hjalmar's life). His ambition was not to become a scholar but a writer, and since his father was a patron of the well-known actor-manager August Lindberg, whose touring company regularly visited Örebro, Hjalmar's early ambition was to be a dramatist, a dream he never relinquished. It is noteworthy that three of his major novels observe the dramatic unities of time and space and were subsequently successfully adapted for performance. In 1908 Bergman married Stina, the youngest of the Lindberg daughters. Much could be written about their marriage. Hjalmar, with increasingly troubled nerves, needed one person in the world whom he could trust implicitly; he suffered from pathological jealousy and seldom let her out of his sight. Until 1926 they were never apart, mostly living abroad, while he worked prodigiously. By 1927 he had in some sense broken free, had friends in theatrical and film circles (he wrote film scenarios and even in 1923 spent four unhappy months as a scriptwriter in Hollywood, which he hated). At the end of his life, while desperately ill, he struggled to fulfil work commitments, including reading on Swedish radio the final two chapters of his swansong and broadside aimed against 'Show Business', *Clownen Jac* (*Jac, the Clown)*. He died on New Year's Day 1931 in Berlin at the age of forty-seven.

Bergman's brother-in-law, the publisher Tor Bonnier, wrote to him after reading the manuscript of *Memoirs of a Dead Man* that it was a 'chilling book' and that he considered as unrealistic the myriad inescapable 'musts' or imperatives besetting mankind and welcomed by greedy entrepreneurs as exceedingly lucrative, and Bonnier concludes: 'despite your eloquence, which I admire, I do not believe in your "musts".' To this Bergman replied, 'So you believe, dear Tor, that still in this year of grace 1918 we with a modicum of shrewdness and obstinacy – or let us more elevatedly call it reason and *good will* – can steer or contribute to steering our own fate and that of others? I, too, believe in reason and good will, treasures guarded behind seventy seals somewhere in outer space and it must be a faint belief in this treasure which still impels us to join the dance, the reflection of a reflection of its glimmering light which we persist in calling "the rosy dawn of a new day". In this we are eternally the same, eternal in the way that numbers are. We are cards in the Almighty's game of patience, the King of Spades remains King of Spades (with his sombre majestically wrinkled brow) the Queen of Hearts remains Queen of Hearts however often the packs are worn out and replaced. And we are revenants of revenants and our human story must perforce be a ghost story – provided we see it from a sufficient distance.' *Memoirs of a Dead Man* is at heart concerned with determinism – and a possible transcendant release.

In December 1918 he wrote to his friend Algot Ruhe, who admitted to having had some difficulty with reading *Memoirs of a Dead Man*: 'It is based on a philosophy of life, rather particularly mankind's relationship to his actions. I believe that a person's actions, particularly of course the more decisive ones, are to some extent independent of him, that is to say that they are manifested *in* him rather than *by* him. For I believe that the *will* is by no means the constituent part of the personality (the "self" or whatever we choose to call it) which it is generally assumed to be. On the contrary, I assume – (though this is no solidly elaborated "system" [...] but at the very, very most "a nascent system"!– I would assume that the will can affect but not be affected by the self's twin kernel, reason and emotion (terms between which I see no fundamental difference). In other words, the will is the instrument by means of which the action takes command of the self. I need not tell you that behind this process I sense the Unknown One or perhaps the Unknown. Except to add that my basically optimistic and practical view of things has induced me to believe in a certain and naturally wise "purpose" in this vast system of human actions, which we in totality can call the history of mankind and which I thus regard as being *instilled* in us by the will – not something *produced* by our human will. That the "purpose" of this system is to influence the real "self" (reason-emotion) is so "theological" a conclusion as to be self evident.' This idea, he writes, is based on observation of himself and others, and particularly of families. Indeed the novel's opening motto is a variant of the familiar words spoken by God in *Exodus* 20:5-6, who visits the iniquity of the fathers upon the children until the third and fourth generation of those who hate him and shows mercy unto thousands of them that love him and keep his commandments. The narrator's father, about whom the first thing we are told is that he is an atheist (consumed by an obsessive ambition to repossess the estate which his father was wickedly tricked into losing and which can be seen as a link in the destructive chain binding two families of successive generations), finally abandons this quest and becomes after his death a gentle mentor to his son. He comes back as a revenant and gatekeeper at the sinister Hôtel de Montsousonge, and when in danger his son Jan can reach out and hold his father's hand through the gatekeeper's window.

Bergman's fertile imagination constructs a plot spanning several generations between 1792 and 1913, beginning with the murder in 1792 of King Gustav III. That same day one of the regicide plotters, General Count Arnfelt, is murdered as he flees to Norway, having allowed his illegitimate son to grow up as an inferior steward who only now learns of his true parentage and (we must assume) bribes his father's lackey to cut the Count's throat. Dire consequences ensue, an ongoing series of murders and acts of treachery – and sometimes strenuous efforts to avoid committing them (for some individuals do not *wish* to be slaves to the family's homicidal will) – involving two branches of the same family, the aristocratic Arnfelts and the family and hangers-on of the steward, who changed his name to Arnberg. This may seem vaguely reminiscent of ancient blood feuds, but Bergman had genetic factors in mind as well. In one respect, there is a striking resemblance to Dostoyevsky's *The Brothers Karamazov*, in so far as the murder of the cruel Karamazov father is committed by his illegitimate son Smerdjakov, whose brother Dmitri confesses to the crime because he himself had wished to commit it and now wants to atone for it. We can note that Jan's father as wise revenant reminds Jan that when he as a child was afraid of who might be lurking in the bushes: 'in the whole world there is only one evil and cruel person, only one thief and killer. You yourself'. We fear the violence we bear within us.

The narrative pace quickens, danger increases, we sense an ultimate, transcendent hope encapsulated in the words 'you and I are not of this world'. For Jan's father died having relinquished all vain imperative striving, and Jan himself succeeds in divesting himself of the imperative to act as the hired assassin of a rich guest to be disposed of at the Hôtel de Montsousonge and, more importantly, succeeds in escaping the imperative to kill his rival Mikael, despite the fact that Mikael has stolen his beloved Léonie. For a promise made out of love is binding, so when Léonie appeals to Jan to protect her errant husband she makes it impossible for him to join in with the band of brigands who all regard Mikael as their prey. And in a delightful twist Jan's stepmother Hedda helps him to solve his quandary, for she asks him for a temporary loan to save her small hotel from sequestration. She has always been poor and worked for others, and her invariable response to something she herself might need is: 'we can reduce that'. Inspired by Hedda, he undertakes four tactical 'reductions' and sends her the money she needs. But it is not until the last minute that Jan deliberately abstains from avenging himself on Mikael who has not only stolen Léonie, but represents the firm which ruined his father. We recall that Jan's father passed through severe testing, and that when he fell ill from excessive striving due to his imperative that he 'must' regain the family fortunes, he resigned and spent the last months of his life with his son Jan, then about ten years old, in a state of peaceful quiescence. Shortly before his father dies, Jan's cousin Léonie came to visit them and the children were sent by Jan's father to look at the fountain in the park of the fine house they were swindled out of, and told to note at what time the rainbow appears in the water. It turns out to be at the exact time that Jan's father dies. And the reader recalls that when the biblical flood receded, God promised mercy to his people and that never again would there be a flood to destroy the earth, saying 'This is the token of the covenant which I make between me and you and every living creature that is with you, for perpetual generations: I do set my bow in the cloud, and it shall be for a token of a covenant between me and the earth' (*Genesis* 9:12). After his death, Jan's father becomes first the tattooed sailor, then Father Johannes, the gatekeeper at the decadent Hôtel de Montsousonge. Having entered eternity he is, to quote Christ's words, 'not of this world' (*John* 8:23).

There is a large element of mysticism in the story. 'Not everyone who lives is alive; nor is death a portal that only opens in one direction' is one of Father Johannes' sayings. Most memorably, his closing words to Jan are: 'when you feel yourself condemned by your will, you shall know that it rests in His hand, who has given you the bow in the cloud as a sign. So do not fear your will, for it is not your tool, but His who guides you.' In Bergman's terms, 'your will' equals your genetic makeup, your unavoidable heredity, but The Unchangeable One holds you in his hand.

Bergman was a virtuoso style imitator, demonstrated in *Memoirs of a Dead Man* by his pastiche of Biblical diction and of American advertisement slogans, clichés which had also been adopted by Swedish enterprises and are horrifyingly parodied when Johan Arnberg's benign healthfood is transformed into Dr Arnberg's worthless Tuberculin, claimed to own miraculous healing powers.

The handsome and devious Mikael Arnfelt appears for the first but by no means last time in Bergman's fictional world in *Memoirs of a Dead Man*, where he comes to a bad end; as he also does in *Kerrmans i paradiset* (1927: *The Kerrmans in Paradise*), having partly redeemed himself. So, too, does his grandfather, a descendant of the regicidal plotter of 1792 in *Memoirs of a Dead Man* with whom the murderous actions were set in train, and who in *The Kerrmans in Paradise* shows himself under his proudly unbowed exterior to possess a heart that breaks when he hears of Mikael's death, just as the sybaritic Mikael is revealed as a lonely little-boy-lost who has only ever loved his grandfather. We must hope that both of the Arnfelts gained transcendental peace.

Notes

11 *Upsala:* an archaic spelling of Uppsala.
11 *the conspiracy against Gustav III:* King Gustav III, a champion of both the Enlightenment and absolute monarchy, was assassinated at a masked ball in Stockholm's opera house on 16 March 1792.
11 *W.:* in his next novel, *Markurells i Wadköping* (The Markurells of Wadköping), published in 1919, a year after *Memoirs of a Dead Man*, Bergman identified his favoured fictional setting as Wadköping. It features elements of the towns of Örebro and Västerås, in which Bergman respectively grew up and went to school. Both towns are in the central mining district of Bergslagen.
26 *Contrexéville:* Water from the spa resort of Contrexéville was believed to alleviate bladder and kidney ailments.
36 *Robert Koch:* German bacteriologist and Nobel Prize-winner (1843-1910), discoverer of tuberculin.
41 *Axel Borg:* Swedish painter (1847-1916) most famous for his paintings of elk.
57 *Swedish-Norwegian:* Sweden and Norway were in a political union between 1815 and 1905.
78 *Freebooter of the Baltic:* The title of an historical novel (*Fribytaren på Östersjön*) by Swedish author Viktor Rydberg, published in 1857.
130 *Gustavian:* Someone sharing Gustav III's cultural and political ideals. Also (p. 335) denotes the period of Gustav III's reign (1771-1792).
145 *a fat ironmaster and his skinny driver had been eaten by wolves:* A story from Bergman's 1914 novel, *Två släkter: Komedier i Bergslagen I* (Two Families: Comedies in Bergslagen I).
147 *Lasse-Maja:* The nickname of renowned thief Lars Molin (1785-1845), hero of many folktales in Bergslagen. He often disguised himself as a woman, hence the nickname.
153 *Andersen's story*: In Hans Christian Andersen's story

'Reisekammeraten' (1835, The Travelling Companion), the young Johannes' father dies, and he is mentored by a ghost who accompanies him on his travels.

176 *Haben wir das alles gethan?*: 'Have we done all this?' A line attributed to King Fredrik I of Sweden (1676-1751; originally Prince of Hesse, he reigned 1720-51 after the abdication of his wife, Queen Ulrika Eleonora) in response to an excessively flattering speech in his praise.

203 *window-mirror:* Swedish *skvallerspegel*, lit. 'gossip mirror', a mirror mounted outside a window in such a way as to allow the occupants of a house to see what is happening further along the street.

243 *HAPAG:* The 'Hamburg Amerikanische Paketfahrt Aktiegesellschaft', the largest shipping line in the world at the outbreak of the First World War.

252 *Leporello list:* In Mozart's *Don Giovanni*, Don Juan's servant Leporello has a list of the women his master has seduced.

253 *St. George:* A district of Hamburg.

318 *Smith:* Joseph Smith (1805-44), founder of the Mormon Church.

330 *Bulwer:* British author Edward Bulwer-Lytton (1803-73). Among the many genres in which he wrote were occult mysteries and ghost stories.

331 *Anckarström:* Jacob Johan Anckarström (1762-1792) was Gustav III's assassin. He was publically beheaded five weeks after the assassination.

331 *Odhner:* Clas Theodor Odhner (1836-1904) was a prolific author of historical textbooks.

332 *the cat would collect chestnuts for the monkey:* Refers to the fable 'The Monkey and the Cat' by Jean de la Fontaine (1621-1695).

335 *Jean Jacques:* Jean-Jacques Rousseau (1712-78), known in part for his ground-breaking pedagogical theories. See *Émile* (1762).